DECEPTION
Of SEVEN
Sacred Vows

DECEPTION Of SEVEN Sacred Vows

TRANSLATE FROM MOST FAMOUS HINDI NOVEL

"SAAT PHERO SE DHOKHA"

KAMLESH CHAUHAN (GAURI)

Ordering Information:

For orders and inquiries, please contact:
1-888-404-1388
www.goldtouchpress.com
book.orders@goldtouchpress.com

Printed in the United States of America

CONTENTS

This is the second novel by Kamlesh to be translated and edited by me. The First One Across the seven Seas is a Great Success. The Current Novel can be taken as a sequel to the first one.

Fiction is for entertainment, but according to the definition of Sahitya in Hindi or the literature in English good fiction also has some message to convey, some purpose for the good of humanity, for it is confined to oneself to "Art for the sake of the art. The fact is that "Deception of Seven Sacred Seas" is a novel by women, of women and for women' which is only highly entertaining but also conveys a message very boldly.

The novel deals with the life of Indian brides who have married away to Indian American grooms the parents of the girls with the fond hope and in most cases firm belief that they were sending the daughters to the world of all happiness and to a world of perpetual spring where flowers bloom around the year. But the moment most of these hapless girls see the foot on the foreign soil, their problem begins as happens in the life of Rita, the protagonist of the novel. Kamlesh's couplet on page14 of the novel sums up the theme of the novel. "Ham Jab Bhi Roye, Jaar Jaar Roye, Ham Jab Bhi Roye Khud Ke Sath He Roye" (Whenever I weep, it was to weep Inconsolably and to weep alone)

The Newly Wed Bride hardly finds time to live her dreams on the foreign land when she starts getting glimpses of the type of life that awaits her. The husband who has had taken vows to live and die for her is the first one is the first one to give her a cold shoulder and to her horror, she finds that the so-called true love was just a flimsy flake of snow that melted with the first whiff of foreign air, The Rita, the heroine finds that she does not command the same respect and importance, other members of Sudhir, her husband family does.

She is constantly persecuted by her husband and his family. In desperation, she tries to run away from this hell of a life but only fails. Her Romantic encounters with Parkash, Dr. Vimal, and Ravi are all failures. Though they all exploit her emotionally or physically, Ravi is the worst. He is the villain through and through, He exploits Rita not only emotionally but also financially.

She was too tired to struggle anymore and manipulated circumstances to have Sudhir by her side at the time of the marriage of the children. Sudhir Repents for his mistake by only mumbling a few cliches and the novel is made to have a precarious happy ending which is much like the silence before another storm breaks. That is a brief story of the Novel.

Kamlesh Chauhan needs no introduction in the world of literature and art in America and in India. She has done justice to the subject and this Novel is a clear improvement on the last one. I am sure the novel will be enthusiastically received by the readers like the last one and enjoyed. I wish her all success in this noble literary endeavor.

Prof, M.S. Verma.
Head of the Department of English
Bhagwan Mahaveer Institute of Engineering and Technology,
Sonepat - 131001, Haryana

ACKNOWLEDGMENT

I would like to express my sincere gratitude to those that helped me bring this book to life. They have Listened to me, provided me with a shoulder to lean on, assisted me with editing, Proofreading, and much more. Thank them for their endless support, as this journey would not be possible without my family, My sisters, Their Kids and friends.

I dedicate this book to Ashwani Kumar Rajput, Preet Kaur Rajput, Sulkshana Rajput, Ashoke Rajput, Late Budhdev, Surishta Sehdev, and Harsha Sehdev.

A special Thanks to a little girl with a beautiful smile - Sahana Khushi Rajput. Riya Rajput and Little Angel Naaya Rajput

I am thankful to my family - My Unique Son Ranjun Kalu Chauhan, who has always been there for me. He is also part of the life of the real character of this Novel. Which is a Dhanush- Rita. Special thanks to my loving daughter, Kiren Minu Chauhan, who was also a real Character - Rita When Rita Cried, then her daughter Kiren Mine Chauhan Cried.

Then Come the Late Dream Girl, an Actress and Singer Sunita Singh, whose memory will always be fresh with me. Special Thanks to Mirjana Macdonald, who always listens to me and understands me.

My Special Thanks to Lou Tretola - My dear photographer, I am thanks to my relatives Surbhi and Kamal Verma along with their children Palak and Sahil.

This book Could not have completed without the moral support of Dr. Parvin Syal, Harshi Syal Gill, Rajesh Shukla, Late Praful Vyas, Jaya Sharma, Vikram Singh Bhadoriya, Ruchir Tiwari, Vikram Singh Bhadoriya also sometimes correct my mistakes and help me. He is a source of encouragement.

I am also thankful to India west, India Post, India Journal, Patrika from Bhopal, Bhaskar as well, Suman and Balbir Rajput and my Late Loving Parents named Laxami Devi and Pritam Dass who had encouraged me for my writing this book. My Late Sister Surrinder and her Husband Krishna Dev, My Sister Raj Rajput and her daughter Susheel Rosy and My Both Brothers Sumit Kuamr, and younger Brothers who was a Stage Preformists Deep Rajput.

Kamlesh Chauhan (Gauri)

vi

PART I

CHAPTER 1

She walked like a robot, taking small steps, oblivious of the world around her and even her two kids who moved with her, holding her hands on both sides. Suddenly she stopped; took out a small mirror and looked in it at the scars on her face which once were spotless and shining. The discoloration was still very much visible. Everything around her swam. She was shocked. Could it be an earthquake? She wondered. Her legs seemed to give way under her. She had lost sense of time and space. It was exactly at this moment that strong male hands held her by the shoulders from behind.

"Hello dear! Why are you started? It is only me." She turned around and looked at the person. He was a tall, handsome young man. His hairy arms and muscular body were attractive. But she felt uneasy to see him. He asked, "Where do you live these days? It has been ages since we last met."

"Oh, just somewhere close by," she said, a little embarrassed.

He at once noticed the expression of disapproval on her face but ignored it. He continued, "What happened to your right eye?" He pointed a rude finger to the blackened eye. Then added, "Oh, perhaps at night…there has been an argument with your hubby…. Sari Raat Kushati Karati rahi ho … (you have been having a wrestling bout with your husband.) …I mean," he said arrogantly, with a twinkle in his eyes. He was smiling as he scrutinized her face like an accomplished actor in Indian films.

"Do I look like a wrestler?" Rita pressed her lips in disgust and turned away from him.

"Who knows? After all you are a tagdi (sturdy) Punjabi Kudi (girl)," he retorted mischievously. "You could fight even a man much stronger than your hubby if you had no mind to oblige him…in…er… what he wanted from…er…his wife…at night," he said mischievously, his gaze fixed on her face.

She could sense that he was talking not only to show that he had noticed the scars but also was appreciating her attractive face and to him the scars had added to the charm of that face. To him she was only a young woman, strongly desirable to the male in him. His words had been well chosen and had a definite target of attracting her attention to him as a peacock does when peahens are around, strutting, implying he was around if she found her husband inadequate in his nocturnal duties and not to her taste. But his tone and his attempt at making little of her anguish and pain added salt to her injury.

She experienced the pricking of a thousand needles into every pore of her body. Her face twitched with distaste and she pretended not to have heard his absurd prattle. She turned away from him and didn't notice her children who had moved away the moment they saw that their mother had company and were playing or pretending to be playing close by. She was over protective of her children, her only object of attachment in life.

She called aloud, "Bhanu, Dhanush where are you? Come on children. Let's go home."

Bhanu was about eleven but she had a fashionable long dress frock on and Dhanush, in his kid outfit, only about five. The children came running to her as if they had been expecting her summons for a long time. Holding them by their hands she tried to leave. But she had hardly taken a few steps when the man again overtook her and impudently brushed against her. Then, like an actor, very sweetly and in a matter-of-fact tone he addressed her, "Oh I see. By the way, I recall having seen you modeling the other day. As I would like to take a few pictures of you, I thought of giving you a ring. But I didn't have your number, you know."

His hungry gaze was surveying her luscious body inch by inch and savoring the charm of her soft silken skin; her more than ordinary height; her slim figure; long dark waving hair; a Roman goddess-like nose on a high cheekbone – a handsome face. She was dressed in a red Punjabi dress - the preferred color of brides. He was overawed by her more than usual beauty. He heaved a wishful deep sigh, cleared his throat and said incoherently, almost stammering, "God has created you matchless… I mean, to be a model! By the way, I know some modeling agencies in Hollywood and will show your pictures to them…." He paused and his gaze was fixed at her face. She felt interested but hid her feelings and said, "Why are you trying to pull my leg? You know, I am nearing 30 and have two children. Don't you see I am past the modeling age or, as Jane Austen, the famous English novelist, would put it 'My dancing days are over.' As regards the day you saw me, they hadn't found any professional model, so I just acted as a substitute and did a little modeling." She said this mechanically, as if she were uttering a dialogue without any personal involvement in the words.

"Then what was wrong in it? I highly appreciate women who are career conscious even after marriage…," he said, almost flattering her.

"I don't think highly of modeling as a career. In Indian society, models are looked down upon. At the same time, after marriage, a woman's life turns into servitude and an object of satisfying someone's lust and a machine to produce children." Her bitterness was apparent in her words. "One loses poise and figure; becomes mentally sluggish and misses the zest to do anything significant," she added, as if impelled by some inner force. The initial disgust that was visible in her demeanor while talking to him was absent now.

"What is the matter with you, Rita? Why are you sad?" he addressed her by her name this time. He was serious now.

"Oh, it is nothing, Ravi," Rita said, with her head lowered and acknowledging familiarity with him for the first time.

"There must be something. Please let me know so that I may be able to help you one way or the other."

"No, thanks." Then, looking around, she said. "Where are the children?" She looked about trying to terminate the fruitless dialogue.

"Look, they are playing over there," Ravi said, pointing to the children a little distance away. "Rita, please tell me what is bothering you? Believe me, I care for you a lot," he said, with a touch of seriousness in his tone. "Here, have my card. If you need me, please don't hesitate in giving me a call. I am worried about you and please…"

She extended a hand and accepted the card without looking at him. Without saying anything, she took the children with her and moved to her car.

Ravi was eying her with a sympathetic look now. To Rita this behavior on Ravi's part was puzzling. The acquaintance with Ravi had been very limited. He had once come to their house with her brother Navin and on another occasion, they had met in a Gurdwara (a religious place) and these brief encounters were hardly enough to make people friends. Rita had a nagging feeling that Ravi had found out everything about her life and its problems. Her elder and younger sisters-in-law lived in Los Angeles.

One of her sisters-in-law, Kanta Rani, who lived in San Francisco, would make fun of Rita by calling her stupid before her friends. It must have been from one of the sisters-in-law that he could have learned about her. He was a bachelor and there was no other way for him to get the information about the present situation she was in.

That night she just tossed in her bed, without any sleep. Ravi and his visiting card took turns in her mind. She felt like ringing him up to ask what right he had to sympathize with her. He was an uninvited trespasser into her personal life trying to foist himself on her and an intruder on her privacy.

Once, on Diwali (a Hindu festival), Rita was modeling on the stage and Ravi standing in a corner. He was taking her pictures. It was for the first time that Navin had introduced Ravi to Rita a little before Rita had gone on to the stage. Ravi was a little startled to see Rita modeling. Rita also recalled that he had smiled briefly and Navin didn't like it. But such incidents were hardly enough to make her sleepless. Her heart was keeping its own counsel and she hadn't learnt the trick of interacting with it. Struggling with these thoughts, she fell asleep.

In the morning the telephone rang and she was awakened a little befuddled from sleep. It was her brother Navin on the line. "Is everything fine, Navin? I was scared to hear the bell ringing so early in the morning."

"Morning? Just look at the watch; it is noon already. Where are Bhanu and Dhanush?"

"They are probably watching TV in their room."

"What sort of mother are you? It is noon and you are still sleeping, least bothered about the children. You seem to have lost your bearings."

"Navin, talk some sense please. It is not India, where the mother gets up early in the morning and makes breakfast. American children prepare their breakfast themselves and don't expect their mother to do it for them."

"Exactly, and that is why they don't care for their mother. And maybe that is why Sudhir…"

"Navin, do you intend to pick a row with me in the morning? Please come to the point. Why did you ring me up so early in the morning?"

"This evening there is a party at Dr. Mahesh Sharma's and he has invited Bhanu and Dhanush. He wants to give Bhanu an award."

"Award! But for what?"

"Everybody liked the poems of Dhanush and the singing of Bhanu at the function. That is why they say that the children should be encouraged."

"Well, it is Saturday today and we can come to it. What is the time of the party?"

"Be ready by 6' o'clock and Anju and I will …"

"Navin, don't hang up the phone I like to ask you, If you don't mind.

"Go ahead ask"

"Are you serious about Anju?"

"No, Didi, I am not serious about anyone, including Anju, yet. She is just a friend. And please don't be disturbed. As far as marriage is concerned, I shall go to India and marry an Indian girl."

"Look here, if you are not serious about Anju, don't give her false hope as when she comes to know the truth, she will be heartbroken, it will hurt me."

Navin had come to America only a year back. He was younger than Rita by about three years. He had been admitted to a medical college recently. He was short tempered but he loved his sister Rita. He never liked anybody to interfere with his affairs but could hardly ever keep away from other's' affairs, especially Rita's.

In the evening the party proved to be a great success. One of the invitees was Prakash. He was a very good photographer. He was much sought after at functions for taking pictures. Ravi had also come but minus his camera. The function was to thank the artists who had participated in the recent Baisakhi Mela.

After dinner and the prize distribution, Dr. Mahesh Sharma addressed the audience, "Ladies and gentlemen, besides Bhanu and Dhanush, their mother also deserves a prize for grooming her two gems of children so commendable. But instead, we expect to be rewarded by her. She is a writer, a poet and an accomplished actor. I request Rita Verma either to sing a song or recite a ghazal."

"But Dr. Sahib, I don't know any song or ghazal."

"I am not taking a 'No' from you. You can't excuse yourself like this." Seeing his insistence, she said, "All right, I shall recite a short poem," Rita said modestly.

"Ok. Ladies and gents, Rita has come to attend a party here for the first time. So, as a concession, we shall make do with a short poem."

Rita came to face the guests and said, "This is my own poem, ladies and gentlemen:

> Whenever I wept, the tears did not console,
> Even though they were my company's sole.
> My harried looks searched for a tiny place,
> But saw nothing except an empty space.

She had hardly finished the lines when Navin chipped in impatiently, "Didi, please! Avoid such absurd couplets." Rita's face became red. She was staring at Navin when she heard a familiar voice, "Rita, please complete the poem."

It was Ravi who was watching her closely. After the disruption by her brother Navin, Rita had lost her zest to recite any further. The lines which she had liked so much sounded insipid to her now. They left the party and during their way back home, Navin kept quarrelling with Rita.

He said constantly, "In future I shall take only Bhanu and Dhanush with me to a party. I feel so mortified with your rubbish that you call poems which I can't make head or tail of." Navin grumbled, a final sign of his impudence.

"If one can't recite a poem, then a poetic gathering is itself absurd and meaningless," Anju said to Navin.

"You stay out of this, Anju. Women will always side with women. My sister is a mother of two children. Do childish things behoove her?"

"What if she has children? Is it a taboo for her to have a little enjoyment in her life?" Anju retorted.

"I don't like modeling on the stage. People make fun …make fun, do you hear?" he said, almost shouting and laying stress on 'Make Fun'.

"If you listen to people, you will never reach anywhere in life," Anju said boldly.

"But will modeling ensure progress and could you erect palaces with your poetry?"

"These so-called palaces have robbed people of their happiness. In trying to build them, their dreams have crumbled to the ground. I don't need any palaces. Navin, you are younger than me. In future, I would like to request you, my younger brother Navin, to show due respect to your elder sister while talking or you had better keep away yourself from your sister," Rita scolded Navin.

"Didi, (Sister) I confess you are instrumental in my coming to America; finding a job for me; teaching me to drive a car. You bought me a used car, but have you ever lovingly invited your brother to a home-cooked lunch? The fact is that I was destined to come to America, and here I am."

"Thank you, Navin. After all, you retain the sense to acknowledge what you have received from me. Anyway, we have reached my apartment and I would like you to drop me here."

Navin dropped Rita, the children and Anju in front of the apartment building and left. He was the only brother of Rita. Once, when she had visited India, her father had pleaded with her quite a few times to petition for her brother and sisters to migrate to America. "It will add to your stature, Rita, if you settle them in America. All of us will forever be obligated to you. When Navin is settled in America, he will settle us too there and we shall have a comfortable old age."

Rita lay in her bed thinking about the ways of the world. The next month her sisters were also coming to America. Their husbands accompanied them as well. They would have to be settled in America. But the one who was settled here had already forgotten the good done to him by his sister. However, he never forgot a single word which was not to his liking. He was selfish. Well, one has to do a good turn and forget it. As wise men have said, "Neki Kar Kunvay Mai Daal" (Give, forgive and forget it.) She finally fell asleep at 2 am.

She was awakened by the telephone bell and took the call, still half asleep. "Hello!"

"Hello, is this Rita?" someone asked from the other end.

"Yes, speaking."

"Your photos are ready." The voice sounded familiar.

"Who is this?" she asked anyway.

"Don't you remember me? This is Prakash."

"Oh! Hello, Prakash." Sleep had deserted her now.

"God be thanked that you have recognized me. I had least expected this."

"I am sorry." Saying this Rita laughed.

"Sorry won't do. You will have to come here to see your photos personally."

"If you don't mind, can I come this evening?" Rita said casually.

"Wonderful. What about dining with me?"

"No, thanks anyway."

"Why not? Come on, I am a good cook and promise that you won't return hungry from my place." He laughed in the mouth piece.

Rita was torn between two emotions. One told her to keep away from strangers, especially of the male variety, but the other impulse forced her to move away from the rut of this miserable life after separation from Sudhir. But life can sometimes be very demanding. The urge to continue with minimum physical or mental discomfort is paramount.

"All right, if you insist," she mumbled, still oscillating whether to go or not.

"Fine, I shall be waiting for you."

She replaced the receiver and called Sudha whom she had befriended in the office. She worked as an engineer in the office where Rita was a clerk.

When Rita had seen Sudha for the first time, she had mistaken her for a Spaniard, not an Indian. On the other hand, Sudha had taken Rita for an Iranian. When they crossed each other in the corridor, Sudha had moved on to her errand with just a hint of a smile. By and by when they came to know that both were Indians, they came closer and started taking some interest in each other. Rita felt ill at ease with this increasing intimacy in the early stages. But gradually the proximity between them increased and turned into friendship.

Rita mentioned the name of Prakash to Sudha and told her that in the evening she was going to see him along with the children.

Sudha asked who this Prakash was. Rita said, "Once when I was modeling on the stage, a man named Prakash had approached me and after a handshake, had told me that he was Prakash and that he had taken some of my pictures. If they turned out to be good, he would let me know. It was then that I had given him my number."

"What followed then?" Sudha asked eagerly.

"Nothing much. Occasionally he calls to find out how I am."

"Then why has he phoned today?"

"Initially he had asked me to accompany him to see movies but I had turned down the invitation. But today he has asked me to collect some of my photos; I felt that there was no harm if I went."

"Why didn't you go to see the movies?" Sudha joked.

"Sudha, how could I have gone to the movies? If Sudhir had come to know…, God be merciful! I have two children and ladies don't …"

"How much is your life worth now anyway? You have ruined your life."

"I had little idea that Sudhir, to whom my parents had married me, would one day beat me like a dog and turn me out of his home?"

When Rita recalled the horrible scene of the beatings, she started crying.

"Why didn't you send this man, a husband of yours, to jail? He has done everything to mutilate you physically and emotionally. On the other hand, you still wish him well. Besides, do Bhanu and

Dhanush mean nothing to him? Is he not their father?" Sudha said contemptuously.

Then she continued, "Just look at the Americans. They readily bring up step sons and daughters. Among most of us, I don't mean to say all Indians, sometimes it is the man who after marriage rapes the woman and deprives her of her virginity, but it is the woman who suffers the consequences of the rape with child birth. I suggest you leave Bhanu and Dhanush with him so that he also has a taste of children's upbringing," Sudha said very indignantly.

Rita looked at Sudha uncomprehendingly. Then she grasped the import of her words, and said, "No, no, don't say this. After all, I am their mother. My children love me very much. I don't want them to live as motherless children. Do you know that whenever Sudhir beat me, they would weep on my account and quite a few times they were even stunned? That's why they don't let me return home."

"Who asks you to go home? But what would you do with that cruel man? Ok, look here, you now go to Prakash without bothering your mind," Sudha assured her with a pat on the back.

"Sudha, I am a little afraid and confused. These days when I am living away from Sudhir, I find myself losing faith in the male species. You just wait. Shortly, in order to make an exhibition of his maleness, he will start maligning me everywhere to prove that men are never wrong. He will imply that I was responsible for all the bitterness that affected my conjugal relations."

"You milksop, he won't eat you. You are in America where a woman can satisfy her sexual needs with not one but a dozen men if she so wishes."

"What are you trying to say to me"

"Let a beautiful woman just click her fingers and she will find a queue of studs waiting at the door for their turn."

"Huh?" Rita was confused as Sudha continued her preaching.

"Nobody would raise a finger at a woman as society does in India. Here your private life is fully recognized. You are the master of your body."

"I am still married to Sudhir in the eyes of the Almighty as well as in the society which has made the norms. Uff!" Rita was puzzled again.

"Sudhir has nothing to do with how you prefer to live. You are living separately. You should not be unduly obsessed with your Indian moral scruples in America."

"What are you talking about Sudha? Just let me know why I should sleep with other men. I am not out of my mind. No matter where I live on this earth, I will remain Indian with my Indian sanskar (moral values). God save me from stooping so low!"

"No! But Rita, I didn't mean this."

"Then, what did you mean?" Rita got a bit furious.

"I meant that to us you are a woman called Rita and nothing beyond that. It is none of our business how Rita leads her life and nobody should sit in judgment over others' private lives."

"Sudhir…"

"Let Sudhir say what he pleases about what you do with your body but nobody would care. Everybody has the right to live their lives according to the situation and time."

"But…"

"Just think over what I have just said. Anyway, I shall take care of Bhanu and Dhanush. You needn't worry. However, yes, wear that maroon-colored Punjabi dress. No, just a minute. You should wear your blue jumpsuit. Be a little late just to test how impatiently he waits for you. I think there is no harm in teasing a prospective friend."

"Friend? Parents don't allow girls to visit even the closest female friends in India. I was so naïve that I missed school for two days once. A girl classmate of mine had a male name, Jatinder. She had written a sad letter to me and it fell into my elder sister's hands. Lo and behold! All hell broke loose because of this. They started thinking a lot of things…you know what I mean."

"That it was a letter from some boyfriend."

"How do you know?" Rita asked, surprised.

"Well, that is the way things happen in India. But the Indian dos and don'ts haunt you not only when you are awake but also when you are asleep. Your mother and sister went to Jatinder's house and found out that it was a girl not a boy. They complained to her parents that the character of the girl who wrote such letters would not be good. Acting upon this observation, her parents forbade her to meet you."

"But how do you know all this?"

"This haunting theme of all your childish prattle about your past and particularly the moral principles have become a public topic. Well, you have told your school time stories a number of times. You dwell in the past a bit too much"

"Those childhood incidents are so much related to my present."

"After all, what is the use of recalling what is past and is gone? Why do you suffer from bitterness again and again?" Sudha continued. "You are an American grown-up woman and don't need a nanny to look after you. But the problem is that you have convinced yourself that by seeing some man other than your so-called faithful husband Sudhir, you will commit the original sin and will reserve a seat in hell."

"No, Sudha, though the memories of the past are vague, I find solace in relieving them, by recalling and following them while bringing up Bhanu and Dhanush. I would do everything to save my children from the American libertine ways. I live because I have them. Except in their company, I haven't had a single moment of happiness since I was married."

"Rita, nobody is happy in this cruel world. The sufferings of some become public and everything about them becomes public property. While there are others whose life remains under covers and they quietly suffer pain and misery."

"But I am suffering from within and outside. I am on fire from every side every minute of my life."

"Yes, I agree with Rita. Your husband has deprived you from all the social norms, harmed you intellectually and emotionally. He has humiliated you publicly. He has exploited you physically. The book of your life is open to all eyes to pry into. It is exactly for this reason that I suggested that you make a fresh start. Go ahead. See this Prakash and …well go ahead with whatever the promptings of the heart are. I can imagine what he or for that matter all the handsome men you meet expect form a beautiful woman like you."

"Sudha, it will take some time for me to learn this language of the heart or the Americanized heart. But your philosophical narrative has reminded me of an incident about Sudhir."

"Shoot."

"There was a time once when a friend of Sudhir's came to our house to meet him. I cooked for them and after eating, there was the usual chit chat. I made a joke casually and he said, "Dear Sudhir, your wife is very smart.""

Sudha was listening to her recurring story attentively.

"Would you guess what he said? He was shaking his head again and again showing his disagreement with what he had said."

"In other words, Sudhir didn't like his remarks about you."

'No, but that is only the partial truth. In addition, the remarks sowed the seeds of distrust in his mind. He started distrusting me."

"Or, so to say, he was so overconfident that he thought you were stupid besides being of a loose character. The other possibility could be that he felt so insecure that he couldn't swallow that other should find you smart."

"But why should he think like this?"

"Keep it for some time later. Now if you continue this old mantra of your past, you will never be able to go to Prakash. Look, it is already six. Hurry up. Get ready at once."

Rita got up and lent Sudha a hand in attending to domestic chores. This done, she took a bath and dressed herself in a blue jumpsuit, colored her hair slightly, and applied a dark red colored lipstick to her lips. She was about to leave when Sudha again intervened, "Oh… why haven't you applied nail polish? Apply red nail polish and put on red shoes to match the lipstick."

"You are making me up as if I were a sixteen-year-old girl. Look, my hair is already graying." This refrain of the graying hair had become a standing joke among Rita's friends and acquaintances.

"Rita, why do you have to drag the gray hair in everything? If unsavory circumstances have hastened the graying of your hair before its time, it doesn't mean you should give up all interest in life. You are hardly out of your youth. But I find that you are incorrigible."

"According to Indian standards, I am old.

"Yes, I know you are aging by the second whereas others age in years. Why are you obsessed with being thirty, may I ask? Do you think that number thirty makes one old?"

"I feel old, not only old, I feel very unattractive. After giving birth to children, physically women lose their allure."

"In your subconscious mind you keep debating whether the eligible males you intend to attract with your looks will find you sexually desirable or not. Motherhood adds beauty to a lady. Even sixty, seventy-year-old women have desire in them."

"I disagree with you, Sudha. Sudhir always reminds me of my brea...."

"Forget Sudhir, talk about yourself," Sudha got irritated with Rita and continued with her thoughts.

"Somehow or other you suppress the real feelings. Age has nothing to do with the feelings and desires of the heart, mind and soul. You see, I was twenty-four when I was married." Sudha laid stress on 'twenty-four'.

"Why does not age Sudhir used to say that girls that marry after twenty to twenty-two hardly ever retain their virginity. They can't find suitable matches either."

"How smart of him! He has just be fooled you with his sermon. I also feel how very obsessed he is with his less than attractive looks. If, like you, I had been married at seventeen, today I wouldn't be an engineer."

Rita had been busy with her make up while the two friends conversed. She was ready and surveyed herself in the dressing table mirror. She exclaimed, "No Sudha, these red shoes, the red with graying hair lady."

"Goodness gracious! If I were a boy, I would...make love to you! She moved toward Rita with arms spread to embrace her and lips readied to impart a kiss on her lips. But Rita moved back laughing. "You naughty girl! Bye, I am going."

Sudha watched Rita leave. She was thinking aloud how beautiful she was. Sudhir was hardly a match for her. She wondered why she thought so highly of him. She was about to shut the door when Ginny turned up.

"Who were you talking to?" Ginny asked her.

"Hi Ginny! Oh, I was just thinking about Rita's lousy husband and was loudly cursing him."

"Yes Sudha, her husband is an insensitive automaton totally devoid of human emotions. His two sisters-in-law and both the brothers have brainwashed him to a point where nobody can argue with him about anything sensible."

"Have you seen her husband recently?"

"Yes, he came to our home this morning."

"Did he say anything?"

"He had hardly anything to say. But he looked happy. He said that if Rita wanted to return home, she would have to do so of her own accord. Otherwise, he would divorce her. He could find another wife anytime."

"Oh my God, Is he so cruel?'

"Where is Rita?" Ginny asked, without making any attempt at satisfying her curiosity about Sudhir.

"She has gone to collect some pictures from a photographer. She was reluctant to go, but I forced her to go."

"Is that Prakash?"

"How do you know him?"

"I was with Rita when he gave her his card. He is a very handsome Gujarati."

"But his name sounds Punjabi and I have noticed that Gujrati names are different from Punjabi names."

"Yes, but his mother is Punjabi. He is an engineer. Photography is only his hobby. His demeanor betrayed that he is in love…with Rita."

"Ginny, Rita has a right to have a relationship with any man she prefers."

"But Sudha, Rita has come from a very orthodox family. She is not the type who would have relations with any man. Then she has created an invisible barrier that at thirty and with grey hair she has lost the right to befriend a stranger even if she likes him."

"Yes, I know other women in her situation would have kept chasing men whereas Rita doesn't. But if Rita's husband is a beast who will never reform, then is Rita bound to live her whole life in misery?"

"Sudha, Rita is the mother of two children. Who will accept her as wife? I regret that Indian culture is burdened with so many dos and don'ts. In India, a father of four children can marry a sixteen-year-old girl and if one happens to be an American Indian, one could have even a younger bride. But if a young woman happens to be the mother of two children, it is very unlikely that she could find anyone who would marry her. If someone does marry her, he would divorce her after obtaining a green card."

"I strongly feel that I should go to India and expose in the papers the doings of these Indian born husbands," Ginny said indignantly.

"It won't help. Our compatriots are not going to change so easily. On the other hand, every Indian man does not act like Sudhir. He is rare on this earth. Look at Dhanush You can see he will not be like his father Sudhir at all."

"I agree on that one. Rita really talks to Dhanush how a man should act and understand women. Dhanush will be a remarkable man when he grows up."

"So, why do we label all Indian men as bad as Sudhir? Well, leave it and let me have a cup of tea," Ginny said despondently.

Sudha had hardly got up to make tea for Ginny when the phone rang.

"Hello,"

"Hello Sudha…" Rita was calling from a public telephone booth.

"What is the matter, Rita? Where are you calling from?"

"I am calling from the gas station on the corner of the 101 Freeway."

"Has your car broken down?"

"No, I phoned just to tell you that I aren't go to see Prakash. I feel very nervous and almost afraid."

"Rita, you are out of your senses. He is sure to be waiting for you. Anyway, here is Ginny, talk to her." Sudha gave the receiver to Ginny.

"Look here Rita. You just collect your pictures today since you are going to see him and then you needn't go again and don't worry. We are with you."

Ginny replaced the receiver. Reluctantly Rita turned her car towards Parkash's house. She was reflecting over the vicissitudes of her life.

Before marriage, she had scrupulously avoided the male company of strangers, whereas there were other girls in her class who had boyfriends. She hated such girls from the core of her heart. To her having a boyfriend meant tarnishing the good image of one's parents.

Once in her high school days, there was a girl named Sita Sharma in her class. A love letter from a boy of her neighborhood was found in her book and all her classmates had made fun of her to a nauseating point. Ultimately the letter had reached the principal. The irony was that the poor girl had no idea who the letter was from. It could have been a mischief of someone from her own class. But it cost the poor girl so dearly. She was expelled from the school. As Rita recalled this incident later, she cursed herself with a guilty feeling as if she was herself responsible for Sita's expulsion. Her present lot was perhaps the consequence of Sita Sharma's curse. If by chance Sita Sharma crossed her path now, Rita would humble herself before her and ask for her forgiveness. When the chest of past memories is opened, they tumble out in heaps like old skeletons. It happened to Rita today.

Lost in the past, she didn't realize that she had reached Parkash's apartment. Absent-mindedly she rang the bell.

"Who is it?" a voice called from within.

"It is me, Rita." Rita cleared her throat and said timidly.

"Oh, great! Please come in. Today Lord Kishana Himself is visiting the humble abode of the pauper."

Prakash gazed at Rita without batting an eyelid. He was oblivious of the fact that she was still standing outside and he hadn't made way for her to step in.

"I have come to collect my pictures. Please give them to me," she said, not meeting his gaze and showed no inclination to enter.

"But won't you even come in?" Prakash said, holding her by the shoulder.

Rita brushed his hand away from her shoulder. A faint mischievous smile played on Parkash's lips. He lived in a small apartment. To the right of the entrance was a small kitchen. Rita moved past him, got into the room and sat down on a sofa. She felt as if she was sitting on velvety cushions. The fact that since her marriage eleven years ago, Sudhir had never brought in decent furniture came to her mind. Whenever she asked him to buy good furniture, he would taunt her saying that she hadn't come to his house with truckloads of cash from her parents, "I hardly earn enough to meet the bare minimum needs of the family. If you are so fond of good furniture, you may as well ring your father up and tell him to send new furniture of your choice." As Rita recalled this, she got up at once as if it were a sin to sit on a good sofa. She looked at Prakash, a very handsome man dressed informally yet looked dashing. Rita then pictured Sudhir in her mind and compared him with Prakash. A deep sigh escaped her.

"Rita, what is this? Why have you got up from the sofa?"

"Oh" She realized what she had just done unconsciously.

"Please sit down; I have brought tea for you." He was carrying a teapot in his right hand.

Rita, who had been reflecting on her predicament, was jolted back to the present world of reality. She said, "Oh Prakash, why did you bother to prepare tea?"

Prakash said nothing. He poured tea into a cup and handed it over to her. He realized that Rita was ill at ease for being alone with him in his apartment. To mitigate the awkwardness, he brought his slide projector.

"Why have you brought out your slide projector?" Rita said, futilely trying to hide her nervousness.

Prakash had guessed her discomfort. He said, "Calm down Rita. Don't worry. I shall first show you the pictures for you to select and then I shall enlarge and mail them to you. I have already put the small ones in an envelope which I shall give you now."

"Oh! I see." Rita heaved a sigh of relief, putting the partially empty tea cup on the table.

"Rita, there is no need to be afraid of me." He smiled, looking at her.

"No, no, why should I be afraid?" She attempted to laugh.

"I really don't know why but it is a fact that I have a great compatibility with beautiful married women. I emphasize 'beautiful.' Last time when I saw you on the stage, for example, I could not have imagined that you are the mother of two children. When I did come to know of this, it was a great surprise for me. I couldn't believe this."

"Well, you know it now. I was married at a very early age. I was very good in studies and would finish two classes in a year and I completed B.A by the time I was hardly eighteen. I had just started coaching when I was married."

"Wow, what a lucky girl! I wish I had met you in India…"

"What then?" She smiled as if urging him to utter the implied but unuttered words. He paused for a moment as if to think of something that could flatter her and he would find a detour to escape saying what he really had on his mind and what this desirable beauty expected him to say. She, too, was making an attempt to avoid saying what she wished in order to escape the sense of guilt, her chronic problem in the matters of the heart.

"Well, err… I would have taken your pictures and shown them to well-known Bollywood Producers Raj Kapoor." "And then…?"

"You would have outclassed Nargis, Hema Malini and Rekha."

Rita was laughing. She knew very well that he was flattering her but she still liked this compliment. Suddenly he asked her, "Ok, please tell me how the boys and girls addressed you in your college days?"

"No special name," she said innocently.

"It is next to impossible. Well, anyway, truly tell me which Indian actress in the Indian movies do you look like?"

"What do you think. Why does it matter?"

"You look like Madhubala one minute, Nargis the next moment and dimple the…"

"Well, ok…ok. Don't over indulge in this flattery. Still, since you insist, I tell you that in high school, girls teased me by calling me Saira Bano. Later, when I was in college, they compared my smile to Madhubala's and my chin to Vaijayanti Mala."

However, he was comparing her with all famous Indian film actresses. He was really dreaming about her being an all-famous Indian movie actress of the sixties and seventies era.

"And your poses too in your photographs are like Vaijyanti Mala. To be realistic, I regret that the beauty of most Indian girls never reaches the big screen. Instead, they get married and waste their life in a dead insipid routine. I wonder why it persists even in the modern age."

Rita didn't see through the game of flattery. She was sure of his seriousness.

"It is simple. A girl is like the slave of her parents before marriage. After marriage, she is the slave of her husband. The parents are the slaves of society..." They were talking like old pals now.

"But in my case, it will be different. When I get married, I shall..."

"Cut out this rubbish. All men make tall promises before they marry."

"But I assure you that I shall not put any restrictions on my wife's freedom when I get married," he asserted.

"Oh, but how long can we keep talking? It is already eight." Rita made a move as if to rise from her seat.

Prakash got up first and suddenly switched off the light and the room became totally dark. Rita was puzzled and apprehensive as to what was to follow. Yet she was awaiting male hands to grope her. She would not like to be groped and pinched, pressed and kissed madly, all the time convinced that all that was to happen against her consent. She had nursed a sense of guilt so big that only aggressive male behavior could justify it. Her body was tense. Prakash started the projector and there were pictures running on the wall that served as a screen. Rita was disappointed but said nothing and the darkness hid her face and feelings.

Prakash first showed her some beautiful snaps of scenery of nature like butterflies, the blue sky, deep dancing waves of oceans, and snowcapped mountains of the world which convinced her that nothing of the sort she had expected was to happen. She pretended to be sharing the slides he was showing to her, little caring that she was alone with him in the dark room. The scenery clips over, he starts showing Rita's pictures one by one and delaying each frame for a few seconds before switching to the next one. Rita felt ashamed and embarrassed within. She was anxiously waiting for the show to end so that she could hurry home. All the slides had been shown but Prakash just sat by her side in the dark. Rita suddenly realized that Prakash had been holding her hand since God alone knew when. But now the undefined frenzy for something she was eager to meet had passed away. Her mouth felt dry. Freeing her hand, she got up and switched on the light. There was a glass of water on the side table.

She tried to take it and, in her haste, tumbled the glass over, spilling the water all over and onto her clothes.

"Oh my God, your clothes have been drenched. But never mind. I shall dry them up in a moment." He quickly brought a blow dryer for hair and began to dry her clothes.

The hot current of air moved slowly up and down her body raking forgotten old fires. The wet clothes had clearly outlined the firm curves of her body. Prakash felt a strange sensation stirring and a tingling in every pore of his body. But Rita, like a puppet character in a show, just watched him dry her clothes. His gaze lingered at some vital stops down her body. When the clothes had dried, she picked up her purse with the intention to leave but Prakash took the purse from her and said, "I have a reservation for dinner at a Thai restaurant. You seem to have forgotten that I had invited you for dinner."

"But I am not hungry. Please let me have my pictures. I want to go," she said, showing little inclination to match her words with action.

"Well, here are your pictures, but I insist that you must go for dinner with me." He pressed her to stay.

Finally, Rita gave in and agreed to stay. She had not been to a restaurant for ages. She felt it would change her mood. She recalled the day when she hadn't had any idea how to use a fork. Her parents had never allowed her to go to a restaurant.

They went to the restaurant and had hardly occupied their seats when Rita said, "Do you know that before I married, I couldn't eat with a knife and fork?"

"But why not?"

"My father had brought me up with lots of restrictions. Once, a female friend of mine, whose father was a doctor, took me to a restaurant. After dinner we went to his clinic nearby and her father hired a comfortable rickshaw for us and I returned home. I found my sisters and mother very angry. I told a lie that I had by mistake left my books at the house of a friend and had gone to her place to collect my books. For the time being peace was restored. But one day..."

"One day what?" Prakash was taking great interest in Rita's narrative. He welcomed every move that delayed Rita's departure.

"My cousin, who must have seen me with my friend, reported the incident to my mother. Now all hell broke loose on me. My mother and sisters gave me a severe beating that put me out of shape."

"In which class were you studying in those days?"

"I was in my second year in college. After the incident, I was not allowed to go to college for a long time."

"I can understand. It is usual with parents. Mine is almost the same story. My parents were also strict with me in such situations."

"How many sisters do you have?" Rita asked. The experience of the dark room was gradually fading.

"I have two sisters. One was two years older and the other was two years younger than me."

"What do you mean by 'One was?"

"Yes, Rita I had an elder sister who committed suicide by burning herself."

"Why did this happen?" Rita asked anxiously.

"Leave it for some other day. I don't want to spoil this dinner now. It is getting cold. Start eating."

"What does your younger sister do?" Rita continued.

"She is just a housewife. She is leading a happy married life."

"You are yourself an eligible bachelor, quite young. Then how is it that your younger sister got married first?"

"In India, girls of marriageable age are married before their elder brothers. As for my age, I may look young but in fact, I am the same age as you."

"I don't believe it," Rita said.

"Well, if you would like, I could show you proof. And if I am proved right, you would have to accept my condition."

"I don't accept conditions."

"In other words, why don't you admit that you are afraid of losing the bet?"

"I am past the stage of giving thought to winning or losing, you know," Rita said boldly.

"Then would you like to bet on this?"

"Yes, I would," she said casually.

Prakash took out his driving license from his purse and showed it to Rita. She was genuinely surprised when she saw his date of birth.

But concealing her surprise, she said, "But the date of birth can be wrong."

"Why should it be wrong?"

"Why not?" I was a minor at the time of my marriage, but my father obtained a fabricated certificate adding two years to my real age."

"But your looks show that you are younger than what you claim to be your real age. Well, accept that you have lost the bet."

"Ok, I concede defeat." Rita tried to end the matter there.

"No, you can't go Scot free so easily," he said.

"What do I do then?"

"You will have to go to see a movie with me."

"No, I am sorry. It is already ten o'clock and I shall be very late."

"Then it is not fair."

"Then is it fair to force a woman to stay against her will? You know it isn't, but because of this silly bet, I shall accompany you to this movie of yours." Destiny favored Rita mysteriously that day.

"I am obliged." Prakash made a chivalrous bow to her.

Convincing herself that she was doing all this against her will and feeling embarrassed, she took the seat beside him in the car which had a sporty look and was spotlessly clean. As soon as she was seated, she observed, "Your car looks quite new." It was more like a futile excuse to divert her mind from the nagging feeling that she was doing something which bothered her, than a sincere appreciation of the car.

"No, I changed it six months back."

"You changed it six months ago? What do you mean?" She was puzzled.

"I change cars every six months."

"Do you know what people say about those who change their cars frequently?"

"No, what do they say?"

"That the people who change cars so frequently also change wives like cars."

"Meaning…?" Prakash, like an accomplished actor, looked askance at her.

"You are a slippery fish. How convincingly you act. Well, here is the movie theater. Let's hope the movie is good."

They occupied their seats. It was a movie meant for old romantics. Henry Fonda, Jane Fonda and Katharine Hepburn were the main actors and the title was On Golden Pond. As they watched the movie, Prakash placed his hand lightly on Rita's shoulders. Though she didn't like it outwardly, she didn't make any move to remove it from there, wondering what the other spectators would think if she protested even slightly. After a few moments she casually tried to move his hand away from her shoulders but Prakash whispered into her ear, "I am just extending a hand of friendship and nothing more. Please don't misunderstand me."

Rita relaxed and quietly watched the movie. There were romantic scenes in the movie and when there was one on the screen, her heart went racing and she felt as if she were still a virgin, an unmarried girl, surrounded by sex hungry hunks who would ravish her, with the only difference that when she was really a virgin, her parents protected her virginity, but today there was none around to look after her. This loneliness and helplessness were shared by her children too. As the thought of her children came to her mind and she wanted to ask Prakash if they could leave, he placed his lips on hers, simultaneously holding her firmly.

"Oh, great heaven!" The long thirst had after all received some drops of nectar. For some time, she forgot everything and time elapsed since the kiss had started. Their lips remained locked, relishing each other's intensity of passion.

Finally, she became conscious of the situation and felt a jolt, regretting what she had done. The old sense of guilt hit her. She felt an urge to run away from the theater, but it was not possible. Another hurdle was that her car was parked at Parkash's place. When the movie finally ended, Prakash again held her hand and led her to his car, opened the door and helped her in.

He switched on Hindi movie songs. "The lines ran, 'Come along my darling, I shall take you to the heaven of dreams.' She felt that Prakash had deliberately played that song for her to feel that what had been left half way could still be finished if she wanted. Her eyes became tearful but she hid them. Prakash too said nothing. He had no intention to hurt her with any of his gestures. He had realized that the incident in the theater had been enjoyed by her like the forbidden fruit as much as him. As soon as they reached Parkash's apartment, she got out and ran to her car. In her confusion she didn't even thank Prakash. He stood watching her depart and thinking when the half-finished business, he had planned would be completed to the entire satisfaction of them both.

CHAPTER 2

Rita left Prakash staring after her. She could feel his gaze piercing her back through the rear glass of the car. She found it difficult to analyze her ambivalent feelings towards him. She had been in lip lock with Sudhir hundreds of times and was the mother of his children but the experience in the theater was unique; it had left a mark on her mind which was difficult to describe in words. It had touched her body and mind and it lingered, permeating her whole being.

Simultaneously her past upbringing in India always haunted her. Her conscience was crying out loudly, a sinner, a sinner. What would those in India say if they had just had an inkling of her feelings and of what she had done? Her past was, she felt, an imposition that seemed to side with her mind but the heavenly sweet flavor of the forbidden fruit in the theater sided with her body. She had an internal tug-of-war that was tearing her into two.

"Oh Lord, tell me whether I have sinned." A voice from inside said that she hadn't but a voice came loud and clear from across the seven seas that she was the fallen legendary Eve.

She was disturbed and agitated, and in this state, she raced the car at a very high speed. She was struggling to control the flood of tears that welled up in her eyes. She was reflecting: though Sudhir was not very good looking, yet he was her husband and she viewed him as her only love. She was unaware of certain things which most married women consider to be normal in their life in this country, such as how to meet a stranger openly or clandestinely, how to write love letters, how to respond to the sensation of accelerated heartbeats, how to become intoxicated with love, how to cater to the physical needs etc. These things clashed with her conscience rooted in Indian mores which were dominant in the present situation. She found herself sinking in self-pity and considered herself to be a woman of easy virtue. The life of such a woman, she thought, is like that of a fruit that drops from a wayside tree and which anyone can pick up and eat.

In the circumstances that prevailed, there was always a likelihood of someone doing the same to her, exploiting her physically and discarding her contemptuously as they do with the rind of fruit. Prakash was just one such person from the crowd. Something from deep inside her protested, "No, you simpleton. He is a desirable male. What has divinity created the two sexes differently for?"

The words of her father, while she was being married away to a total stranger from a foreign country, echoed in her ears, "Dear child, don't do anything that could give anyone an excuse to raise an accusing finger at our integrity and honor. Always remember the sacred marriage vows. It is heard that in foreign countries women may marry not one but dozens of men whereas Indian culture allows only one husband and the woman's body is solely for him."

She cursed herself for the indulgence in Parkash's company and lost in these ideas, she reached home. Sudha was still up and was anxiously waiting for her. When Rita opened the door with the latch key, Sudha could hardly wait to know the reason for her late return, but instead of answering her, Rita put her head on Sudha's shoulder and started crying. Sudha felt uneasy and gently led her to her room. She said, "Rita, if you are disturbed at the moment, then go to bed and have some sleep. We can talk later." Saying this, she left the room, closing the door behind her.

Rita spent the night weeping silently without clearly knowing why she was weeping. Then she reflected on whether her prolonged stay with Sudha was justified. She was a self-respecting woman and would never be a burden on anybody. She decided that she would find a job and would share a room with someone like-minded and companionable. The morning came and Sudha brought her tea.

"Well, Rita, would you like to share with me what happened last night?" Sudha asked.

Rita looked at Sudha for a long moment and then said, "I just didn't feel good about last evening's visit."

"Did he try to take advantage of your vulnerability in any way?"

"I would say, yes and no."

"What do you mean?"

"To tell you the truth, I had an enjoyable evening. But the problem with me is that I can't be an American. I can't forget my Indian roots and upbringing. Though Sudhir has turned my life into a virtual hell, yet we have been married by going round the sacred fire seven times and we have taken solemn vows. Am I to cheat him after all this?"

"By enjoying an evening out with a young healthy male, do you think only you have violated their sanctity?" Sudha said. "Why do you forget that Sudhir too has gone back on his marriage vows?"

"I should follow the seven sacred vows of my marriage." Rita was feeling unreasonably guilty.

"He had married you of his own accord whereas in your case it is your parents who had decided your marriage with him. It was he who accepted you as his wife against the wishes of his brothers and sisters-in-law and now he has turned you into a laughing stock. Then where is the rationale for you to bemoan what you did or he did. Stop this line of thinking and don't accuse yourself for what has happened," Sudha said a little indignantly.

Rita decided not to continue with this discussion. Instead, she said, "Sudha, from tomorrow, I intend to start looking for a job and would like to share accommodation with some woman with whom I can adjust myself well."

"Oh! So, I have been a poor host! When did I say that I would have a problem in putting you up? As for finding you a job, I think I can help you with that too. The manager of the Bank of America is my friend. I shall talk to her about giving you a job."

"Please talk to her. It will be an obligation to me."

"By the way, what have you decided in the matter you referred to last time?"

"Which matters?"

"Would you like to reconcile with Sudhir and go back to him or… divorce him?"

"Oh Sudha! For God's sake don't utter the word 'divorce'. I never mentioned 'divorce'. It stabs me like a sword in my chest and is nothing less than pronouncing a death sentence to me." Rita almost deep sighs in anguish. "Well, ok. But what about the present situation which must be tackled one way or the other?"

"Next week two of my sisters are coming to stay with Navin. I would like to have their opinion too."

"They will never advise you to divorce Sudhir and would either persuade you or compel you to go back to him."

"I would rather wait for that situation to arise. Let me first find a job. In the meantime, I shall collect the few clothes that are at Navin place.

Sudha had been holding the ground bravely so far but the pathetic condition of Rita made her lose her calm, "What a pity that your brother too has alienated himself from you. I quite often feel sorry for you."

Tears rolled down Sudha's cheeks as she talked. Rita's eyes too were moist. She wiped the tears with the back of her hand and said, "Well, fate serves a different dish to everybody. Sudha, sometime ago I had written a couplet:

"What was it?" Sudha showed eagerness to hear it.

"It was:

One, who I thought was just mine, he   is no longer mine.

Why complain about those who were never meant to be mine."

"Wow! With a little coaching you could become a famous poet."

"So now you too have joined the ranks of flatterers." Rita laughed in spite of the seriousness of the occasion.

The girls talked for a long time. Rita decided to dedicate herself to work rather than to moping. After sometime she found the job of a cashier in a bank. There was a small community of Indians. Rita managed to move with her kids with a Maharashtrian lady. The schools were closed for summer vacation. Rita left her children with an American lady who was a lawyer in order to go to work. She also arranged coaching for the children in swimming and modeling. Bhanu was very fond of modeling and she could also sing a little. The American lady also had children of the same age as Rita's kids. All the children found each other's company pleasurable.

One day Rita returned home quite tired. The American lady, whose name was Julie Smith, said, "You know, I took Bhanu and Dhanush for a contest."

"What contest?" Rita asked her, surprised.

"There was an audition for a talent contest. Dhanush will participate in the talent contest and Bhanu in both beauty and talent. The fee for the contest was fifty dollars."

"But there is a problem, Julie. Their father won't allow them to participate in the contest."

"Please Mom!" Both the children chorused.

"Ok, ok. Julie, here are the fifty dollars."

"Thank you, but now they will have to receive some coaching from a professional," Julie suggested.

Rita wanted to say something but hesitated for a moment. Then she said, "But Julie, their dad doesn't give me any financial help and I can't afford to hire a coach for them. But anyway, how much is it likely to cost?"

"It is not much. Only about two months' coaching would do. It may cost just around a hundred dollars."

"Well, I shall arrange this by borrowing from some friend."

Rita's sisters from India had arrived along with their husbands. Before they came to the USA on the way Both sisters had been in Canada with their families for about two months and had been staying with some relatives from their in-laws' side.

They intended to stay in Canada for some time more. The place where Navin lived belonged to Rita and her husband but no tenant paid Rita any rent as Sudhir had influence over them and they paid the rent to him, so much so that even Navin paid the rent to him. Sudhir had promised Rita's parents that he would help Rita's sisters in settling them in Canada. But nothing had been done yet. They felt that it was Rita who was not doing much in this regard and Rita's mother wrote her a letter out of anger which Rita didn't like. However, she didn't react to this and kept quiet.

Time passed. One evening Rita went to the Navin apartment to borrow some money. As she was about to knock at the apartment door, she heard some loud noises from inside. She decided not to knock but listen to what was being discussed.

"Look here, Anju I am not yet settled in life and find it difficult to make both ends meet. Two of my sisters have already come to the

USA and I shall see to it that they are settled properly. Only then shall I think of marrying."

"Navin, you are too young to bear such burdens on your own. You have an elder sister Rita who is married and has two kids. Her husband rolls in wealth. Why doesn't she help you?"

"Neela, that sister of mine is a blot on our family's fair name."

"What do you mean?"

"She is frivolous and has left her husband over some trifle. Rita should conduct herself according to her husband's wishes. A woman should not forget that she is after all a woman and should never assume herself to be a man."

"Sorry Navin, I differ with you here. I fail to understand why a modern young man like you should hold such opinions. Most of the Indian community knows that Rita's husband ill-treats her ..."

"If the wife dared challenge her husband, she would naturally..."

"But it is the husband who forces her to open her mouth against him. I wonder what men like you take women for," Anju said indignantly.

It was enough. Rita had no desire to meet Navin now. She hurried back and got into her car. She was just driving aimlessly on the freeway. It was ten o'clock when the car halted in front of an office. But even at this late hour, the lights were on.

She was puzzled. It didn't occur to her that it was a press printing office where work was done even at night. Without anything particular in mind, she rang the bell.

"Who is this?"

"It is me, Rita."

"The door is open. Please come in."

"Is Mr. Ravi in?"

"No, he is out of town."

"When are you expecting him back?"

"He may be back in a couple of days. Do you have any message for him?"

"No."

Rita felt that everything was for the best. If Ravi had been in his office, she could have done something unpredictable in the state of mind that she was in and most probably wasted a lot of time. She didn't even pause for a moment to ask herself what impulse had drawn her to Ravi's place. Then, as she drove back, she remembered that more important than visiting Ravi was the great event in which her children were to participate. She felt guilty that she hadn't paid the attention that the event deserved. With this realization, she heaved a sigh and accelerated the speed of the car to reach home as early as possible. Back home, she hung Bhanu's dress for the beauty pageant on a hanger. She then ironed Dhanush's suit.

By the time the day of the contest came. The contest was to take place in a big hotel. Rita took her children to the venue. She found that most of the white American parents had already arrived and were readying up their children for the contest and Rita was doubtful of the success of her children among those white, blue eyed, lovely, very sharp children. She felt she and her children were out of place in that scenario. Rita noted with chagrin that some white parents didn't like the presence of Rita's olive-skinned children, the only ones among the white majority. Their disapproving looks at them and their mother were very discouraging. But Julie encouraged her not to lose her self-confidence.

The contest began. People occupied their seats. The contestants were given numbers showing the order in which they were to appear on the stage. First very young children, boys and girls, came to the stage turn by turn. greeted the audience, introduced themselves, bowed to them and resumed their seats. They were followed by older girls who came for modeling. They looked like bundles of grace and charmed the audience. The boys went next. After the boys had had their turn in the introductory appearance, the talent show was the next contest item. Bhanu sang an American song and danced along. Rita's heart almost burst with joy and pride at her performance. Despite Bhanu's being an outsider in this community of whites, she drew applause from one and all.

The other girls too displayed their talent. Then it was Dhanush's turn. He sang sweetly and the control over his voice was admirable. Although the performance of her children had been excellent, Rita had mixed feelings of happiness and sadness and found it hard to hold back her tears, whether of joy or pain she herself was not clear about.

Julie was sitting beside her and noticed this. She reassured Rita that Bhanu and Dhanush were sure to get some prize in spite of the cute American kids' performance.

"But Americans are far ahead in talent," Rita said.

"You should trust your children. They were born in America. I know that the situation of your family is far from being ideal for the upbringing of the children. You should keep the kids busy so that they are not affected by the unhappy environment of home but manage to make a mark in their lives," Julie said

Their conversation was interrupted by loud music, a sign for all to take their seats. The results were declared. Bhanu and Dhanush had won the first position in the children's talent contest; Bhanu was even selected as the beauty queen among the girls of her age. Most of the American mothers came to congratulate Rita. There were a few others who were burning with jealousy. They couldn't stomach the fact that children of immigrants should defeat them in their own country.

Some of them scoffed at Rita and the children as they passed by. But Rita kept quiet and waited for Julie in a corner of the hall. It was then that a white American approached her and said, "Hi, my name is Drake. I own a talent agency. I'd like to introduce your children to the movie industry."

"Yah, yah Mom, we would like to act in movies," Bhanu and Dhanush exclaimed with joy simultaneously.

"Thank you very much for the offer, but I am sorry that my husband doesn't like this," Rita said a little sadly in reply to the American gentleman.

"Here is my card. If you change your mind, do call me." He was moving away but paused again, looked at Rita, surveying her figure and observed, "By the way, you are also a beautiful lady." Then he strode away.

Rita returned home and played with his card unconsciously shifting it from one hand to the other. The children were very excited. Noticing their eagerness, she registered their names with the acting agency.

Occasionally Bhanu and Dhanush were given small roles as extras in films. Each child would usually earn around five hundred dollars a week.

Months passed but neither of Rita's sisters tried to contact her even once Since they arrived in the USA. One day, Rita chanced upon her elder sister in the shopping mall. As soon as she saw Rita, she embraced her and started crying. This could have continued for quite some time but Rita managed to ask her sister, "Bina Didi, I had sent for you to America but I find that after coming here, you didn't try to contact me at all.

Bina told her meekly that Navin, Sudhir and her husband had forbidden her either to see or phone Rita.

"But why, Didi? Has the fact that my husband is my enemy turned the whole world into my enemies?" Rita couldn't help crying.

"No, dear sister, don't waste your tears. Even when your other sister wanted to see you, her husband Ashwini threatened to divorce her if she ever met you or saw you."

"Have I defiled myself so much? Am I so unlucky…"?

"Bina…," Bina's husband Naresh, called her aloud.

Bina left without even waving goodbye to Rita. Rita became thoughtful. There was a time when both Naresh and Ashwini, her brothers-in-laws, loved her as a younger sister-in-law dearly. But because of Sudhir, both had started ignoring her. Even her sister Bina had left her so unceremoniously, without even once looking back. Rita stood rooted to the spot for a long time. Finally, she woke up to the present reality, took her car and drove straight away to Sudha's place. Sudha's brothers Jolly and Joy had come to see their sister Sudha.

They treated Rita as their real sister. Occasionally they took Bhanu and Dhanush for an outing. Jolly noticed that Rita was off-color and in order to humor her he said, "Rita, there is a party at our friend's place this evening. Why don't you accompany us? You should also take the children along."

"Jolly, among you unmarried young men…?"

"Oh, leave it Rita. What if we are unmarried? There will be many who are not bachelors like us.

"Who are they? I don't know them."

"Isn't it enough that you know me? I am your brother, not a stranger. "Jolly Said.

"Ok. What time is the party and how am I supposed to dress?"

"It is a disco party. Wear a skirt and blouse. They will suit the occasion."

In the evening Jolly took Rita and the children to the party in his car. Party was at the place where three sisters were living together. They all were not married. Rita met them and they soon became very friendly with her.

"Rita, are you in any business?" one of them asked her.

"No, I don't have any business. I work in a bank."

"Which bank?" asked the other girl.

"It is The Bank of America, in Culver City."

"This sister of mine is the manager at the Riverside branch of the bank."

"Really?" Rita turned to the fourth sister. "Do you also work at The Bank of America?"

"You live in Buena Park and work in Culver City…at such a distant place?"

"I had no alternative. I couldn't find a job close to my residence."

"Here is my card. I shall help you. I hope to arrange your transfer to a place near your home."

"Oh, I shall be very thankful. I am so glad to meet you. Would you mind telling me your name?"

"I am Vaishali, this is Sunali, the third one is Sohali and the fourth one is Sharmili."

"Oh, goodness gracious! Every name excels the other in sweetness and so does the beauty of each one of you," Rita laughed.

"But only knowing the names is not all. Now listen to our professions. I am a bank manager, Sunali is a dentist, Sohali is a psychologist and Sharmili is a computer consultant."

"Wow, all of you are so highly educated! But alas poor me, a mere graduate from India!"

"It is all a matter of luck which favors you in some other way if not in education. See, you got married even though only a graduate whereas we continued adding to our education. But even after this high education, not one of us has been lucky enough to find a suitable match."

"Why not? If you make an effort, you are sure to succeed. With God's grace you have everything, whiteish radiancy in face color, good looks, education…"

"Rita, the thing is that after good education, one tends to become independent in ideas and cautious in approach least one should take a wrong decision," Vaishali observed philosophically.

"What does your husband do?" Sunali asked Rita seriously.

"He is an engineer but…"

"What do you mean by 'but'?" Sohali looked askance at her.

"We don't live under the same roof. We don't see eye to eye with each other," Rita said, trying her best to sound casual and not betray her sadness.

"That is the point. That's why I don't want to marry. I would prefer the life of a spinster to being the slave of some silly man," Sharmili said sharply.

"But Sharmili, all are not alike. A woman's life is meaningless without a family, dharma and society…," Rita said, almost apologetically.

"You opted for a family life for dharma and society but what did you do for yourself?" Vaishali asked Rita. She continued after a brief pause, "There was a time when your dharma proclaimed that woman was created only to please her husband and procreate to perpetuate his lineage."

"No Vaishali…" Rita couldn't say anything more. She didn't find words to argue against what Vaishali had contended.

"Your disagreement in this regard doesn't impress me, Rita. The truth is that the modern woman wants something more than being a mere child producing machine. She wants to free herself from the shackles of old traditions and taboos and do something worthwhile without any hindrances in her path."

"But we…" Rita muttered something.

"A modern woman doesn't want to be confined within the society-sanctified four walls of the home and be content with just being a silent spectator of the male world. "But even this modern woman is weak and lonely and …," Rita again mumbled something.

"She is not weak at all. She is exploited in the name of dharma under a well-planned male conspiracy," Sohali said offhandedly.

"Her forbearance and shyness are an aspect of her beautiful nature." Rita claimed again in a subdued voice.

"Forbearance is essential for all, whether man or woman, and as for shyness, it should be in the eyes and the heart not in words alone," Sharmili observed cheerfully.

"When a girl is married, her husband is her armor. A woman who defies dharma and does not respect her husband is never forgiven by society and maybe even God. But what sort of woman am I that forever indulges in her husband's character assassination? There is no way society and dharma would respect me," Rita said with moistened eyes.

Jolly had joined the girls by now. He had heard what Rita had said. He came closer to Rita and said, "Rita, for God's sake don't cry. You simpleton, you are weeping because of your woes that have deeply affected your body, mind and your feelings. It is not wise to wash you dirty linen in public, as the saying goes." Jolly soothed her and put his hand across her shoulders. He slowly led Rita away from the company to take her back home. Rita turned and waved goodbye to the sisters.

After Jolly had dropped Rita at her apartment and was returning to his car, he noticed a shadow-like figure running away from near his car to hide himself in a cluster of nearby bushes. The man had in all probability taken his license plate number. Jolly felt uncomfortable. He ran back to Rita's apartment and knocked at the door. He heard footsteps from behind the door and shouted, "Rita, take care and be alert tonight."

"Why? What is the matter?"

"I think your husband has been chasing us. Where is your car?"

"I have hidden it in a neighbor's garage."

"Good. Take care. Your husband has saved himself within a hair's breadth from getting thrashed by me today." Jolly went back to his car and got in.

Blows of fate descend on one in heaps. Rita was passing through one such phase of life. A minor incident would affect her immensely.

Once when she was about to leave for the office, her car refused to start.

The next time she couldn't find a babysitter. Sudhir had come to know where she lived. He, however, didn't know where she parked her car. He was also unaware of her work place location.

One day, in desperation, Rita went to Sudhir's place to collect a few things for the car like a map and stuff that had been left behind when she had left the house. She knew that Sudhir was not at home that day but as ill luck would have it, unknown to Rita, Sudhir had returned unexpectedly and was secretly watching Rita when she was parking her car near his place. He had been waiting for the day when he could steal Rita's car in order to make her suffer and her spirit break so that she would fall at his feet and beg for forgiveness.

As soon as Rita opened the door to enter, she noticed a shadow hiding in the corner, watching every step she took. She panicked and ran to her car, screaming. Dhanush and Bhanu too were with her. They were also scared. In no time Sudhir rushed forward and managed to open the hood of the car. But without waiting for his next move, Rita started the car and with its hood still open pressed the accelerator. She looked in the rear-view mirror and saw Sudhir following her in his car. Rita stopped the car and requested a few passers-by to close the hood of the car. A few good souls moved to oblige her and approached the car but Sudhir didn't let them close the car hood. Defeated in her attempts, Rita moved on and somehow reached Jolly's house. She honked her horn again and again. Jolly and Joy came out but, seeing them, Sudhir made a quick exit from the scene.

"Rita, what is wrong with the car?" Jolly asked, a little frightened.

Before Rita could reply, she noticed a gun in Joy's hand. She was frightened and said, "What do you intend to do, Joy?"

"I shall shoot the bastard. Doesn't he see that you have two kids with you and needn't have been chased like this mindlessly?"

"Please, Joy! For my sake…"

"I would gladly spare him for your sake but for justice's sake, I would shoot the son-of-a-bitch. Tell me where that insect, your husband, lives."

"Jolly, please calm Joy down. Such a rash action is not advisable in the situation." Rita pleaded with Jolly with her hands folded.

"Sister dear, you should give up the habit of weeping so frequently."

Jolly consoled and advised her. Then, turning to Joy, he said, "Come on, Joy, and give up your anger. We shall think of something better than shooting him. But for the moment, take the children in and give them some nourishment."

That day an ugly incident was averted. But the next day Rita took the car for repairs to some Indian who also had his own gas station. Unluckily, he happened to be Sudhir's friend. He didn't do a satisfactory job. On the other hand, he charged her four hundred dollars.

Rita knew that she was being over charged deliberately but she kept quiet.

Jolly was with her at the time and he felt angry but Rita restrained him from doing anything in the matter.

What had happened was not enough. The cruel fate had much more in store for Rita. As a precaution Rita had given her phone number to a select few, very close to her. She was sure nobody would ring her up but she was surprised when in the morning the phone bell rang. It couldn't be Jolly who hardly ever phoned so early in the morning. There had been no contact with either Ginny Sudha for a long time. Then who could be phoning her so early, she wondered. She took the call and said "Hello."

"Rita, where are you?" the caller asked.

"Who is this?"

"It is Ravi."

"Oh, hi Ravi. How did you get my phone number?"

"I see. It seems you want to live underground."

"No, but you tell me first how you got my number."

"Ugh! What difference does it make from where or from whom I got it? Listen, I wish to take you out to dinner this evening."

"I am sorry Ravi. As a rule, I never go out with anybody."

"Are you sure you never go out with anybody?" Ravi asked meaningfully.

"Yes, I seldom find time to do so. Believe me Ravi, I am very busy. I have enrolled Bhanu and Dhanush in acting classes. I watched them learning how to act. I am also taking some movie production classes.

"Taking lessons in theater production is a very good idea. But have you resolved to kill yourself in a rabbit hole? Do you know what? I love your children as if they were my own. They are darlings, to tell the truth."

"Oh ho," Rita said, laughing. Then added, "But Ravi, when he, who is their father, doesn't care for them, what can a total stranger like you give them?"

Ravi didn't appreciate this remark. He managed only to say haltingly, "Please come. I have heaps of things to talk about with you."

"No, Ravi, I can't. Why do you insist? Haven't I clearly told you that I can't come? Why do you force me to do what I can't do?"

"Look here Rita, I have something very important to discuss." There was a pause for a brief moment and then he continued, "It seems there is something wanting in me or I am not good looking. It is also possible that you take me for an unscrupulous person." Saying this Ravi disconnected the phone.

Rita melted a little. She thought that she should ring him up and tell him she would come. She expected him to ring her again but he didn't.

She sat there holding her head on her palm with a blank mind. Then languidly she took up a sheet of paper from the side table and scribbled a few lines.

Oh Lord! My life is in dark slum
Please give me a sturdiness
Endure gloomy night of life
Bless me little ray of Sunshine

She read them a few times to decide whether to tear the piece of paper into bits and throw them into the garbage as she would gladly do that to her life.

CHAPTER 3

Ravi didn't call again. Heretofore, Rita reconciled herself to what was not to be. She searched her heart why she was expecting the call in the first place but found no reason whatsoever. Ravi's words, 'Am I not good looking?' intrigued her. Even the thought that she could be deluding herself into not believing that in some corner of the heart she cared for him didn't occur to her. Like a rising and falling wave in the sea of the heart, images of Sudhir, Prakash and Ravi rose and fell turn by turn. When the image of Sudhir rose, she ran to him with an extended hand, but he didn't hold it. The image of Prakash followed.

She tried to hold on to him, but the image slipped away from her hands and the image of Ravi replaced it. But he just gazed at her with an offended look and the image faded. With the passage of time the images disappeared and moved to some remote corner of her memory.

She realized that the human heart always gives precedence to the essentiality of survival over the matters of the heart. She learned to push the sense of loss to some dark corner of the heart and move on to live life as it comes, moment by moment, day by day and so on. The immediate present called for attention. The children were growing fast and she needed to look after them properly. In looking after them, Rita's routine was getting busier steadily. Joys and sorrows alternated in her life and time passed. It was against this scenario when she came to know that both her sisters worked during the day and attended school in the evening. Both her brothers-in-law had also found work in some power supply company and looked after their children during the day in the absence of their wives. They made up for the lost sleep when the children were away from school.

Rita impatiently wanted to talk to her sisters and to pour out her woes to them and to receive some consolation but all avoided Rita like an outcast. Even Navin avoided seeing Rita. He would occasionally take Bhanu and Dhanush out and after the outing, drop them near the house. Rita was a prisoner of her loneliness now.

Once there was a party at the house of one of Jolly's friends in San Francisco. His friend had also organized a short fashion show at the party. Jolly came to see Rita as he wanted her to attend the party and do a bit of modeling. Jolly told Rita that his friend was a famous doctor named Gursharan. Going to a party with the children meant expenses and Rita was not financially well off. Hence, she thought it proper to know the amount of the fare etc. of the journey to and from San Francisco.

Hesitantly she said, "Jolly, you know I cannot go alone. My children would have to accompany me. Naturally I shall have to consider the expenses for the journey. How much shall I have to spend, Jolly?"

Then, without waiting for his reply she said, "Another problem is that I feel giddy when traveling long distances by car. So, I would like to be excused because of my inability to manage in these circumstances."

"You don't have to spend anything. I mentioned to Dr. Singh that you were to accompany me with your two children and the good doctor informed me that he was sending air tickets for all of us. He has read about Bhanu n Dhanush Performance in southern California. He also knew that they were celebrities among the Indian community and would be glad to have them at the party."

"What about our stay there?"

"At his house, obviously. His wife is a very good hostess."

"Is she a doctor too?"

"No, she is an art graduate and doesn't work anywhere. She is neither very beautiful nor a good conversationalist. When she blabbers, one feels the urge to seal her lips with an adhesive tape. But the irony is that her husband loves her very much, the most important thing for a woman in life. In addition, she speaks so loudly that one can make neither head nor tail of her speech. But…"

"Why does he love her then, may I know?"

"She has a heart of gold."

"A rare quality indeed in our so-called modern world. Well, Jolly, the party must be quite a big affair and a large number of people will be coming." Rita spoke her thoughts aloud. Then she said, "When are we going to go?"

"It is on a Friday, about two weeks from now. Make it a point to take good dresses along..."

"Though nobody is poorly dressed in such parties, yet why do you stress this point?"

"Because there will be other doctors who are bound to take notice of your beau..."

"You...u...Jolly, shut up! You just arrange things with your doctor friend and inform me about the details. I'd better leave now." With these words, Rita left.

Two weeks later, Jolly took Rita and her children to the party at Dr. Gursharan Singh's house. The doctor's wife, Surrinder, though chirpy, was a very nice lady. In no time, Rita and Surrinder became chums. She also had two children, both girls. The house was an imposing rambling structure on a hillside. It was like a big palace surrounded by fortress-like walls on all sides, enclosing not only the main building, but also a couple of lawns. A marble-covered pathway led to the main entrance. It was decorated with beautiful flower pots on both sides. Inside the house, there were two big halls which were meant for important families. Today's function was to celebrate the couple's marriage anniversary. Just in front of one of the halls was a big lawn and in the center was a circular white wooden hut. This served as a bar and drinks were being served to the guests from here. To the back of this hall was a swimming pool. Artistically designed benches surrounded the pool.

Exactly at 8 p.m., people assembled in the hall. The festivities started with dance performances by children. More dancing by young girls followed. A Fashion show was next. One by one American born Indian girls, wearing dresses of different Indian states, came walking and smiling broadly. They offered a rose to each of the guests. Rita was the last to come to the stage. She had a Muslim lady's dress on, comprising a light blue chiffon dress, light pink tight pajamas and a Nawabi cap on her head. She wore shining embroidered shoes to match. She was smiling and had half covered her beautiful attractive face with a pink net dupatta (a cloth to cover the face and shoulders, a part of a woman's dress). She mesmerized the audience.

She tossed petals of Rat ki Rani (the queen of the night) at the audience. Gradually she moved to the exit but noticed Ravi taking her pictures. At his sight, her legs refused to move. She stood rooted to the spot. For a brief moment she even forgot where she was. But soon she became conscious of the situation and still feeling unsure of her steps, she started walking, following a different route and made her exit. She felt her heart go thumping under the ribs. But she had no idea why it was happening to her. From a model, insensitive to the scrutinizing gaze of the audience, she was transformed into a woman, with every pore in the body oozing life, and every inch of her flesh quivering with a weird sensation even when there had been no exchange of promises of love. She had not been serenaded either.

The singing competition was next. When Bhanu and Dhanush sang, they not only received applause but also five to ten dollars from quite a large number of spectators, boosting their performance. They received hundreds of dollars in this way.

Rita recalled how Sudhir had forced her to live the life of a pauper. He grudged her even small amounts for her personal needs. Hardly a day passed when Rita and Sudhir didn't have a fight over money. If it were within his power, Sudhir would not let the children even breathe freely. But today in this gathering of doctors and other respectable guests, the children easily collected over a thousand dollars each of the children.

When the show was over, Rita looked for Ravi but he had slipped away without even a hint to Rita. She didn't like his sudden departure. His indifference added to her misery. There was a sense of humiliation. She would not admit to herself that Ravi had any place in her life but the heart and the head seldom agree on certain matters.

Most of the guests had left by now. A few had settled with playing cards and Jolly had joined them. Bhanu and Dhanush were tired and were soon asleep. Rita felt lonely and lost. She was carried away to some other world. The bitter past haunted her, overshadowing the present.

But sooner or later one has to return to the world of reality.

In this state of mind, she went to her room, changed and came out to the open verandah. There was a big marble fish surrounded by multicolored lighted bulbs. The fish spouted water from its mouth. It was a moonlit night, yet wandering white wisps of clouds now and then covered the moon adding to its poetic beauty. The clouds also caused a rainbow-colored halo around the moon. Rita watched the moon with fluctuating luminance. This phenomenon made her again go to the past.

She recalled the days when she was in college and boys passing by showed their appreciation by comparing her to the moon. Normally she ignored these remarks. One day a boy sang, 'God alone knows where this moon will spread its brilliance and who the lucky guy will be to own it.' Rita preferred to ignore these things. Another would sing a few lines from an old Hindi movie, 'If I take you for the moon, I notice that it has a blemish. If I compare you to the sun, it too had fire in it.' The line had hardly ended when someone started showering blows with a shoe on the mischief maker of the mischief. Rita turned to see who it was and found her cousin beating the boys. Rita didn't pause. She quickly left the scene.

Rita was very sensitive to the scandals such incidents created. There was nothing very unusual in such incidents in her college days. But that was long, long ago. How much bigger things had happened to her? There was not a single Indian family in Los Angeles that didn't know that her husband Sudhir cared a hoot for her. It was very scandalous but Rita had learnt to live with scandals.

When she was at her parental home, nobody dared raise an accusing finger at her conduct and if ever anyone was audacious enough to do so, not only her parents, but also the neighbors would break that finger. But now she was an orphan, bereft of a home, thrown out of her own house by her own husband. This was passing through her mind when clouds covered the moon. Ironically the rest of the vast expanse of the sky was clear. Stars twinkled dimly in the sky, reminding her of the expression, "When the cat's away, the mice are at play." Some evil eye had blurred the faces of the moon, just like Rita's name. Her own relatives had conspired against her out of jealousy. While the world rejoiced, Rita was mourning over her cruel fate. She found herself in complete desolation with no soothing touch around. She covered her face with both hands and started crying, silently roiling in her misery. The moon would come out of the cloud but Rita doubted if the cloud that had cast its shadow over her fate would ever clear. She wept outside while her brother Navin was engaged in playing cards with his friends, as if in juxtaposition to her helplessness. It was then that, unknown to her, a shadow approached her.

"Are you from Los Angeles?"

"Yes, I am." Rita looked at the figure. Then she added, "Who are you?"

"I am Dr. Vimal Kumar Rai. Why are you standing outside alone?"

"Oh, just to have a look at the moon. You know, it is a full moon night and the moon looks very enchanting and mysterious today."

"But how could you be watching the moon with your face covered with your hands? You were not looking at the moon."

"Oh!" Rita felt embarrassed.

Rita didn't take the trouble to look at Dr. Vimal Rai. She tried to get rid of him and return to the house. But Dr. Rai said, "I saw you alone and with the desire to talk to you, I came out. But I see that you are hardly inclined to communicate with me."

"No, there is nothing like trying to keep away from you. It is 2 a.m., you know, and I am tired. I am leaving for Los Angeles early in the morning. But I don't remember ever having been introduced to you," Rita said without bothering whether it was appropriate or not.

"Never mind, I shall introduce myself. I am a doctor. But I am alone without a companion, I mean a companion in life."

"Oh, I see." Rita pretended to be feeling sleepy. She stretched and yawned.

"Jolly, just … a little."

"Jolly what?" Rita was all attention now.

"Jolly talked a little about your life, er…"

"Dr. Rai, I prefer not to discuss my private affairs with strangers. Now, if you will excuse me, I would like to retire to my room."

"Rita, can't strangers become friends? Everybody knows that even husband and wife are strangers before marriage but initiate a new life and become friends."

Rita paused at these words. She inexplicably found herself interested in what he was saying. "Dr. Rai, may I ask a question?"

"Yes. Shoot."

"Was it Jolly who persuaded you to come out onto the verandah and talk to me?"

"No, Rita. Jolly has nothing to do with my coming here. The fact is that when you were modeling, I noticed a peculiar pain in your countenance. Then I gathered a little information about you, a bit here and a bit there because I was interested in you and wanted to talk to you."

"What was it that you asked of Jolly and what did he tell you about me?"

"Look here, Rita. Please don't blame Jolly for anything. In fact, I am the culprit. You know that I am a doctor and can diagnose a disease at a glance. Please forgive me…"

"How strange that a doctor should apologize for diagnosing the malady of a patient! Anyway, tell me, what am I suffering from?" Rita laughed.

"Woe to your enemies, you have no ailment at all. But I was thinking of something unusual. I feel sure of one thing - that you are a victim of male chauvinism."

"What are you trying to imply?"

"I mean to say that divinity has been very generous to you and bestowed on you a beautiful figure, a sweet nature and lovely children. But from what I have heard about you, your man didn't recognize your worth."

"It is one's destiny which no one can change," Rita muttered a bit sadly.

"I don't agree with you. We can make our own destiny and can better it if we will to do so. By the way, Rita, I am going to Los Angeles next week. If you don't mind, I would like to see you there."

"Why not? Here is my phone number. Please give me a call when you plan to come."

"Well, it is quite late now. You are catching a flight early in the morning. Nice talking to you," Dr. Rai said, shaking Rita's hand.

Rita returned to her room but sleep evaded her. She was reflecting on her tortured existence with Sudhir on the one hand and Ravi's tall imposing figure and his taking Rita's photos from different angles on the other. The retrospection of the recent past sent a sweet sensation through every pore of her body. Then Dr. Rai's sympathy too made her feel good, almost as the gentle rain drops quench the thirst of the cracked dry earth. But when she thought about the bad behavior of Sudhir, which had stuck as a chronic pain in her psyche, she was convinced that men were the same everywhere and were to be kept at arm's length. But this brief encounter with Ravi seemed to make her change her attitude a little.

She saw Bhanu and Dhanush sleeping peacefully on the next bed and her heart ached with motherly love for them. They had done no harm to the relatives but never got anything akin to love. They had seen only their mother's tears, her lying awake the whole night, and had heard her cries and witnessed her suffering. She fell asleep at about 5 in the morning and slept till 9. Finally, when she was awake, she had no mind to leave the bed but somehow, she got up and readied herself and the children for the return journey and they all came out. She found Jolly ready to take them back to Los Angeles.

"Well Memsahib, so you are ready to leave?" Surinder asked.

"One has to, Surrender. Such is life." Rita sighed. Then she went on, "To be frank, Surinder, I immensely enjoyed the time with you. The children too have become so friendly with your children that I wish I could stay with you forever."

"If you decide to stay with Surinder, the Rolls Royce of Dr. Singh that has been waiting for you for a long time will go back to the garage," Jolly said cheerfully.

Sudhir had not bought Rita a car. Neither had he said that he couldn't afford one. After all he was an engineer with a good income. Still, he loved using old battered cars for no particular reason or perhaps his sadistic nature found in his not buying a car a ploy to torture Rita.

On the contrary, here was someone, a total stranger a little while ago, who had offered his best cars to travel from the airport to his house and back to the airport. On their journey to San Francisco, the children had enjoyed the trip in Singh's limousine and now there was a Rolls Royce to drive them to the airport.

Finally, they were aboard the plane. The children counted the money they had received as a token of appreciation of their performance at the party. They prepared long lists of toys and clothes they wanted to buy. They reached their place and when Jolly dropped them at their door, Rita found Navin, her two sisters and their husbands waiting in front of her apartment.

The moment Rita saw her sisters, she forgot her troubles. She ran to them and embraced them turn by turn. But when she greeted her brothers-in-law, they turned their faces away. Still, to avoid embarrassment, Rita turned to Jolly and said, "Jolly meet my brother Navin, my sisters Bina and Mina and their husbands Naresh and Ashwini," as she unlocked the front door of her apartment.

"Namaste. I am very glad to see and meet the family together. By the way, count me in as well as in a way I am Rita's brother too."

All tensed up and their eyes were focused on Jolly with suspicion in them. But their suspicious looks didn't escape Jolly.

"Jolly, if you are so close to Rita, then why don't you come upstairs? Why are you leaving like this?" Navin said, trying to sound relaxed.

Jolly was aware that Rita's relatives didn't know her pain, or maybe they were intentionally trying to ignore her pain. Rita, unseen by others, gestured for Jolly to leave but he ignored the signal. He made Dhanush sit across his shoulders and lifted Bhanu in his arms and moved into the apartment, throwing away all formality to the winds. He spoke loudly enough for all to hear, "Dhanush and Bhanu sang really commendable last evening at the party."

"Where are you all coming from?" Navin asked casually.

"From San Francisco," Jolly said.

"Did you drive there?"

"No, Dr. Singh gave us air tickets."

"How long have you known Dr. Singh?"

"Ever since I landed in America."

"Jolly, I respect you for considering our sister as your sister. But what name would society give to this non-existent relation?"

"People will never recognize this relationship and will criticize it. But what is regrettable is that our own Indians, our own so called near and dear don't understand us or don't want to understand this pure relation.

"What are you trying to suggest?" Navin retorted a little angrily.

"Do you know what your sister is going through?"

"Yes, I do. I admit Sudhir occasionally beats her but my sister too is not a specimen of virtue. She has a big mouth and most of the time she deserves the beating."

"How deplorable it is, Navin, that Sudhir always nags her and seldom lends a hand in the kitchen beyond pointing out to her where she should keep ingredients and spices for cooking. Then wife bashing has become a routine with him."

"Such things are usual in a home and between married couples and I firmly believe that the wife should follow the husband's directions."

"I agree with you to the extent that the wife should obey her husband but even after Rita obeys him in everything, Sudhir criticizes her. With such behavior even a dumb person would find it hard to keep mum."

"Sudhir is an educated man and is not out of his mind. He has been in America for a long time. In these circumstances if he occasionally pulls Rita up, it must be for her own good."

"Do you think that thrashing her is just pulling up? After all, there is a way of getting things done. A woman is not an animal, a donkey or a dog that needs to be beaten with a stick. You are Rita's brother. Why don't you intervene in her favor and take pity on her?"

"Who says we aren't concerned about her? It is out of our concern for her that we are here today. Sudhir wants to have her back to live with him and we support this, as naturally we should."

"It is up to Rita to go with him or not. She is a woman first and a wife next. If she believes that Sudhir can reform himself and would treat her humanely, she can go to him. Ok, Rita, good luck. I'd better leave now." He turned to leave.

Although Rita was tired, she put something to cook on the stove and started cleaning up. Both the sisters busied themselves in inconsequential chit chat about school or college days. Navin began to play with his sisters' children. During the little time Rita found to be with her sisters, she learnt that both her brothers-in-law scoffed at them on account of Rita.

This information didn't go well with Rita and she didn't talk to them till after lunch. All talked and laughed and enjoyed each other's company with the exclusion of Rita but no one used a word about Sudhir's excesses against Rita. The sisters also did not talk to their brother.

The time passed without any disturbing incident till evening. At seven when they were about to leave, Rita's phone rang. Navin at once took the call and said, "Hello, Navin speaking."

"Oh hello. How are you, Navin?"

"Thanks, Ravi, I'm fine. What made you call this number?"

On hearing Ravi's name, Rita was stunned and stood still as if mesmerized on the spot where she was.

"Well, not for any particular reason. It is just that I had taken a few pictures of Bhanu and Dhanush in San Francisco and I wanted to inform Rita that she should collect them."

"So, you too went to San Francisco. Anyway, do not bother to call my sister in future," Navin replaced the receiver.

"Navin !!!!!!!" Rita screamed at him, with a lot of confusion.

"I see! So that is why you don't want to make up with your husband. With him not being around, you have found a way to enjoy life…well as we can see, this way."

"Navin, don't cross your limits and leave this place at once!" Rita shouted. Her face had gone ashen with anger.

"Great, you are telling all of us to leave your place," Ashwini observed sarcastically.

"Please Jija ji, you are older than me and I have respect for you. All of you know that I mean no wrong to any one of you but you pretend that you don't."

"On the contrary we see you in your true colors. One man claims to be your brother and the other one…" Naresh didn't complete the sentence.

"I shall take this up with you at the right time, but for the time being, please let me be alone and leave at once."

"Oh yeah, and you may also note, young lady, that this is our last visit to you. We will never cross your threshold in future," Ashwini threatened and went away.

Rita pleaded with her sisters to believe that nothing was wrong in her relations with Ravi or Jolly, but they were helpless as they had to follow their husbands. Sudhir had given them money as a brother should when sisters visit him but Rita had hardly anything to offer to them.

Selfishness is the order of the day. Everyone has their own axe to grind. Parents were particular about their good name, sisters and their husbands wanted to settle down in America, Sudhir wanted to prove himself as a nice man so that all found fault with Rita and persuaded her to go to Sudhir. Rita felt as if they were telling her to go to hell.

Once she agreed to live with him, he would again start treating her like a slave and would make her do what he wanted. Finally, all left and Rita was alone to face the hard realities of life as usual. She went to the children's room and switched on the TV and turned the volume loud. Then she went to her room and started weeping loudly. Artificial dams don't hold long. She had built such a dam to hold back her tears and wails. But now she opened the floodgates and the stifled cries and howls shook not only her body but also her room. The flood of tears slowed down a little after some time. She recalled one of her own poems:

'The wound I try to soothe betrays me and bleeds time and again. The things I shun are uttered insolently like a song's dirty refrain.'

She fumbled about in a drawer and found the incomplete poem. She held it in her hand and on an impulse rang Ravi.

"Hello."

"Hello, Ravi, it is Rita."

"Well, well, I wonder what made you call me so late at night. Rita, I'd like to apologize if I have created any problems in your family life. Navin is …"

"No, it is me that should apologize, not you. By the way, I have come to know that you own a press."

"No, it is not mine. It is just a rented one. Anyway, what can I do for you?"

"Then who owns it? I had heard that you publish 'The Healer Magazine."

"Dr. Rai of San Francisco has opened it for giving medical advice to his patients. But occasionally he publishes new writers' short stories or poetic compositions."

"I, too, now and then, dabble in writing a few lines of poetry."

"Great! So, you too are a poetess."

"It means you know someone who writes poetry besides me."

"Yes, my mother writes too and even helps budding poets."

"Oh, that is very encouraging. I am also very fond of writing. I wish my poems would appear in papers. May I ...next Saturday...?"

"I'll feel privileged to welcome you here. If you come to this poor man's humble abode, I shall cancel millions of engagements to receive you." Ravi sounded very chivalrous.

"It is fixed then. I shall come at 5 in the afternoon next Saturday. Many thanks."

"No thanks are due. And listen, you will share this humble man's food also."

"No, there is no need to go out to dine. Rather I would like to cook something and bring it over with me."

"No, don't cook anything alone. When you are here, both of us shall cook something together."

The clouds were dispersing now and Rita felt good to hear this. She laughed and hung up. Though she had fixed the appointment with Ravi, yet she felt that she shouldn't go to his place. She felt perturbed now after she had committed herself to visit him. She tried to think of a few excuses to cancel the appointment, so much so that she found it difficult to concentrate on her work. But subconsciously she felt a strange sensation and flutter in her heart. She gave up the search for excuses as the inner urge won. She couldn't define this new feeling and it was absolutely alien to her. So, she went to Sudha's house with her children in the evening on Friday. Sudha noticed her unusual absent-mindedness and asked, "What is the matter, Rita, that you are lost in yourself? I hope everything is ok."

"Yes, I am fine, Sudha, except that I feel a bit tired. By the way, are you free in the evening tomorrow?"

"My husband, Dev, is away on a trip and I am planning to take the children to watch a movie. Why don't you and the children too accompany us? It will afford the children a change."

"But, Sudha, I have another engagement. I would like to leave my children with you tomorrow in the evening. Is it feasible?"

"Sure, why not. Is Prakash...?"

"No, it is not Prakash. It is Ravi, you know..."

"But...Ravi." Sudha hesitated for a moment and then went on, "Ravi doesn't enjoy a good reputation. He has had ... with thousands of girls."

"I have heard this. But I am not going on a date. I am just taking a few poems of mine to him."

"He is an able-bodied young man in spite of the insinuating whispers about his reputation. But since you insist on going, I won't stop you, but don't be taken in by his flattery."

"Don't worry Sudha. I am not an inexperienced young girl of sixteen."

"Of course, you are not an inexperienced girl, but you will be alone there besides being lonely in life and a lonely person seeks the company of sympathizers and is open to be deceived with a few words of affected sympathy. Well, I am tired and would like to go to bed early. You may stay here tonight," Sudha requested Rita.

Rita rolled in her bed without any sleep. A crescent moon peeped through a few isolated, dimly shining stars. Rita felt the crescent moon reflected her incomplete life. The beauty of the waning moon made Rita wonder whether like the beauty of the moon her beauty too would ever be waning and never be waxing.

Then she thought that the moon was a rare creation of nature and it waxed and waned turn by turn. But human life has no going back. From birth to childhood, then to youth followed by old age ending in death, human life follows a single one-way track.

Then suddenly the chain of her thoughts was disturbed. It seemed to her as if she was about to step into some unknown and unexplored pathways of life. What golden dreams or her destiny hold for her. One had millions of desires that were never fulfilled. But they still simmered in one's heart. Today Rita was inclined to reach for the moon. But the obligations and the circumstances of the family held her feet to the ground. These thoughts pestered her and she could not get any sleep.

The following day she took the children for an outing in the morning and in return she spent time playing with them.

After a long wait finally, it was evening. She told the children that she was going to see Ravi in order to get her poems polished by his mother so that they could be published in the paper. Sudha will be babysitting for them. They nodded their understanding but said nothing.

As she was about to leave, Sudha beckoned her and again cautioned her against Ravi but Rita recited an old couplet:

" Sarfiroshi Ki Tamana Abh Hamare Dil Mei Hai . Ham Kissi Ki Kaya Bataye kaya Hamare Dil Mei hai "

"Warriorship in our heart today, what can we tell from now, what is in our heart"

"But this is not your couplet."

"Exactly, that is why I might be reciting it wrongly and I am not at all inclined to disclose in advance what I have on my mind," she said a bit naughtily.

Sudha was not so blind as not to have read the writing on the wall.

"Ok, bye! But be careful." Sudha accompanied her to the car.

As She reached the apartment building where Ravi had rented his apartment. That building was quite an old apartment building. Rita approached the apartment nervously. She thought for a moment of retracing her steps and she had just turned to leave when Ravi shouted from the window, "Rita, have you forgotten the number of my apartment?"

"Oh!" Rita said in an uncertain tone. She was taken aback by this sudden call from Ravi.

"Please step in. God be thanked that you have come; otherwise, this humble abode would have been deprived of the chance of your visit here."

Ravi had the buoyant mood of someone who had no cares in the world. He fixed his gaze at Rita who was a bit shocked and puzzled to see this rusty bachelor apartment. It was almost falling to pieces.

A few books lay scattered all over the place. There was an old sofa along a bare wall.

The dining table was covered with a sheet of cloth and there were a couple of empty dishes. Rita preferred to sit on the sofa. For some time neither said anything. Then Ravi broke the ice and said, "Dinner is ready. Let's first have food in our stomach and then we can settle down to talk."

"Where is your mom? I have brought a few poems to show to her. You had told me that…"

"My mom lives in San Francisco. I shall send your poems to her. I talked to her a little before you arrived here," Ravi said, sitting down on a dining chair.

"But I had planned to have a long conversation with your mother." Rita showed a little disappointment in her tone as she assumed Ravi lived with his mother.

"You can talk to me as much as you like instead, darling," Ravi teased her. The word 'darling' made Rita immobile for a moment but she betrayed no emotion.

"Who cooked the dinner?" Rita asked, putting some food in her mouth.

"Don't you like it? Well, after all I am a lonely bachelor."

"No, in fact the food is delicious. It is just to remind you of the promise you made on the phone as we were supposed to prepare food together this evening. Do you remember?" Rita complained.

"Agreed, but is it proper that a guest should cook when she visits you for the first time?"

"Men can be good cooks, no doubt, but the problem is they hardly ever appreciate the good cooking of their wives."

"Why?" Ravi looked at her peculiarly.

"Because most of the men are so arrogant that they would never admit that wives can also cook well. They must criticize them just to subjugate them."

"Maybe, but I shall see to it that I appreciate everything my wife does as she is a lifelong companion and one should learn the art of keeping her happy," Ravi said with gusto.

The meal was over but they still remained sitting at the table long after. Ravi's gaze was fixed on Rita's face. She was dressed in a brown rust colored sleeveless long dress as her bobbed haircut hung down her face. This old style looked amazing on her oval shaped face. Her total persona made her femininity very inviting. Ravi felt a strong urge to remove the curls that covered a part of Rita's brow, away from her face, and look into her eyes and ask why she was so sad, but he withheld the urge.

Ravi was dressed in a yellow-colored T-shirt with the upper two buttons left undone, exposing the dark growth on his broad chest. Rita noticed it and blushed visibly. This reflex action of Rita didn't escape Ravi's sharp eyes. Rita also became aware of the effect it had on Ravi. In order to hide her discomfiture, Rita, with her eyes lowered, took up the used dishes to the sink in the kitchen. Ravi quietly followed her. With trembling hands, Rita washed the dishes and Ravi dried them with a towel and placed them in a cupboard. She was a sensitive lady and even small incidents offended her.

When she was with Sudhir in a similar situation, he would have nagged her a million times and made her clean the plates again and again. She recalled an incident when it was just the first month of her pregnancy with Dhanush. But Rita was so naïve that though she had had the experience of bearing a child, she was unaware that she was to have another baby.

Once, it was early morning, and she was still in bed when her sister-in-law, her husband and their son visited them. Sudhir roughly shook Rita by the shoulder and awakened her. He asked her to prepare breakfast for them. She was not in her normal health and was a little slow in getting up. But Sudhir was very impatient and without giving her a moment to get up, he held her by the hair and shouted angrily, "Will your body never be purged of the dirty blood of your family in your veins? Don't you see we have guests? Hurry up and prepare breakfast for them."

The derogatory references to her family were a regular practice with Sudhir and every time he dragged her family into day-to-day petty quarrels, it pained Rita to no end.

Sudhir's taunts had been increasing since the birth of Bhanu. If a girl had been born to her, how were Rita's parents to be blamed? Rita's father was mentioned for his gentlemanliness in society and was held in high esteem by everybody. Most probably Sudhir could not digest this fact. Another reason for Sudhir's bitterness towards Rita and an excuse for him to malign Rita's parents was an incident concerning her cousin, the daughter of her elder uncle. She was harassed by her in-laws for dowry.

When she was expecting her first child, they stepped up the persecution. When she couldn't bear it any longer, she left all her belongings, her clothes, ornaments etc. with the in-laws and returned to her parents without making any fuss. She never went back. She was well educated and had a nice job. She lived with her parents with dignity. But the in-laws had spared no efforts to malign Rita's family.

Sudhir's brothers and their wives fed Sudhir with the misinformation that Rita's cousin had left her in-laws because of Rita's parents' innuendos. Even Sudhir's younger brother's wife, who was from the relations of the elder sisters-in-law, also added to the baseless tales of accusations. Rita was surrounded by enemies, not relatives, she felt. Because of what had happened to her cousin, Rita's brothers had always forced her to stay with Sudhir, irrespective of the adverse circumstances.

This indulgence in self-pity would have gone on and on but Ravi deliberately placed a dish noisily onto a shelf in the cupboard to pull Rita out of her reverie.

After cleaning, Ravi had placed a kettle on the stove to prepare some tea. Rita took out a few pods of cardamom and put them into the boiling water. Rita said, "How did you know that I like tea?"

"You had been quiet for over half an hour. Your hands were unsteady. You were desperately trying to hold back your tears. The lines of misery on your face were vocal enough to convince me that you needed tea badly."

"You seem to love to speak dialogues as they do in movies." Rita made an attempt to cheer up the atmosphere.

"My mother has always insisted that I should become a doctor but I am interested in becoming a movie director."

"Are you serious?"

"Yes, that is why I am always practicing by taking pictures and am working for a degree from Columbia University in film direction. I am also learning how to write scripts for films and am going to direct a stage play in college for which I need a female character."

"What is the title of the play?"

"It is Mukh."

"But it is a Hindi title"

"What difference does it make? I have modified it into Hindi. Infact I am writing another short film script too."

"But what is this…about my playing a role in any of your movies, Ravi I…?"

"Don't hesitate. Have you ever acted in any play in school or college?"

"Yes, I acted once as Desdemona in Shakespeare's Othello in my College days in India."

"Great! Look here, we rehearse from 3 pm to 6 pm on Saturdays and Sundays and you can manage to attend the rehearsals. Furthermore, there are roles for Bhanu and Dhanush too."

"Oh, I am so glad and thankful to you for all this. I will come to the rehearsal." Rita could hardly conceal the joy she felt.

"So am I that you will come." After a short pause, Ravi said, "By the way Rita, may I know, if you don't mind, why do you live separately from your husband?"

This unexpected question caught her off her guard. But she managed to hide her reaction and in order to avoid answering the question, she said, "Many people talk a lot of unsavory things about you and my friends advise me to keep a distance from you. May I know why? Simply put, they tell me not to get thick with you."

"What do you say to them then?"

"Well, you see, I know very little about you and I am hardly in a position to give a proper reply." Rita's inadequate knowledge of the ways of the world had made her say something which prudence would have checked them by this utterance she had made her vulnerable to the crafty approach of Ravi.

"People always need something to talk about or indulge in gossip mongering. It is a human weakness. But do you notice that although I am not very handsome and rich yet a large number of girls are my friends. They are fully aware of the fact that I can't often take them to expensive restaurants. If I were as bad as people make me out to be, these girls would have vanished long ago, leaving me alone. But leave it. First you answer my question and tell me why you live alone at this age?"

Rita waited a moment or two and then said, "It is a long tale and I fear you will be bored listening to it."

"Rita, I like you and really care for you. I know that you are not happy. But be assured, I will not take advantage of your loneliness. Trust me," Ravi said, taking Rita's hand in his.

Rita quickly pulled her hand away. Ravi was wearing a dark purple shirt. The top two buttons of his shirt were open from collar to chest. Still in the brief moment she had again noticed the thick dark hair on his arms. The hair on his arms and chest displayed his immense virility. She felt an urge to hide herself in the dense growth of the dark hair while Ravi put one arm sportingly on her back and with the free hand, he wiped her tears very delicately. Rita wished he would shield her with his hairy arms from the gaze of the cruel people around her everywhere. That her credulous nature was her biggest enemy was not known to her. As if reading her thoughts, Ravi said, "Rita don't be scared. I just intend to share your sorrows." He patted her head in a petting manner. Apparently, he was soothing her troubled mind.

Rita realized that we as humans seldom trust those who, with genuine concern for us, try to put our distorted perspective of things straight. Rita wouldn't have opened up to any of her friends who really cared for her. Like others, she would have taken such advice as if the adviser hadn't fully comprehended her pain. But with Ravi, it was different. She forgot the forewarning of her best friend Ginny and, throwing all caution to the winds, she opened up before Ravi, the universally branded flirt who had fully mastered his art. He had the patience to wait to ensure the success of his pounce. No spider could have been more cautious in catching a fly or no chess player would have been more patient before slamming down the final piece on the board than Ravi today.

His showing very convincing concern for Rita was a cue for her to unburden her grievances against life and Sudhir in particular. She was like an old dusty volume from a library that was opening up after eons. She stepped into the room and sat on the sofa; she started to ask herself whether she should expose herself to Ravi or not and began telling her story. She felt a shudder and a wave of fear crept into her. With vacillating hands, she picked her purse and with swift and uneasy strides left the room.

Ravi called after her, "Rita! Rita! Please stop, Rita, why are you running like this with fear? Am I some kind of monster?" Ravi was puzzled as he saw her running in fear. Her whole body was shaking as if she would fall anytime. Rita was not into her senses and she was unable to hear anything. The words of her friend Sudha were trouncing her mind. She was visualizing Sudha warns her, "Rita, beware of Ravi, he is not a man of integrity. He is a known womanizer among his peers. Beware! Beware! Beware of Ravi." Even the air surrounding her began to echo with the noise "Beware! Run as fast as you can. Beware! Beware!" In an obvious mood she stepped down to the parking lot.

Now Ravi couldn't restrain himself; he rushed after Rita and stopped her by standing in front of her, and making his voice as soft as he could, said, "Oh Rita, your face is so pale and frightened as if I am not a man but a tiger that will eat you up. Rita, please don't take me wrong, And I want only to become your friend in difficult times. I want to help you anyway, as much as I can."

Rita was now trying to soothe her thumping heart and hammering in the brain and gradually coming back to her senses when she realized that Ravi was all in tears, kneeling down to Rita's feet, his arms stretched wide towards her, and he was staring at her without blinking. Again, her memories flashed back to Sudhir, a man whom she had loved as a husband and as a man more than her own life, but he was so cruel, mean, and hateful to her. Now here was Ravi, still a man like others. 'Oh! No! No! No man can ever understand a woman's heart, Nooooo, I must not trust him; she should not allow a stranger like Ravi to intrude into her private affairs to mock her pain and suffering. But she came out of her thoughts as Ravi interrupted her; she observed Ravi asking her not to go away like this.

"Rita, I have lost my elder sister to the cruelties of her husband, who burnt her alive for no fault of hers. Since then, whenever I see a woman suffering like my sister, my heart gets tormented and I become eager to help her. So for God's sake, Rita, please don't misunderstand me and leave my place in such distrust. I want to hear you; share with me all your joys, your agony, pain, and suffering which you have experienced in your life. That will make me understand you, understand all your troubles; be a good friend to you. For the sake of my dead sister, have pity on her soul and trust me, let me be there for the tough time of your life."

Rita realized how God created the heart of a woman? Whenever she sees a few drops of tears, a few words of sympathy for her. she melts down like nothing else in the world. Rita, who just a few minutes before was scared of Ravi, now was looking at him as a very near and dear friend and her savior and a hero.

Rita leaned forward, took Ravi's face in her tender hands said with moist eyes and a choked throat, "Ravi, yes Ravi. Forgive me, please! I was not aware of your sister's episode. Yes, Ravi, I trust you; however, I don't know how you would be a help for me? I won't hide anything from you now and will share everything about my life.

"I promise you no matter what you share with me will stay with me. I will always be there for you in thick and thin. Trust me. Allow me to be a trusted friend.

"I shall go home. It's already Late for me." Rita was still hesitant to go back to his apartment. ``

"I won't force you to stay, please drive carefully. Remember what I promise you." Rita nodded her head.

CHAPTER 4

I was 21 years old when I was married. I was doing my Master's degree when my marriage proposal came upon me to change my entire destiny. I have been fond of writing since the early days of my life. Occasionally I felt like adopting acting as a career. My very high hopes and dreams as each parent, friend, and teacher's admiration spoiled me due to their constant admiration of good looks. It won't be a boast to say that God had been very bountiful in giving me the bliss of the good looks of mind and body. My daddy was a police officer. He loved me immensely even though my mom was strict with me and kept pulling me up constantly for this thing and that. I had liberal ideas in those days.

While my mother told me to be interested in domestic duties. I felt I had better ideas and ambitions than to devote myself to ordinary tasks. I had entered a phase of my life when young girls of my age took an interest in boys that much. Somehow, I never found them equivalent to my dreams. If by chance some boy tried to follow me, I would take off my shoe and threaten him, telling him that my father was a police officer and I would get Romeo arrested if he didn't desist from following me. He never pestered me again.

Our ancestral house was very big with dozens of rooms. I had two elder and two younger uncles. All occupied their separate rooms and kitchens. But they lived under one roof. All uncles and my father earned humble salaries with the result that my aunts did odd jobs such as stitching etc. Two of my older sisters embroidered women's headscarves to boost their family income. Two of my older sisters embroidered women's long scarves to increase their household income.

The daughter of one of my elder uncle's taught sewing to others and earned a little more money. I also did a bit of this work now and then. In this way, we managed to live comfortably. We were living in a very historic city called Amritsar. There we visited the Golden Temple, the holiest Sikh place of worship, and the morning was our daily routine, irrespective of the fact that we were Hindus. The most praiseworthy thing in Amritsar is that there is great unity among the Hindus and the Sikhs. Many of my Sikh friends went to the Hindu temples dedicated to Hanuman, Lord Shiva, and others. They also observed fasts as religious rituals in the names of various gods and goddesses.

I particularly remember an incident of those days. I was very naughty when I was in high school. My older brother would make some fashionable clothes for me to wear. Our teacher, who taught us sewing in the school, wanted all the students to learn sewing through private tuitions from her only. But all the girls in my school preferred to learn this from my sisters. I was more interested in studies than in being a seamstress. Out of jealousy, the sewing teacher started a campaign to malign me regarding my character. But I had no clue of it.

Once, one of my friends from another school came to see me and told me about the scandal against me that was making the rounds. It was spread as a rumor that some boy had written me a love letter. I was extremely perturbed. When I reached home, I was very dejected, so much so that I had a fever. In the evening the same friend came to our house and told everything to my sisters too. My mother held me close to her heart and patting my head soothingly said, "My dear child, when God gives one beauty, people become jealous. The gift of beauty can be a curse sometimes for some people. You are in the prime of your youth and it has also added to this predicament of yours. Even angels would be tempted to visit the earth to take a look at your beauty."

I remonstrated, "But mom, I have no boyfriend. I go to school on time and return home on time. I don't know who has written me the love letter."

"Where is that letter?" asked my mother.

"I have no such letter. My friends tell me that it is with the said teacher."

"You needn't worry. Your sisters have gone to see this teacher of yours incognito. They will go to the root of this entire nuisance and find out what gave birth to this scandal."

I said nothing for some time, then said, "Mummy, I would prefer not to go to school anymore."

"Why not? You have done nothing wrong. But as your mother, I will consider it to be my duty to give you a few tips to prevent such ugly situations in the future. Beautiful girls should desist from laughing aloud unnecessarily in the class and making fun of their teachers. People feel jealous of young girls who laugh a bit too much as the wise people saying goes, 'A bride who loiters about and the daughter who laughs too much unnecessarily, are sure to be led astray and would invite calumny. "I said nothing in response but tried to digest its significance.

However, soon the teacher's mischief was exposed. My father met the principal the next day and talked to him in this regard. He in turn issued a warning to everybody against indulging in such malicious and baseless acts against anybody. He also cleared my name of this disgrace. From that day, I started going to school and returning home with the principal. When everyone noticed how close I was to the principal, I gained esteem in everybody's eyes. In those days I actively took part in dramas in school and always secured good marks in examinations.

Time passed and the day to join college came. To tell you of my haughty nature then, I'll give an example. On the day I was going to the college to get admission, I collided with a cyclist. Without looking at the person or trying to know who he was, I took him to task and hurried to the college. The naughty days of school were soon over.

I had hardly become a college student when the marriages of my sisters were fixed. In about a fortnight the marriage of the daughter of my elder uncle too was fixed. Fixing the date of three marriages in such a short time made everybody extremely happy. I devoted time to getting new fashionable clothes and trying new hair styles. The joy of all this was immense. I sang and danced to my heart's content.

I gathered the neighboring girls and ladies together and had a great time of fun and frolic. Finally the marriage parties arrived one by one. It was fun to hide the shoes of the Jijas (brothers-in-law) as was the custom and return them only after receiving a hefty penalty in cash.

My antics and frolicking were the topic of discussion among the members of the marriage parties. Relatives even suggested the proposals of my marriage. But I bluntly told my mother that I was in no hurry to get married. I was not to be treated as a dumb animal to be tethered to a stake whenever and wherever they wished. Mummy was annoyed at my blunt response but said nothing. Finally, this hustle and bustle ended and the day to go to college came.

A day before I was to go to college, I visited the bazaar and acquired a pair of goggles, apparently as a protection against the glaring sun, but a piece of fashion in fact. I put on a light-yellow half sleeved shirt with a dark dupatta, salwar and matching black shoes.

I bedecked my wrists with black and yellow bangles. I scrutinized myself a number of times in the mirror. Thus, made up and satisfied with what I had done, I cycled to college.

It was an intensely hot summer day. The first period was English. The professor in English was quite young. He had curly hair and looked gorgeous in a white shirt, navy blue trousers and white shoes. He introduced himself saying, "I have been teaching in English in S.N. College for two years. Everything had been fine. But about two weeks back I had an unpleasant experience. On my way to the college, by chance my cycle touched some insolent girl. She was so impudent that she started berating me without for a moment giving me a chance to explain my side. Finally, she left. On such occasions, it is usual for the people to take themselves as models of public morality. An elderly man approached me and without saying anything slapped me. My protestations didn't help me and the man left, showering indignation on me in so many words. Today the incident is fresh in my mind and I am in a cloudy mood today. Why don't some girls bother to understand that people can be decent and not everybody is a street, Romeo? I am a good brother of nice sisters. I expect due respect from my students in the class. Some of you may like to know my name. Well, I am Kanhayia Lal."

Somehow, I had never expected a 30-year-old English teacher to have such an old-fashioned name and I couldn't help bursting into a guffaw. He felt very angry and shouted loudly, "Who is this impudent girl? She should get up at once."

I looked about and saw the accusing glances of my classmates fixed on me. I had no alternative but to get up.

"You should watch your manners, young lady. Good students don't behave like you. Be careful in future."

Saying this he started the lecture but I noticed that his eyes carried a lot of contempt for me whenever our eyes made contact. But I could not be cowed down so easily and maintained an arrogant countenance.

If there is anything in the world that never pauses or waits for anybody, it is time. Gradually I came to realize that the name Kanhaiya Lal, sounding as if fished out of some ancient attic, had hardly affected the English professor's personality. He was a very handsome young man. His sharp features and large eyes, set ideally on his fair colored face, lent a unique charm to his personality. I had never before seen such a handsome man in my life. Exams were round the corner and girls went to him for guidance, sometimes with genuine questions or under mere pretexts. But I maintained my distance from him scrupulously. I hadn't even exchanged a word with him. Whenever our paths crossed, we avoided each other and went our ways. On the other hand, all the girls made much of his good looks and personality. They surrounded him whenever the opportunity came their way. In the common room they would mob him and would indulge in all sorts of girlish tricks to attract his attention. This went on. By and by the exams were held and I passed the first-year exam with good marks.

After the exams, I again started learning tailoring. It was at that time that my elder uncle's daughter, following differences with her in-laws' family, left them and came to live with her parents. She was pregnant. Her coming back from the in-laws had cast a shadow of gloom over the entire family. Ours was a joint family living under the same roof. As time passed, I came to believe that my mother was more concerned about this cousin of mine than me. I was totally ignored in the family now, so much so that I passed my B.A. exam too but no one had even a word of appreciation for me.

One day, it was raining heavily. Water had entered the college building and all the girls were crowded in the common room where the water hadn't reached. Most of them were very wet. They enjoyed themselves by exchanging jokes among themselves. Some of them were singing in a chorus.

Suddenly Kanhaiya Lal entered the room. He was drenched and his clothes clung to his handsome physique. He looked extremely attractive in this condition. Wisps of his curly hair hung down onto his brow. I felt sweet sensations run through my whole being. The girls who were wet had loosened their hair and with their fingers they were futilely trying to give the hair some sort of order. Ignoring the fact that their wet clothes stuck to their bodies and highlighted their assets, they slowly but steadily surrounded Kanhaiya Lal and pressed him to sing some film song. Kanhaiya Lal was in an obliging mood that day. He agreed to sing but with a condition.

"What is the condition, sir?"

"I shall sing only after one of you sings first," he said, eyeing me.

I bowed my head out of embarrassment. There was a long pause and no one volunteered to come forward to sing. Then Kanhaiya Lal suggested a way out. He said that the girls should write their names on slips and put them in some cardboard boxes. One of the slips would be taken out as in a lottery draw and the girl whose name was on the slip would have to sing. Accordingly a slip was taken out randomly and it had my name on it. Although I had been a regular singer in school, I rarely sang on the college stage. But I had no nervousness on such occasions.

Hence, I sang well and everybody clapped. But Kanhaiya Lal didn't respond. He kept looking away, ignoring me. I felt humiliated and burnt with indignation. Though it was raining outside, I was burning inside. I had an urge to shout at him for showing this indifference to my singing; to me actually. But, after all he was my professor, and I couldn't have shouted at him. Now it was his turn and he sang a film song that ran as follows:

'You are present with us, yet are so aloof. You are angry not only with us; it seems, but also with yourself.'

He sang on and I felt my anger melting away. He had an excellent voice. The song was over, there was loud cheering but he didn't wait to acknowledge the applause and at once went to his office, leaving all of us staring after him.

The heavy downpour had now turned into a mere drizzle and the girls started leaving in ones and twos. But I had no friend to go with and was left alone. I had a very heavy heart and felt lonely. My routine had been to go straight to college and after the classes, to return home. I had no liberty of any sort. Mother didn't even allow me to go to the cinema. But that day, as if hypnotized and defying all scruples, I moved to Kanhaiya Lal's office. I didn't enter but kept moving to and from in front of his office in the drizzle.

My clothes and hair were wet. Kanhaiya Lal saw me through the window but didn't ask me to come in. In about five minutes he came out with his umbrella, took his bicycle and was leaving when I ran after him saying, "Sir, please sir, listen to me." He paused and looked at me but said nothing. "You talk to the other girls, share a laugh with them but avoid me as if I were a pest. What is my fault after all? This is not fair." Kanhaiya Lal listened to me without looking back. Then he again moved on. I ran and caught up with him.

When I was in front of his cycle, I slipped and fell down. I was besmeared with dirty water and mud. My hair was soiled with it and I felt like crying out of helplessness but all this didn't move Kanhaiya Lal. He surveyed me without any feelings for a hapless girl.

I looked at him pathetically and somehow got up onto my feet. I saw a water tap nearby and went to it to clean myself. Some girls happened to pass by. They came to my help. One of them was a little bold. She turned to Kanhaiya Lal and said, "Poor Rita has slipped and fallen down before your eyes, but you didn't even lend her a hand in getting up, sir?"

"Those who are destined to slip and fall down cannot be helped," Kanhaiya Lal observed cynically.

"You are very insensitive, sir, that you didn't feel an iota of pity for her," another girl observed. Kanhaiya Lal said nothing; took his bicycle and pedaled away.

I cleaned myself and my clothes as best as I could, got onto my bicycle and rode towards home. There was a small park on the way and people stood under trees to escape getting drenched. I saw that to one side, under a tree, stood Kanhaiya Lal. The clouds thundered and there was a flash of lightning.

The drizzle changed into a heavy downpour. My hold on my bicycle was loosened. But I didn't stop and peddled energetically on. Then I heard Kanhaiya Lal shouting after me, "The rain is very heavy, Rita. Wait a little till it becomes lighter." But I ignored his warning and tried to move on even harder. But he rushed on and stopped me by coming directly in front of my bicycle. He said, "Are you bent upon committing suicide? Look, the road is under knee deep water. That is why these people are waiting here till the rain stops and the water recedes a bit."

I looked up at him, betraying my indignation on the face and said, "Sir, you are a nice man. But if you start to stop the girls in this manner, the way you have stopped me, who would call you nice? By the way, for your benefit, I may as well tell you that my father is in the police department."

This threat had become a refrain with me even though it sounded childish. Kanhaiya Lal was not intimidated.

"Great, simply great! However, if a civilized act deserves jail, I would gladly accept it but in no circumstances would I let you go a step further in this condition as the weather is so ferocious."

I found myself fumbling for words to say something, but found none.

Finally, he lent me his umbrella and made me stand under a tree. He turned his face away and stood to one side as it rained. I couldn't hold myself any longer now. I stammered and said, "Sir, why are you angry with me? If you are really angry, as I feel, then please forgive me."

"Forgive for what, Rita? In spite of your outward show of hot headedness, I find you an absolute simpleton. You are so naïve."

"If I am that simple, why are you so harsh with me?" I said, moving a bit closer to him.

It was for the first time that we exchanged glances. I noticed that the curls of his long dark hair hung loosely down his face, hiding his big dark eyes. I had an urge to remove those curls away from his eyes but the presence of strangers around prevented me from doing this but I kept looking into his big dark eyes without batting a lid. My wet clothes were plastered against my body but I didn't pay any attention to them.

A cold wind was blowing and it sent shivers through my wet body. As in Indian films, I was subconsciously dreaming that I was dancing with Kanhaiya Lal, my hero, around trees.

But the shivers brought me back to the reality that it was raining and I had a long distance to cover through knee deep water in order to reach home and that Kanhaiya Lal was not at all interested in me as I was in him. Occasionally the wind sprayed everything around with cold drops, adding to my discomfort. There were people under almost every tree. Most probably that was why Kanhaiya Lal didn't hold my hand. I consoled myself with this idea which comforted my ruffled ego even if it was my delusion. Simultaneously something rankled in my mind that I was, in fact, being ignored by the handsome teacher; I felt very miserable. As if to soothe my pain, I saw my father and uncle riding along in a tonga (a horse drawn carriage). I took my bicycle and ran after them shouting aloud.

They heard me stop the tonga and soon I was riding in it with my bicycle too on it. In my haste, I didn't even show any courtesy of thanking Kanhaiya Lal for lending his umbrella and protecting me from the rain. I kept looking at him as long as he was in sight but he didn't even once look at me. On the way my daddy and uncle asked me, "Who was the man with whom you were standing?"

When I told them that he was my English teacher, they asked nothing further. Because of exposure to the rain, I had a fever and could not sleep the whole night. The fever dragged on and I became very weak. I missed classes for a whole week.

After the end of the week, I went to college. I found the girls congratulating Kanhaiya Lal. When I asked the reason, I was told that he had been betrothed and was very happy. It shouldn't have been any of my concern, but strangely enough, I found the ground from under my feet slipping away. I felt like running away out of the classroom. The urge to leave increased so much that I couldn't stay there any longer and, pretending to have a headache, I went to the first aid room. But strange are the ways of fate. Kanhaiya Lal too followed me there. He approached me and said, "Rita, you have been very ill and are weak. The exams are approaching. If you need any guidance in English, you can come to my office."

"Congratulations, sir," I said, looking at the floor. But there was no response. I looked up but Kanhaiya Lal had vanished.

Thus ended my immature teenager's one-sided infatuation. I felt cheated, dejected and lonely. But time doesn't stop. By and by I passed the 2nd year exam. Nevertheless, even till I was in the 3rd year, I hadn't been able to shake Kanhaiya Lal off my mind. I felt very sad. In the meantime, Kanhaiya Lal had married and gone to Toronto, Canada. In his absence, I felt lonely the whole time in the 3rd year. Life had become a drag. At home I spent time playing with my little baby niece.

Finally, I graduated. At that moment the question of my marriage bothered everybody. My daddy had always wanted me to do MA in English.

Consequently, I started studying for an MA in English. It was sometime during those days that one day suddenly the idea of going to America entered my head. Soon it turned into an obsession. My Mausi, the sister of my mother from Kolkata, was visiting us; she observed fasts to appease the goddess Santoshi Ma. In order to try my luck with the goddess and to test the efficacy of such fasts, I too started observing these fasts. I had observed only three fasts and was one day jotting down notes in my study when there was a knock at the door.

"Who is it?" I asked, without getting up to open the door.

"It is your Bua (father's sister) from Bangalore. Where is my darling beti (daughter)?"

I loved the Bua from Bangalore very much. I at once got up, opened the door and put my arms around her neck. But she was not alone. There was a stranger standing by her side. He was a short man with small eyes. He was not at all good looking by any standard. He was eyeing me closely. I felt as if my privacy were being violated. Hence, I removed my arms from around Bua's neck and quietly went back to my room. Bua didn't enter my room. She went away with the stranger.

After about a quarter of an hour, my cousin, the daughter of my elder uncle, came to me. She told me that the stranger was from

America. He was no match for me if looks were to be the criterion for comparison. But he was adequately educated.

"If he is educated, looks shouldn't be a big issue," I said off-handedly and a bit unenthusiastically.

"In that case it is up to you to decide whether to marry him or not. But he likes you and is ready to marry you."

"What is his name?" I asked her casually.

"Sudhir," she said.

Sudhir was one of our distant relatives. My mother had already apprised him of my cousin's problem with her in-laws and had told him that the family was inclined to give Rita to him in marriage only because he was one of the distant relatives and would not like the repetition of the cousin's ugly incident; otherwise, there was no dearth of matches for me.

Sudhir said to my mother that she was not to worry about my happiness.

"You need not worry. In America we get ready to eat food and there is no need to do the washing as washing machines take care of it. Even if Rita likes to study further, there should be no reason for concern as the couples work during the day time and attend school in the evening."

In a few words he had defined what a happy life in America meant. His words were a guarantee that I was not to be a living robot that would have to labor to run the house. It never occurred to me that some further assurance of the wife's happiness was required.

My cousin was very clever. She wanted to make sure that I approved of Sudhir so she played a prank on me that my mother wanted to see me in our drawing-room. So naturally, I have to go to meet my mother in the drawing-room. What was so urgent that she had to see me in the drawing-room.

The moment I entered the room as soon as Sudhir and my mother were shocked to see me, as Sudhir closely surveyed me from top to toe. I felt nervous and to hide my awkward feelings I said, "Mummy, when will Daddy return home?" My mother said nothing and I went back to my room. As a matter of fact, my mother was in no hurry to get me married. Sudhir happened to be a relative and this fact had aroused her interest.

Another growing intention of my mother is that they have shared close family ties with each other. There was something impressive in his conversation that my mother found him a suitable marriage companion for my carefree attitude. God alone knows what?

Marrying Sudhir meant that I would have to go to America with him. But my father was not in favor of sending me away to America. However, persuaded by Sudhir, my mother assures my father to marry me to Sudhir for my better future in America.

The following day my parents got ready to see Sudhir's parents. Sudhir returned to his village and with his people, waiting for my parents to meet his family there. My father intended to take one of our relatives with him on his way to Sudhir's village. Hence, he was late in reaching his place. His family waited for my parents the whole day.

Ultimately, their bus reached the bus stop to his village. My father found Sudhir waiting at the bus stop. He was relieved to see my parents after the long wait.

He had lost hope of their coming. Finally, when my parents arrived. He was happy to take them to his house. As his mother had died when Sudhir was just a kid, his father talked to my parents and my marriage to Sudhir was finalized.

The following day my parents got ready to see Sudhir's father. Sudhir returned to his village and with his people, waited for my parents there. My father intended to take one of our relatives with him on his way to Sudhir's village. Hence he was late in reaching there. His family waited for my parents the whole day.

Ultimately the bus reached the bus stop. My father found Sudhir waiting there. He was relieved to see my parents after the long wait.

He had lost hope of their coming. He took them to his house. When Sudhir was only four-year-old, He lost his mother. He did have two older brothers and younger brothers who were already residing in the USA, when his father talked to my parents and my marriage to Sudhir was finalized.

Until then I had had no information about these developments. I heard of this development later. In the afternoon on a Saturday, I was informed that my engagement to the American Indian was being solemnized.

I felt sad as Sushil was not as handsome as I expected. My dream man was not Sudhir. I recalled Kanhaiya Lal and his big beautiful eyes, his wet curls playing on his brow in the rain and his nice figure. But the stone-hearted man had not uttered a single endearing word to me. On the other hand, Sudhir had approved of me so quickly. In marrying him, I would have my dream of going to America fulfilled. I had dreamt of America for a long time and now the dream was getting translated into reality. I felt happy. With all alacrity, I washed my hair with shampoo and sitting in front of a mirror, I applied black eyeliner and some moistures. That was the only cosmetics I used at that time.

There was a great hustle and bustle in the house. In the afternoon, punctually at 4 o'clock, Sudhir arrived with both of his sisters-in-law. The elder one was almost of my mother's age and the younger one was as old as my elder sister. The elder one was absolutely uncivilized but very strange. However, she was all sugar and candy when she talked. The younger one lived in America but was an arrogant for unknown reason to me.

Though fair complexioned, she tended to be somewhat hefty. Her name was Kanta Rani and her father was a male nurse, who was considered a doctor without a medical degree.

Sudhir was in talking to my sisters in drawing room upstairs and I wanted to have a look at him unobtrusively. I was cautiously climbing the stairs when Sudhir sensed my steps despite the precautions, I was taking very slow steps coming up on the wooden stair of my house. I felt embarrassed and was turning back when all of a sudden, he came behind me and caught hold of my arms. My face reddened but he held my arms tightly and led me to his sisters-in-laws. I was looking down and couldn't raise my eyes even though I tried my best to greet them. I was feeling so shy. Nonetheless Sudhir was holding my arm as if he had known me for years. I was wearing a light green plain silk sari, a dark blouse, green and black bangles and matching sandals. I must have looked stunningly beautiful as my cousins told me that evening. When those women saw me, they stiffened for a moment as if they didn't like me. But the next moment they looked relaxed and started making jokes, something I didn't even understand. They were not funny to my taste.

I had a nagging feeling that with my upcoming engagement, only Sudhir was happy, but not his sisters-in-laws though apparently, they were mingling with my family. It was only a ruse to cover their bitterness. Sometimes everything seems to connive to add to one's happiness if the person is happy and nature looks sad when he is sad. It was happening that day. The sweet music playing on Jullundur, a city in the Punjab in India Radio appeared to be playing a song to celebrate my engagement. Song was Like this: "The King of many palaces arrived at your doorstep to take your daughter away as she will rule the kingdom."

It seemed as if this engagement was unique and divine joy had come only to me and Sudhir in the world and to no one before us and the divinity was showering rose petals from the heavens above to bless us. The evening was very magical and enchanting.

Sudhir looked at me again and again as if overwhelmed with his bountiful luck. I was also elated at the important event in my life. With our union Sudhir and I had made everyone happy.

The following day the guests were getting ready to leave after lunch and I wanted to have a good look at Sudhir before he left. The truth was that since his coming, I had not raised my eyes to have a good look at him till the time for his departure arrived. If the girls in the college asked me how my fiancé looked, I would have nothing to tell. Preoccupied with these thoughts, I went to the kitchen. Hardly had I stepped in when I received a slow punch on the back. I was startled and turned to look at who it was. It was Sudhir. I had been tired from the exertion I had borne since the guests had come and my body felt sore. But when I saw that it was Sudhir who had punched me, the pain vanished at once. He held my chin with the index finger and the thumb of his right hand and raised my face up. I was sure he would kiss me and I didn't know how to fend for myself but he made no move to kiss me and merely said, "Will your highness allow the slave to take leave now?" I hid my face with both hands. He touched my eyes with his fingers and said, "What is the meaning of this shyness? It is unfair."

This gesture made blood rush to my face and I blushed visibly. I tried to move away from him. But he put his arms around me and pulled me to him. It was the first time that I had been touched by a male figure who was going to be the man of my life forever. I felt my resistance giving way but I futilely tried to put some distance between me and him. In doing this, I toppled some pots and pans which fell down clanging, but the noise was heard by Sudhir's sisters-in-law downstairs. They burst into guffaws. Then they shouted loudly to make fun of me. I realized that Sudhir's coming to me was a part of a clever plan. Finally, he left with his people.

Sudhir had left but I found myself constantly dreaming of him. Strange are the ways of human nature. I was dreaming of my rainbow-like future with a person whom I had not even properly seen and known. I saw myself as a newlywed bride and started thinking of the various little things that sweeten the life of newlyweds. I wondered how he would feel offended over insignificant things and how I would persuade him to forgive me. In turn, I too would feel offended even for the sake of fun and he would do the same with me. Not a single moment passed without my thinking of Sudhir. The pangs of love of an almost stranger made me suffer with sweet nothings intensely. But strangely, a feeling of some mysterious unnerving fear also pestered me simultaneously. It could be the fear of impending separation from my parents. My heart seemed to be playing tricks with me.

The date of marriage had not yet been fixed. One day I was combing my hair on the roof of the house when the post man called my name aloud and threw a letter into the courtyard of our house. I came down at once and picked up the letter. It was from Sudhir. My cousins saw this and burst into giggles. They started making fun of me. I ran to my room and read the letter:

My dear Rita,

Lots and lots of love.

I have just arrived in Delhi. I decided to write a few endearing words to my prospective wife. Believe me, I find it impossible to live without you. Your lovely innocent face is always before my eyes. In order not to prolong our separation, I have thought of a way out to cut it short. Let me know the date of marriage and we shall have a court marriage to facilitate obtaining a visa without delay. Please send an early reply. Oh, by the way, please send your measurements so that I may order bridal dresses for you. But… guess what? I know your measurements already. I have a very sharp eye, you know. Well, the rest when we meet on the golden night.

Your husband is waiting, your lover.

Sudhir

Outside, all my cousins were enjoying themselves at my cost. I hid the letter in my books so that no prying eyes could read it. Days passed. One day all the girls were cleaning the house. Our clothes had become dirty.

A teenage girl from the neighborhood came running to my mother and whispered something into her ears. My mother looked at me and smiled meaningfully. Before I could make out anything of this mysterious glance, Sudhir turned up unexpectedly. He was standing before me casting amorous glances. He had an enchanting smile playing on his lips. I made an attempt to go away but he at once held me by the hand. Everybody around was amused. I was annoyed at this show of mirth at my expense. I forcibly freed my hand and ran away to my room.

Everybody busied themselves in making Sudhir feel welcome. In the evening everyone decided to go to the park. I did my best to keep a distance between me and Sudhir but he always managed to come closer and walk by my side. Finally, the sun was setting in the cold evening, night was approaching, our walk was over and we returned home. In the evening I was cooking in the kitchen when Sudhir came there and started lending me a hand. I felt nervous but could do nothing to keep myself away from him. For the same of modesty, I would utter a few words now and then but mostly kept quiet. Whereas, ignoring my silence he said, "Rita, why didn't you reply to my letter?" Then without waiting for a reply, he said, "Anyway, let's have a court marriage."

"A court marriage?" I looked askance at him.

"Didn't I mention in the letter that it would help in getting a passport early? Later we can have a full-fledged marriage according to Hindu rites."

"But I am to take an examination. How can I go to America at such short notice?"

"Forget the exam. Now you can complete your studies in America."

"Will it be possible to go to College in America? Who would attend to the domestic chores?"

He laughed and said, "Don't you know that in America, husband and wife both share such work at home?"

The next day, Sudhir talked to my parents about the court marriage and my elder sister Bina did her best to make sure that it was arranged, but it was not to be. Sudhir had to return home empty handed. Because of Sudhir's urgency, my family also became conscious of the need to hasten the marriage.

As such the date of marriage was fixed earlier than planned. The hustle and bustle of such an important event started. All the relatives and my friends made every passing day very colorful. Every moment was an occasion for celebration. Eventually the day came when the marriage party arrived at our door. I was made up and dressed very elegantly with the help of my friends. But the import of a minor incident that was to become very significant later in the coming days escaped me.

At the time of the jai mala ceremony (the groom and the bride garland each other), Sudhir didn't have a jai mala. Anyhow, in order not to delay the ceremony, my sister brought a flower garland from somewhere and gave it to him.

This negligence on his part for an important ceremony was a shadow of the events that were to come in my life. It became significant how casual he was about doing small things that add spice to life when it was his turn, but how very big the same things became when it was my turn to do them. This aspect of his nature was to poison my whole life. But at that moment, fortunately, its ignorance was bliss.

I moved with the jai mala to put it round his neck. He craned his neck and kissed my hands right and left. He said loudly enough for me to hear, "You have dressed to make a kill today. Everything is mind boggling. You look like someone whom I have always dreamt to meet but had never seen or known before. I don't believe my good luck that this rare diamond is to be mine for life."

It was one of those occasions when all eyes are on the groom and the bride. Sudhir had shown scant regard to all present around us but I was not that bold. Hence, I could say nothing. The necessary rituals of 'the seven sacred vows' by husband and wife, followed by the ritual of going round the sacred fire seven times, commenced.

Sudhir was an easy target for many a volley of jokes by my sisters. There was a girl among the members of the marriage party. She was tolerably good looking. She would smile whenever Sudhir looked at her and in turn, he too returned the smile and said something by way of a joke. My sisters didn't approve of this annoying play. But I ignored it totally as I was confident that my cousin made me think that I am far more beautiful than her. My simplicity in trusting my tolerable looks and education was enough to make me feel secure and blind to certain biological realities of life.

The ceremony was over, all rested as best as they could. In the afternoon at the wedding reception guests were enjoying the lunch offered by my parents. I was to have lunch with Sudhir. But I refused to do so.

However, Sudhir was not so easy to put off. On his insistence, one of my sisters-in-law Kanta Rani came to escort me to him at the wedding reception Lunch. She was behaving very insensitively. A bride needs to be escorted with proper delicacy with a slow gait.

But here she was, running ahead of me as if chased by some beast. She had put a long distance between me and her. I found it difficult to catch up with her in my heavy bridal dress. I looked more like a bride running away from home evading the ceremony than going to share her first lunch with her groom. I dare not call her to slow down. Anyway, I reached the table where Sudhir and his relatives were sitting and enjoying the feast.

The hour when a palanquin takes the bride away is the most touching of all. The only difference is that a car has replaced a palanquin. The euphoria of marriage had left me. I felt as if my soul were being separated from the body. The tensile but invisible bonds of parental love were very painful to break. I had an uncontrollable urge to fly to Mom and Dad, shouting that I would not accept the marriage and would not go away from them and from the home where I was born and had grown up. I would not leave my parents' caring umbrella. But I didn't do any such thing. I found no strength to fulfill this urge. Still, I could not control the tears welling up in my eyes. My mother had moist eyes but she consoled herself with the idea that I was going into a family of relatives. Sudhir noticed that I was silently crying. He engaged me in inconsequential chit chat so that my attention was diverted and I would not miss the family and the old parental home. Now, after years, I wonder whether the lamb being led to the slaughter house had any idea of its impending fate.

CHAPTER 5

The marriage party was traveling in a chartered bus. It stopped at Jullundur City in Punjab, India and all got off the bus for some reason unknown to me. Some relatives of the elder sister-in-law of Sudhir had arranged lunch for all at some place. I was at a small party house. But the Kanta Rani didn't feel like attending the lunch. She stood aloof to one side.

The good-looking girl, who had indulged in flirting with Sudhir when the ritual of going round the fire was on, was standing nearby and Sudhir was insisting on her accompanying him to lunch. I didn't like this. But I didn't unnecessarily pay attention to it either. Now I could also hear the noise of the quarreling of the middle sister-in-law Kanta Rani with someone. A few relatives surrounded her now. She was audibly crying. I stood looking at the scene. I was puzzled at such a scene immediately after the great event of marriage and felt lost when Sudhir came from behind and holding my hand, led me away to the venue of the lunch by a different route which passed through the bazaar.

The shopkeepers looked at us quizzically. Mostly in India, many small Shopkeepers keep the Radio to get the attention of the buyers to come to their shops. Somewhere from some shops a song was playing on the Radio I heard at the time of my engagement song by Noorpuri in the melodious voice of Punjabi Famous Singer named Surinder Kaur: "The rhythmic tickling of anklets of the beloved is beckoning the lover to her." The mood which I was in, made me believe that I and Sudhir were the beloved and the lover of the song. I was convinced that God was very kind to me. With a heart saturated with these sweet romantic reflections and hopes, we reached the venue of the lunch.

The hosts had made a very elaborate arrangement for the welcome of the marriage party. The venue was lavishly decorated and professional dancers had been engaged to entertain the guests. Somehow, I happened to look at the Kanta Rani. She was staring at me with the looks of a stranger. This quick and unexpected change in her attitude made me nervous. She came unduly close to Sudhir and I noticed it. As if in response to my feeling, Sudhir embraced me in a tight grip of his arms, making a show of his love for me. Kanta Rani probably got the message and with a nasty look at me, she moved away from Sudhir.

After the dinner the reception was over and we returned to the bus again. The elder sister-in-law occupied the seat next to mine and the bus sped on. There was hardly anything worth mentioning on the way till we reached Sudhir's village. As we reached his house, children started shouting, 'Bahu aa gayi…Bahu aa gayi." (The bride is here) … Elders and other members of the family came to receive me. But Sudhir was not in a mood to leave my side. Womenfolk from the neighborhood gathered around us. Sudhir would ask them what they felt about the bride.

"Well, how do you like my bride?'

"She is the very moon herself descended to the earth. You must have given pearls in charity to the poor that you have merited such a beautiful wife."

"That surely, she is. Aunty, do you notice how I have fished out this lovely fairy? You wouldn't find a more beautiful looking bride even if you were to search the whole world with a lamp."

"You naughty one, move aside and let me have a hearty look at the bahu rani (the bride). You are most likely to harm her with an evil eye," she said, as if shooing away evil spirits.

A neighborhood lady chimed in, "My dear young man, she belongs to you and we know this. She is yours and will always be with you and you can see her whenever you like. But we are neighbors. Let us see her first."

The elder sister-in-law was happy and was chatting with the womenfolk cheerfully but I heard the Kanta Rani middle-sister-in-law saying loudly and emphatically, "I will leave for my mother's tomorrow."

"But how can you leave so early? Tomorrow the bride is to be taken to the temple."

"All of you can manage it without me. At the moment she is the apple of everyone's eye. Even though I come from a rich family, I have little respect in your eyes now."

Now the jealousy that burnt her was apparent. Sudhir heard this and whispered into my ear, "Never mind if they do not give you your due. I am here to appreciate your beauty. For me you are a rose petal imported from Kashmir." He took me into his arms.

I hadn't been able to digest this attitude of the middle sister-in-law Kanta Rani for some time. But I noticed Sudhir looking at me with admiration in his eyes.

As long as a woman has her husband's love, she needn't be unduly perturbed about such minor things as starting sisters-in-law at the husband. Armed with this philosophic idea, I looked into his eyes and felt the misgivings disappearing and I was lost in rosy dreams natural to a newly wed bride. But the proximity of Sudhir still made me shy. I would shrink and tried to cover myself in the bridal head scarf. My bashfulness overwhelmed me and I dare not look up.

The special night for which every girl waits eagerly, the night for which she treasures her virginity, was approaching fast. I felt every passing moment was taking ages. I had woven dreams of the first night. On this special occasion the silk soft luxurious bed is covered with fragrant flower petals which make it so inviting. Literature and movies highlight this feature and make it more romantic. But I found myself staring with disbelief at my bare bed lacking all these embellishments without a touch of romance. But romantic hearts are very innovative. I painted with my imagination a bed of my dreams. It was covered with multicolored petals forming kaleidoscopic patterns of a fairy land. But I dare not lie on it without Sudhir by my side. Instead, I spread a bed sheet on the floor and lay down on it waiting for the prince charming.

Sudhir was a very well-to-do man. The only thing he was deprived of was maternal love. The mental state that I was in had made me very empathy to others' pain. I felt pity for Sudhir. He had lost his mother when he was very young. If he had had his mother around, the room would have looked a lot different, I argued to myself. These thoughts preoccupied me when Sudhir turned up. I felt a cotton wool like soft touch on my face and heard a sweet voice exuding romance and love. He ruffled my hair abruptly. I felt an electric current passing through my whole being. With my henna bedecked hands, I covered my face with my doubly folded Anchal. (Scarf)

Sudhir lowered his face, almost touching mine and softly spoke into my ears, "What is this, Rita darling? Won't you speak to me?"

My heart was pounding. The fire of desire burnt my whole body. I was doing my best to bear the sweet pain expectantly but the bashfulness and excitement of the long-awaited bliss that permeated these precious moments was too much to bear. Still, I was struggling to hold on. The body was shrinking imperceptibly out of modesty and not a single word escaped my lips though every muscle in my body quivered. He put his strong arms round me. Oh heavens! What was going to happen? What was this heavenly experience, the sweetness of which no poet had described in his best romantic composition? What was this inaudible music that was benumbing my senses? Had some divine being descended from heaven that was wafting my feather light body away across the clouds to some dreamland? Sudhir caught both my hands by the wrists firmly without hurting me and slowly removed them along with the dupatta from my face. I didn't make any attempt to resist now. Then he kissed my virgin eyes passionately, I don't know how many times. The curtain of coyness and fear, built in layers upon layer since I had stepped into puberty, was giving way to Sudhir's hands. I was face to face with the mysterious agony of love, to which I was a total stranger. Finally the crucial moments came when the two bodies lost their individualities and merged into one. Sudhir was very considerate all the while as wave after wave of untold pleasure flooded my whole being. I had lost count of time and the surroundings. The earth moved. The storm raged. But gradually it had to subside as all good things in life do. We lay side by side on the bed and Sudhir was playing with my hair. I had surrendered my body, virginity, innocence, simplicity and most of all my flowering youth to Sudhir. He looked no less than an angel to me. I clung to him to feel his body of warm flesh to ensure that it was all a reality. I was afraid lest this visit to heaven should turn out to be a dream.

No night in my life had been shorter than this. The morning was coming a bit too early, I felt. It was almost dawn when sleep overcame me. But hardly had I dozed off when there was a loud and impatient repeated knocking at the door. Sleep fled and I felt the usual shyness overtaking me. Sudhir helped me straighten out my rumpled dress hurriedly and went to open the door. It was his sisters-in-laws who had chosen to visit us so early.

They came in and scrutinized me from top to toe as if it was the sole aim of their visit. Their eyes lingered at my dress and the combed hair. Without any preliminaries, they started pulling my leg and making fun of me. I regained my composure with great difficulty. Every word they uttered took me back to the moments of the sweet pain shared with my husband a little while ago and which I was futilely trying to hide.

The guests settled down, taking seats of their choice. I hurried to the bathroom and had a hot bath in order to get ready to go to the temple as is a custom in Punjab, India. Having grown up in Punjab, I had always worn shalwar–kameez (dress typical of the Punjabis) dresses and didn't know how to wear a Saari (Indian long cloth for ladies).

Hesitantly I requested the sisters-in-law to help me in putting on a Saari, but they just ignored my request, making faces at me and adding to my awkwardness. Left to myself, I managed somehow to put on the Saari, obviously not the way it should have been.

The elder sister-in-law observed, "Rita, is that how one wears a Sari?" I shyly confessed that I had never worn a saree before and requested her to help me adjust it properly. Before she could say anything, Sudhir turned up and, as if sparing me the embarrassment, said, "My dear wife is very innocent. But I am sure in a short time she would learn all these minor things."

The elder sister-in-law said, as if mocking me, "Do you believe that college educated girls, especially those from cities, are innocent?"

Her remarks had the effect she had desired. I was provoked to say something unsavory but I didn't, even though I would have preferred to tell her that I knew a lot more about village girls than she did about city girls. It was they who mostly indulged in chasing fashions and were heavily made up as if they were coming to the college not for studies but for a film shoot. I decided to ignore the remark, thinking that neither are all the town girls simple nor are all the village girls clever. The thing ended there. After taking some refreshment, they left the room.

A little later, with Sudhir by my side, I was walking over an uneven path leading to the village temple. The sudden twists and turns of the path and the uneven road reminded me of an equally uneven path of my life and I trembled with some inexplicable premonition. If I slipped a foot, I thought it was my life that had slipped and would go down into an abyss. But one is just a puppet in the hands of destiny and life offers no choices at certain junctures of life. I, too, was a puppet being propelled by my destiny. Finally, I stood facing the idol of the deity. I silently prayed, "Oh God almighty, grant me the boon of a happy family life." There was no apparent reason for my feeling of uneasiness. Normally newlyweds carry heaps of happy dreams, but here I was with a feeling of uncertainty in life. One nagging feeling was that I had been burdened with responsibilities a bit too abruptly.

Sudhir noticed my uneasiness and said, "Well, what did you pray for of the Almighty?" Moving a little closer to him, I said, "Just your love."

"You needn't doubt my love for you. I am a man who believes in giving women their full due. There is nothing but happiness in my life and in yours obviously." It was enough for me. All the uncertainty about my future disappeared. The following day I visited my parental village for a day as is the custom, but the flying visit to my parents ended so quickly. We returned to Sudhir's village the very next day. The days that followed were spent in unrestrained enjoyment giving in to the whims of the heart. We went to the cinema frequently. We traveled by cars, buses and all modes of transport that came our way just for fun. Sudhir's infatuation for me knew no bounds. He would embrace me in buses with amused passengers staring at us, and why not, as such scenes are rare in India. Once I heard someone saying with a sigh, "Hey Bhagwan, (Oh God) only lucky people get beautiful wives."

Sudhir, too, heard this and looking at me, he smiled broadly. I lowered my eyes to hide embarrassment.

My days and nights passed with Sudhir constantly by my side. His love for me was so overwhelming that I seldom missed my family and parents. I forgot the affection of my siblings. Here, I had become a little friendly with the elder sister-in-law but for some unknown reason, she preferred to talk about the middle sister-in-law and her relatives.

I mentioned this to Sudhir and the mystery cleared. He said, "The sister-in-law and her brother had planned to get their younger sister married to me but my preference and ultimately marriage to you had upset their apple cart." I trusted Sudhir. The elder sister-in-law made numerous comments about the sister of the younger sister-in-law but I was in the least interested in them.

The reality now was that Sudhir and I were husband and wife and there was hardly any unshared secret between us. Sudhir fully opened up before me and these things had made me totally surrender my body, heart and soul to him.

One day some relatives of the middle sister-in-law came to see her. She cooked eggs for them. I was a vegetarian like my parents who, being of a religious background, shunned meat or eggs. We were sitting in the compound along with the guests. The cooked eggs were served. Instinctively, I shrank to one side. Sudhir's elder brother noticed this and said, "Sudhir, how long can this go on? You are a non-vegetarian and hardly a day passes when you do not have eggs and meat. But some people are hypocrites. They make a show of being vegetarians but these so-called saints relish meat and what not behind people's backs."

It was a valid cue for Sudhir. He picked up a piece of a boiled egg and against my protests put it into my mouth. I didn't like this act of Sudhir in the presence of these people and I felt offended. It encouraged his elder brother and he boldly started condemning my deity. The middle sister-in-law was inciting Sudhir and he was playing to her tune, totally insensitive to my feelings.

It was the first time in my short-married life when I felt angry with Sudhir but he made a demonstration of his love and my anger subsided. I realize now that I must have been a very credulous being to have trusted him again and again. As time passed, the incident was forgotten and it was hardly a month since it had happened when the visa for America arrived. All of us, including my parents and brothers and sisters, came to Delhi. The incident of forcing me to eat eggs now meat was added repeatedly.

The middle sister-in-law Kanta Rani and her husband persuaded Sudhir to make me eat meat in the presence of my parents. My eyes became tearful because of my helplessness. My parents didn't like this. But instead of showing their dislike for the act, they tried to mollify me. They consoled me, "Trust God. He will set everything right. You should convince Sudhir of your problem with love and he will come round to your point of view." Actually, my elder sister Bina told Sudhir out of affection for me, "Rita is a bit over simpleton. Please don't feel angry with her." Sudhir took her words literally and was convinced that I suffered from some mental abnormality although it is a common practice among the elders in the Punjab to call youngsters as devils out of affection. The proof of his conviction of my mental abnormality came the next day.

At the airport, I sat down on Sudhir's leather bag by mistake. He rebuked me before my parents and the relatives of the middle sisters-in-law. The sister-in-law reacted with a hearty laugh and as if to release Sudhir of this misplaced anger on someone else, she observed, addressing nobody in particular, "Sudhir is short tempered, you know."

Her defense of Sudhir had little ring of conviction in it.

The time of our leaving for America arrived. We were to have a break in our journey in Hong Kong. When we were aboard the plane, Sudhir started making a show of his love for me. It clearly implied that he had realized his underserved anger for me; at least that is what I took all his amorous play to mean. My dream plane took off and after four hours our plane landed at Hong Kong airport. We got off. Sudhir's elder brother and his father were traveling with us. Sudhir, accompanied by his brother, went to look for a car and a hotel for us to stay in. My father-in-law and I sat on chairs, and waited for them.

A minor and insignificant but amusing incident occurred. It was the first of its kind for me though it must have been a routine affair at the airport. A Chinese man appeared from nowhere and started pestering me and my father-in-law in Chinese which we didn't understand. He was probably a beggar or a tout of some sort. I saw a young Indian man standing a little away from us. I hurried to him and explained our problem about the Chinese. He obligingly came and rebuked the man in Chinese and then sat down beside us. He stayed there till Sudhir and his brother returned. We heaved a sigh of relief. Sudhir thanked the Indian man for his kindness and he left for his destination.

We reached a big hotel in Hong Kong. Sudhir's brother and his father went to their rooms. Then suddenly Sudhir took away my bridal Scarf and blind folded me with it. I was frightened. I said with a quiver in my voice, "Ugh! What are you up to?"

"Don't worry, my darling fairy queen. It is just a sweet little American custom."

He led me blindfolded to our room and pushed me onto a velvet soft bed. I removed the blindfold and saw red bed sheets all around. A big poster hung to one side with 'Happy Honeymoon' written on it.

I looked around, wonderstruck. I hadn't even seen a small hotel in India but here we were in a big hotel in Hong Kong, the splendor and size of which dazzled me. I didn't know that our room was on the twentieth floor. I ran onto the balcony and looked out. I almost fainted because of giddiness when I saw the road below. Vehicles crawled like tiny toys and human beings were just like beetles.

Evening was approaching and the city was illuminated beautifully. To one side was the sea with rows of boats anchored near the shore. I forgot that I was a newlywed bride and shouted almost like a kid, "Wow! I would like to do some boating. Let us go there."

"There is a small boat right here, my butterfly. Let us first enjoy ourselves in it." He pointed to a large bathtub and before I could respond, he started unbuttoning my blouse. I dodged him and ran round and round in the room. I managed to say breathlessly, "No, I won't sit with you in the tub without clothes on."

"Then come along with your clothes on." He again rushed to catch me.

"My clothes are so fine and expensive that I won't spoil them."

"I again tried to escape him but this time I couldn't. He caught hold of me and gradually and methodically undressed me. Then, showing a little prudence, wrapped a towel around me to cover my nudity. Blushing broadly, I entered the bathtub. Sudhir turned on the hot water shower."

The water was rather hot and I got up to turn on the cold-water tap.

In the process the towel dropped off. Sudhir didn't let me cover myself again. He held me with his left arm round my back and using his right hand to raise my face, started kissing me all over, beginning with my forehead, then coming down to kiss my lips and neck. I closed my eyes. He carried me to the bed and what followed was nothing short of pure bliss that made me forget the count of time. I hate to recall when we dozed off.

It was around nine o'clock in the morning when the telephone bell rang. Sudhir took the call. He said, "Hello."

"Sudhir, I have been trying to contact you the whole night. I have had acute stomach pain."

"Oh, sorry. The handset was knocked off the cradle accidentally and we received no call." Sudhir sounded a bit perturbed.

"What is it?" I asked him.

"My Joginder Bhaiya (brother) has been ill the whole night. But he is better now."

He replaced the receiver and eyed me amorously. The next moment I found him on me, totally gripping and crushing me as he pleased. I just yielded and relished every gesture, pinching, biting, twisting, squeezing and all that with lots and lots of oohs and aahs. All stiffness had gone out of my body as if massaged by a professional masseur. Sweet pain pervaded every pore of my being.

We took a bath and got ready to roam about in the bazaars of Hong Kong for shopping. We shopped for woolen sweaters, pearl decorated purses, tape recorders, cameras etc. Then we spent time on boats.

We yielded to every whim a young newly married couple in love would do. People say 'Enough is enough' but for us enough was not enough. The bodies and the mind craved for more, more and a lot more. Sudhir held me by the hand and with his free hand he held me by the back possessively as if I would run away from him. Occasionally his fingers found their way from under my armpit and pinched a spot that sent thrills through my body. He was being naughty to no end.

We ate at Chinese restaurants and spent time in all sorts of indulgence. Our nights were stormy and thunderous and the dreams, if any, were no match to what we were living.

We spent a week there and then sailed to Honolulu on Hawaii Island. I got my green card there. Our stay there was just for a day. Sudhir and his brother hired a taxi for the day. We passed through sugarcane fields and reached the beautiful beach where most of the time was spent. The exotic scenes were bewitching.

When I was looking at the beauty of the ocean waves and green scenery, I was stunned to see a girl in her birth suit; she had nothing on and was stark naked. She sat there totally oblivious of her surroundings. I was shocked and covered my eyes with my hands.

"What an audacious girl! How shameful she is!" I said, conceal my face in both hands.

Sudhir and his middle brother Joginder noticed my reaction. He looked away, but Sudhir Forcefully removed my hands and kissed them. He kissed my eyes while his father and Joginder enjoyed the beautiful scenery of Hawaii. Still, their presence was very uncomfortable. In India, we don't have the liberty to show our romance in front of our elders. His act made me upset. I looked angrily at him, but he rewarded me with a painful pinch on my back. He just smiled at my discomfort. The following day we flew to Los Angeles.

All the friends and Siblings of Sudhir came to receive us at the airport. Joginder had a son who was nearly 3 years older than me. Coming out of the airport, I don't know why Sudhir made me sit within Sunil Car, the younger brother of Sudhir and his Young Nephew Prabhat. I was sad even though it gave me a chance to get to know Sunil; and Prabhat. The first time I sat by myself without Sudhir after our wedding. I felt forlorn. Sunil broke the ice.

Older siblings Gyan and younger brother Sunil of Sudhir were living together. They rented that apartment with a living room and large kitchen, One bathroom.

It was so sweet when he addressed me as Rita Bhabhi Instead of addressing my sister-in-law or by my first name.

"Here you are Rita Bhabhi. It is our America, A land of white-skinned people."

I had hardly had time to know him. But made a bold counter to his assertion and said, the brown-skinned Indian girls are more loyal and obedient than white girls who could divorce without any compunction whereas the Indian girls never think of divorce after marriage. What then is the merit in having white skin?" Soon I realized that I should not utter such racist words.

Rita Bhabhi, don't say such words. Divorce is meaningless here. It's common practice. Couples divorce on the slightest opportunity. We can't change any country's culture. I would prefer to say "Made in Rome like the Romans."

He said nothing further, but I was shaken from inside. I got so fearful as If Sudhir had already divorced me. I was getting kind of nervous. Something is hurrying me to open the car door and jump out of the car and rush to Sudhir and tell him not to divorce. I prayed in my heart "Oh Almighty God, never let Sudhir leave me. He's in charge of my life now."

No one was aware of what was going on in my heart. Being ignorant about how I feel. They all engaged in making jokes just to have a good time. By the time all the cars reached the apartment complex, I saw Sudhir coming down from other cars. I ran next to him. Everyone was laughing about this. Sudhir Observed. "Well, my beloved, my innocent nymph." My wife who made marriage vows cannot bear to break up with me for a moment."

Anyway, the problem was over for the evening. After dinner, we went out shopping. It was a new world opening up before my eyes. Though I was an alien here, I hardly found time to feel homesick.

The apartment became crowded with friends of Sudhir. Who was in place as though by some secret signal? Meanwhile, I went to get refreshed. I bathed and prepared to mix with the crowd of friends that came to meet us. I was very hungry. I was dying for Indian food after this whole trip. I was amazed and disappointed to see the main dish as the beefsteak was served as the main dish for lunch. Sudhir noticed as he realized my situation at that time; he got up and brought me fruits from the kitchen table. But for no reason, Joginder Brother got upset and said." Sudhir, it's not fair, she better start eating meat. Western meat is the only food available in all restaurants and at parties" Luckily, Brother Gyan and my father-in-law pulled him up. They said that I was new to this place and gave them some time to adjust to her. You can't make her eat meat

Anyway, The Problem was over for the evening. After lunch, we went on a shopping spree. It was a new world, A different world opening before my eyes/ Although I was a stranger here, I missed the earth where I was born. It made me feel homesick.

I noticed that Joginder Bhaiya was a man of a cheerful nature. He was fond of music. On the other hand, Sudhir was reticent and had little liking for music.

Joginder and Sudhir were poles apart in their nature. I also noticed a peculiarity of Sudhir's nature. He found fault with people over minor things and would flare up for no apparent reason. It pained me but I preferred to keep mum. He was also adamant by nature. But these shortcomings were compensated for by his love for me.

Two days later, Sudhir, Joginder of Sudhir who had travelled with us from India, we all took a plane to see San Francisco. Joginder Brother was a resident of San Francisco. He owned a house there. We all stayed in his home while his wife Kanta Rani was still in India for another vacation. Everything except, the most attractive things were the pictures of his son and daughter decorating the walls of the house. He was probably a very forgiving father. I felt it all. We remained in the house with Brother Joginder for several days. He brought us all to Lake Tahoe, almost near my favorite spot in India like Kashmir.

Joginder and Sudhir were separate poles in their behavior. I also notice certain peculiarities of Sudhir's Behavior. He nagged, Fault finder, and would flare up for no reason. It hurt, but I was helpless to say anything. He was so playful in his demeanor. But these failures were counterbalanced by his love for me.

One day a friend of Joginder invited us to dinner. Meat was served here too. However, I could not bring myself to eat it. But this time I could not escape. Joginder put a piece of meat into my mouth and I felt like throwing up. I excused myself and went to the bathroom and spat the meat piece out. Joginder again rebuked Sudhir.

That night Sudhir was sulking and didn't even speak to me. It was too much for me. His anger seemed to deprive me of my happiness. I tried hard to persuade him to forgive me but he had turned into an insensitive piece of stone. Frustrated, I started crying. But a much unexpected thing happened. He gave a forceful slap on my face. I felt the heavens come crashing down.

That night Sudhir was sulking and didn't even speak to me. It was too much for me. His anger seemed to deprive me of my happiness. I tried hard to persuade him to forgive me but he had turned into an insensitive piece of stone. Frustrated, I started crying. But a much unexpected thing happened. He gave a forceful slap on my face. I felt the heavens come crashing down.

As the night passed, Sudhir realized his mistake in the morning, but the slap became a horrible shock to me.

As the night passed, Sudhir realized his mistake in the morning, but the slap became a horrible shock to me. This might be an omen for future events. Gone was the romance that had preceded this slap. I fell to the ground like a bird hovering in the sky would if its wings were suddenly cut off.

The following day we returned to Los Angeles; I still am carrying the hangover of the undeserved slap. This slap was a sword on my back as Sudhir had promised my parents that he would keep their daughter safe and happy.

A month and a half passed. I was upset because of the new development. At times I felt nauseous in the morning now, but was not unduly disturbed as there could be nothing more than simple morning nausea. I had not learned cooking at home, but had been trying to do so here and was almost near perfection. But the

I was a little nervous about Sudhir's bad habit. He would come to the kitchen and criticize me. It was hard to endure these everyday events. But I calmed them down.

About two months later, Sudhir's middle sister-in-law, Kanta Rani, came to see us. One day we were sitting in the room and she unexpectedly said, "Are you taking medication?"

"Medicine, what medicine?" I asked, a bit puzzled.

"To delay the arrival of an infant," she said.

Till that time, I hadn't given any idea or thought to the issue of having or not having a baby. I was totally unaware of the existence of any such medicine. Neither my sisters nor my mother had told me anything in this regard. In Los Angeles, Sudhir's friends constantly made fun of me, but I had ignored them.

Bhabi, be a bit more precise. I have no idea what you're talking about."

"Tell me if you have had a period this month or not."

"It is a bit late this time. But usually, my periods are always a little late."

"There is no question of 'usually' now. You are going to have a baby."

I was a little nervous about Sudhir's bad habit. He would come to the kitchen and criticize me. It was hard to endure these everyday events. But I calmed them down.

About two months later, Sudhir's middle sister-in-law, Kanta Rani, came to see us. One day we were sitting in the room and she unexpectedly said, "Are you taking medication?"

"Medicine, what medicine?" I asked, a bit puzzled.

"To delay the arrival of an infant," she said.

Till that time, I hadn't given any idea or thought to the issue of having or not having a baby. I was totally TOM unaware of the existence of any such medicine. Neither my sisters nor my mother had told me anything in this regard. In Los Angeles, Sudhir's friends constantly made fun of me, but I had ignored them.

Bhabi, be a bit more precise. I have no idea what you're talking about."

"Tell me if you have had a period this month or not."

"It is a bit late this time. But usually, my periods are always a little late."

"There is no question of 'usually' now. You are going to have a baby."

"Was that all? Listen, come here. I am thirty and you are twenty-one."

"But I am not yet ready to be a mother. I know nothing about such things."

"But you are not alone. I am with you. In India, child bearing may be a problem but it is damn easy in America."

"I agree, Sudhir, that I am twenty-one but I was brought up like a pampered kid in my family. I am still like a teenager."

"That was my point too when I told you that you behaved like a child. But never mind; now do as I advise you."

"Yes, yes, I hear you; who else do I have in this country who can understand my feelings? I will do as you tell me to do," I said, vigorously nodding.

"That's like a good wife." He held me in a tight embrace.

At that moment someone started knocking at the door impatiently. It was the five-year-old son of the Kanta Rani. We heard Bhabhi Kanta Rani, saying, "It is very much like them. They always sit in their room with the door shut."

The next moment, Joginder Bhai pushed open the door saying, "Err... I have heard that a little baby is expected into our family. Congrats Sudhir. I have heard people say that if the husband is sexier, the baby is likely to be a boy and if it is the other way round, the baby will most probably be a girl. Which one of you is sexier?"

Sudhir said nothing and out of embarrassment, I sat crouching where I was. In the meantime, the middle sister-in-law Kanta Rani had come into our room. She said, "I think it is Rita. She always sits behind closed doors. Take note. It is going to be a girl."

"I don't care whether it is a boy or a girl. I only want the delivery to be normal," Sudhir answered adamantly.

The Kanta Rani cooked meat regularly, ignoring my protests. I couldn't bear the smell of meat but Joginder Bhaiya and Kanta Rani forced Sudhir, who started forcing me to eat meat and if I objected, he would be angry and feel offended. Whenever he stopped speaking to me, I felt as if my world had come to an end.

The middle sister-in-law Kanta Rani played many dirty tricks to persecute me. When Sudhir was planning to return to Los Angeles, she suggested that he should leave me with her for a month. At that time Sudhir had no job. America was suffering from a recession and engineers were jobless. The space industry was facing closure. In these circumstances Sudhir agreed to let me stay with the middle sister-in-law and added that she was to train me in cooking. To this request she retorted, "Why should I bother? Have I opened a training school for cooking? If she is interested in cooking, she should learn it herself."

When Sudhir was leaving, his brother Joginder said, "Sudhir look here, your dear sister-in-law has cooked Kababs for you. Come along. Taste them yourself and also help Rita to eat." I signaled to Sudhir not to eat the kababs and sat down on a chair.

The middle Kanta Rani caught hold of my hands and Joginder tried to push a piece of meat into my mouth. I turned my face away but Sudhir opened my mouth and pushed the piece in. I felt very vulnerable and weak. I was convinced that Joginder and the Kanta Rani were making a laughing stock of me, exploiting the simplicity of Sudhir. I did not know how to convince him not to force me to eat meat. When we were alone, he could be persuaded not to force me into meat eating, but with his brother and the middle sister-in-law around, he behaved differently. He would forget that he had promised not to force me to eat meat.

My mother's advice relevant to such situations was to persuade him with love and not by quarreling. Well, Sudhir left me with the middle sister-in-law for a month. Now the situation was that whenever I asked her to cook something new and to give me the recipe, she would put me off with some excuse. But when I was not around, she would cook the dish. Well, somehow the days were passing. I spent time in the company of her children.

One day the Kanta Rani began talking about the eldest sister-in-law of Sudhir. She said, "When you were in India, you always chased the eldest sister-in-law of Sudhir and hardly had time to spare for me."

"No, there was nothing like that. The fact was that you were always preoccupied with your children and Joginder Bhaiya and I don't believe in encroaching upon others' time. That was why I couldn't talk to you."

Changing the topic, she suddenly asked, "Where are your sarees and jewelry?"

"I have none. Sudhir gave them to the eldest sister-in-law without even telling me."

"Including those gifted by your parents?"

"Yes, all. There were a few sarees with colors of my choice. But Sudhir always has his own way, disregarding my feelings. I hope he doesn't do such things to hurt me deliberately."

She looked at me for some time as if savoring this information and then with emphasis on every word she said, "But my husband, you know, is a very nice person. My happiness is always uppermost in his mind. He worships me. He would never do such a thing even in dreams. I am really sorry for you."

I could see very well that this feeling sorry for me was just a barb aimed at my most vulnerable spot, the heart. This observation of her had its desired effect and it hurt me more than she had expected. But I didn't react and calmly added, "Sudhir is a little impulsive and short tempered but these things are natural in life. I prefer to keep quiet on such occasions as harmony in my life is more important than a few sarees." She felt a little disappointed. I wondered at my own composure and the spirit to hit back.

"But how long can you keep quiet? My husband has assured me, even to the point that only those whom I approve of, can visit us. I have a box full of jewelry and I keep wearing them with frequent change according to my liking," she said, clanking her glass bangles at me.

"For a woman the choice of her husband in such matters is very important to win his love. Sudhir likes simplicity and urges me to wear American dresses and I feel happy in them."

"But I find you can't see things beyond your nose. If a girl is born to you, what would you have to give her? Why don't you ask the eldest sister-in-law to return your saris and the jewelry?" she advised.

I blurted out something that I shouldn't have. "You are not on good terms with the eldest sister-in-law. She usually talks of you and your family."

"What did she say?" she asked angrily.

"Oh, it was nothing. Leave it," I said meekly, regretting what I had said.

"Look here, Rita, we are in a foreign land. Here you are like my younger sister. Don't hide anything from me." She was so sweet and solicitous now.

"Please, forget it. It just slipped from my lips. And your...," I checked myself half way. I was sorry for my mistake.

"I know she was interested in getting her younger sister married to Sudhir and I was interested in doing the same about my sister. Naturally her remarks must have been about the old tale."

"If that was the case, why did you take Sudhir to your parental house first after you landed at Delhi airport?" I asked.

I realized that I had been very foolish. Sudhir had clearly forbidden me to say anything in this regard even though I had had a constant nagging feeling that somebody was trying to poison my life by snuffing out every bit of happiness from it. But I was unaware of the perpetrator of the mischief.

The sister-in-law Kanta Rani said, "My younger sister is too beautiful for Sudhir. When something is out of reach, people say that grapes are sour."

To this I said nothing and went away to my room. Away from Sudhir, I missed him and would have liked to fly to him. But that day I was a bit off color. I lay in my bed when I heard the middle sister-in-law Kanta Rani calling me. "Rita, there is a call for you from Sudhir."

I rushed to receive the call and spoke into the mouthpiece, "Hello Sudhir, I want to come back home," I said before he could say anything and started weeping loudly.

"What is it, Rita? Are you homesick or sad?"

"Yes. I feel lonely without you. Take me back home. Please!"

"Has anything happened?"

"Yes, something has happened."

"All right. I shall ask Joginder Bhaiya to put you on the plane for Los Angeles tomorrow."

Kanta Rani came to know of this development and felt offended. In spite of her anger, I reached Los Angeles the following day.

Sudhir had come to receive me at the airport. As I stepped off the plane, he took me in his arms and kissed my face and eyes again and again. He wiped my tears off with his palm. We got into the car and Sudhir had me sit very close to him. On our way home, we talked a lot about everything that had happened and much more which I don't even recall now. In the apartment, Sudhir laid the table. He told me that in future I was not to be afraid of either of the sisters-in-law and was to mince no words in dealing with them.

"They are elders and it will not be appropriate to answer back to them." I spoke.

"Look here Rita, I liked neither the elder sister-in-law nor the younger sister-in-law Sisters. But I had a slight liking for the sister of Kanta Rani. Bhaiya had once mentioned her to me. I visited her place and we indulged in a little flirtation too. But I found you and my search for a life partner ended there. Now you are everything for me."

"Sudhir, am I permitted to say something?"

"A dozen darlings, why only one." Saying this he escorted me to the bed.

"Whenever you play the movie of our marriage before your friends, why do they tease you when they see the sister of your middle sister-in-law?" I asked him, simultaneously cooperating with him in undressing me.

"It was because they believed that the middle sister-in-law could persuade me and I would agree to marry her sister," Sudhir said, exposing the upper part of my body and then loosening my hair.

"Sudhir, do you remember the promise made by you the day following our marriage?" I was helping him in the preliminaries of fulfillment of his intended act that I felt was imminent.

"Yes, certainly I do. It was that I would remove the girl's photo from my album. I shall remove it right now. She is nothing to me after all." He kissed me on the lips and my entire wholesome. Our soul and body merged with each other once again.

Then what followed obviated the need of conversation. Two hungry bodies got what they had been deprived of for almost a month because of the separation. I forgot my moroseness with his stormy crushing of my body. I became a baby doll yielding, nipping him on the exposed skin and cooperated with him in every move he made to enhance the pleasure I had missed for a month. Finally, I clung to him with my embrace and my legs as if we were two bodies but one soul. The storm was the natural consequence. But Sudhir was not satisfied with one stormy bout of libido. He churned me again and again as if we had not had sex for years. The night seemed to be insufficient for the total quenching of the thirst of the two bodies. Dawn was peeping when we fell asleep."

CHAPTER 6

Fate can, sometimes, lead us on to indulge in acts that had better be avoided. It did this to me now. The following day, I don't know what bug bit me that I wrote a letter to the elder sister-in-law asking her to return my jewelry and sarees. But before this I had already informed Sudhir of my intention.

In the meantime, everybody, including Sudhir's friends and his relatives, had come to know of my pregnancy. Everybody had a different joke to make. There were myriad suggestions for my successful delivery. I had no choice but to listen to them without reacting in any way. By now I had also learnt how to cook. But Sudhir had a weakness. He would always find fault with everything I did and would scold me before his friends. Occasionally he would not speak to me for days even when I was not to blame and I had to forget the injustice involved. I tried to tempt him with womanly tricks or sometimes acting difficult-to-get strategy. But nothing worked. I had hardly realized that the slave lamb was nearing the slaughterhouse.

A lady doctor saw me after three months, as earlier she had not been available and I was reluctant to be examined by a male doctor. When I saw the doctor for the first time, I asked her in all naivety, "Doctor, which way will the baby come out?"

The doctor just smiled at my ignorance. I thought that I was stupid enough to deserve this. It was true that I had never till then seen a baby being born. I knew only that it was very painful when it did come out. She called Sudhir and told him to buy some books on pregnancy for me, saying, "Buy some pregnancy guide books for her. She is very ignorant in this regard and must equip herself with the necessary knowledge."

"I have already bought a lot of books for her but she doesn't like to read any."

"Well, every Tuesday, we have exercise classes for expectant women and we also show movies about childbirth. Make sure you come along with her."

On the way home, I was disturbed lest Sudhir should be angry. But in the car Sudhir asked me, "Well, what would you prefer, a boy or a girl?"

I hadn't given any thought to this aspect till then. My only feeling was that I had some minor health problem and my body was undergoing changes. I put my head on Sudhir's shoulder and mumbled, "What do you want? I would like to go with your choice. God knows that my happiness lies in yours."

Sudhir kissed me and said, "Truly, I have been blessed with a very innocent and simple wife. I am really very lucky."

"Sudhir, believe me, when you are angry with me, I feel as if the whole world is angry. Then I miss my parents and wish my mother were with me." As I said this, tears flowed down my cheeks.

"Rita, please don't start weeping so easily. When you weep, I feel sad too. If you miss your mother, the loss of having never known a mother's love starkly confronts me and I feel that fate has been very cruel to me."

When I saw Sudhir sad, my heart melted. I put my free left arm around his shoulders and said, "Obviously the loss of a mother's love can never be made up but I would do my best to make you forget that loss."

The primary aim of divinity was to create a mother in a woman and to reach that ultimate goal, she must first be a wife. But the mother instinct remains in the background and the wife's role is ubiquitous. I felt the warmth of his body while he focused his eyes on the road ahead. As we approached the apartment, I jumped out of the car. Sudhir noticed this and said, "Rita, please be careful when you get down, otherwise our baby doll will be scared."

"A baby dolls? You mean a girl?" I was surprised.

"Darling, you are not alone now. There is another life with you. So, you should take care of her too."

"But who is she?' I hadn't yet comprehended the significance of his remark.

"She is my daughter, the baby doll, you know, in your womb."

"Oh!" I took time to digest this. Then, after a little pause, I said, "How do you know that it is a girl?"

"I know that it is a baby doll, I mean a girl. I want her to be just as beautiful as you are."

"If she turned out to resemble you, I won't even touch her," I said pettily, reclining my head on his shoulder.

"Oh, I see. Love adds luster to beauty but in turn beauty is determined to belittle love," he said.

"Wow! You are turning into a poet."

We had hardly entered the apartment when Gyan Bhaiya wished to talk to Sudhir alone. I became nervous and went to my room. I heard them talking loudly and knew that all was not well. I came out of my room to see what was going on when Gyan Bhaiya gave a resounding slap on my face saying, "You dirty offspring of a pauper, who the hell do you think you are that dare write to my wife so impudently? I say, Sudhir, if you don't keep her under control, she will make your life hell and you will suffer throughout till your last breath."

"Sorry, Bhaiya, she is poorly-informed. I shall educate her. Please calm down."

I felt outraged to hear Sudhir say this and, concealing my anger and tears, returned to my room... He had said nothing to his brother, rather he came to my room and told me sternly to apologize to Gyan Bhaiya.

"Apologize? But why me?" I asked, astonished.

"It was I who had given the jewelry and the Saaris to the elder-sister-in-law and had received her letter at my office address."

"But it is hardly a month since you found a job. How did she, then, have your office address? I would like to read that letter," I said and started looking for it. I found the letter had a cone from India and quickly read it as the eldest sister in- law of the family who was supposed to be the mother figure for all the four brothers of Sudhir's family. It contained a lot of unsavory things about my sisters, brothers and parents who once trusted Sudhir and his family. The sister-in-law, Gyan Bhaiya's wife, had also said a lot of objectionable things about my parents and my kinfolks' moral values.

I said, "Sudhir, I had always been convinced that we two are together and there were no secrets between us but this letter...?"

"Rita, you have committed a blunder by asking for your things from Gyan Bhavya's wife, the eldest sister-in-law. Now come on and apologize to Gyan Bhaiya."

"But I had asked for only what rightfully belongs to me," I said, weeping.

"Rita, don't be adamant. Don't make me angry. Come along and apologize to Gyan Bhaiya." He almost shouted as the apartment walls started shaking.

"But Sudhir, your brother slapped me in your presence. It is for him to apologize. His wife accused me baselessly, wrote incriminating letters full of rubbish against my parents and abused my father. Don't you know they are all innocent? It is for these people to apologize to them."

While I was arguing with Sudhir, Gyan Bhaiya had come into the room unnoticed by me. He shouted, "So this offspring of a hobo will humiliate us in the eyes of her despicable people!"

On hearing this, Sudhir at once started beating me mercilessly as if I were an animal. I felt everything go dark before my eyes. A single slap had by and by led to this severe beating. While Gyan Bhaiya didn't make any effort to stop Sudhir's beating on my weak, helpless and unhealthy body.

All my ambitions of a peaceful life, all my dreams and hopes came down crashing to the ground. My world was crumbling like a house of cards. Sudhir was behaving like a heartless lunatic. I spent the night crying but Sudhir, who was around, showed no inclination to calm me. Rather I felt that the more I suffered, the greater was his joy. I saw this sadistic aspect of his nature for the first time.

In the morning, he left for work without having any breakfast. But my Devar ji (youngest brother-in-law) and his elder brother's son Prabhat helped me to cook and had their breakfast. I ate nothing. Then Prabhat left for school.

When my Dever ji and I were alone, he said, "Bhabi (sister-in-law), you are still very immature, whereas both my elder sisters-in-law are very crooked. You had better keep away from them. As for Sudhir, he has always been short tempered. You know what? When I was very young …"

"What happened then?" I was suddenly alert.

"Sudhir regularly beats me. Once he had beaten the elder sister-in-law too. Gyan Bhaiya's wife. He has always been free with the use of his hands to inflict violence on others. But she will surely avenge herself on him for the beating."

"Why did he beat her?"

"She hadn't cooked lunch on time."

"Please tell me when Sudhir hit the elder sister-in-law, did Gyan Bhaiya not intervene to help her?"

"No, on the other hand he scolded her and forgetting that entire episode she still continues washing Sudhir's clothes."

"I look upon you as my younger brother rather than a brother-in-law. I seek your advice about how to deal with Sudhir and his anger."

"It is beyond you to handle him. You have to deal with a devil, not an ordinary human being."

My brother-in-law left, leaving me to ponder over this highly disheartening information. I was totally friendless in a foreign land. He, who was supposed to be mine and protect me, appeared to be a total stranger now. My heart sank to think of my helplessness. Every inch of my body ached. In order to relieve the pain, I went to take a hot bath. When I undressed, I saw black and blue spots all over the body. I could not control my tears. I wept loudly.

Fate could not have been crueler than this. The line of fate on my henna bedecked palms was fading before the henna did. The bridal red headscarf had holes in it. I felt the tinkling anklets going into pieces before they had done their duty. The black spots on my body turned into black ink and took the shape of snakes to put their fangs into the white soft skin of the cursed bride. Where had destiny dragged me, I wondered? Here all were concerned with settling their own scores and my pain was nothing to them. How was I to live my life? The community knew Sudhir and his family but I was a total stranger here. Married girls happily lived their lives. But here I was with no one to turn to for help. I had no privacy. Even my conjugal love was unbearable to my relatives; every domestic discord was an excuse for them for diversion and was highly entertaining. Gone was the time when I would spend a few relaxed moments with Sudhir. Now I hardly ever spoke to him. Also, I had a mortal fear of Sudhir now. A man may be strong or weak; he is always strong for his wife. If any stranger had beaten me as Sudhir did, I would have sucked him dry of his blood but now it was my heart that was bleeding.

A new life was growing in my womb. My father-in-law had gone to live with Kanta Rani. The elder brother Gyan Bhaiya too had moved to some other city. When I had come as a newlywed, I had to cook not only for the family but also for Sudhir's friends whom he invited without any notice. I felt sick almost every night. There were arguments over minor things. The arguments led to quarrels most of the time. I would feel miserable. I wanted to flee this scene if it were within my power to do so. My coming to America had proved to be a big tragedy for me.

Once I accompanied Sudhir to dinner at his friend's house. The friend's wife, a very beautiful teenager, was a very clever girl. But the most noteworthy thing about her was her sharp tongue that worked like scissors. Reportedly, she was from Bombay. She indulged in vulgar jokes about her first sexual encounter with her husband. She drew applause with such cheap tricks and attracted everybody's attention. I could not fully comprehend some of the jokes. Even otherwise I hated vulgar jokes and I had no stomach for them. When I remained aloof, Sudhir's friends complained about this to him. After dinner, when we were on our way back home, Sudhir was very angry. I was cheerful but Sudhir sarcastically answered every reconciliatory humorous remark I made. When I could not bear all this, I made bold to ask him, "What is it, Sudhir, that you are bent upon picking a quarrel with me for nothing?"

"I had hoped that you, being educated, would know how to conduct yourself in a get together," he said morosely.

"But I did nothing objectionable in the party," I said.

"The impudence and insolence that you exhibited today was unprecedented, you know," he said angrily, looking at me. Then added, "The girl from Bombay, though much younger than you, is so smart and can make very humorous and interesting jokes. But on the other hand, you, an unsophisticated village girl, don't know what to make of such parties and just sit gaping like a fool. I curse myself over the day when I committed the blunder of accepting you as a wife."

"Oh, I see. So, you had no common sense when you married me and which you regret now. Ok, so be it. I shall write to my mother asking her why she married me to a person who is out of his mind." The words just escaped from my mouth.

"Shut up!" Sudhir roared with indignation.

But that 'shut up' was enough to make me feel miserable. I had always detested girls who were mere chatterboxes. While making girls beautiful, the Creator also gave them bashfulness. Now my modesty and humility were turning into my enemies. I wiped my tears again and again but they wouldn't stop.

We reached home and found the middle brother, his wife and the children waiting for us. As soon as they saw us, the brother said, addressing me, "How strange that you go out alone! The minimum you could have done was at least to take your brother-in-law Gyan and nephew with you." He looked at me with an unpleasant smile on his far from handsome face.

Ignoring the remark directed at me, Sudhir said, "The children are reluctant to accompany us of their own accord." Then he continued, "How long have you been waiting?"

"It is over two hours now. But Rita had not thought of cooking for her brother-in-law and nephew," Joginder Bhaiya observed.

"I don't keep well these days," I promptly said.

"But you feel fine if it is to go to a dinner party?" Joginder added sarcastically.

"Look here, Rita, if you can't adjust yourself with us, it will be very difficult to live in this family," Kanta Rani chipped in.

"Sudhir!" I called Sudhir loudly as I saw the turn the ugly situation was likely to take.

"Look here Rita, you have hardly ever kept fit since you have come to America," Sudhir said.

I could clearly see that he was taking sides with his family. I thought it best not to argue with this family, as it would mean an avoidable quarrel. But feeling powerless, I began to shed tears upon my naivety. I regretted that if my mother had given me a course on motherhood, I could have avoided being a mother so soon after marriage.

A man satisfies his lust at the cost of a woman with consensual or forced sex. Later, when the fruit of his sexual pleasure ripens, it is again the woman that has to nourish it irrespective of the fact whether it is sour or sweet.

I was fed up with the interference of the relatives in my small world and Sudhir never bothered to support my cause. On the nights when I had no mind to share his bed, Sudhir would just slap me a couple of times and force himself on me which was more a rape than a conjugal love making but I had no choice. I felt like an insensitive organism and yielded to his lust. He could as well be raping a dead body than sharing time with his beloved wife.

I found myself eight months pregnant. Noticing that a baby was soon to be added to our family, the manager of the apartment served a notice on us to vacate the apartment, as he would not allow a family with a kid to stay in his apartment. As such we started to look for another apartment. My elder brother-in-law's son Pradeep had graduated from high school. He planned to go to live with his father. The youngest brother-in-law, my Dever ji, Sunil, wanted to join college which was quite a distance away from where we lived. So, everybody was to go their own way. I was also expecting my life to change with the arrival of the baby.

At that time Joginder phoned at night. He said, "Sudhir you should keep Sunil too with you. What if the college is far away? Can't you control Rita to put him up with you?"

The phone was taken away from Joginder by the middle sister-in-law Kanta Rani. She said, "Woman is just like a pair of shoes which you can change as you will. She should not be allowed to sit on your head."

"Don't say this. Rita is not of this type. She follows my wishes." Saying this Sudhir replaced the receiver.

"What has happened? What fresh mistake have I committed again?" I spoke.

"Joginder suggested that we should put the younger brother up with us."

"Well, I have no objection but you know that with the arrival of new baby of us, there will be additional work to do. Furthermore, I am to join school, you know," I said.

"Yes, but by then my daddy will have come to stay with us and when you go to school, he will take care of the baby," Sudhir said.

"I don't hate your younger brother, Sudhir. But he is unmarried. He neither washes his clothes nor makes his bed himself. When I have cleaned the bathroom, he uses it and dirties it again. This aspect of etiquette has to be explained to him."

"Rita, in India women do all the work. They look after the needs of the father-in-law, do the laundry, make yogurt, take care of the baby and still manage in a small room."

"Sudhir, don't forget that even in India the times have changed now. Educated working women don't find this possible now," I said.

"Well, let the time come. We shall find some solution then." Saying this Sudhir pulled me to him in the bed.

I regretted that brother Joginder, although a hustler, was jealous of others who lived independently. Even today his wife does nothing. The husband himself fixes something to eat. In the evening, on return from work, he takes care of the children, shields his wife's weaknesses, and doesn't allow anybody to criticize her. He adores her ugly body all the time. She has failed thrice in the matriculation examination. However, I am educated, beautiful, and liberal in my ideas. But that couple is always interfering in my life. I have no idea what hostility they have against me.

When Sudhir had left for work in the morning, I phoned the middle sister-in-law. She took the call.

"Hello Bhabi ji, how are you?" I said affectionately and respectfully.

"Rita, what is it? I was asleep and you have disturbed me in my sleep." she said rudely.

"Sorry Bhabhi Ji. I had something very important to discuss with you," I said, ignoring the annoyance in her tone.

"It could have been discussed in the evening. What was the urgency that you chose to disturb me?"

"No, Bhabi Ji. It couldn't wait till evening. When I found that the matter had crossed the acceptable limits, I decided to ring you up. Why do you and your husband interfere in my personal life, may I know? I can't digest this," I said firmly.

"Shut up, I say," she shouted in the mouth piece. "You have come from a poor family of paupers. How dare you talk like this to us?" she said, boiling with anger.

"Look here, Kanta Rani, though I belong to a poor family, yet am always respectful to you. But I have not compromised my self-respect. Why do you compare me to a pair of shoes?"

"I never compared you to a pair of shoes. It is a lie. Sudhir must have lied to you. He is a dissembler," she said angrily.

"My Sudhir never tells lies," I asserted proudly.

"Look here, woman, I said nothing. Now stop this nonsense and go to hell." She banged the receiver on the cradle.

Well, I didn't ring her up again. Sudhir returned from work. I didn't mention the incident to him. But he looked morose. I thought it better not to broach the issue. Sudhir lay in bed with his back to me at night. Consequently, I also didn't find sleep. In the morning when I was preparing breakfast for Sudhir, I dropped the toast by accident. Sudhir burst out angrily, "You don't know how to cook; don't know how to respect the elders but you are adept at insulting my elder brother. You are stupidity personified."

"You have been angry with me since last evening. Sudhir believes me, it makes me very nervous," I pleaded with him very humbly.

"But you were not nervous when you abused my brother on the phone," he retorted sarcastically.

He caught me by the hair and pulled me back mercilessly from where I was standing. He showered abuses on me freely. Then he hit me with something on the head. I felt everything going dark before my eyes and I was sure that I would collapse. However, I gathered strength with great effort, clung to Sudhir and started apologizing to him.

"Sudhir, please don't beat me. You know I have nobody whom to call my own. For God's sake, spare me this beating."

But all my pleadings fell flat on his unhearing ears. I don't know how Jeth Ji, (brother in law) Gyan Bhaiya and his wife Kanta Rani had poisoned his ears. He continued kicking me with his shoes on. He freely boxed me wherever he pleased. Even a butcher would not be so heartless. I had never before come across such a cruel man in my life. I don't know when I fell unconscious. Leaving me lying on the floor, he left for work.

When I regained consciousness, I found myself still on the kitchen floor. I had no strength left to rise. I just lay there and stared at the ceiling like an animal in a trap. I was surrounded by a pack of wild beasts, not human beings, with Sudhir and his family. The beasts were advancing to tear me to pieces. My throat was dry and I could not even cry. My head was like lead and when I tried to get up, I fell down again like a disoriented being. My limbs felt heavy like stone. There was rumbling in my stomach. My whole body was sore.

After a considerably long time I managed to get up and poured some water into a glass. My hands were shaking badly. My legs were swollen and unsteady. I sipped a little water and dragged myself to bed.

I was now able to weep and made no attempt to control it.

"Oh, mother of mine, why did you hand me over to these beasts? I am an orphan here. I, whose giggles added charm to your home, have forgotten the meaning of happiness. The promising bud nursed by you is drying up. I am dying slowly but find no one to share my pain with. I shed oceans of tears; no one came to dry my tears. You must be under the illusion that your darling daughter is happy in the foreign land so called America, a land of opportunities, but here all in the family chosen by you for my well-being are my enemies. Only if my brothers were here, only if my father was here, would they break the hands of this Satan who dares to beat me so mercilessly."

I just kept weeping with no one around to wipe my tears and console me. The one who was supposed to protect me was now an enemy. A cry of anguish rose from my heart, "Oh God merciful, please don't let any woman have a cruel heartless husband!" At about three in the afternoon, I got up somehow and went to the bathroom and took off my clothes. I noticed blue marks all over my body. My hands were getting swollen. There were lines on my neck as if someone had tried to strangulate me. I tried to straighten my hair but it came off in bunches. I was shocked and began to weep loudly again.

A feeling rose in my heart that I hated Sudhir from the core of my heart. I decided to leave him and this earth forever. I bathed, packed a few clothes in an attaché case and came out of the apartment. I was determined to do something boldly and dangerously.

Suddenly I saw a car coming towards me as if to run me over. I tried to dodge it but it came straight towards me and stopped, blocking my path. It was my Dever Ji, the younger brother-in-law, in the car. He had seen me and realized that something was unusual. I was in no mood to see anyone from Sudhir's family and was thinking how to react when he said, "Rita Bhabi, where are you going?"

"Wherever I am going is none of your business." I went around the car and tried to move ahead down the road again.

"You must have had a quarrel with Sudhir. Come on, get into the car," he said emphatically and forced me into the vehicle.

"I hope the quarrel was not about me. Joginder told me that you don't want me to stay with you," he said.

"Joginder and his wife, your so-called Sister-in-Law, know nothing except ruining others' lives. They have no life except stir problems in people's family life," I said indignantly.

"You know, Bhabi, I want to live with my friends but they are forcing me to live with you."

"I have no objection to you living with us if you are interested. But I don't understand their strange behavior. They prefer to live alone and have nothing to do with how I lead my life. But they never miss a chance to disturb my life and don't understand why they try to be the mediators between you and us. I have no ill will for you but it is your middle Bhabi and her husband who are instrumental in making Sudhir and me quarrel. What harm have I ever done to them?"

"Rita, you are over sensitive and too innocent. The Kanta Rani is crooked and then Sudhir is also very short tempered. He is easily provoked by her clever machination. You'd better keep Sudhir away from her. Don't say anything to her."

He drove me back to the apartment, made and served tea to me. In the evening when Sudhir returned from work, he was still angry and not repentant. I also kept mum. When he was settled on a sofa, my brother-n-law said, "Sudhir, I want to live with my friends but Joginder is forcing me to live with you."

"Has Rita been talking to you?" Sudhir reacted with obvious anger

"Sudhir, I'd just say that your attitude towards Rita, an attitude which you're prompting others to follow, needs to be changed."

"You mind your own business. Got it?" Sudhir told him angrily.

"Do you know that your wife had left your home to commit suicide? If I, were you, I would never harass my wife to the extent you do? I wouldn't even let her see my brothers and their wives if they were antagonistic to her."

"What makes you think that she was going to commit suicide?" Sudhir sounded a little troubled.

"I saw her going away down the road. If I hadn't stopped her, you would have regretted how you have treated her and would have probably been in jail," Sunil told Sudhir. Sudhir went to his room to go to bed without waiting for a response.

I was in my room close by and heard the conversation fully. I shuddered to think of its consequences. I was convinced that another severe beating was in the offing. I wanted to die before he started laying a hand on my body once again.

Prayers rose up from the bottom of my heart and God must have heard my prayers and taken pity on me as Sudhir didn't come to my room against my expectation. I also felt it safer to stay in my room.

It was the dead of night and I hadn't had a wink of sleep owing to my agitated mind and my not having eaten anything the whole day. I quietly left the room and went to the kitchen. I switched on the light and extended my hand to take out a glass of juice from the refrigerator. I had hardly touched the glass when Sudhir turned up there. I was frightened and a loud scream escaped my lips. But at once Sudhir covered my mouth with his palm softly and before I could react, took me in his arms. I was too weak to free myself from his hold though I did my best to free myself and run away as quickly as possible. I was conscious that I had intense hatred for Sudhir. But the more I struggled, the tighter became his embrace. He started kissing me. But the lips that were always a source of bliss in conjugal love were like the lips of a venom-throwing reptile. I was no longer a life partner of this man who used to be my husband till last evening. I was a prisoner in the arms of a cunning male animal. All strength had left my body. I wanted to push him away from me and escape but didn't know how. I felt as if I was getting molested, raped by the man I didn't know any more.

In the morning my brother-in-law left for work but Sudhir stayed back and didn't go to work. I hadn't had any sleep the whole night but at about six in the morning I went to sleep. Sudhir didn't awaken me. I slept till noon. I was still in bed when Sudhir awakened me and brought my lunch, he had himself cooked. I told him that I was not hungry.

He said, "Rita, you won't believe me but the fact is that I love you very much. Why don't you do as I tell you to do?"

"The people who love their wives do not thrash them as if they were animals. In your house I am nothing more than an orphan. There is no one whom I could trust to be mine," I said, staring at my toes, for I had no mind to make eye contact with him.

"I am," he asserted.

"No, you are not mine. I have nobody here, I have no one," I said again and again, to no one in particular, in a pitiable voice, and started weeping loudly.

"Please Rita! Please forgive me. I know I lose temper very easily but I become senseless in anger. Please don't do anything that makes me angry. Why do you make me angry?" he said, blaming me.

"You had promised that you would let no one come between us," I said between sobs.

"I promise that I shall never see Joginder Bhaiya and Bhabi in future and never listen to them," he assured me.

"I don't want to alienate you from your brothers and sisters-in-law but I will not see them in future," I said with finality in my tone.

"Ok. Don't see them. Are you satisfied now?" he said, and started kissing the sore spots on my body. He also fomented my sore body with a hot water bottle. Then he applied oil to my disheveled hair. He also gave me a towel bath.

As the day advanced, I developed pain in my back. It gradually came to my stomach. I started moaning. Sudhir rang up the doctor but he was not free. Sudhir filled a bathtub with hot water, sat me in it and washed my hair. He helped me out of the tub and dressed me. He did everything to share my pain. But the frequency of pain increased. Instead of every half an hour, now it was coming every fifteen minutes. Sudhir drove me to the hospital. An x-ray showed that the birth canal was very narrow and that because of some shock, the baby had moved to an abnormal position. In that position a normal delivery was out of the question. An operation was essential. I was afraid of an operation and began to weep. On such occasions, one always thinks of something going wrong.

I said to Sudhir, "In case of my death, please don't remarry if my baby is alive," thinking about how my baby's life would be hell if I died.

"Rita, we are in America, not India. An operation in these circumstances is just a matter of routine and there is no reason to be afraid."

"Ok, it may be so. But do promise me," I insisted.

"Yes, I promise. But I assure you that nothing will happen to you and the baby will be normal." Sudhir allayed my fears.

At that moment a nurse and two doctors came there to escort me to the operation theatre. Sudhir stayed outside. In the theatre, I was made to put on blue paper overalls. The blue cap slipped away again and again and thinking that it was an essential part of the process of operation, I straightened it again and again. The nurse noticed this and smiled. She said, "Good, you're a good girl."

Then I realized that a doctor was giving me multiple injections on my spine. I screamed with pain but the doctor rudely told me to shut up. I was cowed down. I stuffed a corner of a bed sheet into my mouth whenever a scream was about to occur.

In the meantime, the doctor to whom I used to come for checking arrived. She saw me writhing with pain and the cloth stuffed in my mouth.

She scolded the doctor who had told me to shut up and said, "You are very rude to my patient. Please get out. Don't you see that she is new to this country and is very young and innocent?"

By then my body, from the stomach down to the toes, had gone numb. I had no idea what was happening there. It was an hour before I heard the shrill cry of an infant. Soon a nurse said, "Congratulations. It is a girl." I saw the long dark curly hair, big eyes and fair color of the baby.

The mother in me took over. I saw my daughter for the first time, a new life, a part of my own being. I was impatient to hold her against my bosom and spread my arms to the nurse to let me have her. But she said that I was to wait a little before I could get her. I must have become unconscious under sedation for I don't know when I was taken away from the operation theatre to my private room. I was under sedation the whole night and had no knowledge of what happened during those hours.

In the morning Sudhir came and lightly brushed my face with a bunch of African violet flowers to awaken me. I opened my eyes and when I saw Sudhir, my face glowed with contentment. He bent down and kissed me. He said into my ear, "Did you know a baby girl has come into our family?"

I pretended to be ignorant and said, "Really?"

"Yes, she is so cute," he said sweetly.

"Which one of us does she look like?" I casually asked.

"Of course, like you; the same fair skin color, big eyes, curly dark hair…"

"But my hair is not curly," I said, smiling naughtily.

"Oh no, the curled down eyebrows and the curly hair are like mine."

"Are you glad that it is a baby girl? Everyone was of the opinion that it was to be a boy."

"It is our baby. There is no reason why I shouldn't be happy. Rita, the baby is very beautiful. What name should we give her?"

"Monika," I said.

"No, it is a name like that of a dancer. It should be Bhanu. Vijya had suggested this name to me."

"All right, let it be Bhanu, if you like it," I said a bit sleepily.

At that moment the nurse brought Bhanu in. Sudhir was right. Bhanu was extremely beautiful. Sudhir took her from the nurse and handed her over to me. I held her tightly to my bosom and began to weep.

"Rita, don't squeeze her so tightly. She is just a few hours old infant and is likely to be crushed if you hold her so tightly." He at once took Bhanu back from me. "I have phoned Joginder Bhaiya and the middle sister-in-law. Actually, I had phoned Daddy but they also took the call."

"What did your daddy say?"

"Daddy said that it was really auspicious that a girl was born. She is a goddess, the goddess of wealth, Lakshmi, but the sister-in-law said that she doubted if it was a girl."

"Now, why does she think so? She herself used to predict that a girl would be born to me."

"Well, leave it; because of your poor health, she is coming here to help us tomorrow."

"Where is the need? You have taken leave from your work and can manage without her. She is coming only to show that she helped me when…"

"No, it was my daddy who forced her to come here against her will. But I see you are feeling sleepy. Go ahead and have some sleep now."

The nurse took Bhanu away. I was really feeling sleepy. I don't know when Sudhir left the room.

The wound stitched after the caesarian section pained much. I felt a burning sensation even when I laughed a little. Whenever the nurse told me to set foot on the ground, I felt a current-like pain run through my body. I couldn't suckle the baby properly. But gradually I felt better. Sudhir had rented a new apartment. I had to stay in the hospital for ten days.

When I was discharged from the hospital, we came to our new apartment. I found the middle-sister-in-law and my younger brother-in-law Sunil waiting there for us.

Sunil took Bhanu, looked at her closely and said, "Rita Bhabi, you have produced a gem for the family."

The observation of Sunil made the middle-sister-in-law burn with jealousy. Her daughter was hardly good looking. But considering that children are tiny angels, I thought of her as very cute. This daughter of my sister-in-law was looking at Bhanu and smiling. I smiled to see her smiling and said to Sunil, "Devar Ji (brother-in-law) why don't you get married too now?"

"Alright Bhabi, if you insist, but Rita Bhabi, I shall have a wife who will bear only male babies."

"My daughter is no less than boys. She is our first child, you know," Sudhir said.

"Never mind, another will follow in due course," the middle-sister-in-law Kanta Rani observed icily.

I had never seen a more ill-mannered woman in my life than her. I looked at Sudhir but he threw a kiss at me.

Sudhir was on leave. Bhanu's room had been decorated with red balloons. Numerous toys littered the floor. I looked around and had a fleeting glance at the scattered toys and then reflected over the recent past.

The middle-sister-in-law had left after spending a week without any earth-shaking incident, which was a miracle to me. Before she had left, it came to be known that she was expecting her third child. Now with Bhanu to look after, my responsibility had increased. But even then, Sudhir never disturbed me. Rather, he himself got up and bottle-fed the baby. He changed her diaper. He made a lot of fuss over Bhanu. I had forgotten the beating by now. Bhanu was the focus and subject of our conversation all the time.

Sudhir almost daily brought a new toy for the kid. Bhanu's arrival had changed the whole environment around the house and added a unique charm to our life. She was undoubtedly the cutest kid among the kids of the Indian community around us. She was so attractive looking that the onlookers found it difficult to take their eyes off her.

Sudhir's daddy had come to live with us. He was eighty-four years old then but had good health. Like Sudhir, he too had the habit of nagging. The eldest sister-in-law living in India used to tell people that Sudhir's Dad used to beat his wife. I had also heard relatives and acquaintances say that Sudhir's mother was also beautiful and had modern ideas. Sudhir's father treated her harshly and nagged her constantly. Well, anyway, he was the age of my grandfather. I took the liberty of talking to him lightly and sometimes even ignored him when he found fault with anything. But he never backed out and would tend to enter into an argument.

A little before the time of child delivery of the Kanta Rani, Sudhir sent me to her house to take care of her. Her majesty, Kanta Rani, hadn't condescended to come to us when my delivery was due but I went to her about two weeks in advance. I worked tirelessly with Bhanu in her crib.

Noticing Bhanu looking at her, the middle-sister-in-law would say, "You little pixy, if a girl is born to me, I shall twist your dirty neck." It made me burn inside and I didn't know what prompted her to say such cruel things to the innocent infant. But God be thanked, she gave birth to a son.

When her infant was a month old, I returned to Los Angeles. I was again with Sudhir. At night Bhanu would sleep between us. We were content with our small family. But whenever I wanted to start going to school or to start working, Sudhir put me off, saying that Bhanu was very young. Although Sudhir still found fault with many things and even scolded me occasionally, now I would be bold to answer him back. Life was on the tracks somehow.

Bhanu was nine months old when we heard that Gyan and his family were coming to America. Gyan had asked Sudhir for a loan of a few thousand dollars. Sudhir had given the money to him without informing me. I didn't like it. I didn't mind that money was given but what hurt me was that Sudhir had bypassed me. Well, we argued a lot, had a quarrel or two but I accepted these things as my destiny.

A month later the first elder sister-in-law Leela, the wife of Gyan Bhaiya, came to San Francisco with her five children. I also visited San Francisco with Sudhir, Bhanu and Sudhir's daddy. Leela returned some of my jewellery and sarees. But a few articles were missing. She didn't return my earrings and was wearing them without any hesitation. I felt like asking her to return them to me. Kanta Rani was also urging me to take them back but out of fear of Sudhir, I desisted.

Gyan had rented a house in New City. He lived away from Joginder Bhaiya. We came to his house and Sudhir again left me with Gyan Bhaiya's family in San Francisco. I had adjusted myself according to the nature of the Kanta Rani. We had a good time together. We dressed alike, used similar lipsticks and so on and so forth. Now she introduced me as her younger sister, so much so that I myself came to look upon her as my real sister.

One day Sudhir told me over the phone to go to stay for a week with Leela, wife of Gyan. I said nothing to him. Kanta Rani said, "What had you written in your letter to the Leela?"

"Nothing in particular. Why? Has anything happened?"

"In the first letter you had asked for your saris. What had you written in your second letter?"

"I had asked why she had written a confidential letter to my Sudhir and had also plainly told her that even death couldn't separate me from Sudhir."

"Well, she was making fun of this thing. Not only this, she has been to the in-laws of your cousin who has left them."

"But why? She had no business going to see them."

"She says that your cousin doesn't have a good character and that her husband had realized this the very first night after her marriage," Kanta Rani said, smiling.

"Oh my God! What a grotesque lies! The problem concerned dowry and had nothing to do with her character." I began to weep.

"It is said that her husband married another girl without divorcing your cousin and ran away to England."

"Really? But the other girl can't be his wife. She is just a mistress."

"Yes, and your sister could have him sent to jail."

"Who?"

"Her husband of course. Who else?"

"My Cousin is educated and is the mother of a girl. She knows what is good or bad for her."

"Rita, please don't get me wrong. Why don't the educated girls pull well with their husbands? Why can't they handle their husbands properly?" The Kanta was pulling my leg to have fun at my cost.

"Sister-in-law, the educated girls are busy with their studies and don't learn the maneuverings of uneducated wives who are fully armed with crooked tricks and petty politics that happen round the hearth and which they learn through trial and error by watching the likes of them," I paid her back in the same coins.

As she heard this, she pulled a long face. I didn't like this attitude of hers and went to my room. A week later I was changing Bhanu's diaper. Having done this, as I turned round, I found Sudhir standing there. I felt very happy. I rushed and clung to him. I complained why he hadn't phoned before coming. He said that he had been in New City for the last two days and added that there were certain important things to discuss with the elder sister-in-law. He told me to get ready at once and to accompany him to New City.

"No, I won't go there," I replied without hesitation.

"Rita, don't answer me back and do as I tell you to do." There was the usual annoyance in his voice.

In order to avoid a quarrel, I went to New City with him. Nothing untoward happened there and we returned to Los Angeles.

During those days, Sudhir was again out of job. Some relative of the Kanta Rani, Krishan Verma, had come to America with a selection of Indian clothes to sell. He came to America on a Business Visa. He claimed to be my relative also and intended to start an import and export business in clothes. Joginder advised Sudhir to join him in it. I wrote a letter to my father who informed me that Krishan Verma was a run-away smuggler from India.

I communicated this information to Sudhir but nobody, including him, was prepared to accept this information about Krishan Verma. He came to stay with us in Los Angeles. He was quick to notice that Sudhir nagged me over trifles. The elder sister Leela, wife of Gyan Bhaiya, too, had stuffed Sudhir's head with a lot of rubbish. Consequently, Sudhir started criticizing my family regularly. Whenever he spoke against them, my blood boiled. I was facing new problems day by day.

Gradually Sudhir was becoming a stranger to me and I was drifting away from him. I didn't know when and where he went with Krishan Verma. When I questioned him in this regard, he would quarrel with me so much that one day my father-in-law said to me, "Young lady, your duty is to mind your kitchen. You have no authority to ask him where he goes and what he does."

I was reminded of the famous saying - Like father, like son.

Bhanu's good looks were also not palatable to the relatives. My in-laws lost no opportunity to find fault with her and in her looks. Sudhir, however, loved the kid very much.

In the meantime, my love for Sudhir was cooling down, whereas his love for me had degenerated into mere sexual lust for his own selfish urges. I was a female body or could even be an inflatable doll with a hole between its legs and two boobs for him to squeeze, a sex toy that people bought over the counter in America. He was no longer my husband. He was just an enemy who hated me. He had only anger, contempt and pain for me. I felt like a sex slave who is only there to satisfy my master whenever he wants.

One day, early in the morning, Sudhir and his father had gone out for a walk. I was sleeping with Bhanu in my room. Bhanu was a year and a half old now. I was disturbed in my sleep as I felt someone touching me. I thought it might be Sudhir. I was startled and looked up. Krishan Verma stood stark naked before me. I covered my eyes with my hands and said, ""Uncle you are like my father. Don't you have any shame left in you?"

"My dear Rita, what has shame to do with it? Your husband doesn't care for you. I pity your youth fully in blossom. What if I am of your father's age, but see how youthful I am. A beauty like you needs a lot of male company and well…what man and woman are meant to do to each other."

"Get out!" I shouted. I was terrified and ran out of the room screaming. Our apartment manager saw this and phoned the police. They came and took Krishan Verma away. Sudhir returned in an hour. Before I could have spoken to Sudhir about this incident, the manager had already informed Sudhir. He said, ""Your guest was going to rape your wife." Sudhir was shaken. He came and embraced me. I started weeping and requested him to turn that man out of the house.

"Sure, he can stay with us no longer. I shall give Joginder Bhaiya a ring."

Sudhir dialed the number. Kanta Rani took the call but instead of listening to Sudhir, she started narrating how the younger brother-in-law, Dever Ji, had got married in India. She went on to say that the girl was more educated than me. She had a Master's degree in politics. Now I would be placed where I belonged. My bragging about being highly educated would come to an end. But Sudhir was not listening. He shouted into the mouthpiece, "Forget the marriage. Will you let me speak? This bloody Krishan Verma of yours has turned out to be a rascal."

"What has happened?"

"He tried to rape Rita."

"Are you mad? Why do you forget that he is closer to Rita than he is related to me?"

"Anyway, he can't come to our house now," Sudhir retorted angrily.

"Look here Sudhir, don't blame him alone. There must have been encouragement from Rita too."

"Will you please shut up, Kanta Rani.?" Sudhir said and replaced the receiver.

Sudhir was very angry.

He was called Kanta Rani by a few bad names. By now the attitude of my father-in-law towards me had softened a bit. One month ago, Sunil went to India and had her wedding with a girl chosen for him with the help of some relatives in India. He had to return to the job he had in the United States. His newly married wife, Shanta, would join him when he obtained his American visa.

All four brothers had started a small milk dairy together. Gyan Bhaiya,s family moved to Los Angeles now. Sunil lived with us in the small apartment. Sudhir was at the shop most of the time. The work at home had considerably increased. The elder sister-in-law wife of Gyan was not very happy to live with the others. Joginder phoned from San Francisco and pressed all to live together. Kanta Rani would ridicule me and would say, "Well, Rita, Sunil's wife Meera has come to stay with you. You must be enjoying the company of the family immensely. My husband would never allow anybody to live with us."

But I had hardly anything to say in response to her and even if I had something, nobody would listen to me. Meera was distantly related to the in-laws of my cousin, the elder uncle's daughter staying with my parents.

Naturally I couldn't mix up and hardly ever communicated with her. I was surrounded by enemies on all sides. Though the wife of Gyan Bhaiya was not interested in staying in a joint family, she incited Sudhir and Gyan Bhaiya by telling them it was I that didn't want to live in the joint family.

When Sudhir heard this, he lost his temper. It was the first day of my menstruation period and I was not well. But such things hardly mattered with Sudhir. He removed the belt from his trousers and rushed at me. I ran to avoid the beating but he ran after me and hit me again and again mercilessly as if I were a buffalo. No rider would hit a horse harder. I was not a woman but just a stray dog. Nobody from the family came forward to stop Sudhir but stood as passive onlookers. Bhanu began to weep loudly. I tried to run out of the house but Sudhir caught me by the hair and pulled me back into the room and said, "You shameless one from a family of paupers, don't dare move out of the room."

At that moment Gyan's elder son, Prabhat, came there. He came to my rescue and supported me affectionately. He said, "Come and stay with me Aunty. Nobody here will ever come to protect you. But come with me and I shall take care of you. I shall work to earn and run the home and you may work as a teacher. You'd better leave Bhanu with her father."

"Oh God, the witch has ensnared my young son!" The Leela started wailing.

Gyan informed Joginder of the situation on the phone.

A drowning man catches at a straw, goes the saying. I at once took a few articles of clothing of daily use and came out of the house with Prabhat without a moment's hesitation. Prabhat was the only member of this family who sided with me. He was almost the same age as my younger brother. He had a soft corner for me as he had witnessed what and how his parents, especially his mother, were damaging my future with her vicious mind games. There was a special sacred bond between the two of us.

We reached the bus stand and waited for a bus but none came the whole night. We had no plan or destination where to go and were least concerned where the bus would take us. My eyes became tearful again and again and Prabhat wiped the tears with his handkerchief. Only in the morning, at about five, a bus came. We were about to board it when Sunil, the youngest brother of Sudhir, came and held me back. I protested a lot but he drove me home. Gyan embraced his son when he saw him. Strangely enough, Joginder had also arrived in Los Angeles from San Francisco. He started berating me before everybody, "So, you were determined to bring a bad name to the family."

"Don't say anything to Rita or else I shall do something which I might regret," Prabhat said angrily.

"Dear son, don't interfere when elders are speaking. You shouldn't answer your uncle back."

Gyan said to his son soothingly, "Son Prabhat, where were you two going anyway?"

"God knows where Prabhat was taking Rita," Sudhir butted in.

Then, addressing me, Gyan said, "Listen to me, next month I am going to India and I shall talk to your parents."

"Please forgive me. Why do you involve my parents in this?" I pleaded with him.

"If your father, the rascal that he is, can feel pain, we too are not immune to it. Don't you see that my son too is feeling miserable?" My Father-in-Law said arrogantly.

I was not a normal woman any more. I felt that I would go mad and kept weeping inconsolably. I was helpless among this pack of wolves. Now Joginder turns out to be as Cruel as Sudhir and the rest of the family is.

I couldn't believe that I was the daughter of a police officer, a college grad girl married to a man who promised to make me happy forever. He let his Joginder brother, let him treat me like a slave? Joginder commanded me. "If you want to be forgiven, draw seven lines with your nose on the ground and ask all of us for forgiveness."

Like a robot, I lay face down on the floor and began to draw seven lines with my nose on the floor. The nephew and nieces started laughing. Having finished this, I took Bhanu up and went to my room.

Now Sudhir and I live like two strangers. Sunil could bear this no more. He rented an apartment and moved to it with his wife Meera. Gyan Bhaiya went to India and complained to my parents against me the way he liked. My parents wanted to have me come to India on some excuse. But on return to America, Gyan Bhaiya didn't say anything in this respect. On the other hand, he said to Sudhir, "Her parents have told me that if she doesn't behave, you can punish her. You can beat her hard to make sure she obeys everyone in the family." I was miserable.

Gyan moved to another place with his family. Only my father-in-law lived with us. The shop had already been closed for some legal reason which was unknown to me.

One of Sudhir's friends had employed him in his company. Sudhir was very popular among the circle of his friends. He would repair their cars and attend to other odd jobs. I was in a fix in these circumstances and all found fault with me. I was still caught in the mire of misery. I couldn't even reply properly when somebody asked me anything. Sudhir also was not very vocal among his circle. I would keep laughing or talking to myself just to hide my unhappiness. Kanta Rani spread unsavory things about me everywhere among her friends. The wives of all of Sudhir's friends took me for being out of my mind and even insane. They sympathized with Sudhir for his bad luck in having me as his wife.

One day Prabhat came driving a car. He came to me and said, "See Aunty, I bought this car with my own money. Let me take you on a joy ride. You should also take Bhanu with you." My father-in-law heard this and said, "No, no, you shall not go out with this young man."

"Aunty, don't listen to this senile old man," Prabhat said, eyeing the grand-dad.

"No, Prabhat, it is not proper to speak to the elders in this manner. By the way, tell me how to learn to drive."

"No problem, I have the necessary papers. Read them thoroughly and get ready. I shall take you for a test."

But things don't happen the way we want. Before I could take the driving test, I had to go to attend the marriage of Arun, my uncle's elder son. Sudhir gave me no money even though he was very generous in sending presents etc. to all my relatives. When Sudhir came to see me off at Los Angeles, Gyan Brother said to Sudhir, " Ask Rita to tell everything to her parents"

"What things is he talking about?" I asked.

"Yes, don't forget to tell everything to your parents," Sudhir said without answering my question.

I didn't understand why they were so adamant about me telling my parents everything. Telling what? That Sudhir had let us all down? I was about to tell my parents what kind of family they married me to. I would urge my parents not to force me into this vicious family.

Within 24 hours, I reached India safe and sound. When I stepped out of the plane onto the soil of India, I found it difficult to believe that I was actually in India. I bowed my head to the land I was born in, my birth place, India. I kissed the soil of India as I bent down to pick up the soil from the land and applied it on my forehead while everyone was watching me.

I was anxious lest it should turn out to be a dream from which I would wake up. My parents and relatives had come to receive me at the airport. My elder brother took Bhanu from me but Bhanu went on weeping. She found the environment new and wasn't inclined to leave me. I embraced my parents, turn by turn, as best as I could, holding Bhanu with one hand. She wept a lot. In the evening we caught a train and reached Punjab. Everybody at home was overjoyed to have me with them. I was again transported to my childhood. Almost all took Bhanu for an American rather than an Indian child.

People tried to take Bhanu in their arms but Bhanu was not going to anybody. She wept incessantly. People offered her toffees, ice cream etc. but she cared for nothing.

I had been married for two and a half years. I found that with the exception of a few, most of my friends were still unmarried. A few girls were working as teachers or doing some other jobs. I tried to meet as many of the girls as I could manage. My cousin's wedding day has arrived. I became a girl again. I danced and sang a lot. I made myself up for the marriage party. Everyone complimented me for my good looks.

The marriage being over, the bride came to our house. I noticed that she was hardly beautiful. But it was the selection of Arun and we could at the most shrug away the matter. It could be possible that she was of good nature. Then it occurred to me that I considered myself very beautiful and perhaps that was why I felt others were not very beautiful. I must have been vain. I felt annoyed over this weakness.

It was two months since I had come from America, but Sudhir had not written even a single letter to me even though I had sent a number of nice letters to him. Finally, a letter from Sudhir came to my father. It was full of complaints against me. My father was incensed on reading it and would have done something to give Sudhir a befitting reply but my uncle advised him against any such step. He said, "Bhaiya (brother), people are bent upon ruining our family. Sudhir may have been fed with wrong things about us. In these circumstances it is better to keep quiet. You had better explain the situation to your daughter."

"My daughter is innocent. Her only fault is simplicity. The son-of-a bitch is older than her by ten years but scoffs at her mentioning her young age by quoting Gautam Buddha in the letters?"

I was sitting there. I said, "Chacha ji (dear uncle), I don't feel at home in America. All around me they have animosity towards me. Sudhir beats me for no fault of mine and I hate him."

"Why don't you call the police and have the bastard arrested?" my aunt burst out in anger.

"Look here, don't give wrong advice to the girl," Uncle scolded the aunt.

"Brother, as a matter of fact it is the decency of our family that is proving to be our enemy," Uncle said to my father.

"Rita, the in-laws of your cousin, the daughter of your elder uncle, met your elder sister-in-law who is thick with them. By the way, why did you send Sudhir to New City alone?"

"Aunty, how did you come to know of this incident in America happening in India?"

"My child, your sisters-in-laws regularly inform their families of everything that happens to you in America. We hear about you and suffer helplessly," the aunt said.

"My child, when you return to America, learn car driving; add to your educational qualifications and find some good job so that you can live on your own," my father advised.

"But Daddy, he doesn't let me either meet anybody or talk to anybody," I said and my eyes became tearful.

"You are behaving foolishly. Serve your father-in-law lovingly and when Sudhir goes away, leave Bhanu with him and learn car driving," the aunty suggested.

My cousin Arun was around. He said, "My friends live in America. I shall write to them and they will give you money. I shall write to them today."

I stayed in India for four months but Sudhir didn't write any letter to me. Occasionally my sisters felt so indignant that they would say, "Don't let the parasite go easily. Don't divorce him either. You are in America. Go ahead and have a boyfriend."

"Oh my God, Didi (sister) what are you saying? If I did any such thing, Sudhir would behead me." I was extremely frightened.

"You simpleton, when one doesn't find love at home, one finds it somewhere else. Sudhir hasn't written a single letter to you for the last four months. Do you believe he doesn't have a girlfriend now?" Didi said.

"Yes, he is most likely to have one. I have noticed him ogling other girls and lavishing praise on them. He praises the Saaris of Kanta Rani and spares no word in praising her cooking," I said and began to weep.

"What is the use of weeping? I smell a rat in the conduct of the middle-sister-in-law," Chachi observed.

"Beti (daughter), at night when your husband intends to make love to you, you have the opportunity to twist him around your finger. It is then that you should have him do everything you want. You can have pocket money too," the elder aunty gave a practical tip.

"Tai ji (elder aunty), he doesn't give me even a single penny. Since the time he has heard how the wife of one of his friends had run away with one of his friends, he doesn't trust me a bit," I said to her.

"The faithless one! Let him not trust you. You should just make a show of love and when he begins to eat out of your hand, demand money from him. Save the money; learn car driving; get more education and find some job. Stand on your own feet," the aunty said. Everybody offered advice according to their perspective.

I returned to Los Angeles after four months. I found a big reception committee line of my sister in laws and his family waiting for me at the airport. I felt angry when I saw the crowd. I spoke to none including Sudhir. Bhanu at once went to Sudhir. She hadn't forgotten her father. The elder brother-in-law and sister-in-law were amused and were looking at each other meaningfully. But the four-month long separation from Sudhir had emboldened me. I was able to see through the cunningness of these people now. We all returned to our apartment.

At night when Sudhir tried to take me into his arms, I pushed his hands away and said, "There is no need to feign love. You didn't care to write a single letter for four months. Do you think I should spend life just as an object of your lust?"

"If that was to be your attitude, what was the need to come to America?" he said.

"I had no wish to come back. But as I am from a decent family, I was sent to you because of the good intentions of my parents," I said firmly.

"But do you find my family inferior? What did you tell your parents about me and the situation here?" Sudhir said.

"What was there to tell them? Both your (sisters-in-law) had been regularly sending full reports about us to India," I said.

"What were the reports about?" he said.

"I shall give the details when I find time. Right now, I am feeling sleepy." I turned away and went to sleep.

In the morning when I woke up, I found myself in his arms. Thinking that the time was appropriate, I said,

"You have never given me a single penny. But I want to learn how to drive a car. Give me a hundred dollars."

"Darling, you are always taut. You are most likely to cause an accident. Postpone learning driving," he said, patting me.

"Please Sudhir!" I insisted.

Sudhir hadn't had his lust satisfied and now was his chance, he thought. He at once gave me a hundred dollars. I also didn't find the bargain bad. Naturally he had what he had bargained for. The auntie's trick had worked. I had returned from India after a long time and naturally I also needed him for other things for my future. Whether he knew it or not, I was a willing party in the love making. But Inside I don't want this physical union anymore. I want to get my education and driving lessons.

We had come a bit close to each other. I had appeared in the university entrance test. Sudhir was very glad to know that I had fared well in it. I got admission to college. I chose nine units. I would leave Bhanu with the father-in-law and leave for college at about six in the morning and return a little after twelve. I had learnt how to make pickles and prepared them for Sudhir. Sudhir was happy with this development. I had also utilized the four months spent in India to learn a little embroidery and sewing. I had learnt driving but needed a little more practice and waited for the license. Sudhir had not visited his elder brother for a couple of months. At that time, I realized that I was pregnant again. I thought it would be alright if the second baby was to come as Bhanu was three years old. The spacing between the birth of the children was fine. Sudhir was looking for a new house. When I was in India, Gyan had bought a new house. Sudhir had lent him five thousand dollars without my knowledge though he had sent me no money.

One day when I returned from college, I found that Prabhat had come. After I had changed, he said, "Aunty, let us go out for a little driving practice."

"Prabhat, I am far from being a good driver. If anything goes wrong, your uncle will punish me," I said.

"Has there been a single day in your married life when you have not been subjected to punishment?" I observed, as if talking to himself.

When I was getting ready to go for practice, my father–in-law told us not to move out at that hour. But brushing aside his objections, Prabhat took me for driving practice. It was routine now that whenever he visited us, he took me out for driving practice. I had asked him not to tell Sudhir or anybody else regarding this. We wanted to give everybody a surprise only after I had been given a license. We also politely requested the father-in-law to help us in keeping our little secret. He was glad that I had the happiness of his son in mind in making this request.

Prabhat told me that his mother egged her on to drive the car near my place so that I would see it and would feel jealous. I was driving the car when Prabhat gave me this information. I was perturbed. He said, "Listen, nobody in this family can bear to see you happy. They take your innocence as foolishness and make fun of you.

"How and why do they do that?" I asked, turning the car to the right.

"Good. you have learnt driving very well. You took the turn like an expert." He tried to avoid an answer.

"Thanks, but do tell me how you came to know that they make fun of me." I persisted with my query.

"Do you know what aunty said on the phone to Meera when a son was born to her?"

"No. What was it?"

"She said, "Rita is jealous of you because a son was not born to her.""

I was frightened. I had never thought of such a silly thing when a son was born to Meera. The boy was like my own child, I had felt. Children are, after all, divine gifts. Sudhir loved Bhanu more than he would have loved a son. She was a priceless gem for him.

Hence when I heard what Prabhat's mother felt about me, my blood boiled. I lost control over the car and it hit the neighbor's house. There were children playing around. My driving with pride led to my bad luck. Destiny hadn't wished that a few hours of driving should turn into my victory. The accident pushed the hood of the car a little upwards and the front part was dented slightly. I started weeping. But Prabhat soothed me and said, "Aunty, you need not worry. The car is insured and the expenses on the repairs will be fully covered. Furthermore, the car is still drivable." He drove the car back home.

I waited for Sudhir anxiously in the evening. At the same time, I was afraid of his reaction. The only relief was that these days my father-in-law was a little inclined to side with me. All in the family were happy with their lives. Father-in-law was a little offended with Meera as since her coming to America, she had not invited him to stay with her. Meera Parents never tried to reach to talk to him. Nobody knows who she is and what kind of family she came from.

My father-in-Law began to compare her to me. In fact, He never approved of her as his daughter-in-law because she was lying about her education and age at the time of marriage with Sunil with a fake Master degree certificate.

He believed that whoever played a role in organizing this match with Sunil wanted only to create discord in the family. Meera's age was given as 22 years, whereas she was actually 27 years old. When he vents his disappointment on this count, I tried to pacify him by saying that Meera had done what her parents had desired her to do and it was not her fault. My father-in-law would murmur, "I don't even believe she has a master's degree in politics. Although I am uneducated, I can sense that Meera's manners do not show that she has a master's degree. In any event, I was not very interested in taking her side because she did not do anything to deserve my sympathy. I had hoped that Sunil's wife, being of my age or older than my age and well educated, could prove a good companion to me and life would become somewhat easy but my expectations were proved wrong.

It was almost nighttime. Sudhir hasn't made it back yet. First of all, he had no idea I was taking driving lessons. Second, it was Prabhat's new car that was damaged due to my neglect during driving. Maybe Gyan and Leela called in a car crash. Probably went to the Gyan brothers' house. Leela might be complaining about me. I checked further if he had come or not.? I was afraid and should Sudhir bully me again?

Sudhir finally arrived at 9 pm. No sooner had I opened the door, he pushed the door in my face and began to hit me with his shoes. He knocked down my head and pushed me out of the house. He cried, You slut, offspring of sin, of the indigent family, then you behaved as expected. You cheat; You were learning how to drive without my permission," he then asked his father, '' Did you give money to learn How to drive? Did you grant her permission to learn to drive from Prabhat?

"Indeed, I did. "I liked her to stand on her feet so she does not depend on anyone. You don't give any money to her. I am going to help her."

"You're my dad helping her? Whose side you stand"

"I'll stand by her. She was born into a good family. I learned after Meera came into our family. I witnessed her treachery with my own eyes and the treachery of others," My father-in-law began to cry.

"She is not innocent. She is stupid. She has no brain in spite of being educated. She has no common sense."

To err is human. I feel pity for Bhanu. Whenever you abuse her mother, she begins to cry. At least for the sake of Bhanu learn to respect her mother. My father-in-law was very sympathetic to me at that point.

It was very confusing for me how older women like Leela and Kanta Rani could instill Sudhir against me so that he could throw me out of the house.?

It was very cold, but I was crying in front of the back door of my flat. Imagine how a penniless woman can survive in an unknown world with a small child who knows nobody abroad?

Most of the night, neither Sudhir came to open the door, nor he permitted my father-in-law to open it for me. Bhanu was too little to know why his mother was expelled from the house.

In the morning he opened the door and showered abuses on me. He said, "Have you lost all the shame that you are still here? Go away and beg on the street. Get away, you dirty bitch.

Bhanu looked out of the window with tears streaming down her cheeks and said, "Ma, ma Papa hit you? don't cry; here, have this piece of bread and eat it."

She repeated the words of Sudhir. His baby words brought tears into my eyes as well, but Sudhir took it by force. I spent two pathetic days sitting or lying outside the door. Where could I go? It made it safer to sit outside my house.

Neighbors and bystanders saw me but preferred to close their eyes. After two days Sudhir relented a little and said, "Apologies to your husband. Fall at my feet and promise to do what I say."

I had no choice. Nobody would believe me even if I complained as all had a good opinion about Sudhir. I did as he told me to do. He had been blocking my path as if I would enter the house against his wishes. Now he moved to one side and I went inside the house.

He had caused me so much suffering; beaten me black and blue and spared no chance to persecute me, but when his anger passed away, he acted as if nothing had happened. He would profusely apologize and flatter me like an animal does to attract the attention of the female for inducing her to mate and would then mount me like an animal and start satisfying his lust with my body as before.

The day I had made up with him, I fell ill. It was late evening. I was taken for emergency treatment. An examination confirmed that I had two months of advanced pregnancy. I had suspected as much myself as I had had no periods for two months and my breasts had been growing larger and firmer. Sudhir heard the news of my pregnancy and felt happy. He brought me home and started looking after me with dedication. He massaged my feet, hands, and head all the while asking for forgiveness.

I had started going to school again. Bhanu was admitted to pre-school class. I wanted a son, but Bhanu wanted a younger sister. Sudhir also supported Bhanu. But I wanted a son.

I would go out of the house at night and looking towards the vast sky and the stars, would pray, "Oh Lord God, our master, our creator, everything is within your power. Just give me a son and then you may not give me another child. I am a cursed unfortunate woman. I have never ever heaved a sigh of relief after marriage. Do take pity on me and bless me with a son."

I would spread my hands to the invisible divinity. At other times I would bend down and rub my nose against the floor in supplication. I would call upon Him, "Oh Lord, just take a look at my body covered with marks left after undeserved punishment. Count the number of the whippings I received. Did my sincerity, innocence, sincerity, and decency constitute crimes? Were you behind all the suffering I underwent? O merciful one, will you kindly show me the account of past karmas so that I don't repeat them again? Oh my, Ishwar, (the supreme power) I have never had ill-will against anybody but all my relatives have turned into my enemies. Why did this happen, Lord?"

I would go out of the house at night and looking towards the vast sky and the stars, would pray, "Oh Lord God, our master, our creator, everything is within your power. Just give me a son and then you may not give me another child. I am a cursed unfortunate woman. I have never ever heaved a sigh of relief after marriage. Do take pity on me and bless me with a son."

I would spread my hands to the invisible divinity. At other times I would bend down and rub my nose against the floor in supplication. I would call upon Him, "Oh Lord, just take a look at my body covered with marks left after undeserved punishment. Count the number of the whippings I received. Were all my sincerity, innocence, truthfulness and decency a crime? Were you behind all the suffering I underwent? O merciful one, will you kindly show me the account of past karmas so that I don't repeat them again? Oh, my Ishwar, (the supreme power) I have never had ill-will against anybody but all my relatives have turned into my enemies. Why did this happen, Lord?"

Time went by at a steady rhythm. I off and on asked Bhanu, "Bhanu, shall we have a new guest in our family?"

She would prattle in reply, "Yes, a little sister."

I would at once pull her up and tell her to say, "Don't say this beta (endearing mode of address for a child) and tell God to give Bhanu a little brother."

Then, scared of my little madness, she would say, "Yes Mama."

I would correct her and ask her to repeat what I had told her. She would close her eyes, fold her tiny hands and say, "God, please give me a baby brother." I felt happy and held her close to my heart. Then I would ask her, "Ok, tell me what your little brother is doing at the moment?"

She felt happy and would say, "He probably goes to the little school in your tummy." I would laugh. To see me happy, she would innocently say, "But I want a baby sister."

When I again pulled her up, she hid her face with her little hands. I pretended to be offended. Then she peeped with her beautiful eyes from between her palms and tried to cheer me up. Then we would start playing.

I scored well in my studies and Sudhir felt happy to see my good marks. He praised me before his friends. He seldom saw his brothers and sisters-in-law these days. Our family consisted of Sudhir, me, Bhanu, and my father-in-law. By now I had made friends with women of my age and if anything threatened the disturbance of peace in the family, their husbands would make peace by intervening between me and Sudhir.

It was the ninth month of my pregnancy. I frequently saw Mahatma Gandhi, Jesus Christ, and mother goddess in my dreams. The goddess would say, "Why are you wearing these clothes inappropriate for you? Come on, get up and put on a red dress. You are going to have a son. The family will have five sons. Put up a picture of Dhanush (a name for the boy)." Then I would dream of a new house.

A tan complexion boy would say, "I am Dhanush, Bhanu's brother."

I would wake up at this point in the dream. I told Sudhir about the dream. He would just smile.

A few days later a son was born to me. What was surprising was that in the nursery where the son was born, five more boys were also born to women thus proving the truth of the dream. When her younger brother was born, Bhanu was very sad and continued to weep for a long time

Sudhir named the child Dhanush. I stayed in the hospital for five days and then we came home. When we returned home, Bhanu approached me and said, "Throw Dhanush into the dustbin." If I forbade her to say so, she would weep. She felt lonely now as I couldn't spare much time for her. I would take her up, fondle her and she felt fine. Gradually she started calling Dhanush 'baby brother' and began to love him. She slept with me.

I was thankful to God that he had given me two children. They were so exceptional but how little they knew they were born in the most violent home and what would be their future. Both kids had beautiful eyes and smiles. I prayed to God to let them live happily ever after. Then I looked at Bhanu and felt happy as she was accepting her little brother to be part of her life. Then I saw Dhanush and was overwhelmed with joy when I found him sucking his thumb, oblivious of his surroundings. My lap was a cushion for the kids as well to play, to sleep, and to rest.

Sudhir had bought heaps of toys for both of his children Bhanu and newly born baby Dhanush. On the contrary, recalling the sad events of the past, I would pray to God, "Oh! God, Oh! The Maker of Our Destiny, save my children from cruel destiny and domestic discord. Always protect them and shower your grace on them!" Life functions that way, zigzagging through a maze of happiness and suffering like a game of hide and seek. I recalled Thomas Hardy's famous quote from a novel: 'Happiness is an occasional episode in the general drama of pain.'

CHAPTER 7

The calendars of man and God seldom coincide. Time and tide wait for no man. My life was no exception, I knew. Sudhir had invested money and earned considerably well. We were a family of four including the two children and needed a good house. Sudhir started to think of buying a house. But he didn't have sufficient funds to do so.

Consequently, he sought financial help from his family. But his relatives avoided him these days like a pest so much so that no one from them had even complimented him on the birth of Dhanush. First, he asked for money from Joginder Bhaiya but he refused to give any. He said, "Some people think that I own a bank from where I can give away money as charity to any Tom, Dick or Harry." Sudhir had never expected this but he could do nothing. Then he approached Gyan Bhaiya for the money he had lent him. But here too he got a negative reply.

On the other hand, Gyan Bhaiya said, "Sudhir, I hope you were serious when you came here. Don't you know that it is you who owe us money? I educated you after arranging money by selling my wife's jewelry. We have waited long enough for you to compensate us for our efforts but you have forgotten your obligation so easily. Now you come knocking at our door asking for more money. We are poor people; you know and can't spare any money for you... Ask your father-in-law from India to send you the money as he is a policeman and has taken Rishvat (bribes) from poor people"

My life has always played hide and seek with me. There was hardly a moment of light when clouds again overcast it. Mine was a mechanical existence. There was almost a perpetual mental drought. The nights served the sole purpose of indulgence in the satisfaction of our physical lust, mostly of Sudhir. We survived to earn, eat, spend nights satisfying animal urges, so on and so forth. One may call this a happy life if one likes. But even this life, with a remote semblance of a happy life, was not acceptable to people around. We moved to our house and organized a Havan.A large number of friends and acquaintances attended it but none from among the relatives turned up. We compromised ourselves to this development.

The children kept me extremely busy now and consequently I missed one semester at school. I also hadn't learnt driving yet.

When things stood at this stage, My Older brother got his visa and came to America. He was eager to find a job but Sudhir wanted him to first obtain a degree either as a doctor or an engineer. Sudhir ignored the fact that Navin could not afford to do this. There was a lack of communication between the two. When I heard my older brother's side, I felt he was right.

Similarly, when Sudhir explained the situation, he sounded right. I had no job and could not help my older brother financially. He knew no one to whom to turn to for help. In order to find a way out, I contacted a friend of mine. He had found a job at a Seven-Eleven of an Indian. But instead of supporting this, Sudhir was offended by him. Both met each other under the same roof, but seldom exchanged any pleasantries.

Sudhir quarreled with me unnecessarily. I understood the situation and preferred to keep mum. I just submitted to Sudhir's angry outbursts. Naveen too was proving a clever player. He didn't want to offend the master of the house. He would complain against me to Sudhir. He would say, "She shirks work and always answers back." Now if I as much as slightly protested against this sort of behavior, Navin would pull me up. He would advise me in the presence of Sudhir, "Didi, why do you answer back to Jija ji (brother-in-law)? You should be obedient to him." Sudhir found his advice very justified and didn't see through his cunning. I was sad that my own blood relative, my own brother, was against me.

He lived here on a visitor visa. Hence, he was not allowed to buy his own car. I filed a petition on his behalf and he found a job legally now. He earned now and gave some money to me. Both of us had learnt driving.

Navin saved some money but not enough for a car. He mentioned this to Sudhir and told him that after he got a green card, he would attend school but till then he could not apply for a loan, implying thereby that Sudhir could help him with money to enable him to buy a car, but in turn Sudhir suggested that Naveen should save and deposit the money with him and buy a car in Sudhir's name and use it himself.

Navin had great regard for Sudhir. Therefore, he agreed to this proposal. Sudhir was gradually returning to his old habit of pestering me. He deliberately visited his brothers' families to hurt me. He always had a frown on his face. Well, Sudhir bought Naveen a car. As a result, Navin was heavily indebted to Sudhir. The car was covered with insurance but Naveen wanted to have the policy in his name but he could not afford it as he had to remit money to our parents in India to repay the installments of the loan taken for his ticket from India to America.

As ill-luck would have it, the car met with an accident. The damage was very insignificant but Sudhir took the car away from Navin. It so happened that one-day Navin went to his workplace. His shift was from three in the afternoon to midnight. When he came out of the office, he found the car missing. Sudhir had taken away the car without informing Navin. He found it inadvisable to report the matter to the police. As such he walked back to the apartment at that late hour. In the morning he rang me up to tell the story and wept bitterly for a long time. I felt outraged but Navin made me promise that I was not to mention this to Sudhir. He made me swear in his name. He told me that it could result in a bitter quarrel in the family.

Well, time moved on. Navin bought an old car fit for the junkyard. I resumed going to school. But I was sad inside and the mind was blank as if it had reached a blind alley. In spite of this situation, I kept myself busy with the children. I forgot my pain in their company to a large extent. Dhanush was very cute and playful. His curly hair covered most of his forehead and partially hid his big angel-eyes.

Bhanu was also a very lovely kid. I found immense pleasure in their company. Though I hadn't finished my schooling, yet I devoted more time to domestic chores than to studies. Dhanush was two and a half years old and was a student at a pre-school. I worked as a teacher's aide in a school. As a practice among Indians, I was to have the first hair cutting ceremony, known as 'mundan' of Dhanush when he was three years old and would need money. So, I started saving money for it. But Sudhir lost no opportunity to hinder my working regularly. He would put the car out of order or would call me at school to disturb my work. He was never short of such dirty tricks. But by now I had become habitual of facing such problems regularly. By and by, I saved some money and borrowed some from Naveen and had the ceremony performed in India. While I was in India for the ceremony, Sudhir wrote to me but this time I didn't reply to any of his letters. Naturally Sudhir had grievances against me on this account.

Gyan Bhaiya had organized a reception program for his newly wed son Prabhat and his bride. He invited us to it. But I hadn't forgotten their shady behavior following the birth of Dhanush. They had never visited us to bless the kid as is customary for the relatives. They had never given any gift to him in spite of the fact that Sudhir had always given their children something or the other. But Sudhir had forgotten this attitude of his family.

On the other hand, when Meera's delivery was due, I had stayed with her and had helped her to the best of my ability. Even then Meera and Sunil hadn't visited us. On the contrary they had suggested to Sudhir that he should visit them and take Meera to their place if they were keen on seeing their newborn son. The family had never lost any opportunity to malign me in every way. But their impudence was to expect me to attend the reception with Sudhir. Naturally I showed reluctance to attend it. It infuriated Sudhir. He stuffed a towel in my mouth to stifle my cries, took me to the bathroom and beat me to his heart's content. Leaving me lying on the floor in the bathroom, he took Bhanu and Dhanush with him and went to his brother's place to attend the reception.

Though Bhanu was old enough to know the significance of such incidents, she could not protest to her father. She meekly followed him. When they were gone, I phoned Navin and narrated the entire chain of events to him. He in turn informed my father who at once rang Gyan up and said, "Will you never be content with tormenting my daughter? You have spared her no persecution that you could imagine. I warn you to desist from such actions. Have some fears from God, He does not spare anyone. Have mercy on your own daughters as Karma can unfold to your daughters too. I don't wish bad for any one's daughters, but you have not spared my innocent child in the USA. What harm have I ever done to you by giving my most precious daughter to my family?"

At this Gyan retorted, "Your son-in-law owes us money. If you are a man with the least sense of shame and love for your daughter, why don't you come here and clear his debt? If you can't buy your air ticket, I shall send it to you." He mocked my father. Then continued, "All know that after having been driven away by her in-laws, one of your daughters lives with you; I think you would like to do the same to your second one too."

Bhanu heard all this and narrated the conversation to me word for word. Later, Sudhir stopped buying groceries for the family.

One day, out of anger, he smashed into bits my old pictures, emptied my purse and pocketed the money. There was some milk in a pot; he threw it out in the street in a fit of rage. He disconnected the electricity so that we could not use the heater and left for his brother's house.

I was lucky that some good neighbors taught me how to switch the power on and somehow, we managed life. I was no longer dependent on Sudhir for such minor things now.

Time passed. I was fed up with such incidents and had learnt to answer back in a like manner to Sudhir. I could use my tongue very effectively to cause pain to him.

One day Sudhir awakened me early in the morning as was his habit, and told me to prepare breakfast. When I was doing this, Gyan rang up and I took the call. I told him to desist from coming to our house. But he was not to be intimidated by the likes of me. He said, "Who the hell are you to tell me not to come to my brother's house? A man can always find a woman and children but never his brothers." What could I say to him now? Admitted that I, being from a different family, was not a blood relation to them and could have another husband. Sudhir also could find another wife. But how could Bhanu and Dhanush find parents?

I was lost in these thoughts when someone started knocking at the door deafeningly. Sudhir had just finished taking a shower. He opened the door and found Gyan standing there. He was furious and as soon as he saw Sudhir, he started abusing my father and my family. As was usual, without giving me an opportunity to explain my side, Sudhir started beating me. The children started bawling. Bhanu was so frightened that she ran away to the neighbors' house. Dhanush also tried to follow her. By now I was bleeding in the head. Gyan had ignited the fire and left but Sudhir was unable to control his anger. He fetched Bhanu back home and beat her too. Then he pushed me out of the house and closed the door.

A gardener plants flowers of different hues and nourishes them lovingly but in my case the gardeners, my parents, had themselves turned a blind eye to the flowers and left them to turn into an unprotected jungle; had stopped watering them and left them to the mercy of the vagaries of cruel weather, the whims of the cruel beasts.

The neighbors had come to know of the commotion in our house and someone informed the police. They came and when they saw my bleeding head, they arrested Sudhir and took him away to the police station. I wiped my tears, took my children with me and left home for good that day and have no information about when Sudhir was freed by the police.

All the relatives were blaming me for his arrest. They were convinced that I had been instrumental in having him taken to jail and as such must be a bad woman. Sudhir was charged with felony. Now you see, Ravi, in these circumstances I resolved never to return to Sudhir. He behaved cruelly and it was unnatural for a father to beat his baby daughter, the daughter he loved the most. The tears and cries of my children could not be borne by me any longer. The children were terrified.

PART II

CHAPTER 8

Rita finished her story and started weeping loudly. As he had listened, Ravi had shown surprise at the intimate details she had shared with him, a complete stranger. He had found her details tedious and boring at times, but had feigned an interest he didn't always feel. He had let her tell her story uninterrupted; she had, at times, been lost in her own world and had seemed unaware of his presence.

When she had stopped talking, Ravi placed his hand on her shoulder and said, "You have gone through a hell of a life. Life and destiny both played a very cruel game with you. Your innocent children never have seen their childhood. They have had to grow so fast to face the punishment of their parents' deeds. Society is also to be blamed - they will taunt them about their parents' actions throughout their lives. Nevertheless, don't worry. I am here for you." He pulled her to him and held her close to his chest.

Rita was a broken-down woman that had hankered after sympathy from someone who would listen to and empathize with her. She trusted Ravi in the moments of agony. After she had narrated her sad story in detail, she had hoped that some of the pain would go. But she had hardly realized that she had unwittingly made herself vulnerable before an unscrupulous person. He had assured her not to worry as he was around to take care of her. But such assertions are uttered non-seriously and on the spur of the moment. Who was he who could share her pains and suffering? She realized that she would never seek his help in anything as herself respect would never allow that.

At the same time Ravi was not the type that could sacrifice his self-interest for the happiness of others. But ignorance is bliss, they say, and Rita had had that luxury of believing that she was sure to enjoy bliss from the burning heart. She had rambled on without a pause. But now that the story was over, she found herself quite drained emotionally and physically. What was she doing there at that late hour with a stranger, she wondered? She was like a person that had awakened from a drug induced sleep and was scared. She wanted to flee the place as far away from this man as possible.

She made a move to leave but Ravi pressed her down with his hand and looking into her eyes he said, "Rita, even though you are a mother of two, you are still so young and beautiful. After I have heard your story, I would advise you to seek your happiness …er…I mean, return to school, finish your education and find some good job."

It was difficult to comprehend how her return to school could ensure her happiness. His breaking of the sentence made it obvious that he had something else on his mind but he changed the idea and ended the sentence in a way that it sounded like the sincere advice of a genuine well-wisher. Rita's credulous nature almost convinced her that Ravi was really concerned for her wellbeing, though a little discretion would have made it clear to her that he was talking to a beautiful female body rather than to a friendly being. Rita took up her purse and quickly left for home.

Rita was feeling miserable through and through. She decided never to see Ravi again. He had told her that she was young but she knew that she had stepped into middle age the day of her adopting the role of a mother. She had become a helpless vulnerable woman the day she became pregnant. She had been a sex toy all along for her husband but without getting any appreciation from him in return. God had been generous in giving her a daughter and a son, two cute chubby children. She was educated and intelligent. But indifferent destiny had deprived her of what should have been her due.

Ravi was not rich. He owned just a small press and did odd jobs including photography for those from among the Indian community who hired him and his total income was a little under a thousand dollars which was not much by American standards. His dream was to have his own studio someday. He had a degree in business management but it had not helped him much. He was younger than Rita by a few years. It was said about him that he had had and still had many affairs and was notorious for his shady doings. But Rita never gave much credit to rumors. People of the same age usually get jealous of each other, she thought. Her own impression about (Next) him was not bad. She was certain that he was an honest man who really cared for her.

Sometime later, some institution known as 'Wandering Artistes' invited Bhanu and Dhanush for a singing session. Rita had no idea how they had come to know about the children's talent. Rita had also been invited to do some modeling. They had also sent three tickets for them. At midnight on Friday, they landed at John Kennedy Airport. They found Dr. Rai along with a few ladies of Indian origin waiting for them.

"What brought you here, Dr. Rai?" Rita asked, surprised. But before he could answer, one of the ladies advanced, extended her hand to Rita and said, "Hello, I am Radha, the president of the Wandering Artistes group. This is my friend Labina."

"Labina is a very sweet name," Rita said, getting into the car.

"She is also a very good dancer," Radha added.

"Very nice," Rita complimented Labina. Then added, "But Radha, with my children, won't you...?"

"Dr. Rai is sponsoring my program. It is he who told me about the talents of your children. He isn't tired of praising you either. Besides, a lot is written about you in the press too."

"Thanks, Dr. Rai," Rita mumbled.

Radha was a good engineer and was a divorcee. The car took them to Radha's house. Bhanu and Dhanush went to sleep as soon as they hit the bed. Rita also managed to have sleep. She got up early the next morning and made preparations for the evening's program which was a party at Dr. Bhatia's place. Rita was informed about it by Radha.

In the evening the party was a great success. The audience comprised around four thousand people. There the children sang. Everybody praised their singing. Then there was dancing in accompaniment with music. Rita was wearing a dark lehnga (skirt) and a choli (blouse). The dance floor was located on the porch outside. Rita presented a dance too. She noticed that Dr. Rai's eyes turned to her again and again.

After the program they entered the house. Inside, in every room, there was French colonial furniture. The pink curtains too were made of French silk. Everything boasted of luxury. The children were so tired that they fell asleep on the sofa. Rita sat down by their side to relax a little She looked around to see if she could lie down for a little while.

"What is the matter, Rita? Why are you so lost and quiet?" Dr. Bhatia startled Rita.

"Oh, Dr. Bhatia, no, there is nothing whatsoever. I was just thinking about tomorrow," Rita said.

"Anything bothering you dear Rita?"

"Just that I am to catch a late-night flight on Sunday after the program and I am afraid to use a taxi to the airport at that late hour." By now Dr. Rai had sauntered in and had joined the two.

"You needn't worry on this count. Dr. Vimal Rai is my buddy. In fact, it was he who had pressed me to invite you," Dr. Bhatia said, pointing to Dr. Rai.

"Dr. Rai, many thanks for introducing me to such a distinguished gathering," Rita said shyly.

"Well, you are young, beautiful and talented. There couldn't have been anything better than inviting you. By the way, tomorrow I am also going to Los Angeles. I shall take you not only to the airport here but will also drop you at your place when we reach Los Angeles."

"Did you too catch a plane from Los Angeles?" Rita asked him.

"No, I am going there for a week in connection with a research project and shall stay in Los Angeles. I didn't come from there," he said.

In the evening on Sunday, there was a party at Dr. Rai's place. Rita was dazzled when she saw his house. It was all made of marble and resembled the White House in grandeur. Even the boundary wall was made of marble. There was a big gate towards the front yard of the house where they had an ivory color fountain with different colors of lights. There was ample parking space which was fully occupied by now. Rita and the children were escorted in by a uniformed servant. Large chandeliers hung from an artistically patterned ceiling. The light bulbs were very big and illuminated the hall like room. Leather and velvet sofas lay in every room. The walls were bedecked with mirrors as in a shish mahal (glass palace). In one of the halls there was a big patio with an over bridge across.

Artistic statuettes surrounded the patio. Water spouted from the mouths of the statues. An artificial hillock to the left of the patio was covered with swings of different types for children to have a gala time. Bhanu and Dhanush could hardly wait to run to the hillock to enjoy themselves on the swings.

Rita had taken special care to dress for the occasion. She had fixed small clips on both sides of her head to hold her boy-cut hair in place. In an orange-colored Pathani (Afghani) suit, with Punjabi shoes and black glass bangles, she looked stunning. As they stepped in, Dr. Rai, the host, came forward and held Rita by the hand and took her around introducing her to the guests. Rita felt highly flattered. All eyes were fixed on her and many a jealous heart missed a beat or two. Finally, all settled down in their seats. Bearers handed around soft drinks in fancy glasses to the guests. Dr. Rai sat next to Rita. He leaned over to her and said, "Believe me Rita, you look stunningly beautiful, surpassing the gorgeous wives of the doctors and others in excellent dresses and loaded with pearls and gold." Dr. Rai was obviously proud to have an educated beautiful woman by his side. This made Rita forget her perpetual sadness for a while.

The hectic evening program was finally over. Rita was standing to one side of the patio alone and other guests were either leaving or relaxing a little wherever they found an appropriate spot. Rita noticed Dr. Rai approaching her. Bhanu and Dhanush were with him.

"Who is driving me to the airport?" she asked, a little puzzled.

"The driver is taking you to the airport but I am to accompany you on the plane to Los Angeles."

"Oh, really?" Rita said, with a little surprise.

"If you have any objection, I will catch some other flight," Dr. Rai said mournfully.

"On the contrary, you are coming with us is a godsend as otherwise I would have had to take a taxi at Los Angeles from the airport to my house"

"Ok. It is very nice of you to permit me to travel with you. I am glad that I am being of some service to you. By the way, Rita, would you mind letting me know how you manage things with your two growing children?" he asked hesitatingly.

"I have a job. Besides, by participating in shows organized by the rich like you, I earn some and all this helps me."

"Rita, the paths of the world are desolate and the journey of life is arduous. Why don't you find some life partner to stand by you?"

"Dr. Rai, I agree that bringing up the kids is a big responsibility. But now I have become habitual to walk the long and difficult paths alone."

"I think you are ignoring the hard facts of life. When the children grow up and are on their own, they are not likely to support you."

"Well, it can't be helped. One can just wait and watch. By the way, it is time to leave." Rita left him and went to look for the children.

The flight from New York to Los Ange

les took four hours but nothing much was discussed by Rita and Dr. Rai in the plane. They came out of the airport and Dr. Rai hired a taxi. When he was leaving after dropping Rita at her place, the children said, "Uncle, it is very late. Why don't you come in and stay with us for the night?" Then they turned to Rita and said, "Mom, why don't you ask Uncle to come in and spend the night at our place?"

"Yes, Dr. Rai, please leave in the morning," Rita said reluctantly, as she was still a bit uneasy about the idea of letting a man spend a night at her house even though she was indebted to Dr. Rai.

Dr. Rai agreed to stay with them and spent the night on the sofa. He was a man of medium height with agreeable looks and couldn't be termed either as very good looking or bad looking. But his education, sweet nature, polite behavior etc. had lent a certain charm to his personality. A natural instinct prompted him to show affection to Rita's children.

After all he was past the marrying age but was without a life partner. If he had married, he too would have had children of his own. Since coming into contact with Rita, he had wished to know much about her life but had resisted the urge to do so in San Francisco. Whatever information he had about her was received from Jolly. He had seen the pain in Rita's drooping eyes. He could have a good idea how sad and helpless she was in life. Some instinct of fellow feeling or maybe some attachment for Rita, he didn't know which, made him contemplate seeing her husband. Dr. Rai felt that the man was a great loser that he didn't know the worth of a gem of a wife. She had made him the proud father of such fine children. God had given Rita everything except a sympathetic destiny. He felt he could transform her miserable life into one of divine bliss only if he proposed to her and was accepted. But he would be the last man to take advantage of a woman who was embittered and lonely. Hence the night passed in these musings. When he got up in the morning, he found Rita ready to go to the office. She was preparing breakfast in the kitchen.

"Rita, I am sorry that I got up late and must have delayed you for the office. I am sorry."

"You can save your apology for some other day. You forget that I work in a bank and banks open at ten. It is just half past eight yet. I have already attended half the morning engagements and have dropped the children at school."

"Wow, you are really very smart. You have already dropped the children at school but I didn't even know that you were up."

"Why, don't you think women can be smart too or even smarter than men?" she said casually.

He took a deep breath and laid emphasis on every word he slowly said, "Nature has done an excellent job in creating a woman. She has added beauty and charm not only to the world but to the whole creation."

"Great! Even though a doctor of medicine, you are turning into a philosopher poet."

"Oh, but besides being a doctor, I am also a human being with a sensitive romantic heart. Do you get it?" he said in a light cheerful tone.

"Hold on to being a romantic man. It is enough. But please go to the bathroom to wash yourself and freshen up," Rita dictated to him.

"Yes Madam," he said, bowing dramatically, and rushed to the bathroom. When he finally came properly bathed and dressed, Rita had already laid the table for breakfast.

"It is after years that I am about to have a proper breakfast at a table."

"Why? Does your wife not…?" Rita left the sentence incomplete.

"Why have you checked yourself half way? Go on and complete the sentence if you can. Destiny rules over us, you know, and today I feel like telling you that not all women and not all men are so bad that they suffer unnecessarily."

"No…no, I have nothing much to …" She halted again in the middle of a sentence.

"What do you intend to do this evening?" he asked, looking fixedly at her beautiful face.

"Nothing much. I have joined a photography class. If you like, I can drop you at the airport, Dr. Rai."

"Drop this prefix Dr. to my name. Address me as just Vimal and remember that I am to stay in Los Angeles for a week, you know."

"In that case you would need my car," Rita said.

"No thanks. I am making a call to rent a car. One thing more, if not tomorrow, let it be any day convenient to you. I would like you to accompany me to dinner."

"Only dinner? I can cook dinner by myself," Rita smiled and said.

"Where else would you prefer to go? As for me, I can turn Utopia into a reality," Dr Rai said lovingly.

"No, for God's sake, consider a big no from me. They, who promise heaven, lead you to hell of which I have had enough," she said with a little shudder.

He noticed how cruelly she had been treated by the world.

"Please Rita; everybody has a unique story to tell. But I plead with you not to be perpetually sad like this."

"I am sorry." Rita at once changed the track.

"All right, I shall ring you up in the morning on Friday. We shall take the children along."

"Ok. You make your call for the car and in the meantime I shall also get ready," Rita said, as if in haste.

Rita was learning photography as she was very fond of taking pictures. Besides, she found it a good hobby. She had a small camera. Along with the children she spent time indulging in the hobby whenever she found time. A week passed after the outing with Dr. Rai.

On Friday evening Sudha and Ginni came but they didn't stay for long and took the children with them left, saying they wanted to enjoy their company for some time and Rita would oblige them to let the children go with them. As soon as they were gone, the phone rang. Rita took up the receiver and unenthusiastically said, "Hello."

"Hi Rita, are you still in bed?" It was Dr. Vimal Rai on the phone.

"Hi Dr. Rai," Rita responded with an unsteady voice.

"Please Rita! Why don't you address me as Vimal?" Dr. Rai said, as if offended.

"Please allow me a little time. I am a slow learner in certain things. I shall learn to call you Vimal in due course."

"I hope you have time in the evening…." Dr. Rai left the sentence unfinished.

"My friends have taken away the children in order to spend some time with them and I am alone. How can I …?"

"Trust me; I won't harm you in any way without the children," he said.

"No no, I didn't mean that. I respect you immensely. When are we going to go? Will you pick me up or will I reach your place?"

"Get ready. I shall pick you up in an hour. Oh, by the way, you are learning photography. Please bring along your camera. After dinner, we shall visit Laguna Hills."

"Ok, but bear in mind that I am still a novice at photography."

"Well, ok. But we don't need experts for day-to-day photography and I am sure you can do nicely. Now get ready; I am coming to pick you up."

"Ok bye." Rita replaced the receiver.

Rita was tired but she managed to have a bubble bath and washed her hair. Then she put on a dark leather-mini skirt and white voile blouse. She adjusted her bobbed hair meticulously and waited for Dr. Rai. It had been a very hot day but, in the evening, a light breeze made the weather a bit cool and pleasant in Long Beach.

The half-moon and the stars in the sky imparted a soothing and romantic touch to the environment. Rita noticed that the moon had a peculiar beauty of its own. Exactly at half past seven Dr. Rai arrived. No sooner did he knock on the door than Rita ran to open it. Her face shone at the sight of Dr. Rai and in a childlike manner, she said, "Hello Dr. Rai, I am ready."

When Dr Rai saw Rita, he couldn't believe his eyes and his jaw dropped. He made an effort as if to swallow something. He felt something churning his stomach and felt as if heartbeats had stopped. Rita hadn't expected this reaction on his part. She was frightened and said, "What is the matter with you, Dr. Rai?"

Regaining his composure, he stammered out, "I was afraid that I might have knocked on the wrong door. I didn't recognize you at all. I had not expected a captivating fairy to open the door to receive me. Even now I feel that I am dreaming and shall awaken from this sweet dream and find that I was, after all, not lucky enough to find a nymph waiting for me." He hastily held Rita by the hand as if she were a hallucination.

"Will you please abstain, pulling my leg?" she said with a faint smile on her lips as she locked the door of the apartment.

"Rita, you have a bad habit which I don't like."

"What is it, sir?" She looked at his serious face.

"You take every one of my observations as untrue," he said as he opened the door of the car for her to get in.

Rita became serious now and countered him, saying, "Life has taught me enough how to discriminate between truth and falsehood."

"You drag in your insensitive philosophy at the wrong moment. I am not inclined to give in to your mood. Forget what life has or has not taught you. Come out of this meaningless hangover of the past. Just cheer up and talk about something that could lend us a few moments of relaxation to make us forget the tedium of life."

"Well, I am inclined to agree with you. Strange are the ways of the world. If you laugh, people laugh with you but if you mope, they turn their backs on you at once, leaving you to your fate." Rita produced a forced smile on her lips.

"You look a lot more charming when you smile. Please always keep smiling," Dr. Rai said, looking at her. His grip on her hand had become tighter.

They chatted in a light mood till the car reached the Queen Mary near Long Beach.

Rita was really amused to see such a gigantic, elegant and royal ship whose history she had read about; it was constructed in 1930 in Clydebank, Scotland.

"Wow, how marvelous and imposing!" Rita exclaimed when she saw the beautiful ship.

"There is a restaurant and a dance floor on board the ship," Dr. Rai said.

"Must be, but I am afraid I'll have to miss the dance floor and would prefer to return home after dinner."

"No madam. It is to dance after dinner and then we are driving to Laguna Hills; you are going to take my pictures, you know."

"You are very unpredictable," Rita observed, occupying her seat.

"You mean mysterious?" he said.

"Sort of."

"All right, I shall solve the mystery in a minute. Go ahead and ask me whatever you want to."

"You are a good doctor, have money and most probably know the art of flirting with girls but you are not interested in getting married. Why so, may I know?"

"I was married but divorced," he said seriously.

"Oh, I see." Rita was surprised and looked annoyed.

"But you seem to have formed a very wrong idea about me," he said, feeling a bit uneasy.

"What idea have I formed; may I know?" She looked at him with apparent annoyance in her demeanor.

"That I have cheated on my marriage vows."

"Yes, it is a distinct possibility. At least that is what one may think about you from your lifestyle in New York."

"What lifestyle are you talking about?" He looked worried and cautious.

"I am sorry. I have no right to interfere in your personal life. I sincerely apologize." Rita regretted her words and attitude.

"Apologize for what? If we are not honest in friendship, it is no longer friendship. Ok, I extend my hand of friendship," Dr. Rai said politely.

"I have hardly anything to give anything by way of friendship. I am fed up with telling my unending insipid life story again and again," Rita said, looking at her toes under the table.

"I shall not ask you anything about your personal life. You just permit me to relate my life tale today." Dr. Rai called the waiter and paid the bill.

"Are you serious that you will not ask me anything about my life?" Rita said after they were out of the restaurant.

"Rita I would like to admit that my marriage was much against my wishes," he said, closing the door after Rita was in the car.

"I don't think I got you. Please explain to me what you are trying to tell me?" She looked puzzled.

"I went to India after graduating as a doctor. My parents didn't give me an opportunity to see the girl and fixed my marriage."

"Did you have a girlfriend?" Rita asked casually.

"I was alone in America. Naturally I had girl friends with an occasional fling with some of them. But there was nothing serious with a special girl."

"That you had girlfriends but were not serious, sounds a sort of conundrum to me." She looked at him askance.

"The idea is that I went out with girls and had physical relations with a few but promised marriage to none."

"Vimal, I still can't get you."

"Well, leave it. My wife was educated but not good looking." He parked the car on the beach.

The half-moon shone dimly in the sky. Waves struck against the shore noisily. Some people were surfing. All of a sudden Dr. Rai seemed to have reached a decision and said, "Rita, may I hold your hand as a friend?"

"Why not?" she said, without listening to what Dr. Rai was asking.

Rita let him hold her hand though a bit reluctantly. She wondered if the mere holding of her hand might not lead to anything that ought to be avoided. She demurred a little and Dr. Rai noticed it. He said, "You need not feel self-conscious. Please trust me, I am a good man and will never cross the limits of decency. Sometimes two friends can hold hands too."

Dr. Rai resumed the narrative of his marriage and Rita listened to it with her head bowed. They kept walking on the beach. The waves moved from here and touched the shore there. Rita reflected aloud, "Events in life behave like waves that have no pre planned movement. The traveler moves from one destination to another.

Her philosophic utterance with a poetic flavor startled the good doctor and he looked at her with disbelief. Rita could notice this.

She said, "Why do you look at me like this?" Then without waiting for his reply she said, "Have you forgotten that you are to drop me at my place?"

"Rita, who is the author of the poetic lines you just uttered?' he asked.

"I, of course; who else can blabber lines? Such lines escape from my mouth when the environment and the weather are appropriate."

"Then I should assume that you write poetry."

"Yes, occasionally I pen a few lines as a hobby. Why do you ask?"

"You know I own a paper and have recently bought a radio station in Canada. I have also selected the announcer. Now I am looking for a title song for it."

"Is the radio program in Hindi?"

"No, it is a multilingual program with two hours for Hindi each day."

"What is the title of the program?"

"Love and Leisure," Dr. Rai said casually.

"You surprise me again and again. You are a doctor of medicine but have interest in art and an emotion like 'love', the opium of life." She laughed a little.

"But are doctors not human beings?" he questioned her seriously.

Rita noticed that the doctor was serious. Hence, she insisted on his taking her home at the earliest. The evening today had been an evening of happiness for Dr. Rai. He visualized a life with her as his wife. It didn't matter if Rita was not a nurse or a doctor. She was beautiful; had a jovial nature. She knew how to move in society. If not today, someday he was sure to make her interested in him. He could educate both her children well and could ensure their good future. He could give them happiness. Rita was not yet divorced but things would change by and by. She would change her mind about him and would be interested in him. He would love her so much that she would herself forget the husband.

Finally, when the car stopped before her apartment, she felt inclined to invite Dr. Rai in. But she was conscious of the inappropriateness of the hour. As he opened the car door, he said, "Look here, don't think of inviting me to have a cup of tea now as I am to catch a flight for San Francisco shortly."

"All right, Dr. Rai. Thanks for a lovely evening." She bade him bye.

Dr. Rai left but Rita was a little uneasy. Her womanly instinct had told her that he liked her as she had nothing but respect for him. But she was tired and went to bed expecting to catch some sleep.

It was a hot and humid July night and the temperature was more than a hundred Fahrenheit. Dhanush and Bhanu were spending the weekend with Sudha and Gauri. Rita was alone in the apartment. She stripped herself of all the clothes and lay down in bed without a stitch on.

For the first time she felt that nobody was around to touch her body and give her what she badly wanted at the moment. She extended her hand and patted the empty space around her on the bed.

She recalled the nights when she had wanted to keep her clothes on but Sudhir wouldn't let her. Then suddenly she felt a tingling sensation in her body. She also remembered the night when Sudhir himself had brought a pink negligee for her. How very sexy it was! With the see-through negligee in his hand, Sudhir had chased her while she ran away from him to escape.

Finally, he caught her and forced her to wear the negligee. He pushed her down to lie flat on the bed and started softly caressing, fondling and massaging her delicate but hot body and methodically began with her full firm breasts, gradually coming down to her belly button and then further down to the vital inviting expectant spot. His fingers lingered there a while, sending waves of pleasure in Rita's whole body. Then the palm of his hand was felt on the butter soft thighs that would melt under the male touch and the flesh quivered. His hands then moved down over the beautiful slim legs and the delicate soles where he tickled her and she burst out in a loud giggle. He brought his hands to place under her shoulders and held her in a firm grip. He bent his head down and nipped the upper part of her body making her scream 'ooi'. Then his hands held the God gifted womanly body, the pride of woman, the precious parts of her body in his cupped hands and squeezed them without bothering to know how hard it hurt her. It was followed by his pressing with his thumb and fingers the stiff and erect nipples once again. He touched her as a signal to part her legs. She obeyed and closed her eyes. Sudhir passionately kissed her lips, forehead, cheeks, eyes and wherever he pleased and then the final thing, the great ecstasy followed.

Rita was suddenly jerked back to the present and found herself lying with legs apart and pressing the breasts with her hands. She blushed and hastily removed her hands. She pulled up a sheet to cover her nudity as if she were being stared at. A deep sigh of helplessness escaped her mouth. The old memories reminded her of the loss and drew tears from her eyes. She felt an urge to phone Sudhir and ask him why he had loosened his hold on her body and the mind; why he had abandoned her simply because others had fed him with falsehood about her.

"You never realized how naïve I was and still I am. I couldn't see through the machinations of your illiterate sisters-in-law. I regret that you could never become the husband in the real sense to your wife. You also missed being the father of your innocent children in the true sense. You had youth, love and children that make life complete but you kicked away all this worldly wealth because of your being short-sighted.

Her stream of consciousness was diverted onto another channel. She recalled the words of Sudhir's brothers and sisters-in-law, "Sudhir and Rita will never be able to lead a harmonious life free from domestic strife. They will always quarrel and their life will have a long history of clashes."

These observations, clearly a curse, had proved to be a very accurate prediction as far as Rita was concerned. The scene again changed. Rita could hear the derisive laughter of the middle-sister-in-law. She was apparently calling her husband but in fact was trying to make Rita burn with jealousy for what she had lost in marrying Sudhir.

The sister-in-law was saying, "Darling, why do you forget that we have three children but your hunger for my voluptuous body hasn't died. You love me as if we were still on our honeymoon."

In response her husband would say, "Madam, consider yourself to be lucky that you have an ideal and loving husband. You are also lucky to have a good brother-in-law. Go ahead; you can do whatever you like. After all you have a claim over him to do as you, please."

"You are right. Sudhir never has any quarrel with me. Do you remember the incident when I had returned from my visit to my parents following our marriage and how I and he...?" She giggled, looking at Rita. She was determined to hurt Rita in every possible way.

"I remember very clearly, when Sudhir cooked potato curry and puris (Indian food item) for you."

"Sure. Sudhir would hardly ever let me work in the kitchen."

In the dark room, quite alone, tears started flowing from Rita's eyes like a flood that could no longer be controlled. The mind continued working.

"Sudhir, you were a brother to your brothers, a brother-in-law to your sisters-in-law, uncle to your nephews and nieces but never my husband. Your relatives never let you be mine. You and your kin won and I lost the battle."

The last thing she remembered before sleep overtook her was whether even dreams would oblige her.

CHAPTER 9

Very few in the topsy turvy unpredictable world have control over sleep or dreams. Rita was no exception. She had fallen asleep weeping and wasn't obliged by any soothing dream. She couldn't even complete her sleep. The time spent with Dr. Vimal Rai was intoxicating enough but destiny had other plans. This great puppeteer can play with men and women as puppets. It was hardly morning when the phone rang loud and clear. With eyes and head heavy with the last night's hangover and less than satisfactory sleep, she took up the receiver and said, "Hello."

"Rita?" she heard from the other end.

"Yes."

"Good morning sweetheart." Some male voice appeared to be serenading her.

The mode of address - Sweetheart - at once rattled her to a full wakeful state. She sat up on the bed fully alert. The sheet she had covered herself with had slipped away. She again pulled it up and covered herself as if the eyes across the line could see her. The voice seemed to change into someone's gaze peering into her privacy. Who the hell could it be to call her sweetheart? Then she recognized the caller by his accent.

"Good morning, Ravi. What induced you to ring up so early?" she said casually.

"Lady, I will never forget you. On the other hand, you don't take a moment to forget others, those who dream of you. You didn't bother to call me even once."

"I was busy. Recently I have also been to New York."

"What took you there?"

"There was a show there in which Bhanu and Dhanush too had participated. Hence, I had to escort them there."

"Oh, I see. Now listen, I have just had a call from Dr. Vimal."

Rita felt a little perturbed. She remembered the warning of Sudha and Gauri against being too thick with Indian men. They are past masters in trapping Indian women with their slick tongues, exploit them physically and enjoy themselves at their cost among their friends. All of them are birds of the same flock. Recently Sharmili had told her that there was a network of bachelors and divorcees of Indian origin. They exploit single or divorced ladies by catching them in their net with sweet talk. Rita thought Dr. Vimal and Ravi could be members of the network. As such she bluntly said, "Maybe, but what has his call to do with me?"

"Rita, don't be angry. He is interested in helping you in the situation that you are in."

"When someone passes through bad times, nobody thinks of doing any service to him or her."

"But this time you are wrong. Please listen to me first."

"Ok," Rita said with apparent irritation in her tone.

"He intends to teach you photography and has asked me to do that. He also wants both of us to work as announcers in the program he intends to start."

"But why?"

"I think it is just a whim of a rich man. These doctors have money to burn and would like to come in the limelight one way or the other."

"How will that help?"

"For one thing, he needs a tax break. Then he will attract people's attention. He also hopes to find a good girl he could marry through this."

"He has asked you to teach me photography?"

"Surely me, one in billions." Ravi laughed.

"So you are to be the boss." Rita also laughed.

"Ok madam, Dr. Vimal Rai is coming next Friday."

"What shall I do then?"

"You do nothing. When the plan is finalized, I shall ring you up."

"When is the radio program to begin?"

"It is scheduled for next month. But we start making preparations from next Sunday."

"What preparations?"

"To finalize the script; to compose the songs; the manner to advertise etc."

"How much do I earn?" Rita asked in a business-like manner.

"It is to be decided by the doctor."

Somebody started knocking at the door at this point. Rita asked Ravi to hold the line as there was a knock at the door. As she opened the door, a man from the United Parcels handed a parcel to her. She opened the parcel quickly and found a Yoshika 35 mm camera in it. It was sent by Dr. Vimal Rai. Rita didn't feel happy at first. She thought of returning it. Then she changed her mind, thinking that next week when the doctor was to come, she could return the expensive camera to him. But she had forgotten that Ravi was holding the line. It was almost half an hour before she remembered this. She uttered, "Oh my God!"

When she lifted the receiver, she found Ravi still on the line. "Is everything ok? I am worried," he said.

"Oh, sorry Ravi. Strange that you are still holding the line."

"Who would be so stupid as to shut his ears when a nightingale warbles? In order to hear your musical voice, I am ready to hold the telephone line for my whole life."

"Cut this crap - your dramatic lines. Listen, Dr. Rai has sent me a camera and I fail to understand why."

"It is good that he knows you can't afford to buy a camera. He has given a camera to me also."

"I shall return it to him. I shall never accept anything so costly from a stranger."

"What a simpleton you are Rita! You never asked for the camera. He has himself sent it to you as a present."

"But what am I to reciprocate the present with?"

"Leave it for some later time. Well, listen to me. Rita you are so beautiful that if you are put among a bevy of beauties, you will be the centre of attention."

"Ravi, you are a bachelor and bachelors are expert in entrapping girls. But don't forget I am not an unmarried and raw girl and will never be caught in your net."

"But now-a-days the married ones are like the unmarried ones and the unmarried ones are like the married ones."

"What are you trying to say?" Rita was annoyed.

"I shall explain when we meet. Well, have you written any new poems?"

"Yes, I have, but it is just an attempt of an amateur at putting together words and ideas randomly and it is not yet worth showing."

"Ok. But at the moment, Rita, may I say one thing?"

"Go ahead."

"Don't underestimate yourself and don't knowingly hurt anybody. If Dr. Vimal Rai wants to help you, there is nothing wrong in it. You have not begged for anything. But if you spurn the good gesture, it is likely to hurt him."

"Ravi, you are much younger than I yet you talk wisdom with such great felicity."

"Hai mein mar jawan! Balle balle. (An exclamation in Punjabi, appreciating someone's gesture etc.) Somebody has after all praised me," Ravi said in a typical Punjabi style.

"Oh sorry. I had forgotten…," she said, a little embarrassed.

The chat continued for a long time. Ravi made Rita laugh with many tid-bits and a funny style of talking. When Ravi hung up, Rita went to Gauri and Sudha and brought back the children. The whole day was spent cheerfully in the company of the children. The old routine followed and Rita noticed that gradually her life was undergoing a change.

The rent of the apartment was running into heavy arrears. After paying electricity and telephone bills, hardly anything was left in her hand. But somehow, she was managing to spend time. Vaishali had got Rita transferred to a branch near her home. Consequently, most of Rita's time was spent with Vaishali and her sisters. But once when Sharmili invited Rita to visit their house, she excused herself saying that Dr. Vimal was to take her out to dinner and she was unable to come.

"Lucky Indian woman, I say, why don't you arrange a date with some doctor for us too?'

"Sharmili, I am not going on a date. He is going to start a radio program and he wants me to work as the announcer."

"But I was appreciating your guts and was suggesting that Indian women should feel free to go on dates with other men. If men have the freedom to go and do whatever they want, why shouldn't women do so?"

"Sharmili, I have two children. If I do such things, I would lose their trust and they might have wrong notions about me."

"Your children are very young. You don't have to be worried about your husband either as you live alone. That's why I tell you to get away from the rut and enjoy life when and as long as you can."

"Sharmili, don't take me wrong. I am interested in the job for the sake of a little extra income. I have to take care of the children's needs, uniforms, books etc."

"In the radio program, do you have some male members too as a co-worker."

"Yes, he is a photographer. But he tries to flirt with me."

"It is a surprise, Rita, that we are unmated heifers yet no stud seeks us. On the other hand, you were mated, bore children and there is still a herd of studs chasing you."

"But do you know why?" Rita became a little informal now.

"Why?" Sharmili asked eagerly.

"The reason you are unmarried," Rita said significantly.

"Well…leave it," Rita said it again

"Look here Rita, what if we don't have the marriage certificates to do what the married women can do without fear. We too have enjoyed sex, the thing the married women do legally. May I tell you what you can do right now?"

"Go ahead," Rita said vaguely.

"You are married. Go out with whomsoever you fancy and have as much sexual pleasure as you can. From your herd of studs, make your kill and get free sex as regularly as you eat and drink. If you get pregnant, nobody would ever know who the father of the offspring is. In this way you can do certain things better than the unmarried ones can. Got it into your thick head, simpleton?"

"Oh gosh! No, I won't do that," Rita said, unbelievingly.

"Why not, may I know? Do you realize how ignorant you married women are who happened to be married in the early seventies era?"

"Sharmili, right now we have a professional company and nothing more. I would like to keep it as it is."

"Rita, you have hit the bull's eye this time. Now don't be emotionally involved with anyone. But at the same time don't push anyone away either. Just entertain him with your womanly tricks and keep them in good humor. If this Dr. Vimal of yours is so generous, let him be. But be careful; don't make anyone your enemy."

"I am afraid lest the children would misunderstand me. Knowing the atmosphere in USA, when the kids grow up, they might throw my weakness on my face in order to get what they want in their lives"

"Rita, listen, my sister-in-law is coming from Canada tomorrow with her children. You can leave the children with us as; all the children, being of the same age, will be happy."

"Well, but Sudha's children...."

"Rita, you had better stop interacting with such settled families. If at any time you go back to Sudhir, these very so-called friends of yours will indulge in your character assassination and irrelevant gossip. All of them do behind the curtain what they criticize in others but a simpleton like you discloses everything thoughtlessly. Learn to respect your privacy."

"Sharmili, now that I have found a guru (preceptor) in you, I am sure to learn fast, so much so that I may even surpass you. It is said, 'Jinhan de guru tapne, chele jan chhapad.'(Those, whose preceptors are capable, are sure to have their disciples even sharper than them.)"

"Ok. Do you have a good dress? If not, please take one from me when you come to leave your children with us."

"Ok. See you on Friday."

On Friday Rita left the children with Sharmili and borrowed a dark blue dress from her. She wore white pearl earrings and a necklace. She was the least attracted towards Dr. Rai. She was paying this visit just as a formality. Punctually at 7, Dr. Rai knocked at the apartment door. Rita was wearing a dark blue dress with matching shoes. Her hair hung loose. As she opened the door, she found Dr. Rai standing with a beautiful bouquet held in front of his chest in both hands. Rita was elated to see the flowers and asked excitedly, "Who are these flowers for?

"For you… and er…for your children."

"The children are not at home. Please don't mind if I take the flowers of their share too."

"Why should I mind? After all, the mother of the children is not a separate entity from them."

"Dr. Rai, I am very hungry today and would eat like a hungry beggar but I would like to foot at least half the bill for the dinner," Rita said.

"Yes, but first you have to eat. The bill comes later. Come on. Get into the car." He had come in his Jaguar. In his formal suit, he looked a picture of elegance. He himself opened the car door and made Rita take her seat. Then he took the driver's seat. On the way he switched on some sweet, light romantic music. A little hesitant, she said, "Dr. Rai, thank you a lot for sending the camera and starting the program. I hope I shall certainly be worth your generosity."

"Rita, how many times do I have to remind you to call me Vimal? Why don't you regard me as your friend?'

"But you are so highly educated and accomplished and I stand no comparison to you. I dare not obliterate the difference in our personalities. I am insignificant before you in every way."

"This is a patent shortcoming in our Indian women."

"What?" Rita was startled.

"The Indian women lower themselves in the eyes of the men folk of their own accord. Rita, you don't know your worth." He heaved a deep sigh.

Rita said nothing. She looked at Dr. Rai and wished it were Ravi in the car beside her.

"What are you thinking, Rita?" Dr. Rai asked, parking the car in front of the restaurant.

""Dr. Rai…"

"Please call me Vimal." He led her into the restaurant.

"See, Vimal, you are taking me to dinner. You presented me with a camera, but in return I have nothing to offer to you. I am crushed under the weight of gratitude."

"I ask for nothing in return. I would, however, like to ask for just one thing."

"What…?" Rita occupied the chair a bit nervously.

The waiter had placed glasses of water on their table. Dr. Rai sipped a little water and said, "Your friendship and a b–e–a–u–t–i–f–u–l smile, you know, can bring the dead to life."

Dr. Rai took both her hands in his and kissed them passionately. She blushed profusely and felt that it was Ravi, not Rai, who had kissed her hands. Clearly it was Ravi who haunted her psyche. She was looking into the eyes of Ravi with all the intoxication that a beautiful woman like Rita could. She had forgotten that it was Dr. Rai, not Ravi, sitting before her. Her lips quivered invitingly. She was awaiting a passionate kiss by Ravi and half closed her eyes. But fancy can't cheat forever, as the English poet Keats says in his Ode to a Nightingale.

She was jolted back into reality. Dr. Rai was still holding her hands in a kiss. Rita said, "Please Dr. Rai…"

"Please call me Vimal, my real name. What is this repetition of Dr. Rai, Dr. Rai?"

"If I address you as Vimal, the flimsy barrier that keeps us in our places will be demolished. I am a married woman and it is not desirable that I cross the limit of friendship."

"Oh, forgive me. Out of passion I kissed your hands. I sincerely apologize. Please don't misunderstand me." Dr. Rai became a bit self-conscious.

After this, there was hardly any intimate and personal conversation between the two. Whatever they talked about was all business.

"Rita, I want not only you're singing but also recitation of your poems whenever you write any."

"The audience will be bored, I am sure."

"No, Rita. There are quite a large number of people who like poetry recitation. But do one thing."

"What is it?"

"Practice speaking in different tones, voices and moods in front of the glass."

"How will that help?" Rita said, having finished eating.

"Undoubtedly your voice is very sweet but practice will lend it a certain depth."

"Why are you doing so much for me?" Rita asked.

"The fact is that I had purchased the radio station much before I met you. I needed an announcer and Ravi gave me your name. Hence, I selected you."

"Thank you, Dr. Vimal."

"Again Dr. Vimal? Now it is time that you gave up calling me Dr. and thanking me so frequently."

They returned to the apartment and when Rita was getting in, Rai said, "Good luck for the show."

"I assure you that I won't let you down in the radio program. I shall work really very hard to make it a success."

"I trust you," Dr. Rai said as he turned the car to go home.

Left alone in her apartment, Rita spent the night turning in the bed without any sleep. She found Dr. Rai to be such a nice gentleman. However, why did the image of Ravi surround her world? Dr. Vimal Rai was very tall and had a broad hairy chest. He had a long nose, slightly longer than it should have been. His big round eyes occasionally looked frightening. But in spite of all these features, Rita didn't know why she was drawn towards Ravi.

The thought of learning photography came to her. She would not only have her wish to learn it, but also the radio program was going to start. The next morning when she went to bring the children home, Sharmili said, "What was the hurry? You could have permitted the children to spend the weekend with us. They were quite happy with our children."

"Yes, they will be more than willing to stay here, but what about me? I feel sad without them. That's why I have come to take them."

"How was your evening?" Taking Rita to one side for the sake of privacy, Sharmili asked her conspiratorially in a low voice.

"Leave it yaar (buddy). These things are beyond me. He is a gentleman but what can I do with my heart?"

"You are letting a rich man go. Believe me, you will starve throughout your life."

"Money is not everything. My husband too earns well. But his habits are not good."

"Are you not divorcing your husband?"

"How can I afford hiring a lawyer for a divorce?"

"Oh, I see. So as long as you don't have money, you can't think of another man."

"The questions: whom the heart appreciates, why it does so, what is happening to it etc. are maddening to me, the mother of two children."

"You are hiding something from me, Rita," Sharmili said, expressing her doubt.

"No yaar. It is just that photographer…"

"Oh, so this is the story. You have fallen for that worthless bachelor? Anyway, what is the delay? Just ring him up and invite him to dinner at our place. You will see how easily I shall catch him, for you of course. I have the patience to wait yet, you can be sure."

"Oh, my gosh! Do you think I am so cheap that I would be chasing people?" Rita said shyly.

"What rubbish are you talking about? It is the twenty-first century and you are in America."

"Please Sharmili, just leave it," Rita said conclusively and called the children.

Rita took the children for swimming and later to watch a movie. The old routine took over and by and by a week passed. Dr Rai didn't ring her up but in the morning Ravi did. "Hello Rita, how are you?"

"Thanks, I am fine. How about you?"

"Good morning, sweetheart," he said sweetly.

Rita was again startled with this mode of address - sweetheart. She was vacillating between two opposites; she liked the way he had addressed her and at the same time she was at a loss to know what had emboldened him to address her sweetheart. But she said, "Good morning, Ravi. What made you miss me so early?"

"I seldom forget you. Whereas you never even think of ringing me up. What are you made of; I wonder? May I know what crime I have committed?"

"Sorry. I was just busy. Dr Rai had asked for a few poems and to write the script of the program. That is what I have been doing and am going to do today."

"Ok dear, finish the poems and be ready to record this evening."

"But how would I do this with the children around?"

"Listen. Bring along the children but come you must."

"Ok Ravi, I shall ring you up again after consulting the children."

Rita asked the children to accompany her to Ravi's place but they wished to see the children at Sharmili's place. Rita phoned Sharmili and she agreed to let the children stay with her overnight. Rita at once rang Ravi up and told him that the children would be staying with a friend and she would come to him.

"Simply great! Now listen, dinner is awaiting you here."

"No, you need not worry. I shall cook and bring it along."

"Dr. Rai has sent me money for the dinner."

"That is not fair. Am I so poor that I can't even have my own meals?"

"Business is business dear. Not only is he paying for the dinner, he has also sent money for the gas of the car."

"I have never had any experience of business. Naturally I am totally ignorant of business etiquette."

"You will learn it soon. But Rita, that day your sad story made me sad too."

"You are just wasting your sentiments for me. I am in the same bubbling health."

"You have become an expert in side tracking things," Ravi teased her.

"You are off the mark. I am only trying to spend time the best way I can," she said seriously.

"Spending time… and that too when I am around? Not only time, would you like to spend life itself happily? With me as your co-traveler, the time will fly. By the way, an idea has just occurred to me. After preparing the radio program we shall go to see the Universal Studios."

"No, no, I am not going anywhere with you. I do not want to earn a bad name by going with you."

"Please cut away all this absurdity. After seeing the Studios, I shall teach you a little photography also. This will cheer you up, I am sure."

"We can postpone the cheering for some other time. Today, we shall do only the radio program." Rita abruptly turned down his request.

"Ok Devi ji (lady), when are you reaching the poor man's shanty?" Ravi said.

"At seven on the dot," she said.

Rita was aware that Ravi was a good photographer and was very popular among the Indian community. He claimed to be an engineer, but his ambition was to be a movie director. Rita's children were interested in acting and Rita was interested in writing. If she maintained the right contacts, her objective too would be easy to achieve. She knew that because of the radio program their meetings were going to be frequent. As such she had promised to go to see him. But she decided to be serious with him as otherwise he could cross the limits. He was a bachelor and his name could easily be linked with her and if it happened, her image in the society would be lowered in esteem. But these considerations apart, as the afternoon advanced, she felt her heartbeats accelerating. She was inexorably drawn to Ravi.

Though busy cleaning her room, she felt as if Ravi stood waiting with his arms open to take her in a warm embrace. She shook herself out of this reverie but like a hypnotized person, she again found herself thinking of Ravi. She was like a snake that dances with the movements of the snake charmer's pipe and who was just getting ready to capture the snake to put it into his box. She found a rosy hue gradually appearing on her face as if a dead body was getting alive again.

In the evening she drove the car as if she were flying a plane. In the car her body was racing faster than the car to reach the destination. An hour's journey was covered in minutes. She reached Ravi's apartment door and knocked at it.

"Who is it?" Ravi deliberately asked from inside to tease her.

"It is me," she said in a changed voice.

"Me who?" He also knowingly showed ignorance about the caller.

"Are you sure you don't recognize my voice? All right then, I am going back," she said, a little indignantly.

"Ok, wait a minute. I am opening the door at once. Modern beauties are so easily offended."

Ravi at once opened the door only to find that Rita was not there. Thinking that she had gone away, he was a bit nervous. Without shoes on, he ran out of the apartment shouting her name like a mad man but didn't find Rita. He was returning when near the entrance of another apartment at some distance away he saw her shadow Hiding. She was wearing a black skirt and long boots. Ravi pretended not to have seen her and looked blankly around him. Rita waited with her eyes closed and a light smile on her face. Ravi tiptoed to her and pressed her in a tight embrace.

She started screaming loudly. Windows of the apartments opened to see what was happening in their neighborhood. When Rita saw strange eyes focused on her, she felt self-conscious. With his hand on her back, Ravi led her into his apartment. Rita was so shaken with embarrassment that even inside the apartment, she was self-conscious. Ravi noticed this and said, "By giving you these bashful eyes and this blushing face how generous destiny has been to you that it made you so beautiful."

Rita liked the compliment and felt proud of her beauty but by way of changing the topic, she said, "I would care for a tea. Where is your kitchen?"

But Ravi seated her on the sofa and went to the kitchen to make tea himself. Still embarrassed, Rita was struggling with her thoughts. She reflected how tortuously life had led her through a maze. She was drawing closer to strange people.

Her perpetual vacillation between the right and wrong of her conduct bothered her. Was it right for her to fall into the arms of strangers after rejection by one man? Had she degenerated thus? She remembered the song she used to hum. It ran – 'Aurat hai jise aurat ki sharam hai. Bas laaj hi to aurat ka dharma hai' (The ideal woman never abandons her modesty which is her religion.) What has happened to that woman in her? Was she losing her bearings? Then the next moment she visualized herself in Ravi's arms. The thought gave her impetus. She was impelled to run into his arms in order to forget the whipping by Sudhir, the pain of which was never to leave her. In Ravi's arms, she thought, was the balm best suited for her injuries. This train of thought abruptly cut itself up and she took out her small pocket diary, one she always carried with her, and scribbled something in it.

"Please Call me Ravi now as your friend. Drop this formality of adding Mr. to my name. Address me informally by my name," he said. "I don't know what keeps you engaged so deeply and what you keep scribbling. But I strongly felt that I should make tea with my own hands and serve my dream queen." Ravi's words of flattery had the desired effect on Rita. A faint smile appeared on her face but she said nothing.

After tea, they settled down to work. Ravi had prepared a script for the program. It was improved by Rita and Ravi together. The songs were recorded. Rita had written a poem while waiting for the tea to get ready. She showed it to Ravi. He liked it and recorded it. The poem was:

Happiness has strayed into my life.
Some desires have invaded my life.
I had crushed my ambitions into dust.
They are stirring up again in my life.
The cruel dragon bares its teeth at me,
Threatening to burn me and my life.
Love is stirring up again in my heart.
A lamp has been lit in my life.
I can't define the pain in my heart.
Who is imparting joy to my life?
Inept eyes can't define dreams.
The feverish pain pervades my life.
Whose footsteps make me feel sore?
The crippled body awaits love in life.
The shyness looks up eager to welcome,
The beating footfalls again in my life.

"Great, simply great. I shall have it vetted by my mother and then publish it in the paper in your name."

"But it doesn't qualify to be published in the paper. It was just a random idea that I jotted down," Rita said.

"Thought is life; it is poetry; it imparts a flavor to life and makes it meaningful." Ravi looked at Rita with hypnotic eyes.

Rita thought it discreet to leave him now. He must have deceived scores of young gullible girls in the name of love. Men like him have nothing to lose and everything to gain. If a girl responds to such people's overtures with a smile, she is a sure victim. He must have befooled many girls. Thinking this, she made ready to leave but Ravi stopped her and said, "Where are you going, darling? You can only come of your own sweet will but you can leave only with my sweet will."

"No, I can't stay any longer. I have to pick my children from my friend's house and if I delay now, it will be very late." She gave an excuse.

"Madam, just spare an hour. We shall drive up to the Universal Studios. The view of the whole Los Angeles from there is stunning," Ravi said with confidence as if he already knew that she would not say 'no' now.

Rita didn't need much persuasion and accompanied him. But on the way she was quite restrained and kept quiet. She was lost in her own thoughts. Finally, the car reached the Universal Studios and halted.

Rita felt as if her heart had missed a beat. But instantly Ravi opened the door and helped her get down. He put his hand round her waist and gently led her away.

A pleasantly cool breeze was blowing and the sky was clear. It was a full moon night which had dimmed the stars. Rita felt as if it were after centuries that some male hand had held her by the back and had moved leisurely in step with her. The environment had its effect and she felt her heart giving way to her sense of pleasure. Her defense against such an eventuality was crumbling as if dry sand were moving away through numerous tiny holes of a sieve. She stole a glance at Ravi. What a tall and handsome figure he had. Ravi's mind was engaged in different thoughts. He must have walked like this on these very paths with hundreds of girls who were young and inexperienced but raw.

On the other hand, Rita was mature and had been with her husband for so many years. Even though her perfect beauty was unmatched. Ravi couldn't detect a single flaw in her form and composure. He pitied her husband who couldn't keep her to him with his love. Ravi was sorry for him and a little later for her too. He wouldn't bother whether he could marry her or not or she divorced her husband or not yet one thing he was sure of was that he would make her experience the supreme bliss that can come only with equally exploding physical relations between male and female of all animal or human worlds, the bliss which makes a woman forget her being.

Her sexual encounters with her husband had resulted in the birth of her two children but he doubted if she had also experienced emotional satisfaction. He could give her both. Most of the time she had been an unwilling partner with her husband in bed and she had been legally raped. But his approach would be entirely different. No girl had ever found his performance lacking in verve and passion.

Rita's old weakness of the sense of guilt that she was married and had children again proved an inhibition. She made an effort to free her hand from Ravi's grip. But he tightened the hold. Rita's ambivalence added to her difficulty. She liked the male possessive hold of Ravi but her conscience told her otherwise. Feeling helpless she meekly mumbled, "Please Ravi."

Ravi looked into Rita's eyes. There was deep despair in them, betraying deprivation of sincere love. Ravi could read the message in the moistened eyes – I need love but I don't know what true love is. Please give me a feel of it. I have never experienced true love. I don't intend to bother about what is right or wrong. I just hanker after love. Won't you oblige me? Rita had never thought of platonic love between man and woman. The satisfying conclusion of the sex act was the end of male/female relations. Like all normally healthy women, she preferred emotional interaction and finally the culmination in the act would mean true love. It was this love she badly needed now and she had a more than willing partner in Ravi. But Ravi was a male animal who enjoyed the act for its own sake and would go to any length to repeat it umpteen times with umpteen women.

Ravi raised her hand to his mouth and nipped one of her fingers lightly. "Did you say anything, Rita?" he asked.

"Ooi! What is this rudeness?" She was annoyed slightly.

This ooi fanned his passion further. He said "Oh! I am sorry. Come on, let me blow on it." He again pulled her hand up.

Rita visualized herself standing in a burning desert, hungry and thirsty, an undefined thirst. Then she saw a shadow which gradually and imperceptibly acquired the figure of Ravi. She felt it could be her succor and moved towards the figure. Her hands moved up to cling to the figure but something from deep inside her pulled her back with a sudden jolt.

"What are you up to? You are married and have two children. You are at the threshold of hell." She heard her own voice.

She was again back with the real Ravi and realized that her hands were very close to his handsome body. She hastily stepped back. She lowered her face, struggling to kill the storm that had risen in her heart. The desert disappeared and the cruel fate faced her.

"Ravi, I want to go home at once," she repeated the only excuse she always found handy, ineffective and unconvincing as it was meant to be.

"No, not yet. I haven't even feasted my eyes on you that are eager to devour you," he said, adopting a sober tone by design. He was gradually becoming quite brazen.

But Rita was trying her best to isolate herself from the thought of Ravi. Her mind was functioning on a different plane. She murmured, "All the doors of my life are bolted and chained. Freedom has been banned from my life."

Ravi, like an accomplished actor, synchronized his words and tone with Rita's and said, "Rita, learn to survive the journey of life with strangers if your co-travelers have deserted you. You can always make the journey happy with a strong will."

"I fail to understand your philosophy. What are you trying to say?"

Without knowing, Rita was seeking a confession of love by Ravi even when her troubled psyche wouldn't realize it.

But Ravi was an experienced hunter. He had heard and dealt with many better ruses than Rita's. Countering her apparently meaningless words, he said, "Why do you pretend to be so innocent? Don't I know that you are deliberately trying to sidetrack the vital issue which both of us fully know? Your eyes betray more than you intend."

"What is my eyes betraying, may I know? They have lost the faculty of discriminating between right or wrong. Don't be misled by their expression." Rita started weeping.

"Why are you bent upon punishing your eyes? Let them see the light of love they have been waiting for. When the moon peeps from among dark clouds, one's eyes turn to have a look at it and appreciate its brilliance and beauty. Even a momentary glance at the moon is like a message promising that the tedious journey of life can be made easy," Ravi said philosophically.

"But I am a lusterless moonlight discarded by its moon."

"Sure, and what I have been trying to do since you stepped into my house this evening is to refurbish the lusterless moonlight in your eyes. I will be your light."

"For God's sake Ravi, don't hold out meaningless dreams to me. I am doomed to live till the last breath in the perpetual dark moonless night. The full moon light is banished from my life. Your words of consolation are meaningless to me."

"Rita my love, you, yourself, are the moonlight that shines forever. Here, come into my arms, waiting to squeeze and crush your warm voluptuous body into my arms. My lips are tingling in expectation of robbing the rose petals, your quivering lips, of their fragrance and color. Why do you deny yourself the bliss that only two hungry bodies can generate? Look here, every passing moment is our loss. The sooner you come into my arms, the deeper will be the bliss, heavenly bliss, I should say. Your body was ravished by a brute, not a man who valued your beauty. Ravi stood with his arms outstretched invitingly.

Rita ignored the passion of Ravi's words and said, "Nothing in the world can populate the deserts and bring up the dead from the graves. What can restore hope to the hopeless cheated by life and destiny?"

"Rita, please! Right now, we can do without some philosophy." Ravi looked into her eyes with great passion for her.

They were standing at a secluded spot where there was no onlooker. They looked into each other's eyes and their individualities began to melt and merge into one.

Though Rita's lips were half open invitingly, she moved backwards, slowly fanning Ravi's passion. He found it extremely difficult to hold himself back now and kept moving on towards Rita. Gradually the distance between the two was getting narrower. Ravi saw nothing and wanted nothing except Rita who seemed to have hypnotized him. The barrier of Rita's inhibition too was slowly crumbling. This game continued for quite some time. But even the strongest defenses fall before determined forces.

She struggled to disengage herself gradually. Ravi realized what she is thinking." Ok, I shall not go to the ultimate limit. Trust me." Ravi tried to convince her.

"Why are you asking me to do the impossible? With you around, how can I be in my senses? Your fascinating eyes and beauty can bring down angels from heaven and I am but a weak human being. Please Rita, don't leave me hanging like this."

"Ravi please, you know…" She just wanted to leave.

"Sweetheart, don't leave me alone in life. Forget your dejection consequent upon a failed marriage. Let me populate your barren flower bed with fragrant and colorful buds. Why are you moving away from me thus?"

Rita didn't prolong the romantic encounter. She moved to the staircase and started climbing down with unsteady steps. But Ravi rushed forward and lifted her in his hands as if she were made of papier-mâché and tried to kiss her half opened rosy lips, bringing her downstairs against her meek protests.

Rita was confused. Her heart shouted to her telling her to sweep aside flimsy and meaningless social taboos. What did it matter whether Ravi loved her or not? Right now, her body was in control of her reasoning faculties and she was inclined to go by its commands. But she suspended the reasoning faculty and stopped resisting the persistence of the mind that told her not to do what she ought not. Ravi said, "Oh! my beauty queen, don't be cruel. Why are you bent upon burning me to ashes?"

"Don't do this. The onlookers will assume I am trying to rape you."

"What is it if not rape?" she said with genuine seriousness this time.

"For God's sake don't make this serious allegation against me. I am expressing my love to my heartthrob." He again tries to get close to her.

Bemused onlookers had already started ignoring these infatuated lovers. Ravi was moving down a flight of steps leading to the ground floor with Rita in his arms. Rita relished every moment of this event. She didn't want to think of the past or the future. She wished the present moment to become infinite.

Despite her being married with two children she was being used as a virgin. A few steps remained to climb down and Rita knew the end of the bliss was fast approaching when Ravi, with her in his arms, missed a step, stumbled and fell down. They rolled down and hit the floor. Ravi's limp body lay under Rita, who was on him. Ravi was immobile. Rita panicked. She looked around for help but there was no one around. She was convinced that Ravi had received some serious head injury. Ravi's limp arms were still around her. She eased herself by removing his arms and managed to rise to a sitting position. She softly moved her hand on Ravi's head and sweetly asked, "Oh Ravi! Please get up. What has happened to you? There is no one around here to help us." But Ravi didn't respond to her pleading. She decided to leave him and summon help. But as she tried to move, Ravi suddenly held her by the hand and pulled her to him. "How can I die with you around? But I hope I have not offended you? I was just testing whether you cared for me or not."

"Chhii. (Bah) This is too much. Do you think it was a joke? I don't want to talk to you." She expressed her annoyance. Tears started flowing down her cheeks.

"Rita, please don't take me wrong. I was just making our outing a bit spicy. The fact is that I would like to be yours forever. Why don't you put all your worldly woes onto my shoulders? It will make life easy."

"You are taking advantage of my helplessness." She kept moving towards the car.

"No, Rita, please don't misunderstand me." He helped her into the car.

"You very well know that I have nobody to call my own except my children. You also know that I am not a teenager that could be beguiled with rosy dreams."

"To translate dreams into a reality is in our hands, you know, only if you agree."

"But what do you know about life? You are a mere young bachelor."

"You too are young, Rita," he said with conviction.

"You are just pulling my leg. This idea of yours to make me your life partner is just bait and I am not a kid to take it. Also, listen, we have recorded four days' program and now you can find some other announcer," she said with finality in her voice.

Ravi had nothing more to say at the moment and decided to keep silent. This ambivalence on the part of Rita was new even for an experienced hunter like Ravi. He, however, was not to be dissuaded so easily by the annoyance of a woman whom he wanted. He decided to wait and see and was sure that she would finally give in to his tactics and would come round. On the way back, neither spoke. Ravi was worried to think that Dr. Rai might dismiss him from the job if he came to know about this development.

Finally, they reached his place and Rita moved to her car. When she was getting into her car, Ravi politely said, "Rita, please don't take today's incident seriously. I meant no harm to you." Rita left in her car. Ravi stood leaning against his apartment door with his hand pressed against his forehead. He was feeling perturbed and cheated for the first time in such a situation though he had had numerous steamy encounters in the past with girls he would pick. Because of Rita's behavior he realized that he needed to change his strategy from now on. Rita had not been fully charmed with his usual ploy that had entrapped many girls in the past. He looked up and found that Rita's car was nowhere in sight.

CHAPTER 10

Rita was reflecting over the incident. Ravi had asked for forgiveness, assuring her that he intended no harm to her. But she found it difficult to decide what he was asking to be forgiven for. She had been waiting for his phone and when it did come, she felt eager to go to him. In whatever words she might have shown her disinclination to go to his place to meet him, she was never serious in her refusals. She decided to visit Sharmili after a week.

"Tell me, tell me. You don't even care to call me to tell you about your romantic encounter with Charmer Ravi. "Sharmili was eager to know if anything serious happened between Ravi and Rita.

"Please Sharmili! You have taken it all wrong. Listen to me first. I don't like to get involved in such affairs. Hence, I refused to continue to do the radio program with him," Rita said.

"Do you believe that he doesn't know how to turn this 'no' into 'yes'?"

"What do you mean?"

"I simply mean that he is not going to let you go so easily. He is surely going to renew his contact and ultimately to get a hold on you."

"Such things don't have any importance in my life. My whole life is concentrated on Dhanush and Bhanu."

"It is natural for a mother to feel this. But Rita, in due course these children will begin to lead their life in their own way, leaving you alone to fend for yourself and with no one around to share your joys, if any, and heaps of sorrows."

"How is that possible? My children already realize how greatly I am sacrificing my interests for them. They will never forget this."

"Rita, if I were you, I would never put my trust in such meaningless expectations. The world is not what it used to be. You live away from the world of reality, or in a fool's paradise."

"I don't think I quite understand you."

"Soon, Bhanu will start nursing her own dreams, friends, pleasures and ambitions totally unrelated to your happiness. Grown up children turn out to be very selfish."

"But you have had no experience of life yet, Sharmili. How can you be so sure of the future?" Rita asked confidently.

"Look here, do you know that my mother regularly calls me to tell me that I should get married, and do you know what my reply to her always is?"

"What?"

"Just that she doesn't want me to enjoy my freedom and happiness. She is jealous of my freedom."

"Oh!" Rita was shocked. "How do you say such things to your mother? I would never even dream of saying such things to my mother."

"I know you won't but I know what you are going to hear, at least from your children. The times are changing fast. The new generation likes to learn things through self-experimentation and experience. Today's generation are self-centered. I would like to be told in this scenario why we should bother what the society and the people are; what they do or say about us."

Rita chose to say nothing to Sharmili. She came home and the time moved on as usual. She was conscious of the fact that times were changing as Sharmili had reminded her. She recalled that there was a time when in India the people took the neighbors' daughters as their own and were ready to defend them even at the cost of their life if an outsider harassed them.

On their part the children too were very particular to see that they did not indulge in anything objectionable that would bring a bad name to their families and communities. But today they cared a fig for the society, religion and the good name of the family. With them, the family or the community was irrelevant in their lives. Now the son defied paternal authority and the father punished the son without any rhyme or reason. In many cases, if the mother was herself unable to ensure two meals a day, what future could she ensure for her children? When the mother could't protect her honor, how could she do anything if the daughter faced the same situation?

Rita realized that if she maintained liaison with Dr. Vimal or Ravi, she could never be honest with her children. Hence, she decided not to do any radio program with them. She had been living separately from Sudhir even though not divorced. But how could she afford a lawyer to file a suit for divorce when she could hardly afford to pay the apartment rent? But strange is human nature. Even in these distressing circumstances and her resolution not to have any contact, she often found herself thinking of Ravi. She was so enamored of the man that she saw him in every man passing by even though she didn't know whether it was her loneliness or love for Ravi. She reminded herself that she had never known or experienced love for a man. But whenever anyone showed her a little of the so-called human trait called love, she was sold to him.

It was over two weeks since either Ravi or Dr. Rai had phoned her. When she was expecting a call, they did not come. One day she started receiving calls from her acquaintances and sisters. They had read her poem in a paper and liked it very much. Rita was unaware of its publication. Such a good thing had never before happened to her. Hitherto her in-laws and relatives had always found fault with whatever she did and never appreciated anything she did. They were always likely to make fun of her for insignificant things. Their appreciation and the gesture to call her were very unusual.

The situation at home, when she was with Sudhir, had been so bad that even when she cooked well, Sudhir never praised it. He always preferred to praise his sister-in-law's cooking. This attitude was not limited only to her cooking. He freely praised the beauty of his middle sisters-in-law though the fat ugly woman had an elephantine girth. She was always very liberal with the use of dark red lipstick and a bindi (dot) on her forehead. She had mothered three children and her body was sagging. She stood no comparison to Rita, slim and beautiful. But Sudhir always sang of the sister-in-law's beauty.

The first broadcast of Dr. Rai's program was praised by everybody in the Indian community. Rita again received compliments from many listeners including her relatives. Though she had decided not to do the program with Ravi anymore, she changed her mind and informed Ravi that she would go ahead with joining the program. But Sudhir came to know of this and didn't like all this.

On the other hand, Rita's brother Navin wanted to persuade Rita to go back to live with Sudhir. In the meantime, Rita had made friends among some divorced women. The radio program had also made her a familiar household name.

Consequently, Sudhir also softened a little and sent feelers through common contacts to make up with Rita.

On the other hand, thought of Ravi, the guilt she associated with such a relationship bothered her. The inner voice, maddeningly loud, hammered her brain - 'You are married and have two children. You sin if you think of sexual gratification with Ravi, who is not your husband.' Still, she imagined herself as Ravi's bride. She had been robbed of all her happiness after her marriage with Sudhir. Accepting a short happy time spent with Sudhir, almost the entire married life had been a nightmare. She was nothing more than a sex object for him. Sudhir and his relatives never spared any efforts to persecute her over one thing or the other. She spent most of her time weeping in desolation. She had forgotten what smiling meant and was drowned in her misery.

Her new, single divorced friends narrated tales of their sexual escapades and urged her to take the plunge. They advised her to enjoy herself with men of her choice. One of them suggested in a lighter mood, "You lucky devil! You are not tied to one insipid mate. You can have variety daily." But Rita was unwavering in her resolve not to follow their advice. She was adamant to limit her interaction with Ravi to the radio program and learning photography despite the urges of her heart.

The thought of Bhanu and Dhanush's life was uppermost in her mind. If she gave way to her physical weakness, she would be presenting a poor example before the children. She would not choose the life suggested to her by her divorced friends. She would also not divorce Sudhir. She would try to manage life as best as she could in the given circumstances. If Sudhir himself chose to divorce her, she would not oppose it but herself she would never do this.

Bhanu was ten years old. One day Navin left Bhanu and Dhanush with Sudhir. That evening Rita was to attend some party and the children were obliged to spend the night with Sudhir. Navin had informed Rita about this. Sudhir took the children to his brothers and sisters-in-law. Rita went to the party and met Ravi there. Rita was dressed in a dark maroon colored suit. She noticed that wherever she sat, Ravi came and seated himself beside her. By and by the singing and dancing hour came. The guests asked Rita to sing but she declined the request with finality.

"Excuse me, I have heard your commendable radio programs and your poetry recitation. I refuse to believe that you can't sing," one of the guests suggested.

"Yes, Rita, please do sing a song," Ravi insisted. Rita relented and took out an old poem she had recited on the radio. It was:

> Happiness has drifted into my life again.
> My desires are budding once again.
> The aspirations I had crushed into dust,
> Have risen afresh like a big gust.
> But I am afraid of the cruel world's claims
> That they may again put my life into flames.
> In the depth of the hearts of heart,
> Love is stirring again in life for him
> I see the light brightening, which was dim.

As the poem was finished, a loud clapping followed and gradually died out. But Ravi continued clapping. Rita's face reddened with embarrassment and indignation. It was shameful. Ever since she had started doing the radio program, there was gossip about her relations with Ravi. Today's conduct of Ravi had substantiated the gossip. She picked up her purse and at once left the venue for home.

This incident was naturally followed by all sorts of whispers. Rita stopped going to parties. Finally, Dr. Rai got wind of the incident and he removed Ravi from the program. Rita didn't like this. But she was in dire need of funds. Money, as the saying goes, makes the mare go. Hence, she didn't give air to her disgust about the incident. Ravi started his own school to teach photography and soon his business flourished. After about three months he rang Rita up.

"Hello Rita, how are you?"

"Ravi, why did you take so much time in ringing me up?" she said in a complaining tone and added, "How do you do?" She felt her heart missing a beat now and then as she talked to him, extremely overjoyed.

"I am a little unwell."

"Well, what is it? You sound all right to me." She betrayed concern for him.

"No, I am a heart patient," he said seriously.

"Oh! You should have consulted Dr. Rai." She had seen through his ploy.

"Dr. Rai diagnosed the disease but gave me wrong medicine."

"Ravi, I have heard that you have an excellent studio." She tried to cut the rubbish out.

"Yes, these days I go to Columbia studio for training as a movie director."

"Really? Do you intend to make a film?" she said cheerfully.

"Listen, I need a story for my school project. Will you write one and oblige me?"

"Why not? But I am not very good at English," she said a bit nervously.

"You needn't worry. I shall help you with it," he said.

"When do you want it?"

"The story should be of thirty minutes' duration at the most. I want it within two months."

"Well, it is a deal."

Ravi replaced the receiver with a simple bye. Many thoughts came to her mind. It was likely that he had found some new girlfriend. The old unease that she was the mother of two children and he was a young bachelor got hold of her. Ravi could not have gained much in marrying her. Besides, he would feel burdened with the responsibility of bringing up two children. She stopped thinking about a close relationship with him and limited herself to writing the story he had asked for.

These days Rita shared an apartment with her new female friend Sneh, a friend of Sharmili. Sneh was a divorcee and had a Sari on her all the time. By this time the story for Ravi's program was completed and instead of calling Ravi, Rita sent it to him by courier.

One day Rita was dusting her car along with her friend Sneh when somebody placed a hand on her shoulder from behind. She was startled and looked at the intruder. It was Ravi. He said, "What is its dear madam, how have I sinned that you preferred to send the story through a courier rather than visiting this servant's humble abode?"

"Oh Ravi." Rita uttered with surprise.

"Rita, where did you hide yourself? I am very angry with you." His resentment was betrayed on his face.

"Ravi, this is my friend Sneh. We share the apartment." Rita tried to squeeze herself out of the situation.

"Hello Sneh, how do you do?" Ravi extended his hand to her.

"Thank you. I am fine. By the way, your voice is very sweet."

"My voice?" Ravi said, a little puzzled.

"Yes, when you were on the radio program with Rita, all female listeners were eagerly listening to every word you spoke."

"Thank you. You are raising the poor man to the sky. In fact, the program was in the name of Rita." He grasped the opportunity to flatter Rita.

Ravi and Sneh continued talking in the parking lot and Rita pretended to be busy dusting her car. In the adjoining shed was the washing machine. Sneh moved to it for a while. Finding Rita alone, Ravi said to Rita, "What is the reason for this coolness? You have written an excellent story and it is beyond my expectations. Your capability as a writer has made you more desirable for me. I can't help dreaming of you. You have deprived me of my peace and sleep. You are so weird."

"What are you talking about, Ravi? Let us please confine our relation to business." Rita turned away from him.

"Rita, that day your poem was so good that I found it difficult to believe that you could write so well. I am a fan of your artistic talents. I had been looking for a girl like you throughout my life."

"I am not a girl. I am a woman and even more, a mother."

"I know, but in my eyes, you are sweet sixteen," he said with a smile on his face.

"Look here Ravi, after today, never try to deceive me."

"But, why? I will be the last man to deceive you."

"You are bent upon slandering and betraying me."

"Why should I be such a sinner?" He was still not serious.

"Ravi, listen to me, do you realize what idea my friend Sneh would form about me? All know that I am not living with my husband Sudhir. But I am a member of a civilized society and I have to bring my children up in this Indian community in America."

"Society! Society! Society! It is a hypocritical society, your damn Indian society."

"Whatever it is, but it is the society where my children are to grow. They will be looked down upon by the people. I won't let them live this life of disgrace. What harm have my innocent children done to any one for them to pay the consequences of their parents' deeds – parents who never paid attention to their sentiments?"

"What has this society given to you? When you were homeless, did society give you a shelter above your head? Did this society provide you and the children with two meals a day?"

"Stop this harangue, Ravi." Rita was furious now.

"But what I am saying is the truth and I know, Rita, that nobody is prepared to hear it."

"I can discriminate between right and wrong. You are nobody to teach me this. No one can change society irrespective of the fact whether it is good or bad." Rita was determined but tears were rolling down her cheeks.

"You can change yourself. When you were whipped and were groaning with pain and were shedding tears, did this society of yours come to wipe your tears? Did they hold you close to their heart?" Ravi came close to her and started to kiss her cheeks, wet with her tears.

"Please Ravi, go home. Don't make me emotional; don't play with my emotions anymore. Go away!" Rita again busied herself in cleaning the car.

"No, Rita, the poem 'Lonely Tears' has made me sleepless."

"In that case, please let me have my story back," she said indignantly.

"No, first give me a reply."

"What reply? I have told you in plain words that I have great regard for society." Rita was weeping now because of helplessness.

"What rubbish do you talk about mentioning society all the time like chanting in temples? When you were kicked out of your house to spend the night in the cold, did your society come to your rescue? What society and which society are you defending before me? Make me understand this double standard of our Indian society. When it comes to their turn everything, they dodged behind the sofa but they do try to control a woman like you."

"Enough is enough. You leave this place at once," she told him with finality in her voice.

Ravi left. Sneh was a witness to the whole drama. Sneh was around fifty-nine years old, but looked hardly above thirty. She was divorced around five years back. She was still very good looking. Rita came to her room and started weeping. Sneh didn't say anything about the incident that night. But she kept working in her office.

Suddenly Sneh heard someone knocking at the door. She looked out of the window and saw Ravi standing there. Instead of opening the door, she went to awaken Rita. She said, "Rita, it is Ravi outside."

Rita was alert but said, "Don't open the door. Let him stay wherever he likes."

"No Rita, he has seen me. Please come out."

Sneh opened the door while Rita went to the washroom and came out after washing her face. Her eyes were red and swollen. Ravi stared at her disheveled clothes and her unkempt hair. He realized that she was still angry with him. Rita said dryly, "Ravi, don't you see, it is midnight. What is the great idea behind your coming here? Two single women, civilized women, in this apartment"

"I want to say something to you."

"But I refuse to listen to you."

"Rita, please…please," Ravi almost begged

"Haven't I made it clear that only two women live here and it is hardly the appropriate time for a man to visit them at this late hour."

She pushed him out of the room saying, "Would you please leave me alone now?" She closed the door behind him.

Ravi walked away without even giving a last look to Rita. Sneh didn't like this untimely visit and the unsavory scene. She said, "I agree he should not have come at this ungodly hour but you too didn't show any pity, Rita."

"Sneh, I ask you whether any man has the right to behave in this manner with a woman who has been abandoned by her man, irrespective of the hour of his visit."

"But I feel Ravi loves you sincerely." Sneh was remembering something of her own encounters with someone.

"When Sudhir proposed to my parents for marriage, he too professed this love so much and look at him now, even though he is the father of my two children. Now my husband and I live separately. How does Ravi fit in this scenario?"

"Ok. Go to bed now. I shall tell you what I have undergone in my life in the morning."

But Rita did not oblige. She held her back and said, "Sneh, I have always wished that no one should face what I have had to face in life. Oh God, am I so self-centered now that I think I am the only one who suffered such ugliness in my life? I am so sorry, Sneh."

"Yes, Rita, I have not suffered as much as you have. I was not battered as emotionally, financially and physically."

"Why did your husband divorce you then?"

"I said it is midnight and go to sleep," Sneh persuaded her sweetly.

"No, I am not sleepy and I don't have to go to work tomorrow anyway. Go ahead and tell me what you have on your mind," Rita pressed her.

"Rita, our divorce was the result of my husband's being a drunkard, gambler and womanizer."

"Really? Why was he so self-destructive? I don't understand, liquor is so bitter, still why do men enjoy drinking so excessively?"

"I was a religious minded girl. If my husband wanted to have sex in the morning when I was still asleep, I wouldn't let him."

"I would have done the same if I were you. If anybody tries to disturb my morning or night sleep, I would hate him as I would a devil incarnate."

"Not only this, he tried to be unreasonable in front of his brothers and sisters-in-law, which I detested."

"I too don't appreciate the public display of romance."

"Well, he was educated in America and was a little westernized. But when I also became a little westernized, he did not like it. I gave birth to my daughter Purnima exactly after nine months and to Krishma after a year of her birth."

"How old are you? Where are your daughters?" Rita asked.

"I am fifty-nine now and I was married when I was twenty-four. My husband doesn't like to have baby girls as he thinks females are too much of a burden to protect from the bad intentions of a male dominated Indian society."

"Huh! But why?" Rita asked, surprised.

"Because both his sisters-in-law had two sons each and they used to tell him how some immoral minded men rape our girls sometimes.

"Only boys were welcome in the family and daughters were not; I don't know why they blamed men as all men are like that. All Indian men are not."

"But Sneh, how are you to blame for this? My husband always told me that it is the father who is responsible for the child's sex, not the mother."

"Yes, my husband knew this but held me wholly responsible for the birth of the girls."

"He must have been a strange man, Sorry to say, his education was no good if he was stuck with old thinking where people used to kill even newly born baby girls in many countries around the world. Even though our Hindus family suffered a lot from the hands of the Mughals Invaders in India. I also know men who rape women, they have no religion. But 99% Indian men are very respectable in India"

"We would leave both the daughters with a babysitter and visit a country club to dance. By the time the girls grew up and understood and needed parental love but my husband had no time for them. I used to sing in gatherings and his friends openly made fun of him about this."

"What was the name of your husband?" Rita interrupted her.

"Ravinder Dutt."

"What is his profession to earn for the family?"

"He is an engineer. We clashed over minor things in the presence of the daughters. I loved the girls very much and felt sorry for them. Once someone asked me to sing on the stage and I obliged him. It was the beginning of a new phase in the household. Now tabla and harmonium can be heard any time in our house. One Satish Verma would accompany me in singing. We came close to each other. While on the other hand I was fed up with Ravinder's nagging over minor things and his hob-nobbing with numerous famous women. My relations with Satish Verma were above board yet my husband could not tolerate this. He mercilessly beat me over this and the divorce was the result."

"What became of the girls?"

"They lived with me. They were attached to me. Till they did their matriculation, they preferred Indian dress, food, music and movies. But as they…" Sneh's voice became heavy and choked. Rita could feel her distress and tried to console her. But Sneh started howling. She was shaking with misery and was saying to herself, "Oh God in heaven, don't make anyone suffer on account of children. It is the severest suffering one can experience."

"Tell me, Sneh, what happened to the girls?"

"Rita, as they entered college, they were led astray by American boys and girls."

"What did they do?"

"The elder daughter found an American who was good in studies. You know how uninhibited American youth are. They do before marriage everything which they are supposed to do after marriage. The Indian ritual of going round the sacred fire seven times or a marriage in the church had no meaning for them. The boy's mother too had had premarital sex with her lover and the boy to whom my daughter was attached, was born to her before marriage.

"After his birth his mother dumped his father and married another man. The young boy was brought up by his maternal grandmother and had never known a regular family life. He was the product of a fractured American society. He often quarreled with his mother. My daughter had known what maternal love is and she mediated between the mother and the son so much so that she left me. Her boyfriend is a freeloader. He does not even have a profession. He lived with her on her earning."

"Why didn't you stop her?"

"I did. I tried to explain to her that Indian society and American society were quite different from each other. But she would not listen to me. I severely reprimanded her but all my efforts to bring her back to our way of life came to naught. The more I tried to persuade her to leave the boy, the more she ignored my advice. To justify her action, she accused me of having affairs with several men and called me names like prejudice and racist. Yes, we lost between two cultures."

"What? For God's sake, what kind of a man is she living with?

"Taking a cue from her, the younger one also started going out with a mutt American. Her American boyfriend also brainwashed my innocent girl and without any information to me my daughters married them."

"Oh, Sneh, I can understand the trauma you must have faced. What about those boys' parents? Don't they tell their sons not to mess with your girls. Born in America has no relevance to American culture; also, it's not about any race or if we like to stay in our culture that we hate any race or culture. Everyone has the right to preserve their culture. Each outsider should understand the culture of the race they are not born in."

"Are you kidding? These parents think I am prejudiced, being a brown colored woman, I am evil. They called me by this name openly in front of an outsider. They don't understand our rituals, traditions and family values at all. They themselves do the same thing; why would they stop their sons to eat and live free on my daughters' account?"

"Sorry to say this, but one day your daughters will regret the pain they cause you. Trust me, these people will leave them on the street. All Americans are not bad; some of them wish they can follow our Indian moral values. They are good people from good families," Rita got very upset.

"You had better not even think about it. My relatives started making fun of me in numerous ways. They also referred to my divorce in derogatory terms.

"Alas! One's own offspring becomes one's enemy. Such kids have low self-esteem. The ones who abandon their family values, lower their standards, blame their parents are the ones who suffer from the so-called lovers they choose."

"It is because the children are produced by the mother but the seed is from an outside stranger," Sneh said with utter pain and tears in her eyes.

"Did the girls ever try to contact you? You know, Sneh, when children go to the outside world, The world will manipulate them and never let them be on the right path. The world is selfish. In the name of love, children are blind. It will be too late when your daughters realize this."

"No, I have also severed my connection with them. I have disowned them. Initially I fell ill owing to separation from them. They failed to see my motherly pain but then I compromised with the circumstances, mustered courage and am on my own feet now."

"How did you do that?"

"I had never had any doubt that I was not responsible for the wrong ways of the daughters. It was all destined to happen and I surrendered myself to the divine will."

"I hope you are happy now, Sneh."

"Yes, I am happy as I have surrendered myself to the will of God. If the children can be selfish, the parents should also try to look after their own happiness. This peace comes only by His grace."

"But Sneh, when suffering invades, even God's name is forgotten."

"Yes, I agree but not a leaf in the world can move without His will. We are insignificant before His might."

"But why does God harass His own creation so much?"

"It all depends on one's actions. We have taken birth to make a reckoning of our karmas (actions). Well, Rita, you had better go to bed now," she suggested sweetly.

"Ok, Sneh, you are like my elder sister. Never feel that you are alone. I am always with you," Rita said.

Rita lay in her bed but sleep had deserted her. She lay looking at the ceiling. She wondered whether one could foresee what the children would do to the parents when they grew up and whether they would turn against their parents. Can our own children be on the path of destruction for the sake of so-called love of the materialistic world? On the other hand, the society blamed the parents if the children went astray. Were the Indian children produced for such a society where they don't understand the pain of their parents?

Then she thought of Bhanu and Dhanush. What if Bhanu was to go the way Sneh's daughters had done? No, she would not let that happen. She would start right from this moment and keep an eye on her.

At the same time if it happened, she would commit suicide out of shame and misery. Then she remembered Sudhir. She wished only Sudhir hadn't turned violent against her. If only he had tried to look into her heart. She could have showered her love on him. But he had staked their happiness for his brothers and sisters-in-law. She wondered whether he had married her for himself or for his brothers and sisters-in-law. "I was not that bad. But you betrayed me before the world, Sudhir," she told him in her imagination and heaved a sigh.

This train of thought shifted to Ravi. She regretted that he hadn't come to her before her marriage and now there was no justification for his wooing her. Her children were her whole concern now and all her hopes were centered on them. She wished he would go away. With him around, she could never be an ideal mother to Bhanu, her dear daughter.

Now Ravi was just a representative of Satan. "Go away Ravi, go away. Leave me alone." Rita closed her eyes and tried to go to sleep again. But a strange face appeared before her eyes and asked, "Will these children ever be yours? Will they ever share your pain? You simpleton, they will love their own life and be responsible for their actions. They will never care for you. They will sneer at Rita, a pious lady. In the world it is one's own blood that causes pain. Julius Caesar had said in the play of the same name when his friend Brutus had stabbed him, "Et tu Brute? Then Caesar falls." The cruelest cut is from one's own people and friends. When your husband abandoned you, what do you expect from your children? They will become selfish and will drop you like a hot potato when they grow up. They will laugh at your orthodox ideas. You will be alone...alone... alone... God forbid, if this should happen, Lord. Oh Lord, you give me any amount of physical pain but please do not take my children away from me." Rita almost cries every night in her dreams. Story of Sneh started to haunt her.

"Come in, Sneh," Rita said, still half asleep.

"Look here, I have brought tea for you," Sneh said very lovingly.

"Sneh, I had bad dreams the whole night."

"Why, Rita?"

"I was troubled when I thought of the future of my children."

"You should have trust in God. Whatever happens, will be for your own good. But whatever you decide to do, please be careful. I would like to say something if you don't mind."

"Sure."

"Don't leave the children with unmarried girls."

"Yes, Sneh, now I shall take the children with me, whenever and wherever I go."

"But it is different when you leave them with women who have their own children. You can't neglect your life too. If you make up with Sudhir ..."

"No, Sneh, how can I do that? He can never resist violence as long as he does not take some counseling. But I am sure he will never leave his brothers and sisters-in-laws."

"Look here. His sisters are not only to blame. But he should have complained against them to his brothers. It is natural. No brother ever abandons his brothers. The brothers should have enough discrimination to stop leaning towards their wives and let them ruining their other brother wife.

"Sneh, sisters are very clever. The illiterate women know nothing except scheming etc. I am caught up with them and am helpless."

"Ok. Listen to me. I won't advise you whether to get a divorce or not but if you intend to continue friendship with Ravi, please keep it secret from the children."

"Sneh, I have nothing to do with Ravi. I have discontinued seeing him."

"How old are you?"

"I am in my early thirties."

"Then I don't see any harm in having friends. But just mind your steps. I feel Ravi is a nice man but you should use your discretion.

Ok. I have to be early at the shop and would like to leave now." Sneh got up to leave.

After Sneh was gone to her work, Rita got ready and brought the children from Sharmili's place. She would spend time playing with the children and was particular that she didn't leave them away from her vigil. At the same time Sudhir and Rita's brothers and sisters kept insisting for her to go back to Sudhir. But she had committed to nothing.

One Saturday, it was raining heavily. Bhanu and Dhanush were asleep by her side. The postman knocked at the door. The rain had made the weather chilly and she was reluctant to leave the bed. She got up and the postman handed over a packet from Ravi. Rita had almost forgotten Ravi.

She opened the packet and found a 'thank you' letter from Columbia College newspaper and the movie department. There was a photo of Ravi in the paper. Rita's story had won an award. Rita was beside herself with joy. She impulsively wanted to call Ravi but she saw the children sleeping and resisted the urge to do so. It was a beautiful picture and Ravi had written in glowing terms about Rita. Ravi's face again haunted her mind. She could hear the raindrops falling on the window pane. There was an inexplicable sensation in her body and mind. Her hand would automatically go to the phone but the sight of the children stopped her. Moments passed but neither Rita nor Ravi phoned. Still, she felt Ravi was around. He, in fact, was with her every moment.

The next moment she found herself alone. Then she became reflective. She did not know why life was such a puzzle. Bad memories clouded the present moments of happiness. Her destiny was very cruel. The next swing in the mood made her feel as if everybody around in a crowd was laughing at her with derision. They were making fun of her present state, her predicament. She heard a cry from her heart, "Oh God, lead me onto the right path or teach me how to love."

She had never been loved by anybody. She was a total stranger to love. She was so naïve and free from machinations that she would never hurt anybody. Then she thought of her parents who were in the process of finding a match for Rita's younger brother. She wanted to have a peep into their planning for his marriage. She would like to know what lay in their heart and what their dreams were. Her brother would have no idea what life had in store for him. He must have come into contact with a large number of girls.

Dr. Rai had not paid her a visit for months. But they were in contact by phone.

She composed a new poem and instead of sending it to Ravi, she mailed it to Dr. Rai. The poem was:

My lips tremble seeking his lips.
Life is ebbing away waiting for him.
The desire for love has rejuvenated my nights.
All the aspirations which were buried deep,
Have come up out of the shroud and grave in the sea.
With great effort, for centuries, long gone
I had burnt my hopes and dreams,
It has again raised its head and has burnt my being.
I wonder if it was just a mirage.
I don't know why life has been so kind to me.

Dr Rai published this poem as free style in his magazine. By and by Ravi also read the poem and he too had a strong urge to see Rita. If Rita was restless without him, he too greatly missed her despite the fact that he had never experienced any dearth of girls. But the feelings for Rita were unique.

No other girls had moved his heart the way Rita did. A storm was rising in his heart. There were two things happening simultaneously. One was rain outside as well as storming inside of his heart. As it was very late in the night, he prudently avoided going to Rita's apartment. Instead, he rang her up.

"Hello" She picked up the phone.

"Rita, please don't disconnect the phone," he pleaded humbly.

"What is the matter, Ravi, that you rang up at this time?"

"God be thanked that I have found you in a reconciliatory mood. I have read your new poem…"

"Dr. Rai didn't correct it. He published it in its original version," she said.

"There was no need to do that. It is excellent." After a few moments he said, "Rita, please, can you come to have dinner with me tomorrow evening? I have something urgent to discuss with you."

"Ravi, please forgive me… I cannot …"

"Rita, why do you want to delude yourself? This love is a double-edged sword. Apology is alien to the matters of love. It is a blessing. Listen; come here straight from work. We shall talk a lot…"

It had been raining for the last two day but Rita left the children with Sneh, who asked no questions. Rita also didn't tell her anything.

On the way she had no time to hear the raindrops pitter pattering on the glass panes of the car. she covered the hour-long journey in half an hour.

The rain was now pouring. She parked the car outside Ravi's apartment and got down but stood in the pouring rain. She was dressed in an open, long chiffon skirt topped by a pink silk blouse. Soon her dress was drenched. Then she moved and her feet virtually pulled her to his apartment. Her hands were cold. She knocked at the door. Ravi instantly opened it. He saw her and without any hesitation, took her in a tight embrace and lifted her up. "Do you know that in the Punjabi love story, Sohni had reached her lover Mahival after fording a river in the rain? My Sohni too has duplicated her act."

Rita's body heated up with the squeezing hold of his arms. Her lips opened and closed disobediently.

"Rita, I will do anything which you won't approve of. I will not disgrace you in the society, just trust me. "

Then he tried to hold her hand and kissed them. Rita's body became a living piece of elastic rubber with throbbing veins. Her body and mind were in unison and the body's urges dominated the mind. All of sudden She pushed him away, staggered to the nearby sofa and sat down weeping. Her heart swelled with indefinable regret for the act.

"I am sorry, Rita, please don't weep."

"Ravi, I am weak through and through. My destiny has wrecked me but you are strong, physically and mentally. While I fall victim to my weakness, at least you should not give in. Please don't do what both of us want to do. Both of us know that what we were about to do was wrong."

"Forgive me Rita, after seeing the beauty of your body in covered clothes, even angels would find it difficult to resist its charm and from doing what I wanted to do."

He came closer. He straightened her disheveled dress and her hair. He went to the fireplace and lit a fire to heat up the room. He put his fingers again in her hair and drew lines randomly patting or setting it. Soon the fire made Rita's face red, imparting it a unique glow. Her eyes still carried the intoxication. She was struggling to control herself. She said in a controlled voice, "Ravi I am hungry. But outside it is not only raining but hailstones are falling. How will we go to eat out?"

"Very simple. I shall shield you in my arms and, holding you against my heart, carry you to the car." He attempted a smile on his saddened lips.

"Oh! only if Sudhir had loved me, respected my liberal ideas, understood my aspirations, worshiped me…"

"Please forget the nightmares."

"How can I do that?"

"Look into my eyes. You will see a promise of a bright life. I want to live with you every moment of my conscious life. Our breath is so close to each other's. I want to play with your hair, doing and undoing them."

His endearing words again pulled Rita to the dream world. Her lips were half opened. But Rita's deep-rooted conscience again jerked her back to the bitter state of her existence. She said, "No, Ravi, no. I am the wife of someone and mother of two children. I can't do this."

"Do marriage and motherhood deprive one of the rights to love?"

"Yes. And in addition, this is a sin in the eyes of the Lord."

"Love is no sin. It is pure and sacred; it is worship. No restrictions are acceptable on love," Ravi urged in a husky voice.

"Ravi, I also hunger for food." She was back to her real world.

Ravi took out an umbrella. He held it on his side. Rita began to think of Sudhir. She would have loved to have Sudhir by her side in this situation. But Sudhir was always in a bad mood. He was edgy and angry. He always tended to nag. He would not let Rita relax nor would he himself relax. Rita had not had any boyfriend before marriage. It was not possible either. She couldn't step out of the four walls of her house without the permission of her parents. Here she was with a stranger, not at all related to her in any way. They quietly moved to the car side by side. Ravi made her sit in the car and occupied the driver's seat.

"Ravi, don't go so fast. It is raining, you know."

"But I am, in fact, driving slowly."

"Oh my God! The roads are flooded. How will I be able to go home?" She was almost weeping.

"Rita, why don't you stay with me overnight?" He braked the car in front of the restaurant.

"No, I have not informed Sneh and the children."

"What of that? Give your friend a ring so that you are staying the night with a girlfriend."

"Oh, I see. So, you have chosen to be a girlfriend from a boyfriend. This hunk is also afraid of society."

"Who says I am afraid?" He pinched her on the cheek.

They occupied seats in a Greek restaurant. In the restaurant, there was dancing with music. It would be slow now and fast a little later. Rita had never eaten in a Greek restaurant. While they both were eating Ravi will feed Rita in between. A Greek couple noticed this romantic display and the woman approached them and said, "Honeymoon?"

"Yes," Ravi said and smiled broadly.

"Very beautiful bride."

"Thank you. I am very lucky."

Rita blushed profusely. She looked angrily at Ravi and he burst out laughing.

"I swear to my mother, you look stunningly beautiful when angry. I would gladly feed on these big beautiful eyes rather than on the food on the platter."

"Why did you lie?"

"I and lie? impossible? Believe me, I never entertain ideas that are true and I don't encourage falsehood either."

"You have become an expert in dissembling and clever talk. I shall never see you after this meeting."

"Please, don't say this. I shall eat poison and commit suicide. Forgive me, my lady. As long as I don't have you as my bride, I shall make-do with your being a girlfriend."

"Don't trust houses made of sand. Times are very cruel. A gust of wind can demolish them in a moment."

"Agreed, but the few moments of love spent with you are going to stay with me forever. Whether I can ever own you or not is in your hands, but I shall never give up hope of meeting you in future too."

"But except prayer, I can give you nothing. These precious moments have taught me how to live again. I don't intend to exercise my mind about tomorrow. Hence, I pray to God to bestow happiness on you forever"

"From today you are my happiness and to keep you happy will be my entire endeavor and duty My dear Miss Rita."

"Ravi, why do you want to get so close to a simple Rita? How come all of sudden you called me Miss Rita?"

"When I address you informally, I love you as one loves kids but when I address you as Ms. Rita, I respect your ideas."

"Ravi, the world of my dreams has sunk deep into the sea. The boat of my life is caught up in the whirlpool of the complexities of life. You don't have any role in getting the boat of my life in untangling from this net."

Rita didn't wait for an answer. She went to the car and got in.

"I am a human being, Rita. Trust me and stop thinking about what is not necessary."

"My life is surrounded by darkness. How can I stop thinking about it?"

"Let me share your suffering and pain. I have strong shoulders and I can carry them along without ever getting tired." By now they had reached Ravi's apartment.

"It is eleven already and I won't go in now," Rita said.

"Don't, please, it is raining hard and I am burning with the fire of love. Please stay with me tonight."

"Please Ravi, let me go. Why play with old toys? I know my presence will soon bore you."

"Beauty can never tire me. I want your company every passing moment. I would like to make you up with my own hands; I would like to do and undo your silky hair. I want to send you to sleep with lullabies of love."

"Oh dear, you have become a poet too!" Rita said, and got into her car.

"Please don't go sonhiye (beautiful one)." Ravi came and stationed himself in front of the car to block her way.

"Do you intend to commit suicide?" Rita laughed at this move.

"Rita, you are good company. In your absence, I shall become sad. Your way of thinking, your excellent understanding, your quick grasp of the situation and unique interpreting skills impress me greatly. Your shining eyes with sudden inspiration haunt me. I wonder at these things. I constantly dream of you."

"My dear love, enjoy your dreams, but now let me leave." She laughed.

"Must you go?" he asked again.

"Yes, I must. Please don't insist on my staying any longer," she requested.

"Ok. But on one condition."

"Go ahead, I am listening."

Ravi approached her. He looked into her deep eyes, took her face in his hands and lightly kissed her. Rita also spread her arms, pulled him down to her and embraced him. She said thoughtfully, "I don't know what my life has led me to, but I promise that one day I shall fulfill your dreams." She pushed his head away from her gently and the car moved away.

CHAPTER 11

Rita had left Ravi in the heavy rain, staring at her disappearing car. She found the tug of war between the head and heart too tough to handle. Her forehead was throbbing with fatigue, sleep and exertion. She reached Sneh's apartment, used her duplicate key and entered as quietly as possible. She found Sneh and the children sleeping peacefully in their beds. There was a huge mirror in the children's room and she looked at herself in it. Everything about her was not as it should have been. Her hair was disheveled; her beautiful dress was a mess because of wetness and tugs and pulls a number of times. She noticed red lines in her eyes that looked swollen. The face had an unhealthy purplish hue.

She looked at Bhanu's innocent face and big eyes that made her look like an angel. Rita felt very sorry for this angel. The child had never experienced paternal love. Daily quarrels between the parents, scolding by the father, injustice heaped on her mother; tears and suffering had been her lot for years since she was old enough to understand the ways of the cruel world. Dhanush lay by her side. He had his thumb in his mouth even in sleep. As Rita could not spare sufficient time for him, Bhanu was the only company and support for the boy. He loved her very much.

Rita squeezed herself between the children and lay down to catch some sleep. She put one arm under Bhanu's head and the other under Dhanush's. She felt love swelling for the children and was proud and thankful to the Lord God that He had given her the little angels that to some extent made her life meaningful and livable as a mother.

Another aspect of her life, the life of a young beautiful woman, was still lonely and unsatisfied. The satisfaction of the maternal instinct was momentary. Gradually the womanly loneliness surrounded her.

But today, as a consequence of her meeting with Ravi, she saw a thin and flimsy and wavering beam of light in the all-pervading darkness. The thin beam of light pierced the darkness and reached her.

The darkness today was not as threatening as it usually was. Consoling herself with whatever it was worth, she dozed off. It was early morning when she woke up. She got ready to go to work hurriedly. She awakened the children, got them ready for school and left them at school and then went to work. She had hardly begun working when Ravi rang her up. She took the call and said, "Hello, Ravi, why have you called so early in the morning?"

"Darling, I haven't had any sleep as the moon face of my heart's queen did not let me have any. But now as I was on my way to the school library, I thought of seeking some relief for the aching heart by listening to the sweet musical notes of my darling's voice."

"I don't agree. I feel the situation is the other way round. It is the young beauties who would swoon on hearing your sweet voice. I think I am no exception," Rita said naughtily.

"But what matters the most for me is what my own beauty queen thinks about this slave as a whole, not his voice only."

"Well, I would need some time to think about this," she said again, with still a hint of naughtiness in her voice.

"Very well, mem sahiba (my dear madam), I shall ring you up at three in the afternoon."

"No, please, it is not proper to call when I am at work, our employers don't allow private calls during working hours."

"All right, then I shall call you in the evening."

"But then Sneh and the children will be with me."

"What am I to do then? Without talking to you, I won't be able to have rest during the day and any sleep at night."

"Oh, so the situation is really very serious. Well in that case I shall ring you up when I can manage."

"All right my nightingale, I shall wait for your warbling then," he said, and replaced the receiver.

Ravi had just given a short demonstration of love and it had added a glow to Rita 's face. Her attitude towards the children too had become loving. The children were surprised but were happy that their mother no longer scolded them as she usually did. Sneh also saw the change and the glow on her face, but said nothing. Now Rita rarely visited her friends and acquaintances. There was no need either. Her routine was confined to going to school, recording radio programs and work at the office and spending time with her children. When she was alone at home, she would talk to Ravi on the phone. If she still found time, she wrote something. Her gait was brisk and a smile always played on her face. She would randomly hum some tunes. She also would recall Ravi's jokes and smile to herself.

In the meantime, Sudhir somehow made acquaintance with Sneh. Sneh had never discussed Rita or her affairs with anyone. Rita also hadn't shared her matter of the divorce with Sneh yet Sudhir would visit her shop on one pretext or the other or would take the children with him to her shop to justify his visits. He was very solicitous to Sneh. He would gladly repair Sneh's car if it needed any or was ever ready to extend any help without her asking for it. His attitude puzzled her but she said nothing.

The schools were closed for vacation and the children were staying with Sudhir. Rita's affair with Ravi was quite infatuating and he phoned her almost daily to ask her to visit him but Rita put him off, making one excuse or the other. One day he found a good excuse to ensure that she couldn't say no. He told Rita that a producer wanted to see her in connection with her poem 'Lonely Tears'.

"Why is he interested in it?" Rita asked.

"Most probably he intends to make a movie."

"Ravi, try not to pull my leg occasionally."

"I am not doing that now. Tomorrow is Friday and there is a swimming party at his residence."

"I can't swim, you know. I shall only be able to dip my feet in the pool and nothing beyond that. Anyway, when is the party?"

"It is at six o'clock."

"But it is very cold in the evening and I am very sensitive to cold."

"The water will be warm darling… as long as I am around."

"Shut up. You are always up to some mischief. Ok, see you tomorrow then."

"Don't replace the phone yet."

"Why?"

"Give me a kiss with your lovely lips on the phone first."

"No…"

"Please…! Ok, I'll do it first. Now put your ripened cherry lips to the mouthpiece."

He kissed the mouthpiece of the phone on his side.

"Here it is then. I will return your kiss on the phone." Rita replaced the receiver.

The next evening Rita and Ravi reached the swimming pool. There were very few people there. Rita had taken it to be a private affair. She was puzzled and asked if it was his friend's house.

"Sorry, you had been putting me off for such a long time. This was the only alternative left with me. I was helpless. I sincerely apologize to my lady."

"I hate lies." Rita was genuinely offended.

"Forgive me, Rita. Ever since I have seen you, I have given up seeing all the other girlfriends. Look here, I have rented this pool for you." But Rita was annoyed. She had come to see him thinking about the movie. She didn't like this lie at all. She said, "Ravi you have made fun not only of me but also of my dreams and ambitions. You have exploited my credulous nature."

"Please Rita, don't take it so seriously. I am your slave. I apologize again." He took her in his arms. As if by magic, this move on his part made her anger vanish. He said passionately, "I love you, Rita, I love you."

"I love you too, not a lover but as friend" she blurted out.

Her self-control was giving way to her desire. But she did manage herself control over herself. She never forgets she is a mother first. She kept the calm.

"The humble man worshipped
But he discovered the real God.
Whereas his ardent love for a mortal one,

Twisted her into a fickle one."
He recited a couplet.

"This is not your own composition and not correct either," she said.

"I agree, but it fully applies to you."

"I am not faithless, Ravi, I am only helpless."

"Ok. Put this swimming suit on and I shall initiate you into swimming." He handed over a swimming suit to her.

"No no, I shall never put this on while you are looking. I feel shy."

"Ok, when you put it on, I shall turn my eyes away to the other side. Rita, why don't you liberate yourself a little in such things? It will make you happy. Go ahead and enjoy life. You are still young and beautiful, not yet beyond the age of enjoyment. Please put on this suit since some people came in that private area, please do use the lady's dressing room on your right side."

"Ok, mister. I will be back shortly"

Rita went to the women's dressing room and Ravi to the men. After about 15 minutes, when Rita emerged after putting on the swimming suit and Ravi, in his trunks, from his dressing room, he looked at Rita. He could not believe his eyes. She was in a dark blue color swimming suit which fitted her extremely well. It outlined every curve of her body. He looked at her face and gradually went down from her breasts to her slim waist. It was a perfect figure with a flat stomach, slim waist like a valley down two mountains. Then his eyes lingered on her hips. His eyes lingered at her breasts, waist and hips, perfect 38-34-38, the legendary hour glass figure. Her legs were full and slender, tapering till the toes and were white. He stared at this beauty incarnate and could not take his gaze off her. "But she has two children. How and where must she have carried them for nine months?" He tried to visualize her being pregnant. He felt deeply sorry for Sudhir who had not noticed this beauty and had beaten her. He must have been very stupid to do this.

Rita was also thoughtful. Ravi had chiseled male features; she noticed his muscular physique and a broad hairy chest. Was this fine specimen of manhood, a bachelor, really in love with her or was he just playing with her sentiments and helplessness? Ravi came closer. He was panting visibly, his chest rising and falling. Both had noted each other's attractive physique. Rita's lips trembled and her breathing became deep and fast. She had forgotten the pool and the swimming lesson that was to be given to her by Ravi. But Ravi came even closer and took Rita in his arms. He softly led her to the pool. He squeezed hand. Rita uttered 'ah' in a very low voice. Ravi looked at her naughtily. She knit her brows, pursed her upper lip and smiled, pretending to be angry. Ravi released the hold on of her hand. They were at the edge of the pool. Holding her firmly now and without any warning he pulled her into the pool. Both fell into the water with a splash.

Rita was afraid, but he supported her with his arms under the belly. She beat water randomly with her arms and legs. Little by little she gained confidence and felt her body getting lighter and floating. Ravi pulled his arms out from under her and told her to swim a little on her own, assuring her that he wouldn't let her drown. She had gulped a little water but spat it out forcefully. Rita forgot the presence of Ravi as her mind was occupied with her new found skill and kept swimming. In the meantime, Ravi watched her supple body.

He suddenly recalled Rita's past life. He imagined looking at her naked skin and Sudhir whipping her mercilessly as she screamed with pain. Instinctively he ran to her and rushed to save her. He put his arms and legs round her body as if to defend her from the whipping. Then he started kissing her wet body everywhere within the reach of his lips. She kept protesting but he didn't heed her protestations. Secretly she was enjoying every touch of his lips on her body. Though her body was in the water, her mind was surveying the world of her dreams. She felt the ghosts of her past, her dirty memories departing. Her body was surprisingly getting lighter. She felt free like a fish with no concern for Sudhir or the likes of him.

All of a sudden, she heard a frightening cry and she shuddered. It was her own. She felt she was drowning. But actually, she was going under the water when Ravi had pulled his hands away from under her. Now he again held her in his supporting arms. The swings of Rita's mood were always unexpected. She would be so pliable a minute ago but so remote the next. She was enjoying every touch of Ravi's body but now suddenly felt that it was too much. She said, "Cut it out, Ravi. I don't like that you keep playing with my body like this."

"What do you mean? Do you know that you were drowning?" He was really serious now.

Her face lost its glow suddenly and she said, "You should have let me drown. Why did you save me? What do I have to live for, after all, in my life? Sudhir will bring up the children and take care of the interests of his sisters-in-laws. As far as you are concerned, you shall find thousands of younger girls more beautiful than me and they would gladly marry you."

"Agreed, Sudhir will bring up the children as he was brought up without a mother. He will take care of his sisters-in-laws also as they had looked after him. As for me, will you believe me that since I have known you, I haven't even rung up a single girl and seeing any is out of the question?"

"Ravi, I am badly confused. I am a married woman and have two children. Do you think it is proper for me to maintain liaison with other men?"

"Rita, I feel exhausted explaining to you that married women too have every right to fall in love. They are not heartless, emotionless and insensitive like a stone. Before you mothered the two children, did Sudhir ask you whether you wanted to be a mother or not? But here you are caught up in this dilemma of right and wrong. You are killing yourself. You will go mad thinking about this self-created problem."

"A woman who has relations of this type with men other than her husband, is branded as a characterless one. I ask you, will my children not be called offspring of a characterless woman? My children are not burdened on me. I am glad they were born to make me happy"

"Why do you call yourself a characterless woman? You haven't sinned in any way. It is your husband who is behind your present plight. Furthermore, we are together as we both need each other. You know that whenever you are with me, my body craves to merge in your body. But the irony is that with both of us as willing partners in the love game, you have not shown the consideration of even showing me your clothes-less body."

"Ravi, the world spares none. I am afraid of this world and society. They are a greater force than a poor unfortunate woman. If

I don't keep myself away from you, there will be rampant gossip at my cost."

"Nobody has been able to defend himself from the gossip mongering by society. But in my eyes, you are a pure and innocent woman. If you chain anyone against his will, is he not a prisoner?"

"Yes, you are right and as long as he is in chains, he is a prisoner. I am blessed with two children. I do not deny this but at the same time I do not want to shirk the responsibility of bringing them up. This is a chain that I would willingly wear round my feet."

"I fail to understand this line of your thinking. Why do you forget that your children were born in America, not in India?"

"But I am determined to bring them up according to Indian culture. It is only Indian culture and character that strengthen one's personality."

"I disagree with you. Man is stone hearted by birth and he does his best to make others live with the same sort of heart."

"In the cruel, insensitive world, if an Indian woman was also stone hearted, then only she would be able to deal with the cruelty of man, a faithless husband and a lover. Men have their own world and its rules. As such, if I am destined to defend myself against such men, I shall gladly do that."

"Rita, if you are determined to fight such men, why don't you divorce Sudhir? You should have no worries. I will marry you the day you divorce."

"Divorce? I am afraid of the very sound of this word. I don't find myself strong enough to put up with the idea of divorce." The suggestion had frightened her and she started shedding tears.

"Rita, please don't keep your tears so handy. I can't see you weeping. I feel my heart going out to you." He held her against his heart.

Gradually Rita and Ravi's closeness progressed. Rita was a woman. A woman's heart is deep and vast like the sea. It hides in its depth rocks, poisonous creatures, beautiful flowers and what not. But the ocean never knows what is good or bad in its store. However, Rita was not taken in by Ravi's slick tongue.

The thing that most touched her was that a cordless kite, that was destined to be destroyed, was considered by someone worthy of interest. She clung to this person. True, she could not surrender her body to Ravi, yet she felt that someone had removed the shroud of the corpse of her dead soul and a dead seed had sprouted again. Spring had again visited this dried up garden in the coldest of winter of her life. It had stirred the dead desire for love and trust. These musings prompted Rita to continue visiting Ravi frequently. But Physically She never gave in.

Ravi made short documentaries these days. Rita wrote stories for them. She also assisted him in photography. Rita could not act, but she wrote a forty-minute-long story entitled 'Divorce: A Call for Death'. She tried a bit of acting with the help of Ravi. She acted in this movie with Ravi, Bhanu and Dhanush. The movie was a hit among the Indian community. But this appreciation did not come alone.

Bouquets are always accompanied by brickbats. Gossip was rife about Rita's relations with Ravi. Sudhir also heard this and he couldn't be a silent spectator to it. He decided to see Sneh and threw her an olive branch to Rita. Hitherto he had had the impression that with two children, nobody would come forward to marry Rita and after rejections she would come back to him. It had never occurred to him that if an injured person is thrown out onto the road, someone will take him to a doctor. Similarly, if a woman was throned out of her home, someone would take her to his home.

One day Ravi phoned and nervousness was betrayed in his tone.

"Rita, I am scared," he said.

"What is the matter? What has happened?" she said sympathetically.

"Rita, if one has no money, nobody likes to have anything to do with him."

"It is no news to me and not a discovery by you either. All know this. Why are you so philosophic today? You have always teased me on this account. Perhaps the company has finally had its impact," she said mockingly.

"My mother used to teach me not to undertake any venture about which you have no knowledge and experience and which ensures you no profit…"

"But if you don't do anything new, how can you learn and gain experience in life? You learn everything by actually doing it," Rita said didactically.

"You know, Rita, I showed your 'Divorce: A Call for Death' to an Indian doctor. He liked it very much."

"Then what..?"

"He suggested that I should make a full three-hour movie on it and he will invest in it. Hence, I have contacted a few filmmakers in India."

"Are you serious?" Rita asked eagerly.

"Rita, I have a strong desire to turn your story into a film."

"It will bore the viewers, I am sure," Rita observed.

"It is out of the question. When the viewers see you bedecked as a bride, shyly hiding your face with modesty, carried in a palanquin, carried by the pallbearers, a million young hearts would imagine a beautiful wife like you."

"But the happiness episode in the story is very brief. When the people watch the oceans of tears that follow, what will they think?"

"Yes, Rita, I shudder to think how Sudhir pricked your flowery body with thousands of thorns. You faced autumn much before the time of the departure time of spring."

"It was destined to happen. I fail to understand with what pen the Lord God above wrote my fate. He cheated me on my sacred marriage vows and wiped out my sindoor (vermillion on the brow of the bride as a mark of her being married)." Rita began to sob loudly on the phone.

"But Rita, I suggest, you should make up your mind to rewrite your fate. I want your life to be put back onto the right track. You can help me with this."

"What help do you want?"

"The fact is that when the doctor promised to invest in the film, I contacted some film makers in India. But the doctor went back on his promise and if I go now, I shall need money for my return ticket, stay in a hotel and other miscellaneous expenses. I have no relatives in India. Hence I can't afford the trip."

"I find nothing new in it. When the time comes, even our blood relations go back on their promise. I think when you also become a famous director, you will forget me, the humble homely writer."

"You are mistaken in thinking this, Rita. I would like to make you an internationally recognized queen if only I had money."

"Sudhir also said such things immediately after our marriage."

"But I will fulfill my promise. Trust me Rita, I can never forget you. Please never ever misunderstand me."

"To give assurances in these circumstances is the way of the world. But when they get famous, they don't look back to recognize you." Obviously in her naivety of the work-a-day world, she could not see-through Ravi's game.

"Oh Lord, what do I hear? How can you think this about me, Rita?"

"Ok. Cut out this morning. What do you intend to do now?"

"I don't know what to do. I am in a situation in which I can think of neither going ahead nor retracing my steps."

"I also find myself in the same situation and can think of nothing even if I try hard to think of a way out," Rita said seriously.

"But I have nobody except you, Rita. You alone know my artistic talents and you alone can help me."

"I…, how can I help you?" she asked, puzzled.

"Rita, Dr. Rai can help you."

"What can he do?" Rita asked nervously.

"He appreciates your art. I suggest you talk to him in this regard; I promise to return the money on my return from India."

"All right. I shall talk to him. If he can't lend the money, I shall give you my gold bangles. You can arrange money by selling them."

"No no, I don't want jewelry. It has many sentimental associations linked with it."

"But this is the only alternative at the eleventh hour and you know I will do anything for you."

Rita replaced the receiver but became thoughtful. She had made a commitment but she did not know how she could arrange the money. She would have taken a divorce long ago if she had money to pay the fees of an attorney. She tried to ask a few contacts to lend her the amount needed by Ravi but all in vain. In such a mental state and a ticklish situation, she impulsively phoned Dr. Rai.

"Hello Dr. Rai, are you happy with my radio program?"

"Of course, I am. If I hadn't liked it, I would have long ago taken it off the air. But I see that you are making a long-distance call from Los Angles, Is everything fine?"

"Dr. Rai, I need your help."

"What sort of help? Are your children fine? Has Sudhir bothered you in any way?"

"Yes, everything is fine. But …I would like to borrow some money."

"Has Sudhir divorced you?"

"No, not yet but a good friend of mine has asked for a loan from me."

"What type of friend is he? He very well knows that you are alone and have to bring up two growing children somehow and instead of helping you, he wants money from you."

The remarks of Dr. Rai made her think. He was right, as a friend would have never asked for money from her. She felt disappointed at Ravi's behavior. But concealing this feeling, she said, a bit offended. "Never mind. If you cannot help me, it is ok."

"Rita, don't take me wrong. I can lend you money for you or the children. But I feel you want to borrow money for Ravi."

"Dr. Rai…!" she said, a little worried.

"Look here, Rita, don't be so defensive. I know Ravi through and through. He is playing with your sentiments and is exploiting your gullibility."

"Look here, Dr. Rai, I am not a young teenager who cannot discriminate between right or wrong. I don't like interference in my private affairs. Forgive me. I shouldn't have phoned you." She banged the receiver on the cradle.

Rita felt immensely offended by this behavior of Dr. Rai. She regretted that Ravi had put her in such an ugly predicament. "I fail to understand him. He very well knows how financially poor I am but he still asks for money from me." Rita compared herself to a tired and wounded roe that had got caught up in a thorny bush. She constantly worried about how to help Ravi. Finally, she went to one of her longtime friends Ginny and told her about her commitment to help Ravi.

"What promise are you talking about? I have also heard this. Is it true?"

"What have you heard?"

"Just this, that you and Ravi…"

"People enjoy gossiping. He is not only my friend, but also appreciates my artistic talents. He wants to promote my talents and is going to India to enhance them."

"Why to India?"

"He is going to arrange funds for making a movie on my story 'Call for Divorce."

"And.?"

"He needs two thousand dollars. I shall give him my gold bangles; he will arrange the money by selling them."

"You will give your bangles to him! Are you out of your mind? The bastard is showing you dreams to rob you of the little security you have."

"Ginny, I have committed to help him. I shall give him the bangles and if he doesn't return them, I shall think that I lost for fake love and friendship."

Ginny did her best to persuade Rita not to give her bangles, but Rita had resolved to follow her will. Her bangles were with Sudha. She collected them from her and came home.

Strange are the ways of the world. The natural craving and biological need for love cast such a spell on everybody, irrespective of age and sex, that they get ready to sacrifice everything to have it. Rita had not experienced romance, dating and real love. Her husband had turned love into a mockery. For him love making was a mechanical act of satisfying his testosterone driven urge for sex caused at the cost of Rita's Body. She would surrender her body to him whenever he showed his desire for the act any time whether night or day. But Ravi, though poor, had given her a feel of romance so much so that she got ready to sacrifice everything for his interest. Bravo the world, bravo nature, you show multicolored dreams to the people to beguile them. A love hungry person turns into a mere puppet. Man was created to do something worthy of humanity and to reform his future, but his desires and lust misled him. It never occurred to him that if he loved God and brought peace and happiness in life, it could change the world for the better.

The following day Rita phoned Ravi and informed him that she had not been able to arrange the money for him but was ready to give him her bangles. He was to collect them from her the following afternoon. Rita's naivety was at its zenith. She had managed to acquire those pieces of jewelry by saving pennies from her meager earnings. She loved them so much. Whenever she asked Sudhir for any new jewelry, he would scoff at her, "What rubbish! Have you ever looked at your image in the mirror? Your ugly face doesn't deserve even brass ornaments, what to speak of golden ones. If you want gold jewelry, tell your father who will send them to you." Rita was lost in these musings when Dhanush came weeping to her. Rita rushed towards him and taking him into her arms asked the reason for his weeping.

"Mama, today when we accompanied Daddy to my elder uncle's house, Daddy beat me."

"Why...?"

"I was hungry. So, I took an apple from the dining table and the elder aunty said something in Punjabi to Daddy."

"What did she say? Dhanush exerted your mind and recalled exactly what she had said."

"She sounded to say 'To hell with this woman. Like mother, like her offspring.'"

"Then…?"

"Then Daddy slapped me in anger."

Rita held Dhanush to her bosom, kissed his angelic eyes and led him to Rama's picture. She said, "Oh ! Lord), please protect my children from all evil. Let no grief befall them. If at all there are sufferings to come, let them fall to my lot not them. Let my flowers never wither." Her eyes became tearful. She was still weeping when Bhanu returned from school and, seeing her home, she asked, "Mom, didn't you go to work today?"

"No, my child. I didn't. It was a holiday today. How did your school go, darling?"

"Mama, do you know what my friend Rena was saying?"

"No, my child. What did she say?"

"Renu was saying that her mother had told her that she would bring an Indian husband for her when she grew up. She had also said that Indian girls don't have boyfriends. Why is that so, Mama?"

"My child, you are very young for such things. At your age it is wrong to think about boyfriends. God will be angry."

"But Mama, why doesn't God get angry with American girls? He gets angry with us because we are born of Indian parents?"

Rita burst out in laughter when she heard Bhanu's innocent logic. She embraced her sweet, the most gorgeous child Bhanu. She cried deep down in her heart when she used to take her anger out on Bhanu. How cruel a mother she could be! How could she have taken Sudhir's abuse on her innocent child Bhanu?

"Yes darling. God has his own rules for such things."

She made sandwiches for the children and made them to eat. All of them then watched TV for some time. Then Rita took out a Hindi alphabet book and started to teach them Hindi.

When a human is broken by the ups and downs of life, he finds sleep evading him. Even when he can manage to go to sleep, real sleep still doesn't oblige him. This was the condition Rita was in. Finally, when it did come, she had nightmares haunting her. She saw herself standing near a mountain with the children, holding them by the finger. She found it difficult to climb up. The next moment Dhanush and Bhanu were no longer around. She was shouting and looking for them. She ran about in different directions weeping and calling them by their names. Then she was awakened. Dhanush and Bhanu were sleeping on both sides and she was relieved to see them. She thanked God.

When you are disowned by your people, you establish links with the outside world. Rita had forgotten whose daughter, whose sister and whose wife she was. But what she knew was that she was the mother of Dhanush and Bhanu and they slept peacefully on both sides. The two flowers were enough excuses for her to keep alive. She prayed fervently, "Oh Lord, take away everything from me but please leave my children with me." She had been shedding tears for such a long time that her past memories had been washed away. Her own people had abandoned her and killed the hope of life. Now she sought to heal the wounds by going for support to strangers. Not only this, she had decided to help a stranger.

The following day she again took leave from work. The children went to school and Sneh to her shop. Left alone, she waited for Ravi. This loneliness in the apartment was unbearable and frightening to her today. She saw many frightening scenes threatening her. Then it occurred to her that she would muster the courage to say no to Ravi and refuse to give the bangles to him. Consequently, even if he discontinued seeing her, she wouldn't mind. After all, who was he to expect so much from her? His was hardly a give and take relationship. She had a nagging feeling that her exploitation had begun. She rang his place up a couple of times but he was not at home. It was something very disturbing and beyond her comprehension.

She had long ago given up the desire to live a good life. She tended to begin weeping about minor things. It was a peculiar situation. Someone had supported her from going down the hill but was asking for a fee. She would have done better by living a life of loneliness. The winds of suffering had torn her nest into bits and blown away the straws. She struggled to collect them again but they were again blown away by the whimsical winds of circumstances.

She was lost in this deliberation when she was startled by the doorbell. She felt her heart skip a beat and the last bit of strength drained away from her body. She had no inclination to go to open the door. Whoever was there would leave. But she could not do even this. Finally she got up to open the door. Ravi was standing with a rose bouquet in his hand. He was smiling broadly. His smile and the roses sent a rejuvenating wave of life through Rita's body. She felt so light that a gust of wind could waft her away like a feather. Her face was competing with the roses in his hands. She was beside herself with joy. Never before had anybody brought beautiful flowers for her as he had done. Ravi held her face with the fingers of his free hand and raised it to face him and said, "These eyes, cups full of red wine, will make me lose my sense of discrimination between right and wrong."

"How is that?"

"These rosy cheeks, the scattered uncombed hair; believe me, I am already out of my senses."

"You needn't fear. I shall assure that you don't face any such eventuality," Rita said, taking the flowers from him.

"But the eventuality has already taken place but you are miles away from me. How long shall I have to wait? Please come closer; I mean into my arms." He invited her in his arms spread wide.

"If that is my fate, I shall always be far away, out of your reach."

"I shall cancel this distance in a minute, in one go."

"No, no." Rita stepped back quickly.

"Who are you afraid of? Who are you going away from?"

"From you…"

"No, not from me. You are running away from yourself. Rita, please let the strong and legitimate but suppressed desires find an outlet. Be bold and learn to live."

"There are hurdles in my way of life. Every one of my passing breaths is burdened with social do's and don'ts; with taboos, customs and traditions."

"Break away these shackles and tell Ravi that you still want to live."

"No, I cannot say this. Not in this situation. I am alone and a vulnerable woman."

"You are no longer alone now. You are my love and I am your love. I am with you." Ravi abruptly pulled her to him and held her in a tight embrace. It was enough to put Rita's body on fire again. The wall of social inhibitions and taboos had collapsed and she wanted to burn him again with the fire she was herself burning with. She was not sure whether these moments would revisit her in life or not but she would like to perpetuate them forever and add to the history of her life a new significant page. She would ensure that Ravi would not be claimed by any other woman in future. But the old cry of revolt of conscience frightened her and all of a sudden, she detached herself from him.

"Rita, please don't do this. Today I won't allow you to be so inaccessible to me."

"Ravi…Ravi…" Her lips were quivering.

"Please just test me. You should know how my body; my soul loves you."

"Is it true Ravi? Are you serious?" she asked him nervously.

"You may plead with me in the way you like, but today I won't …"

"Please, Ravi, let us maintain an appropriate distance between us.…"

"No…today I am resolved to quench your physical hunger and mine. I have lost my sense of right and wrong."

"Oh, so you claim to be bold enough to be wicked?" She looked at him from the corners of her eyes in an enticing way as a challenge.

"Please don't challenge me," he said with folded hands.

Rita moved back, inviting him in. They moved in and sat down to eat. They joked with abandon. Rita had cleaned and arranged the furniture in a tasteful way. She had placed the old sofa she had acquired from Gauri at its right place and the dining table at an appropriate place and sprayed rose perfume in the room. The potato prathas (fried Indian chapattis made from wheat flour) Ravi was eating greedily. He said, "Who has cooked these prathas, my love?" Naturally he was trying to flatter her.

"Rita's ghost, of course," she said, smiling.

"What? Does your ghost live with you?"

"Yes, he protects me from the faithless flirts - ones like you."

"A faithless flirt?" Ravi was a little nervous.

"Oh no, you react as if you were really a…"

"Look here, Rita, never ever take me as faithless." He looked offended.

"You get offended so easily when I take a little liberty with you, but you always keep teasing me."

"But I say, this teasing adds flavor to life. Why don't you enjoy these small things in life?"

Rita busied herself in cleaning pots and pans in the kitchen and Ravi lent her a hand. Rita behaved as if he was her husband and she was his wife. After the cleaning when Rita was wiping her hands dry, Ravi snatched the towel away from her hand and said, "Come on, let me dry these delicate hands with my heart's warmth."

Ravi put her hands on his hairy chest. It maddened her and she started playing with the hairs with her fingers. She felt as if she had known him for many lives. She had completely forgotten her bad times and destiny. Sudhir too was out of her mind. She strongly desired that the two beating hearts should become one.

The desire inflamed her heart and the body. She did not know whether it was love or lust. Then it occurred to her as if she were a female snake dancing to the tune of Ravi, the snake charmer's flute. He was enchanting her with the music of the flute. Ravi too was caught in his desire.

Rita was dressed in a peach-colored sleeveless blouse with dark brown trousers. She wore her hair in a ponytail. This elaborate preparation had cut down years from her age. She was a teenager out to make a kill. This simple dress added to her beauty and charm. This wax doll would like to melt and merge into the male body and finish its identity. Ravi's body heat or her own, she didn't know which was burning her. She started kissing his chest. It was too much for Ravi. He, too, in obedience to her desire, exposed his hairy chest to the full and let Rita kiss it; play with it and do whatever pleased her. He loosened her hair and explored its mysteries with his fingers and kissed it. He looked into her big deep eyes and said, "You are an embodiment of female beauty. You are vintage wine that one may go on drinking without ever feeling satiation."

"I find myself helpless against this storm that is unsettling me from my feet. Please go away"

"Forget the storm, darling. Lose yourself into my arms." He held her in his arms and lifted her up as if she were a child. Rita was conscious of the sweet poison which must be sipped to feel relief from the fire of lust that pervaded every pore of her body. Today she was a volcano that was ready to erupt to burn Ravi. She was beyond the mundane considerations whether it was true love or mere physical lust. She was like a drunkard that went on licking the bottle with no quenching of his thirst. But when the fire was the hottest and love was to culminate in heavenly bliss, the doorbell rang. Both were startled. Rita wondered who it could be as nobody knew whether she was at home or not. Ravi stared at Rita for a brief moment and then rushed and hid himself in the bathroom. Rita opened the door and found Ginny there. She asked, surprised, "How do you happen to be here, Ginny?"

"I saw Ravi coming to your house. I wanted to speak to him. Where is he?"

Rita's face lost color but somehow, she managed to ask, "Did you have anything urgent to say to him?"

"Yes. I wanted him to bring something for me from India. Why is he hiding? Ask him to come out of hiding. There is no need to be afraid of me." Ravi came out in the meantime. He tried an embarrassed smile to show Ginny that he was hiding just for fun. They sat down and talked randomly about insignificant things. Ravi was still embarrassed. After about half an hour Ginny left but this untimely visit had cooled down the fires Rita and he were burning with. Rita took off her bangles and handed them over to Ravi, and said, "Look here, Ravi, I acquired these bangles after grueling hard work and I ..."

"Rita, you have a very large heart. I am convinced of your sincerity. Believe me, if I succeed in my venture, I shall lavish you with riches. Gold and gems will be nothing in comparison to what I would do for you."

"I don't want your gold or gems. Sudhir had also promised them."

"But I am not Sudhir. I am conscious of a woman's wishes. I respect her aspirations."

"Ravi, it is time for the children to return from school."

It was a cue enough for him to leave. "I have no mind to leave you alone, but I shall make this incomplete meeting meaningful in some leisure moments. I shall never let you feel helpless and lonely."

They held each other's hands and began climbing down the steps. Rita slipped her foot and would have fallen if Ravi had not supported her. He said, "Don't keep falling. If I fail in my plan, who will look after you?"

"I slip only when you are with me. I feel drunk without drinking in your company. If ever I took a peg of wine in your company, I assure you to take you down with me."

"I am already down on the ground," Ravi said, getting into the car. Rita became silent. Ravi felt that she was about to start weeping. Although his car had moved, yet when he saw her sad face, he turned round and brought the car close to her. He stared at her fixedly. But Rita kept quiet. He couldn't fathom the depth of her heart and try as hard as he might, he could not know why she was unusually sad that day.

Rita was not perturbed for parting with her bangles. Sudhir didn't exist for her although now and then, when she thought of him and recalled that when he held her in his arms, she would forget herself. But the heaven she had experienced in Ravi's arms was rare and she felt that Sudhir stood no comparison to Ravi.

Sudhir was a weak husband who only beat her. She also had a sort of strange feeling as if it was Rita not Sudhir that was a man. He had abused her and tortured her in numerous ways but she had borne all and tolerated everything, consoling herself with the idea that he was after all her husband. With Ravi, it was different as she was a willing partner in their artificial love game and they had never had any arguments. She would cling to Ravi like a doll and forget the beatings received from Sudhir who now seemed to belong to the past. But what bothered her when she was alone was why she was attracted to a man who was nothing to her. She had no claim to his hand or his heart, soul and body.

"Rita, what is the matter, my darling? Why are you so sad, my soul? If you don't want me to go, I shall cancel my visit to India for your sake."

"Oh no sir, I would be the last to insist on such a move. Why should you put your future in danger? Go ahead and make a good career." Rita pushed him into the car again.

"My future and career is centered on you,". Then he called her loudly "Rita, please come here for a minute. Listen to me."

"What is it now?" she said, coming closer. He implanted kiss after kiss on her lips. Rita again found herself struggling to control herself from falling into his arms. The door of the car opened and she fell into his lap. "One day when you return from India, satisfy the fire that is roasting me alive. I...I..."

"I too shall wait for that day. I love you, Rita; I love you."

"I love you too Ravi, I love you." Rita just said without any reason..

"Rita, I love not only your beautiful body but also your beautiful heart, soul and dreams. Just wait for me."

"I shall wait for you," Rita said very romantically.

The time to bid adieu came. The car came in motion and as it was going away, Ravi kept throwing flying kisses to Rita. She watched the car till it disappeared from sight.

CHAPTER 12

Ravi droves away but Rita didn't move an inch. She kept looking at the now deserted road with unseeing eyes. She wondered whether it was a reality or a dream that had departed leaving her alone. At the most it could have been a long dream, or a mere hallucination. She was seeing dreams that were never likely to be hers. A sweet pain in her heart was the only tangible proof of the time spent with Ravi. If it had been a dream, she would have tried to reconstruct it to find consolation in it but it was a reality that was no longer available to her. Occasionally the bright light of reality dazzled her and she blurred it a bit by closing her eyes for a while and would welcome darkness that was her fate lest she should forget it. After a long time, she returned home with a heavy heart.

Ravi had left but the case against Sudhir for wife beating was still in the court. The date of the next appearance in the court was approaching. On such occasions she needed male support and nobody could have been better than Ravi. But he was gone. She felt lonely. In order to keep her mind busy, she routinely taught classes to small kids to teach them acting, creative writing and directing.

One morning when she had left the children at school and was getting ready to go to work, the phone rang. She answered it.

"Hello, Rita speaking."

"Mrs. Rita?" An unknown voice was heard from the other end.

"Who is this please?"

"This is Roger Davis."

"What can I do for you, sir?"

"I am your husband's attorney. I would like to settle a felony case of felony."

"Mr. Davis, don't worry. I do not want to do anything to harm my husband."

"Good. But you have to come to court and release him from the case."

"When?"

"Tomorrow."

"Well then, I will be there." Rita replaced the receiver.

Every one of her well-wishers that heard this development tried their best to persuade her not to withdraw the case against Sudhir but to have him sent to jail but, though Rita had filed the case in the heat of argument, she had no intention to punish her husband now. She was ready to forget that he had disowned her as his wife and had always persecuted her and the children.

In spite of all this, she didn't want to harm him. The conduct of Sudhir in day-to-day life and the regular beating of Rita by him had ruptured the sacred relation of husband and wife and created a wall of hatred between them. Whenever she recalled the violence against her by Sudhir, the pain was rendered fresh and a cry of anguish rose from her heart that suffered quietly. Everything would go dark before her eyes.

She reached the court with a mind to withdraw the case against him but when she saw Sudhir with his lawyer, the fire of taking revenge on him again flared up. She approached his lawyer and said, "Mr. Davis, I would like to have another date. I have changed my mind. Now I would like to teach my husband a lesson."

"Why, Mrs. Rita? He is very sorry and will never hurt you in future."

"For your information, I want to tell you that he has been sorry umpteen times, assuring me but he never kept his promises since we were married. "Believe me, this time he means this, especially for the sake of your children."

"I don't trust him. He is a very cruel man."

"Believe me, your long separation has taught him a good lesson. Give him one more chance."

Sudhir's lawyer put so much pressure on her that she finally relented. Strange is the female heart that it can be persuaded so easily. The lawyer had pleaded with her so convincingly that she gave in to his persistence. She again started thinking that Sudhir had never known a woman's love. He had lost his mother in early childhood. His sisters-in-law had succumbed to his daily demands for one thing or the other but had later taken revenge for them one by one. The middle-sister-in-law Kanta Rani was hell bent on destroying his family life. God alone knew for what wrong doings by Sudhir she was trying to avenge herself on him. Rita again saw his helpless face in her imagination. He was forty years old with childish habits.

She recalled how, like an insecure child, he would cling to her. One night he had related how he had had no love in life and that his sisters-in-laws were vamps. Out of emotion, Rita had assured him that she would compensate him for the love of a woman that he had missed all along. After all, a woman is a mother, sister, daughter and wife. Rita had assured him to make up for the lack of female love in his life. The ignorant, inexperienced girl Rita busied herself in the role of a grown-up woman to give maternal love to the husband who was much older than her and had always taken her for an immature girl. But she forgot her age in the new role. She pitied him like a mother. She suffered his pain. This reflection on the past again played a trick on her and she said, "Ok Mr. Davis, I shall drop the case."

The words were hardly out of her mouth when Mr. Roger at once made her sign the papers. As soon as she signed the papers, both Sudhir and his attorney changed the tune. Gone was the politeness. They left her at once. But Rita waited foolishly, expecting that she might have to sign more papers. She had never before faced such a situation. Sudhir and his attorney never took another look at her. When she could not wait any longer and was exhausted, she returned home, regretting what she had done.

It was hard to control her tears. Ravi, who could have been the only sympathizer, was in India. She was utterly lonely. Since her marriage, she had never known a life in which husband and wife share the ups and downs of life. She recalled her mother's words. She would say, "Oh God, let there be quarrels and periods of absence of communication between the husband and the wife, but never separation."

Rita's mother was a simple village woman and her love had made her married life successful. On the contrary, modern education has made family life a tough task. In the past a woman's simplicity and her orthodoxy had made her worship the husband and tolerate all cruelty. She had learnt to compromise her own welfare for the happiness of her husband. But education inculcated a sense of self respect that a man could not tolerate.

Absorbed in these philosophical considerations, Rita unconsciously stopped her car in front of Ginny's apartment. She must have had a strong desire to share her experience with someone close to her. Ginny welcomed her and Rita sat down to narrate what had happened at the court. As soon as she started to tell her, Sudhir also turned up there. Rita got up to leave, but Ginny held her back and said to Sudhir, "Sudhir, now you have seen how generous a woman can be. You persecuted her in numerous ways and were cruel to her. Still, she has forgiven you and taken the case back in order to save you from jail. I suggest that now you make a move. Persuade her to come back. After all, she is the mother of your children."

"Yes, I agree she has been generous but I shall never live with her. Nobody will marry her. She is just a second-hand woman with two children..."

It was a disgusting response. Ginny could not bear it. She shouted, "Sudhir...!"

"I am sure to find a girl. In fact, my brothers and sisters-in-law have already found a girl for me. She is a teacher. I am going to get married and I shall again have a golden night with her. The divorce case with Rita will be finalized in about six months. I shall visit India and get married to the girl."

Ginny could not help saying, "Oh, so your relations have succeeded in making you a show piece and a laughing stock forever."

"Look here, she has herself ruined her life. She could not keep her husband happy. She is responsible for her present plight."

"Would you tell us how a woman can keep her husband happy? Your illiterate sisters-in-laws have, with difficulty, learnt how to dress in a western way and make a little conversation in English. What they do is just offer as much sex physically or verbally as they can to please their hubbies. Do you call it keeping one's husband happy?"

"Rita never got up early to prepare even breakfast," Sudhir complained.

"You sing praises of your middle sister-in-law but if making breakfast for the husband is the criterion for being a good wife, does your sister-in-law make breakfast for her husband in the morning?"

"But she is not my wife," he retorted.

"Listen Sudhir, I am just a neighbor and stand nowhere as compared to your middle sister-in-law Kanta Rani. But still, you always describe her ugliness as beauty. She is beautiful neither in body nor in mind," Ginny said frankly.

"Leave it Ginny. I have nothing to do with his sisters-in-laws. Whatever was destined to happen has happened," Rita said tearfully.

"What has happened is just the beginning. Just wait for what lies in store for you. You will learn a lot when your children grow up, get spoiled and beat you with shoes."

"What sort of father are you that think so ill of the future of your own children?" Ginny said again.

"I am not making any predictions. You will see how she starves. She will beg on the streets and if she comes begging from me, I won't give her a single penny."

Rita could bear no more. With tears in her eyes, she returned to her apartment. She pondered why men could marry a number of times without inviting criticism whereas it was a sin for a woman even to look at someone other than her husband. Rita recalled an old wives' tale 'If a woman remained within the four walls of the house, rats would nibble her away and if she moved out, decent people would taunt her.'

Some Indian men, but not all, exploited the wisdom propagated in this cliché. Rita went to relax on her bed but hardly had she stretched out when Ginny rang her up again. "Rita, can you come back for a few minutes?"

"Not at all, Ginny. I have had enough humiliation at Sudhir's hands."

"Listen, Sudhir would like to talk to you politely. I have given him a piece of my mind."

"No, I don't want to talk to him. The arrows of his taunts and foul language have pierced my heart. Besides taunting me, what has any member of his family given me, anyway?"

"Spit out the anger now and…"

"Ginny, even though I was born in a poor family, I had food, clothes and a roof over my head. My parents had never beaten and thrown me out of their house as this husband has done. He is so inconsiderate that he curses me and his own blood to live in misery. Does he deserve to be called a father?"

"What a simpleton you are! If you don't listen to me now, he will use your refusal against you before his relatives. Why do you want to let him have this advantage?"

When pressed by Ginny a number of times, Rita went to her place. On the way she thought of her past with her husband. Sudhir had always had a strange, unpredictable nature of blowing hot and cold in the same breath. He would pick a quarrel for nothing and a little later he would express his love for her.

On the one hand he would talk of resolving differences but on the other hand he would taunt her. He teased her about her inefficiency almost in everything she did and would make her weep. Rita's patience had been exhausted. Hence, after she was seated, she said, "See, Ginny you can never milk a dry cow. He is an absolutely incorrigible man. He can't change and will never be reformed."

"Go to, woman! You think of yourself as being a great reformer, an embodiment of virtue. Have you ever looked at yourself in the mirror?" he taunted her at once.

"Ginny, so this was why you had called me here? He can never change his habit of finding fault and nagging. He is a slave of his nature."

"You had better go to change the habits of that bastard, your father, and your cousin who stays with her parents after leaving her in-laws."

"Shut up Sudhir," Gauri retorted angrily.

"Ginny, I have grown accustomed to hearing taunts. This man is a slave of his nature. Moreover, if he follows the advice of his relatives, he can't live not only with me but also his second wife."

"Shut up. Who needs you? Get out. If one wife goes, a thousand others will come over."

It was too much even for Ginny. Being a little older than Sudhir, she retorted angrily, "You are stupid to miss this chance. I had called Rita with great difficulty so that the differences between you could be resolved."

"Where was the need? Why did she come?" he said angrily.

"Actually, she was not coming," Ginny said, "Sudhir, will you never mend your ways?"

Rita got up to leave, leaving both arguing, but Ginny stopped her and said, "Rita, for my sake, please compromise with him. Accept some of his conditions and make him accept some of yours."

"Ginny, since the day I was married to him, I have always succumbed to his whims. But there is a limit to everything. He has crossed all limits now. He has taken me for a wax doll that will melt with a little heat."

"Ginny what does she expect from me in the role of husband? We have a house, money, and enough to eat. What more does she want? But for all this, she doesn't know how to look after the family. You visit our house and have a look at the stove. How dirty it is!" Sudhir got up in agitation again and again and spoke angrily.

"But Rita has been away from that house for six months. How can you accuse her of such a thing?" Ginny interrupted him.

Sudhir would never listen to the other person when he spoke. He would just persist in what he wanted to say. Fed up with this behavior, Rita returned home but Dhanush and Bhanu stayed with him. Rita again felt lonely and missed Ravi. She was not ready to accept that she was lonely. Love for someone occupied her. She faced a dilemma. She could not live with Sudhir but she also did not want to divorce him. She could not decide why she was afraid of divorce. She was an Indian born woman and could not compromise with the idea of divorce although times had changed. The ritual of going round the sacred fire seven times changed Indian women forever and condemned them forever to be persecuted by the husband.

During the days spent in college, Rita had a friend who was not very good looking. But still she had had lover after lover in her life. Whereas even though Rita was beautiful, she had not been able to win the love even of a single man. This lack of love in her life might have made her lean towards Ravi, who had given her the taste of love. He just showed sympathy to her and she was sold to him. In the deserted lanes of life, someone came to her with a little love and his dreams started haunting her. She had also had a feeling that the dreams were never to be real, but she did not give up dreaming as these dreams had imparted a new meaning to her life.

It was early morning and she was still in bed when she received a call from Bhanu. She said, "Mama."

Rita was alert and anxious. She said with great concern for the child, "What is it, my child, that you have called so early? Has Daddy hit you?"

"Mama, Daddy is not letting me go to sleep. He is pressing me to send it to you."

"Ok, dear, I shall come. Please hand over the phone to Daddy," Rita said. "Sudhir why are you bothering the children? Why are you dragging them into our conflict?"

"Rita, come here at once. I miss you immensely. Without you, I can't sleep."

"In that case you had better call your sisters-in-law. They can sing lullabies to put you to sleep."

"Please Rita! My sisters-in-law can't stand comparison to your shoes even."

"What a funny man you are, Sudhir! Last evening you were so unbending with your inflated ego but now so early in the morning, you are ready to lick the feet of your wife."

Rita hung up. Today's incident was not new. Sudhir had always behaved in this manner. He would forget that Rita was a woman who besides being his wife was also a means of satisfying his sexual urge. But as soon as the sex urge was satisfied, he would again be an aggressive animal who would wait only to repeat the cycle of hate, love, hate, love. Only the love was limited to releasing his accumulated testosterone. He had hardly ever let his emotions be involved in love making. He would just be an animal seeking the female of the species to release his sexual tension. If he picked up a quarrel, the fight would go on.

There were occasional exceptions. Once Rita was so unwell that she had to be hospitalized. This development worried Sudhir and it was a rare phenomenon. He did everything necessary for the wife in such circumstances. When she returned home, Sudhir took care of her comfort so well that Rita was touched. But such phases were temporary. He could suddenly change color like a chameleon.

Once Rita returned home from work very tired. Sudhir was watching a football match. Rita straight away went to the kitchen and began cooking dinner. When cooking was over, she cleaned the pots and pans and felt exhausted. Then by way of some rest she came to Sudhir and lay down resting her head in his lap. When watching a match, he used to be so absorbed with the ups and downs of the match that if a player of his choice was defeated, he would suffer like him and would react angrily. He would feel let down by the player and would start abusing him aloud. If, unfortunately, Rita happened to be around, he would vent his anger on her.

On such occasions she did not know how to react. That day when Sudhir's favorite team was losing, Rita had placed her head in his lap. As such he rudely pushed her head away. Rita could not bear this. Outraged with this behavior, she switched off the TV. This was enough. Sudhir lost his temper at once. He started picking up whatever he could lay his hands on and hurling them at Rita indiscriminately. In the heat of anger, he threw a brass vase at her. It hit her hard on the head and injured her. Blood oozed out and flowed down her temple. She started shouting in pain. Bhanu and Dhanush saw this and ran out of the house with fear and started shouting for help.

Hearing their call for help, no neighbor came out. But someone phoned the police. If such an incident had happened in some village or a town in India, there was likelihood that neighbors would have thrashed the husband. But in this foreign land, even if there is a murder, no one would intervene. Consequently, the police arrived but Rita told them that the injury was just a minor accident as she had slipped her foot and fallen down, causing the injury. The police left. Hardly had they left when Sudhir again burst out in anger.

"What did your police do? How audacious of you to call the police!"

Bhanu watched all the drama, standing a little away. She was shaking with fear. She lay on the ground and beat her head against the floor. She was trembling and crying pitifully. Dhanush too had an inexplicable fear in his eyes. But Sudhir didn't even look at the plight of the children. Bhanu said sobbing, "Mama, I am scared of Daddy. Please, let us go to Sudha's aunt's house."

Rita took the children with her and went to Sudha's house and stayed with her overnight. The next morning, she again returned home to Sudhir.

Rita held the sisters-in-law of Sudhir responsible for such behavior of the man. She could not fathom how she had wronged them. The children were suffering only as a by-product of his overall conduct. The quarrels between the parents were depriving the children of their childhood charm and parental love. They had spent their conscious life helplessly watching the quarrels and the senseless cruelty to their mother.

A number of times Rita thought of divorcing Sudhir but the word divorce scared her. Her Indian sensibility and upbringing always deterred her from making any move in this direction. A divorced woman gets nothing but humiliation for her and the children. Men exploited this predicament of women to the fullest.

Rita was out of a job. She was very weak physically. But the situation in the house did not change. There were frequent quarrels. She often had to flee the house with the children to spend a night with some friendly neighbor but ultimately had to return to Sudhir. Sudhir was a past master in persecuting his wife. When Rita was away, he would change the lock of the house.

One day when she returned home, she found the lock changed. Sudhir was not at home. He had been watching a football match all day somewhere. Rita broke the glass of a window and somehow got in. Sudhir returned home at eleven at night. Rita was sleeping in her room with the children. She had closed the room from inside. But he was so infuriated that he kicked and broke the door and started shouting angrily. Rita was at her tether's end. She got up and with folded hands she pleaded with him, "In the name of God, I request you to spare us this hell. At least take pity on the innocent children.

Why are you bent upon depriving them of their childhood?" Rita was weeping loudly now.

"You bitch, if you had chosen to leave the house, why did you return? I had sent you no summons to fetch you home," he shouted at the top of his voice.

"When you quarrel, the children are scared and tremble with fear. I leave the house for their sake. Then why do you forget that beside you I also own this house."

"You own this house my foot! Does your bloody father make payments for this house? You own this house, how ridiculous! Have you looked at your face in the mirror? You should thank your stars that you got an opportunity to see America."

Rita had a big stock of the old memories, all bitter. She was educated but had to spend life like a house-maid. With two children to look after and not financially independent, what options did she have? Illiterate women were far better than the educated Rita. She came out of the nightmarish reflections that day when Bhanu called her and told her what Sudhir wanted. She did not go at once. But when Sudhir phoned her again and again, she was afraid lest he should again beat the children if she didn't go to him. She knew what he wanted. It was not the first time for Rita. When Sudhir could not contain his testosterone, he would condescend to apologize to Rita as he was doing today. With this nagging fear in her heart, she went to his house. When she stepped into his room, he came forward with outstretched arms and said, "Rita darling, now my heart has softened towards you after I realized how rash I have been towards you in the past. I assure you that in future, I shall never ill-treat you."

A woman can be very gullible. She can be taken in by a little sweet talk of the husband, however intensely she may have been wronged by him. Hunger for love and the need of security pull her again into his arms. Rita, with a badly bruised psyche and body, forgot all her suffering when Sudhir used a few loving words for her and she surrendered herself totally to his lust. In the past too whenever they had quarreled, and slept in different rooms for days together, they would not talk to each other and spend time missing each other. But mad with his sexual craving, Sudhir would make a truce with her and satisfy his lust. Rita also forgot everything and surrendered to his hunger but tonight she had a strange experience. She felt as if his embrace was not as tight as it should have been. She was frightened as if his hold on her body would go lose any moment and she would find herself insecure again. Sudhir's grip was extremely weak today. Initially she had wanted to run away from him but in the end, she gave up the idea Sudhir also persuaded her to leave Dr. Rai's job on his radio program. She passed the day in cleaning and cooking during day time and nights in Sudhir's arms. Sudhir's friends in the Indian community soon came to know of this truce between Sudhir and Rita. Congratulations calls started pouring in.

In India, Rita's parents also heard the news and heaved a sigh of relief. But in the family of her in-laws, everybody was on fire. They were bitten by jealousy. The sisters-in-law started a propaganda campaign that Rita's father had asked for forgiveness of Sudhir. That was why Sudhir had taken pity on the poor parents. The eldest sister-in-law of Sudhir's family would say, "You know what? She has returned to Sudhir of her own accord but tells others that Sudhir has reconciled and decided to live with her. returned or has been forced to return?" The other sister-in-law would observe, "Who would be so naïve as to accept as wife the mother of two children? All have exploited and used her, and when they have had their fill, they just discarded her. Off and on Rita expressed anger at Sudhir on hearing this baseless gossip. But by and by Sudhir cut down on visiting his sisters-in-law. Now Sudhir was so possessive that he would not leave Rita alone for a single day. One day he found Rita sad and asked, "Why is my dear wife sad today?"

"Sudhir, you have turned over a new leaf for the better but sometimes I am afraid of your sisters-in-law..."

"I have nothing to do with them or even my brothers. If they had been so good, they would have never pestered my wife."

"If you again go against me and become angry, be sure that you will find only my dead body going out from this house, not Rita ..."

"Rita, please never ever mention the dying word in future. I have had a motherless childhood. That is why my upbringing has not been proper. I assure you that I shall never use physical violence on you in any circumstances."

"Oh Sudhir!" She clung to him.

"Rita, the day you came here as a bride, how innocent and clean like a white sheet you were. But my nagging and the insinuations of my sisters-in-law have made you suffer to no end."

"But what puzzles me, Sudhir, is what happens to you so unexpectedly sometimes," Rita said. She went on, "When you are angry, you can't bear even to look at me, but when you are calm, you become so nice to me that you won't let me be away from your sight even for a moment."

"I don't know Rita. It has been my nature since I came to know the world. I am a perfectionist, you know. I also want my wife to be perfect according to my perception. Whenever you err in anything, I try to set you right in my own way."

"If you do not share things which you think are right or wrong, who else will? But you start scolding me thoughtlessly. You can correct me with love too. Then it would be in order."

"But I use the methods which were used in my upbringing."

"Sudhir, I want only love from you. My beauty, my talents, every one of my activities craves for approval by you."

"Rita, I don't know why I don't trust womankind."

"Sudhir, did any girl friend of yours ever deceive you?"

"I have had a big painful sore in my life. I have had it there for a long time."

"But why does this distrust exist between wife and husband, my angelic husband?"

"I confess it was very stupid of me never to try to have a peep into the heart of my wife."

"It is still not too late, my love. Just look into my eyes and into my heart. There is nothing but your love there."

"Once when I was seventeen years old, I was spending my vacation with a relative's family. I had two cousins, the sons of an uncle by some distant relation. One of them was a professor in a college but the other was yet a student. My aunt had died and my uncle was away for days together in connection with his work. The wife of the elder brother was very beautiful. Occasionally the professor also accompanied his father.

"One day the uncle and the cousin were away. At night I was awakened by some noise. It was summer and we all slept out in the open. I was surprised and looked in the direction of the noise. It came from a room a little away. Its door was open and I saw something which stunned me. Can you guess what I saw?"

"What?"

"I found the younger brother of the professor engaged in sex with the sister-in-law."

"Oh!" Rita was shocked.

"My cousin, her husband, loved her so dearly. For her convenience, he had hired a servant. He had arranged all types of comforts and facilities at home. His wife had nothing to do except make herself up, go to the movies or go shopping."

"But the younger brother too should not have done this to his sister-in-law even if she wanted to seduce him."

"Yes, he too is to blame. After all she was his elder sister-in-law who is like a mother. He should not have done this to her."

"Maybe the elder brother was…"

"But Rita, he was a very nice husband and worshiped his wife who was one of the most beautiful women."

"Did he never suspect any foul play"

"No."

"But how did this incident affect you?"

"This incident affected me deeply. Another incident was that my real eldest sister-in-law ostentatiously showered love on us but stayed with her parents for almost a year."

"Then…?"

"Still our father washed clothes, bathed us and cooked for us."

"But all brothers treated her like your mother?"

"Yes, but whenever she came to the village to stay with us, she took care of domestic chores."

"What about your middle sister-in-law?"

"I was alone in America. I paid for my education either by earning some money myself or occasionally my middle brother paid for it. After my marriage, he stopped giving any money."

"Listen Sudhir, I am not against your love for your brothers and sisters-in-law. You might have noted that I am in favor of this love between sister-in-law and you, the brother-in-law."

"I had no love for any sister-in-law. I just humored them for my brothers' sake as I had none except my brothers and their families in America."

"Forget all this now. Let us turn a new leaf in our life. If the house belongs to me, it is also yours and the children."

"Oh, my dear Rita, I am so happy now." He held her close to his heart.

Compromises in life are neither difficult nor easy. While it is very easy to dream, it is equally difficult to materialize it. For a brief period, Rita's life was happy. One day Rita again fell ill. Sudhir noticed this and said, "What has happened, Rita?"

"I am not sure but I think I am pregnant again."

"That's great! Congratulations."

"Are you sure, Sudhir, that you want a third child?'

"Why not? This time …"

The atmosphere at home was undergoing change. Suddenly Sudhir was transferred out of the state. It was not feasible for Rita to shift to the Pace where new posting with Sudhir got it. Hence Sudhir joined his duty at the new place leaving Rita and the children back. But no one in his family had any idea about this development. They did not know where Sudhir was. Rita also didn't tell anyone anything. It was the third month of Rita's pregnancy.

One day Sudhir's eldest brother came without any information of his visit. He asked Rita, "Where is Sudhir?"

"He lives out of state," Rita told him.

"Why? Have you two divorced each other?"

"Bhai Sahib, why do you always say inauspicious things?"

"But that is what all say about you."

"You believe in what others say but not in what you see yourself."

"Look here Rita, people are talking even about your character."

"Bhai Sahib…!" Rita said in an offended voice.

"They say that the child you have carried for three months in your womb was fathered by someone else, not by Sudhir."

"Get out … get….out, get out…" Rita shouted. She was panting with agitation and indignation.

Hearing her screams, he made his exit but his insinuating suggestion and derogatory words had affected Rita's heart and body so much that she had acute stomach pain. She had to go to the hospital. She was given some medicine and a sleeping pill. In the morning when she opened her eyes, she found Sudhir standing by her bedside.

"Sudhir, how do you happen to be here?"

"Dhanush and Bhanu are with your sisters. They had rung me up at night and I booked a flight and reached here just a little while ago."

"Oh Sudhir, but why did you take the trouble? It was nothing serious, I believe."

"Did you wait for me before my sweet dream crashed to the ground?"

"What do you mean?"

"You have lost the tiny...son," he said with tears appearing in his eyes.

"What?" Rita said, shocked, and tried to get up, but felt giddy and fell down on the bed.

She began to cry. Sudhir made no move to silence or soothe her. Instead, he said. "You shall stop the new magazine 'Sapna' (dream) that you have started."

"Sudhir, are you sure you should tell me all this at this moment?"

"I have arranged for a nurse to look after you. When you regain your health, we shall sell the Los Angeles house."

"Sudhir, I am sorry Sudhir." She sobbed incessantly.

Sudhir returned to his job but phoned daily. Rita was recovering normally. Gradually the frequency of his calls decreased. Her children were reluctant to leave Los Angeles. The small magazine Rita had started was a source of a little income. She busied herself in it. But what puzzled her was that not only Sudhir had discontinued phoning but also never came to Los Angeles. Rita wrote many letters but with no response. Finally, when a letter did come, it was a divorce proposal.

Divorce, Divorce, Divorce, the word rang in her mind and rattled her whole being. It was an extremely disconcerting term. It sounded like a death bell. Rita felt everything going round and round. There could not have been a bigger deception, she thought. She found herself in a whirlpool that was pulling her down. What had she not done to please her husband and how had she not borne all the punishment by him? She had sacrificed so much for her own family.

She had helped her sisters settle in America only to be told that she had done nothing for them. When the shock of the divorce letter had slightly abated, she started weeping loudly. But by and by it was replaced by a strange strength and determination. She started laughing and talking to herself aloud, 'Get up Rita, buck up. Face this calamity boldly. Today you are free, Sudhir has freed you. There is no reason for you to feel sad and weep. From now on you will be the master of all your activities; you will have unrestricted freedom to do what you please and see whoever you like, absolutely unshackled.'

Another mood overtook her, an unnerving mood. How was she to bring up Bhanu and Dhanush in this foreign land? There is every likelihood of the children of broken families going wrong. How would she handle them? She had no means to pay house rent, car insurance, health care etc. She was lost in these thoughts when the phone bell rang. She rushed and lifted the receiver. It was the middle sister-in-law from Sacramento.

"Hello, so you have the taste of sending your husband away? Now the world will shout from rooftops that your husband has dumped you. Look here woman, now your children too will abandon you. They will openly have liaison with colored vagabonds as you did."

"How have I wronged you, by the way?"

But there was no reply, just a click to show that she had replaced the receiver. Rita spent the evening weeping. A few days passed but the shock still did not leave her. Finally, with the help of some friends, she found a good attorney. She took the divorce papers to the attorney and with the papers in her hand she kept weeping. When Sudhir came to know that Rita's attorney was better than his, he changed the plan. He wrote a letter of apology to Rita's parents and sent them tickets to come to America. It was all done very secretly.

Her parents arrived soon. The same discussions and persuasions followed and as all pressed, Rita again made up with Sudhir. Her parents returned to India. A few years dragged on with these quarrels and reconciliations. Now Sudhir didn't beat Rita but never gave her any money. He also brought groceries according to his choice. In the meanwhile, Ravi had got married. He had returned neither the bangles nor any money. Having been cheated thus, Rita shrank within herself with mortification. Still, even with the passage of time, the story of Rita and Ravi was a hot topic of gossip among the Indians.

In the meantime, Bhanu was growing and change could be noticed in her behavior. She was about fourteen. In order to take care of her, Rita had resigned from her job. She still retained interest in acting. Adolescence marks a period of changes when one is neither a child nor a grown up and the behavior is also unpredictable.

When Sudhir and Rita quarreled, Bhanu would either weep like a child or would also try to persuade the parents to stop fighting in the name of God... If children witness such quarrels daily, they leave a deep impression on their mind. They are hurt. Occasionally children step into the role of grown-ups and the grown-ups behave like kids. The children clearly understood the helplessness of their mother when she was beaten by their father, but what was beyond them was why, after being beaten by her husband, their mother vented her anger on the children. The frequent quarrels affected Bhanu's education. But Rita did not want her to give up her interest in acting.

Sudhir had found another job in another state but he never gave any money to Rita except the rent of the house. Bhanu had become very insistent about having her way in almost everything. She wanted to go out on dates like other American girls against her mother's will. Rita did not like this. To ensure that Bhanu and Dhanush were punctual to and from school, she took up the job of taking care of neighborhood children at their own house. Now, along with studies in school, Rita's children also did small roles in Hollywood films. Rita arranged for their books, clothes and toys with their earnings.

With some savings, an instructor in acting, Ishwar Sigh, was hired. He would say, "Rita, I shall train your children so well in acting that they will surpass famous actors."

"Mr. Ishwar, I feel you are not in touch with the reality around here. The petty politics in the community here are so bad that as long as you don't fawn on artists, doctors and press barons, you can't get an entry in their citadel."

"How is that?" he said, surprised.

"See, though I don't want to criticize anybody, yet you might have heard the name of Sita Devi…"

"Yes, I have heard of her. One Professor Ram Sharma who occasionally wrote a little about the community in Dr. Rai's paper has a little…well, leave it."

"Ishwar, I don't know what sort of relation he has with Sita Devi, but whenever my brother or I do something noteworthy, he never writes a word in appreciation. But he raises Sita Devi to the sky as if she were the Linda Carter of Hollywood."

"In that case you too should learn a little politics," Ishwar said, a little cautiously.

"What politics do you mean?"

"You should try to be in the good books of Dr. Rai and, finding an appropriate opportunity, tell him about Ram Sharma's bias for Sita Devi. I understand Dr. Rai has great regard for you."

"Well, let us cut it out. What do you say if we produce a historical play?"

"Bravo Rita ji! You have no match in your high intelligence. I keep telling my mother that Rita's mind keeps working even during sleep."

A few weeks were spent in holding meetings in planning this play. Finally, it was decided that they would produce a play entitled 'Noor Jehan'. Ads were inserted in papers and a search for new actors was launched. Ishwar Singh was a good director. He was already very well known for producing short plays with Rita. She respected all his decisions. He was a nice bachelor. For 'Noor Jehan', Sharmili undertook the work of sketching a set for the play. She also became a good friend of Ishwar. Sharmili's younger sister had come on a tour of America from Canada. She was thirty years old. She wanted to do a small role in Rita's play. Now Ishwar acted with tact. He was in search of a Noor Jehan and a Jehangir. Bhanu was too young to fit the role of Noor Jehan. Sharmili's younger sister was not considered to be capable of doing justice to the role of Noor Jehan. There was a young man named Rohit. He was tall and good looking. Rita liked his acting skill also. Though very young, he could fit the role of Jehangir.

"Ishwar ji, I feel we should have Shilpa, the new girl, play the role of Noor Jehan and Rohit of Jehangir."

"Rita, why don't you let Bhanu come forward? I see you don't respect the acting skills of your daughter. She is a very promising artist in her young body."

"But uncle, I won't be able to play a big role. I also don't know Urdu," Bhanu, who was listening, said to Ishwar.

"Never mind Bhanu, I shall teach you Urdu," he said, allaying her fears.

"I shall help in sound management," Dhanush offered.

These fruitless discussions continued for quite some time but the problem was still unresolved. Many suggestions were flying in but without any result. One day Ishwar Singh called, "How are you, Rita?"

"I am fine, but have you reached any decision?"

"Yes, I have decided that you will act as Noor Jehan and I shall be Jehangir."

"What??? I...I...I...this time I shall only produce...the play."

"But Rita, you don't know that you outclass the modern young beauties in good looks."

"But I shall be only the producer of the play, you know."

"Listen, I am the director. A good director can never go wrong in the selection of an artist. But you are an artist of a high order."

Brushing aside Rita's refusals, Ishwar gave dates to the actors for rehearsals. There was hustle and bustle day and night. Rita had not only to participate in the rehearsals but also to look after the children of the neighbors. She spent the money she earned in arranging meals and costumes for the artists. Luckily a few not so prominent doctors had contributed some money for the stage. By now Rita was determined to stage the play 'Noor Jehan'. But to get together with the score artists, to arrange food for them on time and other odd jobs was not easy.

Rohit was young but Sharmili lost her heart to him even though he was new to America. He was slightly short tempered and immature. Sharmili tried to attract him with new womanly tricks and flirted with him. Sharmili's sister Gayatri tried a few times to warn Rita in this connection but Rita ignored her warnings.

One day Sharmili said to Rita, "Dear Rita, I like this Rohit very much."

"Oh! No! He is younger than you and I feel he is attracted to Gayatri."

"Rita, you are jealous of me, I think."

"Don't talk nonsense, Sharmili. I love you more than my real sisters," Rita said very lovingly.

"Is it true, Rita? Wow, how sweet you are!" Sharmili soon felt relaxed.

The date of the play had been fixed and it was to be staged only five days later. But a new development was taking place. Rohit and Ishwar often quarreled and Sharmili added fuel to the fire. Rita was totally unaware of Sharmili's mischief. A day before the play was to be staged, Rohit and Ishwar again quarreled. At the eleventh-hour Rohit threatened to quit the play. It scared Rita extremely. Rita requested Sharmili to bring Rohit round to continue to be in the play but unfortunately Sharmili fell foul with Rita.

"Do you know Bhanu is the real cause of this dispute?"

"Bhanu? What are you saying? How could Bhanu be involved in such things?" Rita said incredulously.

"Yes, Rita, please check your daughter. At this young age, she wants to date grown up people."

"Sharmili, I am so much involved in this play, that I have neglected Dhanush and he has become very weak. As regards Bhanu, she sees people only when we are around. What do you think in these circumstances?"

"Keep Bhanu away from Rohit."

Rita at once called Bhanu and quizzed her in this connection.

"But Mama, I have done nothing," Bhanu said.

"But Sharmili has quite a different tale about you."

"Mama, Rohit had said that the old spinster was chasing him, and I told this to Sharmili aunty."

"Why did you tell this to Sharmili?" Rita thundered and gave a resounding slap on her face. Rita had never before been so angry with Bhanu. She beat her unusually hard, so much so that even Dhanush had never witnessed such violence. He started weeping. But Sharmili didn't intervene to stop Rita. After Sharmili had left, Rita wept for a long time and finally she rang Rohit up.

"Hello."

"Rohit, I am not bothered whether you act in the play or not..."

"What are you saying? Sharmili and Ishwar have provoked me against you."

"Why did you say objectionable things to Bhanu against Sharmili?"

"You know, Bhanu told Sharmili what I had said to her. As a result, Sharmili was so angry with me that I was scared."

"It is easy for you to say so but sandwiched between you and Sharmili's jealousy, my innocent child suffered and got beaten by me." Rita started to weep on the phone.

Rohit said nothing but just stayed on the line and heard her weeping. Finally, he apologized for his action. The next day the play was staged and it was a great success. The audience was highly appreciative of Bhanu's acting. An appreciative report of Bhanu, Gayatri and Rohit's good acting was published in Dr. Rai's paper. But Sharmili had written the introduction of the play and the players. The Hindi of the script was not good. Hence there was no mention of it in the paper. For this omission, Ishwar and Sharmili held Rita responsible. There were irritating calls almost daily and then a series of pseudonymous critical letters were published every week.

Ishwar and Sharmili were behind them. Consequently, Rita severed connection with them.

Time again moved on as before. Rita's life was a long sequence of compromises. Hence, one has to move on with whatever one's lot is. Sudhir was also busy with his affairs. Rita was worried about Bhanu and Dhanush's future. The children played short roles in films and so did Rita. As Sudhir was not around to snatch away the little earning the mother and the children made, Rita was able to make a little saving. Our destiny can play tricks with us. Sometimes we have to walk the paths abandoned by people. Rita had received a small part in a film in Paramount studio. One day when she was moving from one room to the other in the studio, someone closed her eyes from behind. She heard, "How long I had been looking for you. Finally, I have caught up with you. Well, if you can tell who I am, I shall accept my defeat."

Rita turned around and looked at the person. It was Ravi. Rita screamed angrily, "Oh, so it is you…Mr. Ravi." She pushed him away.

"Rita, please don't be angry…"

"Look here, I don't know you and wouldn't care a bit to know you. Is it clear?"

"In this film I am playing the role of your lover, you know."

"It is your profession to play roles which are all fake and like what you use in your real life."

"Rita, you can criticize me because I am married…"

"Mr. Ravi, I am a married woman and have two children. Are you suggesting that I am not happy at your marriage?"

"Then why show this anger? We can at least be friends."

"Be a friend with the types of you who can sell not only a poor woman's sentiments but also her jewelry."

Rita had had a complaint against Ravi and it had found expression now. Her eyes became tearful and she ran away from him. She went to the bathroom and looked at her image in the mirror. She talked to herself, 'You stupid, you were expecting love and romance. But what you got was plain infamy and disgrace in the society. You have earned a bad name that will chase not only you but also your children till eternity.' Rita hid her face in her hands and kept weeping for how long, she had no count.

CHAPTER 13

Ravi acted like a blood thirsty leech but human predicament is such that the victim never knows of its nefarious activity. He exploited Rita's sentiments of love and deprived her of the only worldly possession, her golden bangles. Ravi was an unscrupulous man. He had had his eyes on Rita's beauty and whatever money he could exact from her. He was a selfish cheat through and through. The master cheat had finished Rita emotionally and physically, leaving her a pauper. The result was that she was now a branded cheap woman who had lost all virtue and who had two children to bring up in this cruel society. There was no one around to share her pain.

On the other front Sudhir had himself crushed the dreams he had shown to Rita. He had performed the ritual of going round the sacred fire seven times to tie him to Rita with marriage vows in a lifelong relationship of husband and wife. But he had cheated on the marriage vows. Society would forgive Sudhir but what about Rita, a helpless woman? Perhaps even God almighty wouldn't forgive her. She was told once by a priest that it is laid down in the holy books that a woman who even thinks of a man other than her husband is a sinner and is condemnable. But then Rita's conscience would cry, 'Is the man who goes after a woman other than his wife not a sinner? Sudhir had always favored his sisters-in-law. Are they not other women?'

Time is an enigma. It can play many tricks with human beings. People say that all of us have to face the consequence of our actions and the result is a consequence of our karma. But on the other hand it is also said that man indulges in bad karmas also with His will.

For good or bad karmas, it is God who is responsible, not man. If that is true, then why should man be punished? In that case society too has no business to blame anybody for his karmas. But society has great reach.

A helpless woman, abandoned by her husband, can never fight society. Men always side with men, not women. Then the irony is if a woman is bent upon demeaning her own kind, no role is left for God to play in the matter. In human social structure the mother-in-law forgets that she too was once a daughter-in-law. She also had aspirations and ambitions as her daughters and daughters-in-law have. The elder sisters-in-law also forget that they too are women and should not have ill-will for the younger sisters-in-law as their children will have to bear the consequences of their misdeeds.

Shana was the daughter of Kanta Rani who loved Rita and Bhanu. Rita would call her Shan out of affection. One day she told Rita that the daughter of the elder brother who was married about five years ago had no child. As a result, the husband and the wife usually quarreled. Shana said, "Rita aunty, do you know that Chandani didi is facing many problems?"

"Shana beta, we should not discuss others' affairs," Rita advised her.

"But Tao ji and Tai ji (elder uncle and aunty) incite my mother against you."

"How do they do this?" Rita asked eagerly.

"They say that Rita doesn't have a good character."

"And...?"

"And that I should not be allowed to mix with Bhanu as otherwise the mother and daughter will lead me astray."

"Beti, if that's what they say, you had better not come to our house." Rita began to weep.

"Aunty, please don't weep. Do you know what? When I am eighteen years old, I shall live away from my mother."

"Shanu...!" Rita screamed at her. She then said calmly, "Shanu beta, an aunty can never replace a mother."

"But Rita aunty, my mother does not understand me. She doesn't know that I too want to act on the stage."

"What if she doesn't? I shall talk to your mother."

"Mama, Shanu's boyfriend…" Bhanu asked.

"Bhanu, Shanu, you are too young yet to talk of such things. What has happened to you?"

"Rita aunty, what is wrong in having a boyfriend?"

Rita felt as if someone had placed a stone on her head but she could neither remove it nor utter a word. She faced a dilemma whether to talk to Shanu's mother or not. She was in a great fix but she somehow controlled herself and made bold to ask Shanu, "Shanu, who is he?"

"Mama, he is an Afro American," Bhanu said cheerfully.

"You shut up Bhanu." Rita pulled Bhanu up. Then she addressed Shanu and said, "Shanu, you are not yet seventeen but you are taking interest in an Afro American…"

"But Rita aunty, you used to advise me that we shouldn't discriminate among people on the basis of religion, caste, creed or color but today you feel so bad about Afro-Americans."

"No, I don't discriminate against them. But our culture is different from theirs. You are very young. Look, don't do anything bad. Indian girls never share a bed with men before marriage. The girls who do so before marriage…"

"Rita aunty, my boyfriend is not that type. His mother had not married when he was born."

"What…?" Rita couldn't believe her ears. Then she added, "Shanu dear, in what strange situation have you put me? Look here darling; you are very young for such things. Beti, you will have to promise me or I shall tell your mother about your boyfriend."

"What, Rita aunty?" Shanu was scared.

"That you will break up with your boyfriend and will never again see him."

"Ok aunty, but don't tell my mother." Shanu began to weep.

"Don't weep Shanu." Rita held the girl to her bosom.

Rita thought it to be advisable not to mention this thing to Sudhir as he too would believe what others said. In the meantime, she kept advising Bhanu and Shanu about the matter of having boyfriends. By and by Shanu came round and stopped seeing the boyfriend. This affair always remained a secret.

Life is a puzzle. If someone is destined to be always weeping, it doesn't change. Rita recalled her past and shed tears which had become her compulsion. She had had just a few good days but the misery was perpetual. She was convinced that only death could rid her of this miserable life. Hence, she dedicated herself to making the career of Bhanu and Dhanush. When Bhanu was fifteen, she didn't look very attractive as the regular quarrels at home had affected her physical growth and nature. But now Sudhir had a job away from them. The result was that in the atmosphere of peace both the children looked charming. Bhanu's singing and acting on the stage was appreciated by the people. Rita knew a small-time film director Jagjivan. One day he called Rita.

"Rita, I have heard that you have been separated from your husband. Have you divorced...?"

"Jagjivan Sahib, no not yet." She was offended.

"Oh, sorry. Ok then, with Ravi..."

"Mr. Jagjivan, a Hindi movie producer of New York has selected Bhanu." She changed the topic.

"Great! What is the name of the movie?"

"Pardesi Saajan (a foreign lover)."

"If the movie is being produced in New York, then naturally Dhanush..."

"The school is closed for vacation. Consequently, he and I also have minor roles in it."

"In that case, instead of locking up your house, I suggest an alternative."

"What is it?"

"I have an actress with me at the moment."

"Go on. I am listening."

"Here she is taking some classes regarding production."

"What production?"

"Movie production of course."

"So.?"

"She wants to live alone. If you could rent her a room, she will pay for it."

"There is no need to pay. She can live here as long as I am in New York."

"You are great. May I bring her along this evening?"

"Why not? You can bring along your wife, Sitara Devi, and dine with us."

"Do you know the actress?"

"What is her name?"

"Shabab."

"Jagjivan ji, Tamanna too is in New York, I think."

"Yes. She married an American in 1965."

"She was very beautiful. How is she these days?"

"Shabab's mother was a maid in Tamanna's house. Tamanna was instrumental in making her a heroine with the help of her celebrated father."

"If you know so many people, why don't you please help Bhanu?"

"Sure. We shall discuss this when we meet in the evening."

"Ok. See you." She replaced the receiver.

"Bhanu, o Bhanu," Rita called Bhanu happily.

"Yes, Mom?"

"Dress yourself properly and be ready in a way that you look beautiful."

"Why?"

"In the evening, director Jagjivan is visiting us with his wife and actress Shabab."

"Is it the same Shabab whose movie I had seen when I was very young?"

"Yes."

"She is not pretty."

"What has that got to do with us? She will stay here for some time and that will strengthen our contacts with her."

Early in the evening Jagjivan turned up with his wife and Shabab. Sitara Devi Blowing cigarette smoke rings, showing her off infront of Rita. Sitara Devi asked Rita How long she has been in America.

"I came just about fifteen years back."

"Oh, then you must be my mother's age," Shabab said. This surprised Rita, when the first film of Shabab was shown in cinemas, Bhanu was six years old.

"How old were you when you acted in the film 'Mere Kaun Hain Apne'?"

"I was only twelve years old."

"What?" Sitara Devi and Jagjivan were startled.

"The age of film actresses is always below fifteen. It never advances," Sitara Devi observed as she blew smoke rings up.

Well, it was Bhanu and Dhanush's first contact with Mumbai actors. Bhanu was only fifteen years old when she had acted in 'Paradesi Saajan'. Bhanu and Rita loved Shabab very much. Shabab's friend Justin lived in Texas. He occasionally phoned Bhanu also. It was said he too had made a few films in Mumbai. In the society from which Shabab had come, she had become habitual of eating free of cost.

One day Tamanna, an old friend of Shabab, invited Rita, Dhanush and Bhanu to dinner. Shabab had no interest in promoting Bhanu in films. For some inexplicable reasons, she was jealous of Bhanu without the knowledge of Rita and Bhanu. As such, whenever Rita scolded the girls at home, Shabab made it a point to spread this news around.

"Do you know, Tamanna aunty, Rita is forcing her daughter Bhanu to act in films?"

"But her daughter herself tells me that she would like to be a model," Sitara Devi said.

"Oh no, no, Sitara Devi. The woman is out of her mind. She is totally upset mentally."

"Does that man Ravi visit her openly?"

"Ravi, who is Ravi?" Shabab asked, a little surprised.

"Yes, the same Ravi. I have seen him talking on the phone with Rita a number of times."

"Leave it. If she doesn't have good relations with her husband, then what is wrong if she has found some sympathizer?" Tamanna said, showing a little sympathy.

"But then the son would do the same as the mother does. The son will naturally take a cue from his mother," Jagjivan observed.

"Not Necessary," Tamana said.

"They are all against her. They say that she had been bad since childhood."

"Who has?" Tamanna said, a little annoyed.

"Rita called all her brothers and sisters in America and harassed them to no end. But Tamanna aunty, please don't be angry with me."

"What did she do?" Jagjivan showed interest in the discussion.

"Look here Shabab, you live in Rita's house. Don't talk ill of her." Tamanna pulled Shabab up.

"You don't know how bad this woman is. She eats away all my food and steals my clothes." Shabab began to weep.

"Oh my God. Is Rita a thief?" Sitara Devi asked.

"Her husband is a very nice man. She steals his money also."

"Why doesn't her husband send her to a mental asylum?"

"Rubbish! She is fine. I shall invite her to my Thanksgiving party. Don't condemn the poor lady. She is, as far as I think, just a victim of bad luck." Tamanna said sympathetically.

Rita had no intention to go to Tamanna's party. She told this to Bhanu. She said, "I don't know why I don't feel like going to Tamanna's party."

"Mama, let's go there for a little while. Shabab has been there since yesterday," Bhanu suggested.

"My intuition tells me that Shabab doesn't want us to interact much with Tamanna."

"Mama, Shabab has been a failure in Mumbai films and doesn't want me to work there. She never misses a chance to tell me that I am not beautiful."

"Is it true? You know, she used to tell me that she would introduce you to Mumbai producers," Rita said, surprised.

"Mama, I am sure Shabab has stolen the school candy money from my room," Dhanush said.

"What are you saying beta (son)?" Rita asked unbelievingly. But the fact was that since Shabab had come to stay with them, things had been disappearing continually. If it was Rita's saari today, it would be her golden bangle tomorrow. Rita was so busy that she didn't know what had been lost.

One day they were invited by Tamanna for a social party at her house. They went to Tamanna's party. Bhanu looked very beautiful. She was sixteen years old and was tall and slim. She had full lips and a beautiful nose. Dhanush was also thirteen years old. He looked very charming, with a perpetual smile on his face. Tamanna's daughter, Payal, was also thirteen years old. As such, Dhanush and the girl were good friends. They indulged in all sorts of adolescent tricks. By and by the time to go home arrived and Rita asked Bhanu and Dhanush to return home. But Payal insisted on their staying a little longer. She said, "No, aunty, don't go yet. I want to play with Dhanush and Bhanu."

"But dear Payal, both of you are to go to school tomorrow. We must leave now," Rita tried to explain to her.

"Ok Dhanush, here is my phone number. Please keep in touch with me," Payal said. At Tamanna's house, all showed much love to Bhanu and Dhanush. The entire gathering there comprised film people either from Hollywood or Mumbai. Rita was glad that at least Bhanu had a chance to interact with film people. She would learn more with future contacts.

Man's ambitions, dreams and desires have enslaved him. Rita noticed that for some time Bhanu had been neglecting her school assignments etc. This made Rita reflect on the circumstances she had gone through. She had been forced to abandon the traditional beaten path when she was separated from Sudhir.

Rita tried to view things in retrospection; the way things had happened for quite some time. After separating from Sudhir, she had found an alternative to ensure proper bringing up of the children. All along Rita had had a sharp eye on the children's habits and behavior lest they should be led astray by the not so healthy environment in the film industry. The situation at home too was not very healthy. This also must have been a reason for Bhanu's neglecting school work. Whenever Bhanu didn't do homework or was late in returning from school, Rita punished her. Her reactions were far more severe than necessary and Rita didn't know why. But she had no complaints about Dhanush.

Bhanu was passing through a phase of life when she wanted to interact with American boys like other girls and Rita was strictly against it. One day Bhanu put the vital question to Rita which she had been afraid of for such a long time. Bhanu said, "Mama, why don't you let me live my life my way?"

Rita stared at her for a long moment and scrutinized Bhanu's face. Was she the same Bhanu, the kid who would look at her mother for every little need? Had she grown up so fast that Rita didn't notice? But now she was face to face with the reality. Bhanu was becoming independent. Rita was shaken out of complacency by this knowledge. Finally, she said, "Bhanu, as long as you are not able to stand on your two feet, I shall have to live your life."

"But Mama, I was born in America and am an American," Bhanu said firmly, with conviction.

"Yes, you are right, I fully agree, but your parents are Indians rooted in the great Indian culture. Indian culture teaches us tolerance and patience..." Before Rita could conclude the argument against Bhanu's seeing boyfriends, Dhanush called, "Mama, it's Jagjivan uncle on the phone."

Rita took the call, "Hi Jagjivan, how are you? What made you call so early in the morning? By the way, Tamanna's party was..."

"Listen Rita, that day $500 was stolen from Payal's room."

"Oh, I see...," Rita said.

"God knows what school your children go to and what drugs they consume!"

"What are you trying to say?" Rita's voice betrayed irritation.

"Just this, you should keep an eye on the conduct of your children. Tamanna has filed a report with the police about the theft."

Rita felt the ground slipping away from under her feet. Being a mother, no one could be a better judge of her children. Her children could never be thieves. They had never stolen anything at school. They often stayed overnight with Rita's friends but there was no complaint of this nature. But the implied allegation in Jagjivan's words rattled her and she had a nagging feeling that the children could perhaps be thieves. She at once went to their rooms and searched them thoroughly by turning over every article, and their beds, but found nothing. Then she questioned them closely and when they showed ignorance in the matter and claimed innocence, she slapped them to make sure they were not lying. She even became terrified and demanded, "Where is the $500?"

"Which dollars, Mama?" The children started crying loudly.

"The dollars that are missing from Payal…" Rita started weeping.

"Mama, we didn't take them. We don't know."

"Then who stole them? Tamanna, Shabab and Payal all think that…"

"But Mama, we didn't steal them. We are innocent. Please don't be mad with us. Who is ours besides you?" The children wept pathetically.

"Rita felt a shooting pain in her heart. She rushed to the children and held them close to her bosom. She said, "Forgive me my darlings. Forgive your unlucky mother."

"It is us that are unlucky that our mother suspects us. Come on Dhanush, let us run away from this house," Bhanu motioned to Dhanush.

"No, my children, don't abandon me. I am the sinner." Rita was weeping very loudly now. She was banging her head on the floor.

"Don't weep Mama. Don't hurt yourself. Your forehead is bleeding. It is ok." Both of the children started to cry.

Rita resolved never to beat her children thereafter. But the children stopped speaking to Shabab and Jagjivan. Rita quietly told Shabab to find another house but Shabab could not stomach it.

"How have I wronged you that you are angry with me?"

"Look here, I am fed up with you and your Mumbai film people. When all you Mumbai film walas want something, then you are chummy chummy to all, yet when you leave someone, you leave blaming them. It is not in your blood to be loyal to anyone."

"But I respect you like my mother."

"Listen Shabab, I treated you as my daughter and helped you in every possible way. But you thought ill of my children. I wonder if your mother, your friend Jagjivan and Sitara Devi could not teach you the principle that one should not betray the person who feeds and shelters you. If it were someone else in your place, you would have been thrown out of the house by now."

"You are bent upon murdering me knowing well that I know nobody in America."

"Your life means nothing either in America or in India. What would I gain if I murder you?" Rita went on saying.

"No wonder Tamana, the most famous star of Mumbai, the millionaire of Beverly Hills, knew something about you. I will not hold her responsible for this accusation. She does not know me and my children but you live in this house and you know my children are not thieves."

Shabab began to weep. Then she phoned Jagjivan using Rita's phone. "Where have you put me up? I am afraid of this mad woman. She is likely to kill me."

"Put me on to Rita. I shall talk to her. We shall take you away from her house tomorrow."

"She is abusing all of you," Shabab said, and disconnected the phone.

The following day Jagjivan and Sitara Devi came to take Shabab away. As long as they were there, they kept looking at Rita and the children with a strange look. Finally, when they left with Shabab, Rita and the children heaved a sigh of relief.

From then on Bhanu and Rita had a commendable chemistry and had a nice time together. Dhanush was dedicated to his education very seriously these days. In his school, there were Indians, including Sikhs and Pakistani students. Because of Dhanush being the son of Rita, they made fun of Dhanush. Naturally they must have heard a lot of nonsense about Rita from their parents. It meant that Rita was discussed in their families negatively. She had become a laughing stock in the community.

Rita tried to spend most of her time with her children. Bhanu had somehow cleared high school and was in college. She worked part time in a restaurant. She had high ambitions and very rosy dreams. Her strongest desire was to succeed as a model. Hence in accordance with her desire, Rita took her to various modeling agencies but all in vain. She was tired now. Hollywood did not encourage entry to Indians. All who saw Bhanu took her for a model, not an actor. A modeling agency in New York had selected Bhanu but Rita didn't want to send her that far away even though Bhanu requested her earnestly. Rita was apprehensive for some inexplicable reason.

It was in those days when Rita received the marriage Invitation card from her aunty from London . It was the marriage of her aunty son in London. On the other hand, the agency that had selected Bhanu, told her to go to London to join the wedding. Rita and Dhanush also got excited to go to London. The aunty in question bought their tickets.

Sudhir had been out of the country for about three years. When Rita, Bhanu and Dhanush were about to leave for London, Sudhir turned up home without any information. At once the same arguments, quarrels and disturbing activities started in the family. In such a situation, it was possible that Sudhir would do his utmost to stop their departure to London. He was most likely to take away the car they needed. Anticipating this, Rita asked Bhanu to leave the car with a charming singer Binny for the night.

But a day before their departure, when Rita and the children were going to Binny's house to leave the car, they saw that Sudhir was following them. Rita felt her legs shaking. Bhanu and Dhanush were also scared. As a result, Rita was driving the car unsteadily and an accident was imminent. The co-motorists looked at her with disbelieving eyes. When Rita could no longer bear this, she shouted in a pitiable voice, telling some young motorists that she was trying to save herself from her estranged husband who was following her. She also told them that she was very scared of him.

"Don't worry; we shall take care of him. You keep driving on." The young drivers surrounded Sudhir's car and finally parked their cars in front of Sudhir's car. Rita escaped along with the children. She didn't wait to see what happened to Sudhir. The following day

Binny drove them to the airport. The moment Bhanu and Dhanush boarded the plane, they fell asleep as if they had not had any sleep for years. Rita's eyes became tearful when she saw their innocent baby faces.

The old chain of thoughts caught hold of her. What had these kids seen in life in the world? What harm had they done to Sudhir? Rita recalled that Sudhir had been very harsh upon the children. Once when he had returned home after a long time, he had beaten Dhanush mercilessly and tried to strangle him. Out of pain Dhanush had managed to say, "Daddy, what have we done to you that you beat us so much? We love you so much but you show no mercy. You are our father and there is no one else to look after us."

"Great supporter of the mother, aren't you? Like mother like son."

"Daddy I am your son too."

"Get lost. Let me have some sleep. You are a puppet of your mother."

That day Dhanush had wept for a long time. Rita was heartbroken. Then Sudhir had rushed to hit Rita without any cause; Bhanu had come between her mother and Sudhir and said, "No, Daddy, you can't hit my mother like this. Now we are grown up and we won't let you beat Mama."

At this Sudhir had collected all of Bhanu's clothes, and throwing them out of the door had told her to leave the house at once saying, "Now you are eighteen and in America children after eighteen have to earn their living. Get out. There is no place for you in this house." He also called the police. When the police arrived, Rita had told them that the girl would stay where the mother was. The policeman said, "If the mother wants to keep her daughter with her, she can."

"But I...," Sudhir continued angrily.

"Sorry sir. God be thanked that we are not your children. A cruel father like you would make a prostitute of his innocent daughter." Saying this, the police left.

That day Bhanu also wept for a long time. She had said, "Mama, I don't feel as if this were our house any longer. Do we have no house, Mama?"

"No my darling, don't say so. I am around for you. You are not alone, the house I live in is also the house where my children are going to live"

In this short span of time fate had made them face so many unpleasant situations. Do fathers behave like Sudhir? Rita wept and after some time went to sleep.

When she woke up, the plane had reached Heathrow airport. Aunty and Uncle had come to receive them. As soon as they reached home, Bhanu and Dhanush left to see the bazaar. Preparations for the marriage were in full swing. England is a very nice place.

The Indians migrated from Africa and Indians from Africa have different ways of life. Rita's uncle was born in Africa and had received education there. During 1962-64, when the Indians lived there even some of them were born in Africa. Some part of Africa demanded freedom, Uncle, Aunty and the other members of the family had come to England and settled in London. The groom-to-be was also born in Africa and he was called Bawa.

"Here, Bawa, you used to say that you would marry an English girl. What made you change your decision that you are marrying an Indian now?" Rita teased him.

"Yes didi, I really wanted to marry an English girl, but my parents did not agree."

"Then…?"

"I had an English girlfriend. She was very nice. She liked Indian culture very much. She wore a sari and liked Indian music so much that she had learnt even Indian cooking. Her parents too loved me very much. But one day when I brought her home, Mother was frightened."

"Why?"

"Because she was not a white girl, she was black."

"Arre baap! (Father)!" (Oh my God!)

"Why are you so surprised?"

"Bawa, whether they are black or white, their way of thinking is different."

"I don't agree. The British ruled over India and subjected the Indians to untold miseries; still Indians like their white color. Tomorrow if Bhanu found a black boyfriend, what would you do?"

"She may have a white or black boyfriend but if she picks one out of my Indian culture, I shall never speak to her."

"No didi, if he is white, you would feel proud…"

"And if he is black…." Mausi (mother's sister) intervened.

"Didi, will feel humiliated. Indian culture and Indians will say things about such a development."

"Arre (oh dear) please say auspicious words, Bhanu is very young." Rita felt irritated.

"Children grow fast. Please don't speak against Sudhir before them as then they won't respect you when they are adults," the mausi said.

Rita felt giddy when she heard this. She prayed, "Oh Lord, take away everything from me but don't let my children go against me. They have none of their own in the world. I fail to understand why everybody thinks ill of my children. I don't want to have any dispute with Sudhir. Oh God, please let the dreams of my children come true. Protect them from the evil eye. Let them not go astray. Oh Lord almighty; oh creator of the universe, please protect my children from evil people."

"Rita didi, I see tears in your eyes. You have taken jokes very seriously. Have I offended you?"

"No, Bawa, it is nothing. By the way, what is the name of your bride?"

"Rubina."

"Is she a Muslim?"

"No, not at all. Only name is Muslim. But don't tell grand ma…"

"What…?" Rubina wears a sari in the presence of my mom. She goes to the temple; performs aarti of Krishan Bhagwan and recites Hanuman Chalisa. (A prayer in verse to Lord Hanuman, worshipped by the Hindus.)"

"And what does she like to do behind your mum's back?"

"She is fond of visiting pubs."

"What is a pub?" Rita casually asked.

"Pub, a bar."

"In other words, it is a place of unrestricted indulgence, where liquor is served and one can dance, smoke and eat and ..."

"Didi, you are strange. What difference does it make if she occasionally smokes...?"

"If Mausi finds this out after marriage?"

"How will she know? We shall start living in a separate house right from the day following the marriage."

"Have you rented a house?"

"Yes, we have. Rita didi, actually we wanted to marry in court but Mom and Dad didn't agree."

"Dear Bawa, you are their only son. If you marry according to Hindu rites, you lose nothing. The marriage party will arrive, saat phere honge (the ceremony of going round the fire seven times), the bride will be carried in a palanquin and the golden night will..." Rita blushed when she mentioned the golden night.

"Didi, we didn't feel the need to wait for such ...I mean... essential physical requirements and the least of all these elaborate programs to delay important things. We have already..."

"You naughty Bawa...!"

"Lo, here comes Rubina. Rubina, this is my Rita didi from America."

"Namaste didi." Rubina wished Rita with her head bowed in modesty.

"Wow, how innocent and beautiful she is!" Rita forgot everything Bawa had told her about various facets of Rubina's character.

Rubina felt too weak to speak. She was feeling so shy that she took Rita for her mother-in-law. She was tall and slim and physically strong. Her big dark eyes and dark silken long hair added to her charm. Rita could not decide whether she was really as simple as she appeared to be or Bawa was just pulling her leg. In the meantime, Mausi's friend Amita came there with her two children. Rita and Amita had a great rapport. They talked and joked a lot. Her two children and Rita's children were also very friendly with each other.

Amita observed when she saw Rita 's children, "Wow! Bhanu has turned out to be very beautiful. I see Dhanush too has grown very tall."

"You got Beautiful Kids"

"But this is not fair. A marriage is on and instead of adding to the grandeur of the marriage celebrations, they want to go to watch a movie," Mausi complained indignantly.

"Mausi, in Los Angeles they don't go anywhere. But they may go with Amita's children. But I shall stay at home and along with Amita, we shall dance the Bhangra till we fall down entirely exhausted, won't we Amita?" Rita changed the topic.

The children enjoyed themselves a lot and so did Rita and Amita. In the meantime, like in India, Mausi's house was getting crowded with relatives from distant places, who came almost daily. Mausi performed every ceremony. Kirtan and Jagrata were held turn by turn. If it was Maiya now, it was Kangana tying next. Trials and tribulation were almost history for Rita and her children. On Rita, Mausi showered love in abundance. Rita freely used Mausi's saris and jewelry. Rubina and Bawa's marriage was performed with due pomp and show. Rita and the children stayed in England for a month.

It was time for Bhanu to go to Greece. Amita worked for some private airline. Hence, she also made a program to accompany Bhanu with her children.

"Mama, I feel Amita aunt's son Pankaj likes me," Bhanu said to Rita. She said Further "mama I don't want to I am not ready to have a boyfriend yet.But Mama, I am nervous to think of all such things."

"What things bete?"

"That all men are bad like Daddy."

"Bete, if you find a man judiciously, I shall have no objection even if he is an American. Man should not live on the money of his wife. He should Provide everything to the wife or Girlfriend. I don't like free loaders. But I would be very happy if you select an Indian."

"If it is a man from an Indian lineage, his people will talk about Daddy as Daddy does about your family when he abuses them."

"Anyway, now you go to bed, leaving tomorrow's business to the God in heaven."

In Greece Their stay was in a big hotel in Athens. Dhanush was a very straight boy. Bhanu was busy shooting with a modeling agency and in the evening, she went to eat at a restaurant with Purnima, Pankaj, Amita and Dhanush. There was a dance club in the hotel and everyone went for a dance there. In the crowd, Rita and Bhanu felt lonely. One day Bhanu said, "Mama, shall I ever become a good model?"

"Why not? What are you lacking in? But if you don't become a successful model in a year, you shall have to find some other career on the basis of your college degree."

"By inference it implies that I won't be a good model, then."

"I think, Bhanu, you are losing confidence in yourself but want assurance from me."

"Yes aunty, these days she is depressed," Pankaj said.

"Rita, tomorrow let's visit different islands in Greece; it will cheer Bhanu up," Amita proposed.

All agreed and tickets for three islands were purchased. The ferry stopped at every island. The weather was hot and a blue sky added to the charm of the trip. The clear sunlight turned the sea water a green hue. Because of the heat, all felt thirsty. Greece is sprinkled with numerous historical sites. At a particular place, the captain of the boat told the passengers to get off for sightseeing. Amita and Purnima busied themselves in shopping. Pankaj and Dhanush went for a swim in the deep sea. Left alone, Rita and Bhanu sat alone on the shore and were lost in thought. At that moment Bhanu saw a girl swimming without anything on. She said, "Look, Mama, there is a girl swimming without any clothes on."

"Yes, Bhanu, but she looks as if a beautiful fish were swimming in water in the form of a woman."

"In Paris and Greece people swim in the nude."

"Bhanu, in India, the police put such people behind bars."

"But is there any such place in America where people can bathe without any clothes on?" Bhanu asked with apparent curiosity.

"But I don't know why that golden haired girl bathing in the nude does not look obscene to me. It seems God has created a woman's body in a beautiful mold."

"But God has created the most beautiful body of my mom," Bhanu said, and reclined in Rita's lap.

"What is it, Bhanu, that you show so much of love to your mom today?"

"I love my mom more than my life.'

"Oh my sweet baby! My children are my strength and my life too. I can't live without my children."

"Mama, I don't dislike Pankaj but I think he likes me very much."

"My darlings, both of you are very young. My advice is that you just enjoy each other's company and don't think of going beyond it."

The discussion between the mother and daughter would have continued but then Dhanush came there and said, "Mama, Pankaj and I swam in considerably deep water. Now we are hungry and would care for some food. Look, Purnima and Amita aunty too are here."

Amita came closer and said, "Rita, you are a total bore as you are always sad and keep Bhanu too bored like yourself."

"See, it is time for the boat to return to Athens."

While shopping, Amita had bought a lot of eatables too. As a result, as soon as they were on board the boat, they could start eating without delay. They reached their hotel at about ten in the evening but Dhanush and Purnima went to swim in the pool on the roof of the hotel. Pankaj and Bhanu also got up as if to leave. Rita asked them, "Dear Pankaj and Bhanu, where are you two going?"

"Aunty, Bhanu and I are going for a stroll on the beach," Pankaj said.

"How impractical the children are! Dhanush and Purnima went to swim and these two…"

"Rita, let us go to the night club. You know, the hotel manager tries to flirt with me," Amita said, smiling.

"If the manager takes interest in you, you should make the most of the opportunity. But I am tired and would prefer to have some rest and relaxation." All had found something or the other to busy herself or himself. Rita lay down on her bed. After sometime, Dhanush also came and went to sleep with his mother. Purnima went to the club with her mother. Rita was left alone with her memories. Man may run away from worries and sufferings but the scars always stay with him. They cause pain off and on with a light or severe intensity.

Rita recalled an incident. Once some thief entered the house breaking a glass window of the back door. Rita informed Sudhir in Washington about this incident on the phone. But he didn't send any money for the replacement of the glass. She spent sleepless nights for the safety of the children. Sudhir had a habit of aggravating situations without any objective. Rita would try to interpret the meaning of her life. She could not precisely define her existence. Questions such as who she was, what she was, what made her continue with the miserable life etc. bothered her. She would also want to find out answers to who she was fighting with and why she was doing this. But she never found an answer that could calm the agitation of her mind. The only thing that always happened on such occasions was that she would start weeping helplessly. This happened today too.

She now spoke her thoughts aloud, "I wish to run away and keep going without a halt," but another question faced her - where to flee? Her path was strewn with thorns from beginning to end. Every co-traveler left her half way, leaving her in desolation.

"Did you go to sleep?" She heard Amita, who was standing by her bed with intoxication in her eyes and movements.
"What time is it?"
"It is morning. Look, the golden sun rays are welcoming you."
"Oh my goodness! Where are Bhanu and Pankaj?"
"Look out of the window. You can see them coming to the hotel. It seems they are chums now. I think you should warn Bhanu."
"I can trust Bhanu. My child is very understanding and mature."
Bhanu had by now reached them. Seeing that her mother was still awake, she asked, "Mama, didn't you have any sleep? I am sorry, Pankaj and I discussed school and my future..."
"Beta, in a foreign country, you stayed out till midnight..."

"Don't worry, Mama. I am a big girl and I can take care of myself."

Amita was a woman of very liberal, modern ideas. Her nature too was good but it was a mystery what made her seek male company of total strangers. Why did she love to talk to them and hear them praise her looks? She was born in Kenya. She had married in Nairobi. She was also educated.

One day they decided to see Cape Sounion and the Temple Poseidon. This is the most visited tourist spot in Greece. During the summer season, there is scorching heat of the sun as in India. In this season the Greek remain indoors, trying to stay cool and comfortable. But in the evening, when the sun goes behind the hills gathering with it the hot rays, the golden light of sunset from behind the hills looks as. The sea looks green and blue alternately.

"Bhanu, look, someone is looking at you over there. His eyes are dark and his hair is dark, touched by yellow," Dhanush said to Bhanu.
"Let him do whatever he likes. I am not an apsara (a legendary semi-goddess.)."

Bhanu had been very innocent and had never raised her eyes to the sky. She always humbly looked at the ground. Since the day she had opened her eyes, she had seen nothing but her parents quarreling and her mother getting abused and beatings at the hands of her father. After her father had beaten her mother, he would deal with Bhanu in a like manner. Bhanu was growing fast and the attitude of Rita towards Bhanu was turning into friendship from that of maternal love. Now Rita never used her hands to punish Bhanu. Dhanush also was fourteen years old. Whenever Sudhir beat Rita, Dhanush would hide himself behind Bhanu and she would shield him in her arms. Now Pankaj's friendship added spice to the life of Bhanu. Whenever he called her lovingly, her face shone with joy.
"Bhanu, today I would like to take you to the remotest restaurant in Greece."
"Yes, I am ready. Let's take Purnima and Dhanush too with us."

"No, only both of us will go and don't tell Rita aunty," Pankaj said.

"Pankaj, I shall hide nothing from my mother. But why do you want to take me there alone?" Bhanu was uneasy.

"To be honest with you, I am fast getting attracted to you. I love your quietness," Pankaj opened up.

"I don't understand what you want to say. We are too young yet," Bhanu blurted out thoughtlessly.

"Bhanu, just look into my eyes," Pankaj said, looking into Bhanu's eyes.

"No, I feel bashful and afraid," she said, moving away from him.

"In the meantime, Dhanush, Purnima and Amita all came there.

"Bhanu and Pankaj, where have you been?" Rita asked, feeling a bit concerned.

"Bhanu didi, I am very hungry. But all are talking of going to Angor," Dhanush said, clinging to Bhanu.

"Then why didn't you eat anything? But wait a minute. I think I have an apple in my bag." She took out the apple and gave it to Dhanush.

"I am also hungry." Purnima also joined Dhanush.

"Rita, the children are hungry. Let us hire a taxi and go to Angora. There we can do some shopping and also eat in some Greek restaurant," Amita said to Rita.

"Why not walk there? I like the Greek habit of sleeping during the day and enjoying themselves at night," Rita said.

On hearing this all laughed. They reached a restaurant. When they were seated, Rita saw something unusual. Earlier she had heard Dhanush saying that someone was looking at Bhanu. But she hadn't paid any attention to it then. Now she herself noticed someone staring at Bhanu from behind the counter. She got up and went to the counter in order to talk to the young man. But he had disappeared.

"Mom, I would like to go to London," Dhanush said somewhat sadly.

"Why are you sad dear? Ok, after seeing Santorini and Acropolis we shall return to London." Amita tried to cheer him up. But Pankaj had no intention to return to London so early. But noticing that

Dhanush was very sad, all decided to return to London and reached the airport.

"Bhanu, will you forget me?" Pankaj whispered in Bhanu's ears.

"Pankaj, you are my childhood friend. Why should I forget you?"

"You are very beautiful. I am sure all love your fair color, dark eyes and long dark silky hair."

"No, I am not beautiful. Even though I am fond of modeling, I am not beautiful."

"Why do you underestimate yourself?" Pankaj asked her.

"All the girls in Los Angeles are jealous of me for some reason unknown to me. They never encourage me to mix with them."

"It is so because they are jealous of your beauty. Your are taller than most of them. Look at your long slim legs, and the full inviting lips. I would like to kiss…"

"Ahoy Pankaj, what are you doing there? Let us join our family. Look there, Dhanush and Purnima are looking for us."

In a few hours, all were back in London. Bhanu and Pankaj were about to bid goodbye to each other. It was still a mystery why Dhanush was so eager to return to Los Angeles. Finally, the hour came when Rita, Bhanu and Dhanush were waiting at Heathrow airport to take their flight to Los Angeles.

"Mom, if Daddy again quarreled, what would we do?" Bhanu said sadly.

"Bhanu, my darling, I shall just keep my mouth shut. I have also decided to take a few hotels management classes."

"I wish I stayed back in London! Pankaj likes me a lot."

"And what about you?" Rita casually asked Dhanush.

"I don't know Mom, but I feel that I should decide my own way from now on."

In the meanwhile, the passengers started boarding the plane. Rita, Bhanu and Dhanush also occupied their seats. As the plane was airborne, Rita and Dhanush fell asleep but Bhanu was sleepless. She recalled what Pankaj had said. His shadow approached her and said, "Bhanu look into my eyes. What do you see there?"

"Pankaj, I don't know what love is."

"I have also heard of love, but do not know what it is. I just understand that I like you very much and would like to kiss your hands."

"Pankaj, you are just trying to entice me. The girl Riya, your neighborhood friend…"

"Riya is my girlfriend. Occasionally we…, anyway let it go. Since you have come to London, I have not seen her even once. Bhanu, you are almost like my heart beat."

"And when I am back in Los Angeles, will you again start seeing her?"

"Bhanu, why don't you stay with us in London? We shall go to college together."

"Who will bear my college expenses? How will I pay for my meals? Besides, London is very expensive."

"Bhanu, you can work in the evening to earn your living and other expenses. You can stay with us at night."

Bhanu had liked Athens very much but Rita didn't want to leave her alone there even though an agency had selected her for modeling. Rita recalled that the history of Athens is full of thrills and surprises. The Greek value art very much. Images of the legendary heroes are built. They add to the romance of the city of Athens.

One day Bhanu had visited some shop in the central market in Angora with Pankaj. There Pankaj bought a single eyed ring and gave it to Bhanu, he said, "Here Bhanu, have it as a memento. It will strengthen our friendship."

"Who told you that it is a magical ring?" Bhanu queried.

"It is known as Argos, i.e. it is not one eye but millions of eyes."

"What does that mean?" Bhanu was at a loss to grasp the significance of what he had said.

"Bhanu, I have attended a class on the history of Athens. This is my third visit here."

"Pankaj, you are very lucky. I also want to visit the whole world and I would like to study in Milan, Australia, Norway and Holland."

"Bhanu there is some blind faith about Athens. People regard Poseidon and Athena as gods that protect Athens. You are like my Athena and I am your protector."

"I wish I were born in Athens! I feel I shall never be able to go to college. But I will help Dhanush in getting a college education."

"Dhanush is very mature, Bhanu. If you stay in London, we shall see the whole of Europe by Euro rail. It will be so adventurous and romantic"

"Pankaj, why are you pressing me to stay in London? I know your parents will not agree to what you propose."

"My dear lovely Bhanu, you just say yes once and I shall persuade my parents to allow you to stay here." Pankaj suddenly took Bhanu's hand and kissed it. But Bhanu scolded him and said, "Pankaj don't kiss my hand."

"Why not Bhanu? Oh that I knew the language of the stars. I wish that I could serenade you in the soft fragrant moonlight to express my love for you. I would then show you how deeply I love you." Pankaj again kissed her hand.

Bhanu was reflecting this when the air hostess brought lunch. Dhanush and Rita were awake now. After lunch, Rita and Dhanush again went to sleep. But Bhanu was sleepless. Bhanu kept moving around in the plane. Then she went to the first class to read some magazines. The first class section was not crowded. She took a magazine and sat down to read it. A young man came to her and said, "I think you are also a model. The model on the cover page of this magazine stands no comparison to your appearance."

"Thanks," Bhanu said without looking up. Bhanu never looked at any boy. A little later, the air hostess announced that all should resume their seats as the plane was scheduled to land at Los Angeles in about half an hour. Bhanu returned to her seat. It was nine o'clock now. Gradually the plane began its descent. The lights of Los Angeles looked like brilliantly shining stars. They were like Christmas lights or Diwali lights. At night Los Angeles looks very beautiful.

As Rita, Bhanu and Dhanush got off the plane, somebody handed a card to Bhanu. Bhanu was lost in her thoughts and didn't pay attention and care to look who handed the card. She felt as if Dhanush had given her something.

"Dhanush, what is it?" she asked him.

"Where is Bhanu didi?" Dhanush asked in return.

She held up the card and read the words written in shiny golden ink, 'You are my destiny. You are the one who is my destiny, my dreams have been waiting for many centuries. Ah! I found you. You are my soulmate.' She showed it to Rita and told her that someone had given her the card.

"Throw it away. At the most he could be some mad man." Bhanu wanted to obey her mom but she hesitated and didn't throw it. "Didi, I feel the boy who was staring at you in Athens must be the person that has given you the card."

"My dear little brother, how could he be in Los Angeles? He was in Athens."

Rita hired a taxi and reached home. They opened the door and noted that Sudhir was not there. On the other hand, all the furniture and Sudhir's clothes were also missing. His car too was gone. The children recalled how badly Sudhir, their father, had behaved with them. Bhanu said, "Mom, there is nothing here. There are no pots and pans and even the beds are gone."

"Come on. Let's see whether they are in the first-floor room." Rita said with clear uncertainty in her voice. They went up and found a note from Sudhir— 'I have thrown away all our belongings. I have found a job in Korea and am going there. The children are yours and I have no responsibility towards them. You now earn your living and bring the children up. Buy everything you need and run the family.'

Rita put the note into her purse and asked the children to have some sleep. "But the note is by Daddy. What has he written?"

"My dear children, your daddy has gone to Korea. He has found a job there."

"We miss Daddy very much." Both began to weep.

"You must not weep my dears. We shall find out where your daddy is and then you can talk to him," Rita soothed them. As the children were tired, they somehow went to sleep. In the morning Rita bought the essentials including some eatables, sheets etc. She also started looking for a job. The schools were open and the children busied themselves in their studies. Bhanu studied in a community college and side by side worked in the school library.

"Bhanu, I have found a job as manager in a big hotel," Rita said.

"Oh Mom, I am so happy for you."

"Bhanu, Dhanush is interested in training as a doctor of medicine. He has received a letter to that effect from many institutes."

"Mom, Dhanush is good at studies. But unluckily, I could not even go to college."

"Why do you think this dear? You are not to blame. It is my fault."

"How is it your fault? You asked Daddy a number of times to deposit college fees but he never did."

"Yes, but if I had a job, I would have found some good college and helped you," Rita said and tears appeared in her eyes.

"O Mom, Pankaj is coming to see me this week."

"Oh yes, Amita had rung me up."

"Mom, Amita aunty is very nice, but Pankaj had told me that his father doesn't approve of our marriage."

"Marriage!" Rita was startled.

"Yes, Mom, Pankaj says that he has fallen in love with me."

"Love!" Rita got another shock.

Pankaj had been coming to Los Angeles off and on earlier too, but after Bhanu's London visit, it was his first visit. Rita had just thought of Bhanu and Pankaj as mere friends. She had not realized that Bhanu was now a grown-up girl. But she also wondered why Pankaj's father was against the marriage of Pankaj and Bhanu. Bhanu was a tall, slim, sweet, beautiful girl and Pankaj could not have found a better girl. She said to Bhanu, "If Pankaj's daddy does not like the marriage, you too need not mention marriage to Pankaj. There is no dearth of good boys for you."

"Mom, don't be angry. Pankaj is my first love. But we will not marry until he has completed college."

Rita started going to her job. Dhanush had been admitted to Washington University and was receiving a government scholarship. But he was determined to leave to join the university only after seeing Pankaj.

In the meantime, Bhanu was waiting for Pankaj. On the night preceding his arrival, Bhanu found it difficult to sleep. Hope can lead man to strange situations. Bhanu would talk to Pankaj in her imagination, "Pankaj, you have colored my dreams in a way that I feel as if I have talked to you for many nights in a row."

Pankaj would respond, "Bhanu, you don't realize how deeply I love you."

Bhanu would say, "Pankaj, what has happened that we never realized how and when we fell in love with each other?"

He would say, "Bhanu, the day I saw you swimming in the emerald green waters of Grease Sea I resolved that you alone would be my life partner."

Pankaj pervades Bhanu's thoughts. She felt as if he was creating waves in her heart and asking her to buzz like butterflies. She then missed him badly. She took her big pillow and hugged it tight against her bosom. She fell to reflect again. Once when Pankaj and Bhanu were taking a stroll along the beach in Greece, Pankaj had said, looking into her eyes, "Bhanu do you know that when you are reticent, I feel sad."

"Why?"

"I love you sweetheart," he had said and kissed her on the cheeks.

"Pankaj, we are very young. You had better not touch me like this," Bhanu had suggested.

"Love is God and in loving each other, we are not committing any sin," he had said.

"These philosophical dialogues are beyond me, Pankaj."

"I only want to see a sweet smile, you know."

"How long will you love me? The moment you set your eyes on another beautiful girl, you will forget me."

"I will love you till my last breath," he said and again kissed her. Lost in these musings, Bhanu went to sleep. While she was asleep, Dhanush startled her when he awakened her and told her that Amita aunty was on the phone and wanted to talk to her. She rushed to the phone and at once said, "How are you aunty? Where is Pankaj?"

"Bhanu, I have been thinking how to talk to you for a week but didn't know how to broach the issue."

Her voice betrayed helplessness and she began to sob on the phone. Bhanu was frightened. She almost shouted, "Amita aunty why are you weeping? Where is Pankaj? Please give him the phone. I would like to talk to him."

Rita was getting ready to go to work. But before leaving she was getting juice and omelets ready for the children. She called the children, "Bhanu, Dhanush, come along and have breakfast."

"Mom, Amita aunty is on the phone and Bhanu is talking to her," Dhanush told Rita.

At the mention of Amita, Rita picked up the parallel line in the kitchen and said, "Amita, how are you? Why don't you pay us a visit here with Pankaj and Purnima?"

"Mom, Amita aunty is not talking. She is just weeping and is not giving the phone to Pankaj either," Bhanu said into the mouthpiece.

"Amita, please let Pankaj talk to Bhanu," Rita said.

"Amita aunty, does Pankaj not want to talk to me? Is he angry with me?" Bhanu said and began to weep.

"Bitya (a baby girl), Pankaj has become angry with the whole world. He has severed all relations with all of us and gone to the Supreme Father, Lord God, forever."

There was a click and the phone on the other end went dead. "Pankaj…Pankaj…" The receiver fell down from Bhanu's hand and hit the floor. Bhanu screamed, which pierced the heart of Rita and made Dhanush tremble.

Rita was lost. She had no idea what Amrita told Bhanu. All of a sudden Bhanu went numb.

"Mama, I told you I wanted to stay in London. Why didn't you let me stay in London with Pankaj? Only If I had known that this was going to happen, I would have never ever left him in London alone."

Rita felt sharp pain in her words. The man she loved; he was no more. The man Bhanu was planning to spend the rest of her life with.

"I want him back in my world, Mom, he is not dead. No, he is alive. Aunty Amita is lying. He will never leave me alone in this cruel world. I am going to London. Let's go, Dhanush, get ready. Maybe he went to sleep. He will wake up with the touch of my fingers. You watch, Mama, I am going to bring him back to Los Angeles."

Bhanu was totally out of touch with the family and herself. Rita does not even know what to tell Bhanu. How to console her.

CHAPTER 14

'Man proposes but God disposes' goes the saying. There could not have been a worse beginning for the love story of Bhanu, almost an innocent child, who had hardly tasted a few moments of love, the divine gift for Adam and Eve's progeny. Her first love, Pankaj, was killed in a car accident. Bhanu gathered together the pieces of a broken heart, the few pictures of Pankaj with her and a few memories of the moments spent with him. The only thing she was capable of doing was to keep crying inconsolably. Her eyes were red and swollen. Dhanush also knew Pankaj. He, too, missed him acutely but his pain was different from Bhanu's. He had lost a playmate, a warm young friend with whom he had a great rapport and could talk about the new things that lads learn while growing into men. He also occasionally shed tears and was in no mood to talk to anybody. Seeing the children's plight, Rita was herself at a loss how to console them who had never seen the ugly face of death from close quarters in their short span of life.

Rita fell to reflect on the ways of fate. Who had said that man, the weakling that he is, can fight fate? Life is a puzzle. However hard Rita tried to puzzle out the mystery of life, she found it difficult to find a satisfactory answer. God had created the world and put humans as puppets on it to dance to the tune of fate, the tyrant. If God loves creation, why does he behave in such ways that his puppets, his children on the earth, suffer so much? The Hindu philosophy believed in experiencing the consequences of the past actions whether of this life or some past life. Rita didn't remember anything so wrong that entailed this fate. Of past lives she knew nothing. The only thing she saw was the suffering of the children at the loss of a dear friend. Their weeping was too much for her to put up with.

Rita controlled her own grief at the incident and said to Bhanu, "Don't weep, my child. Have courage."

Bhanu just looked at her mother's drawn face and helplessness in her eyes and her weeping turned to a storm. She clung to her mother and both wept for a long time. Bhanu was exhausted and fell asleep in the arms of her mother who did not move lest she should awaken the girl. Both mother and daughter lay in each other's arms for a long time and perhaps Rita too was asleep. God had been merciful to grant them a little respite after all.

When they did get up, Bhanu again started weeping and complained to her mother, "You always say Bhagwan (God) is merciful. But why has He snatched Pankaj away from me? How had I wronged Him?"

But if there had been an answer known to Rita, she herself would not have suffered in life. Consequently, she said nothing.

Dhanush too was sitting close by. He wiped his tears and said, "Bhanu didi, I am your brother. At least for my sake, stop crying."

Those who bid goodbye to the world never come back but leave the living to spend life in tears forever. Time, it is said, is the best healer. The tears finally dry up but the bitterness and suffering sinks in the hearts to stay forever. It was now six months since Pankaj had been killed. Bhanu had imprisoned herself in a cocoon and hardly ever talked to anyone. She had discontinued going to college. Nothing was known of Sudhir.

Dhanush had gone to Washington D.C. for further study in the medical field. Bhanu occasionally talked to Amita and Purnima. They had told her that Pankaj had gone to a party at the club with his friends. The boy who was driving was drunk and the accident occurred.

Once, Bhanu said to Amita, "Aunty, I knew that Pankaj and his friends drank. I had tried to persuade Pankaj many times not to drink but as his friends also consumed liquor, my persuasions had no effect on them."

"Bhanu, if you really loved Pankaj, why did you not...?"

"Don't say 'loved', I still love him and nothing can replace his love as long as I live. But aunty, why didn't the doctor save him?"

"Bhanu, he could have survived but a nurse didn't give him medicine on time."

"What, aunty?" Bhanu again started weeping loudly. She added, "Amita aunty, I don't feel at home in Los Angeles. Can I come to London?"

"My child, you are always welcome but whenever you decide to come here, please take permission from your mother."

"Aunty, I shall ask my mother this evening." She had disconnected the phone that day.

From that day on Bhanu almost always insisted upon going to London but Rita knew that if she once went to London, there was a very slim chance of her ever coming back to Los Angeles. Consequently, she would put her off with one pretext or the other. But one day Bhanu sprang a surprise on Rita. She said, "Mom, I have got admission to a nursing school in Toronto."

"Why Toronto? Is there no school in America? Will you leave me alone here?"

"But Mom, you were unwilling to let me go to London. I also realized that I should not go to London as memories of Pankaj would haunt me there."

"But why do you want to go to Toronto? I will be all alone in the house." Rita was perturbed.

"I want to be independent. If I stay with my parents, I shall not get a scholarship."

"But why go to a nursing school? Why not go to a medical college just like Dhanush? After all, Dhanush is also going to train as a doctor."

"Mom, I am not Dhanush. I would like to be a nurse. Why do you always try to make me feel small? What is wrong with our Indian parents in America? Why are they always pushing children to be a doctor for their own Showing up their status? Anyway, I am going to do the packing," Bhanu said dryly.

"Believe me Bhanu, I am not at all partial to you. Both of you are the same in my eyes. But if you have decided to be a nurse, go ahead and do as you wish. Follow your dream my child, but please never go away from my life," Rita said sadly.

Rita recalled the time she was married. She had left her parents, brothers and sisters and come to a foreign land but her husband was with her. But now Rita's children had left to build their career on their own. Rita lived alone in a four-room, big house. She spent the day at work and didn't feel lonely but at night, back at home, she found the four walls cold and unwelcoming in the absence of her children. Actually, she was married but her life was no better than that of a divorced woman.

Divorced women were free to have some male company and people took pity on the widows and they could find some comfort, but Rita was neither a divorcee nor a widow. She expected nobody to be sympathetic to her. She was a married woman, separated from her husband, and deserved no sympathy from society. Occasionally she visited a temple or went to some movie. At night she would find the bed vacant without the children and lay there sad without her Children. She had realized she is not going to seek love from outside. She had always moved forward and looking back was not a part of her life. Now she had no inclination to again exhaust herself with shattered dreams, broken promises and cruel blows of fate. The fresh gusts of wind that had made their exit from her life were never to return. Uninhabited places promise only ruins. They are not for flowers to blossom. Her laughter of youth, her youth and prime of womanhood had left her for good.

Dhanush had been good at studies since the early school days. Although he the creator had created him in a mood that he was always smiling and cheerful. Away from home, whenever he felt sad, he would call his mom or Bhanu to mitigate his homesickness. But he continued with the tough subjects of medical science.

One day he was exceptionally sad. He went out to the tennis court and began to play tennis alone. He was very engrossed in the play when he heard a sweet female voice, "Hey, are you Indian?"

He stopped and let the ball fall. He saw a beautiful young girl looking at him. Then he said, "Yes, I am. I was born here in America. What about you?"

"Yes, me too. Do you speak Hindi?"

"Of course, I do," he said proudly.

"My name is Savera. May I know Your name?"

"I am Dhanush. Do you study in this college?"

"No, my brother is a medical student here. Mom prepared aloo parathas (fried Indian chapati) for Subodh and I have come to deliver them to him."

"I am also very fond of aloo parathas. Then the name of your brother is Subodh."

"Did you think he was my boyfriend?" she joked.

"I would not be much wrong if I thought that a beautiful girl like you would not be single. Won't you please introduce me to your brother? I am alone here, you know."

"Where are your parents? They are not in America?" Savera asked him offhandedly, ignoring his oblique complement.

"They are in Los Angeles. They live there. But I have residency in Washington D.C."

Dhanush and Savera were engaged in light chit chat when Subodh also turned up there.

"Who are you taking to, Savera?" Subodh didn't approve of her talking to Dhanush.

"Subodh, this is Dhanush. He is alone here. Would you mind giving him one aloo paratha please?"

"Nice meeting you, Subodh," Dhanush extended his hand for a handshake.

"Have you come here recently Dhanush?"

"No. In fact I got residency from Washington D.C."

"Very good. But my residency is almost over. I shall go to New York shortly," Subodh said.

"Congratulations. It is good to hear this."

"Here, sit down and have a pratha with us." When they were eating, Subodh asked Dhanush, "What does your father do?"

"He is an engineer. He works in a Korean firm."

Subodh, Savera and Dhanush became good friends soon. The brother and sister introduced Dhanush to their family, Satnam the mother and Ravinder the father. Now Dhanush had found a new family to interact with. Whenever Subodh's mother had a party at her home, she also invited Dhanush. At one such party where Dhanush was invited, Satnam's sister-in-law (husband's sister) remarked, "I notice that Dhanush is a very nice boy."

"Yes, didi. But Savera was saying that his parents are separated. He is from a broken family," Satnam said.

"What does Savera think about marriage? After all, she is a grown-up girl now. She has also done a law degree," Satnam's sister-in-law asked.

"Just let Subodh become a doctor. Then I shall find good matches from India for both, the brother and the sister, and get them married there."

"What? I shall never go to India to get married. Don't bother to find a match for me in India," Savera told her mother bluntly.

Satnam Kaur belonged to a good Sikh family. She had married Ravinder Dass Gujjar of her own choice. But she didn't like Savera's blunt words, especially before Ravinder's sister.

Savera was older than Dhanush by two years but still she loved Dhanush secretly. Dhanush was a very simple young man. He did not like to have a girlfriend or go to clubs due to his deep interest in finishing his studies first. He also did not want to lose the government scholarship.

On the other hand, Bhanu had arrived in Toronto. One day she had an orientation program. A large number of students from India, China, Philippines and Toronto were present. There were also a few boys to join the nursing training and some doctors who wanted to give the new trainees ten hours' work. Bhanu left the room for a minute and went out to drink water. She came back soon after but by then the orientation was over. She found some familiar written notes on her seat 'You are my destiny. On seeing you here, I am sure that you are made for me.' Bhanu first got a little angry, then she got nervous and frustrated. Who could it be that crossed her path again and again and had been chasing her for such a long time wherever she was? She put the note into her bag unwillingly.

Bhanu got a room in the school. She shared it with another Indian girl, Nadia. (River Hindu name) She was senior to Bhanu by two years. The girls became good friends soon. Nadia had a car whereas Bhanu had never had either a car or a driving license. As a result, she shared Nadia's car whenever they wanted to visit any place.

One day the weather was very fine. The rain had stopped after falling continually for a few days. The sun was shining brightly and the moisture in the air had imparted to the sunlight a golden hue. The Canadians were happy.

Bhanu said to Nadia, "Nadia, I love your name. It is very musical and sweet."

"I, too, like your name, Bhanu," Nadia said.

"That is great. I have an idea. Why don't we exchange our names?" Both laughed.

"Bhanu, do you not have any boyfriend?"

"No," Bhanu responded sadly.

"Are you still a virgin?"

"Yes, I am a virgin," she said proudly, though she didn't like this curiosity of Nadia.

Nadia had many boyfriends. She had been once married too. But she was never on good terms with her parents, so much so that she didn't like to hear from them. Seeing them was simply out of the question.

"Nadia, why do you hate your daddy so much?"

"Bhanu, my daddy has spoiled the lives of two women."

"How was that?"

"My father had first married an educated girl in India."

"Then what happened to that woman?" Bhanu asked eagerly.

"I know only this much that my grandparents were very greedy and wanted a dowry."

"This dowry is evil. The in-laws of the girl expect the girl to bring along a gold mine with her in dowry," Bhanu observed contemptuously.

"I told my grandmother that an educated girl was nothing less than a hen that laid golden eggs. Have her do some good job and give her due regard. She will also prove to be a good housekeeper."

"It was sane advice. But didn't your father want his first wife to do a job?"

"I don't know why he did not let her do some job. My grandparents wanted her to bring money from her parents with which they could clear their debts," Nadia said with dislike.

"Where is your daddy's first wife now? Why has your daddy come to Canada?" Bhanu showed curiosity.

"She is in America along with her daughter, my step sister. My grandfather has a travel agency. He sent my daddy with my mother without getting them married," Nadia told her.

"So that's why your mother gives a wide berth to Indians."

"Bhanu, my stepmother had a very harmful influence on our family."

"What influence?" Bhanu asked.

"I have heard that out of anger my stepmother had written very dirty letters to my father. My grandparents sent copies of those letters to all the relatives of the stepmother, the in-laws of the stepmother's sisters and even neighbors."

"It was really in very poor taste. Exchange of letters between husband and wife is purely a private matter."

"Bhanu, it was exactly for this reason that I did not want to marry an Indian boy."

"If that was the reason, then in what circumstances did your first marriage with an Indian boy take place?"

"My father took me to India on an excuse and there married me quietly to a young man who was an engineer."

"Why didn't you protest?" Bhanu asked in surprise.

"I had protested initially but then I was given a chance to talk to the boy who talked decently. Hence I agreed to marry him. But once in Canada, he underwent a total metamorphosis and showed the ugly side of his nature."

"How did he change?" Bhanu hadn't fully grasped what Nadia was saying.

"Bhanu, I was teaching him how to drive a car. He often committed mistakes and I stopped him. He took this as humiliation. If I asked him to lend me a hand in the kitchen etc. he would protest, saying that I was treating him as a servant. He quarreled almost in everything. He constantly talked to the people in India and never realized that in Canada, the husband and the wife both work. He would advise me to save or spend money judiciously."

"Nadia, did he have any girlfriend in India?" Bhanu asked Nadia.

"Yes, since you mention it, he had a girlfriend that he wanted to bring to Canada and marry after divorcing me."

"You should have made him shift back to India."

"Yes, when I divorced him, the immigration department sent him back to India."

"You treated him appropriately. People think that in America and Canada, money grows on trees for all just to extend a hand and pluck."

"Bhanu, let us stop this. I am bored with these harrowing memories. It is a sunny day today. Let us go out for an outing."

"Nadia, I would like to go to High Park. I have heard that there is a blue water lake and the trees around are very ancient and of various colors."

"But Bhanu, I would prefer to take you to Casanova Castle. Then we can go to High Park too."

"Yes, but the condition is that I shall foot the gas bill."

"Well, ok, if by paying for the gas you feel happy."

Rita worked and saved a little and from the meager earnings she sent small amounts to Dhanush and Bhanu. They had no knowledge where Sudhir was and what he did. Usually when people step out of youth and attain responsible adulthood, they want to forget their time of youth if it had been unpleasant.

Dhanush was a handsome, tall young man now. His brown complexion, curly hair and serious demeanor were his great assets. Off and on he felt very lonely in Washington D.C. But his friendly nature came to his aid to some extent. If he came across acquaintances or friends while going anywhere, he would never pass by without greeting them or asking for their welfare. He also went surfing in the sea to mitigate his boredom. He loved his sister Bhanu very much. Often, he missed her and cried silently.

He recalled how on such occasions when he had been a witness to the severe beating of his mother by his father and he was frightened, Bhanu, though herself disturbed, shielded him in her arms. The old memories hurt him. Sometimes when Rita was beaten, she vented her anger on Bhanu and beat her. All these incidents had left their impact on his nature. They had made him feel that there was no rationality in life and no true friendship and no human relation was genuine. It was against this background that he kept a reasonable distance from Savera and did not let his relation with her go beyond formal friendship.

Satnam invited Dhanush whenever there was a party in the family considering that he was alone in Washington D.C. Dhanush had purchased an old car. It often needed minor repairs and Savera's father taught Dhanush how to take care of them. Dhanush had told Rita and Bhanu how lucky he was to find a nice family comprising Satnam, Ravinder, Savera and Subodh. Dhanush, Savera and Subodh were good friends now. Incidentally Subodh and Dhanush had got residency in the same hospital.

Savera was senior in age to both Subodh and Dhanush. She was a good defense attorney. On the other hand, Dhanush was junior to her by almost two years but there was a mysterious understanding between them
Whenever Dhanush expressed any idea, Savera understood it perfectly as if by intuition. The habits of both were also identical. Savera loved Dhanush but had never expressed this to him. Savera's parents Ravinder and Satnam had had a love marriage. They used to

be engineering students together in university at Timarpur, Delhi, India. Though Ravinder Kumar was a Punjabi, Satnam was a staunch Sikh. Satnam's parents wanted to marry her to a Namdhari Sikh but Satnam was a girl of determination. She proposed to Ravinder to go to Washington, join an engineering college there and marry her in the court. Ravinder showed his disinclination but brushing aside his refusal, Satnam got herself admitted to a college in Washington and married Ravinder. Later, the families of both accepted their marriage.

Satnam was a member of big clubs in Washington and attended big parties. But she was not ready to reconcile with the fact of separation of Dhanush' parents. Dhanush had one more year to complete his graduation in the medical college. After graduation, he was likely to move back either to Canada with Bhanu or to his mother in Los Angeles. Then Savera wouldn't find time to propose to him. Although she had been on dates with many young men, whether Indian or white, even during school or college days, there was something about Dhanush that had won her over. His economy of words, his innocence and simplicity and, most of all, his charming smile attracted her to him. She herself was brownish in complexion, was tall and had very sharp, attractive features. Her long dark hair added to her charm. When she loosened her hair, it could put even dark clouds to shame. She found it difficult to remove him from her mind and wanted the two hearts to beat in unison to create sweet music but hadn't been able to express her love to Dhanush.

One day she made a bold call to Dhanush. She said, "Arre yaar (hey buddy) what are you doing?"

"Savera, I was just collecting my books. I would like to go to see my sister. We miss each other very acutely."

"Oh, will you please let me talk to your sister and mother?"

"Savera, if you had mentioned this earlier, I would have let you talk to them in a three-way conversation."

"Dhanush, you are so cute, sweet and handsome," she managed to say.

"Oh, you are praising me a bit too much but you are telling me nothing new. I already know that I am cute, sweet and handsome," Dhanush laughed.

"Oh, so you are so conceited," Savera sounded offended.

"Savera, why do you mind this joke? Please don't be so easily offended. By the way, will you not cook an aloo (potato) paratha for me?"

"Not today. But today I accompanied a smartly dressed party to my office," Savera almost commanded him. She intuitively knew he would not say no.

"Savera, I don't attend parties. They are so time consuming and I am very serious about my studies."

"Dhanush, I am not taking any excuses. You have a life to study. Be ready by six o'clock. It's a date." She disconnected the phone.

Dhanush didn't realize that she was taking him on a date even though she had plainly told him that it was a date. He liked American girls very much but he never went on a date. He remembered the advice of his mother and sister that as long as one could not stand on one's own feet, and didn't earn a name for oneself, there was no justification for a date or getting married.

Bhanu and Nadia too had become very good, close friends by now. They were almost like sisters. Both attended school and also worked.

Bhanu one day asked Nadia, "Nadia, one thing beats me. Why didn't your daddy's first wife file a complaint against your daddy to Canadian Immigration?"

"I have heard that when my stepmother complained to the Immigration, my daddy's lawyer argued that she was out of her mind and was making a cock and bull story in order to migrate to Canada. As a result the case was cancelled."

"How bad that your daddy told such a gross lie," Bhanu said indignantly.

"Bhanu, I had explained to my mother also that if my daddy could ditch his first wife, he wouldn't hesitate in doing the same to her and me and there was no use of her visiting so many places of worship to prevent such an eventuality. Gods seldom intervene in day-to-day incidents of human beings."

By now Bhanu and Nadia had reached Casa Loma. Casa Loma is a grand castle, built by Henry Platt. It has eight hundred caves and a maze of secret passages. It is surrounded with gardens of flowery trees. Bhanu had the habit of always walking with downcast eyes. She was alerted by Nadia, "Bhanu, look there. A tall, young, handsome man with dark eyes and hair is looking at you."

"Leave it. I am not beautiful enough for anybody to look at. He must be looking at you."

"Bhanu, this man resembles George Conn." Then she added, "Oh yes, he is a doctor who had come to nursing orientation too."

Now Bhanu looked up and saw the man. She said, "Could this be the man who writes notes to me?" Bhanu was obviously nervous. She added hastily, "Let us get away, Nadia. I am nervous."

"Bhanu, why do you flee everybody without any reason?" Nadia said with annoyance.

"Nadia, people of this type are mostly stalkers. They chase and befool innocent girls, write notes to them and trap them. Then they drag them into prostitution or take them to Greece and have them killed."

"For God's sake, Bhanu, don't be so negative. Come on. Let us go and ask him who he is."

"No, not me. You may go alone. I am going into a cave. I shall wait till you come back." Bhanu hurried away to a cave.

Nadia was worried and stood there. But the man had seen them talking. He advanced towards Nadia. Coming closer he said, "Hello, my name is Dmitri. May I know your name please?"

"I am Nadia. Nice meeting you." She added, "Are you Greek or Indian?"

"I am half Indian and half Greek," he said in Hindi.

"You mean you have mixed blood in you. But I see you know Hindi. Where did you learn it?"

"My mom is Indian and my father is Greek."

"No wonder you are so good looking. By the way, have you ever been to India?"

"I went to India to get my medical degree. There I learnt Hindi and Urdu."

"By God that's great. If you speak Urdu, it is natural to assume that you write poetry in Urdu."

"Your assumption is fully justified. I not only read and recite Urdu poetry, I also write it."

"Then God willing, I shall also hear you recite some of your poems."

"Sure, but where is the friend you were talking to?"

"Why are you interested in my friend? If you are chasing her, it means you are stalking her."

"No, I am not stalking her. If you interpret my interest in her as stalking, I assure you that in future if I come across her, I shall close my eyes rather than look at her."

"Ok. Please tell me clearly who you are. My friend Bhanu is a very simple girl." Slight annoyance was betrayed in Nadia's voice.

"Please don't be agitated. But the name Bhanu is very sweet. It perfectly matches her good looks," Dmitri said and moved to leave.

"Please wait. First promise that you will never write any note to Bhanu and will not chase her. If you again stalk her, I may think of calling the police. I can even kick you out of Canada."

Dmitri was a tall handsome man. He had a muscular body with a broad chest and long strong arms. Nadia's threat had no effect on him. Dmitri's mother, Tripta, was an Indian woman from some Rajasthan royal family. When she was still a girl, she had come to Greece as a tourist after graduating from college.

On an island in Greece, she came across a businessman. As they talked about each other, she fell in love with him. She was so mad after him that she didn't bother to find out whether he was single or married. The business man not only married Tripta, but after the birth of Dmitri, he also built a big house for her and started an Indian restaurant. Tripta wanted Dmitri to meet his relatives in India and she asked her husband also to accompany them. It was then that she found out that the business man was already married and had three sons from his Greek wife.

Tripta felt shattered. She could not reconcile with the idea of how she had deceived herself. But she didn't give up. She took Dmitri to India alone. Initially her parents were very angry at her naivety but by and by they accepted the fate and compelled her and Dmitri to stay in India. She left Dmitri in India; came to Greece and divorced her husband. She dedicated herself to learning Greek language, history and culture. She worked very hard and made her name in business circles. She then came to Jaipur and opened a hotel in Dmitri's name. When Dmitri grew up, he shared his time between India and Greece. When Tripta had decided to send Dmitri to medical college in Canada, she had advised him that if ever he fell in love with a woman, he must respect her. She also impressed on him that he was to marry only an Indian girl.

Dmitri was fond of speaking Greek, Rajasthani, Hindi and Urdu. Once, after graduating from medical college, when he was back in Greece, he saw Bhanu sitting sad on the beach. He noticed that she was tall and innocent looking and had dark eyes. She looked forever dreaming. But there was perpetual sadness in her eyes for some unknown reason. As soon as he saw her, he wrote on his palm, 'You are my destiny and getting you is the aim of my life.'

Dmitri was still engaged in conversation with Nadia when Bhanu returned from visiting the caves of Casa Loma. She found Nadia talking to a young man and decided to leave them alone and made a move to go back to the caves but Nadia hailed her, "Wait Bhanu. I am fed up with this vanishing act of yours. How long can you keep running away from life and the world?"

"Who says I am running away from the world? I just wanted to give you time to talk to your friend."

"Bhanu, he has become my friend just now. Wait. He is leaving but I shall have him meet you before he leaves. My friend can also become your friend." Nadia called Dmitri back.

He came back and politely said, "Never mind, Nadia. I shall never meet you again. I am not a stalker at all."

Nadia rushed forward and stopped Dmitri by coming in his way. She said, "If Bhanu is your destiny, why are you running away from her?"

"Nadia, I don't think your words have any significance. Look, your friend is standing aloof with downcast eyes."

"Dmitri, you just follow me. I shall introduce you to my friend." She led Dmitri to Bhanu and said, "Here Bhanu, meet Dmitri.

"Hi, nice to meet you," Bhanu said, with her eyes still looking at the ground.

"Bhanu, you haven't even had a look at me but have just said 'nice to meet you'. People don't meet this way anywhere in the world. Do you think I am a stalker? Believe me, I am not a stalker. But I confess, I am… your… worshiper."

"What?" Bhanu looked up, surprised.

Nadia liked this conversation between Bhanu and Dmitri and tactfully moved away out of the range of hearing. Bhanu looked up and could not believe that a handsome young man was looking into her eyes. His attitude showed as if he had been in search of Bhanu for ages. Bhanu noticed Dmitri's dark hair, eyes and brown complexion. He was wearing a blue jacket and chocolate-colored jeans. He looked dashing and Bhanu felt she would forget herself in front of this handsome man. Somehow, she managed to control herself and said, "Who are you and how are you, my worshiper?"

"Bhanu, for the first time I had seen you on the beach in Greece and heard a voice rising from my heart that you were my destiny."

"Dmitri, I am not a poet. Please don't overdo the act of expression of your love for me. Don't make me vain. Don't show me rosy dreams and don't tell me fairy tales. I fully well know that I am not as beautiful as you tell me. I can be your friend, not beloved."

"All right, you have shown me a little light of hope. I am lucky that you have given me a chance to be a friend at least," Dmitri said, smiling.

"You are welcome as a friend but let us remain within our boundaries. But I think you won't mind satisfying my curiosity and telling me how a Greek can speak Hindi."

"There is no mystery about it. My daddy is Greek but my mother is a staunch Hindu. I have had Indian upbringing and consider myself more an Indian than a Greek."

"You are very lucky. I went to India only once in childhood but never thereafter got a chance to go there."

"Ok. But if luck favors you, after completing your nursing training, you will be able to go to India."

"How do you know that I am studying nursing?" she asked, puzzled.

"Bhanu, I am a doctor. The day you were present in nursing orientation, I was there. You went out of the hall for a while and I wrote a message in your book."

"I don't think it was a gentlemanly act. You are a stranger and a stalker in a sense. You know that if I report the matter to the police, you can be behind the bars. Please don't chase me in future." Saying this, Bhanu moved to look for Nadia.

But Dmitri said nonchalantly, "If it gives you pleasure to have me arrested, I am ready to be arrested. Here, have my mobile phone and call the police. But Bhanu, I know that you are my destiny."

"Oh Lord! Why don't you understand that it is not India where boys chase girls to show their love and stare unabashedly at them? Such acts are called stalking here," Bhanu said impatiently.

"Calm down Bhanu. I have recently come back from India. But I promise that I shall never stalk you. Here, has my business card. If at any time you need any help or guidance in studies, please call me." Handing Bhanu his card, Dmitri left. She stood looking at him.

She made no move to stop him. Nadia had gone God knows where. Bhanu kept looking for Nadia around the place and finally, feeling tired she sat down on a low wall. Nadia returned after a full three hours. As Bhanu saw her, she vented her annoyance at her, "What sort of friend are you, Nadia? You left me alone with a total stranger."

"Forgive me, Miss Bhanu. I had no ulterior motive in leaving you with him. I am your friend first and then anything else. Now let us go home. We have to prepare for the test also."

At night Bhanu found it difficult to sleep. She wanted to ring Dhanush and narrate the entire incident of meeting Dmitri to him. Bhanu rang Dhanush a number of times and left messages on his answering machine, but he was busy in getting ready for going on a date with Savera. Hence he ignored her phone calls.

In the evening Savera came to pick up Dhanush in her BMW car. Dhanush wore a dress shirt and jeans but on Savera's insistence, he put on his black suit, border shirt and long coat. It was snowing lightly in Washington. When Savera came to pick Dhanush up, he noticed her heavily made up for the first time. Though she had long hair, today she had had them bobbed. She had put on long suede boots topped by a long dark blue coat, black hat and full gloves. Savera rarely used lipstick but today she had put on a light pink lipstick and pink blush. She looked almost like a film heroine.

Though she was very informal with Dhanush and interacted with him without any inhibitions, today she had prepared herself for the kill. She wanted to make sure that Dhanush was hers. She was consequently very sober and thoughtful. She knocked at his apartment door. Dhanush opened the door. When she saw Dhanush dressed so magnificently, she could not take her eyes off him. She told herself that she had never known Dhanush to look so dashing though she had spent much time with him on sight-seeing trips to historical monuments in Washington and the museum. His outfit, his curly hair, and the permanent smile on his face had added to his charming personality. Savera had never before seen him in this turnout.

Dhanush also saw Savera for the first time and she looked like the famed Barbie doll. The most attractive and fascinating part of her anatomy was her eyes, like tiny bows. She looked like a fine creation of an artist and at once caught his fancy. Dhanush had been in Washington for about five years but he had not made many contacts. He had visited the Washington monument that looked like an Egyptian obelisk and the highest building of Washington with a few American girls. He recalled how happy Savera was when he had gone to see the cherry blossom festival with Savera's father and brother. Snow white blossoms from dark branches had covered Savera's hair fully. Dhanush gathered them and playfully showered them on Savera. By and by when the bright sun rays had filtered through the dark branches and touched Savera's eyes dazzling her, she had said, "Dhanush I like you as my best friend. Please don't forget this friendship."

Dhanush had also responded in a like manner and said, "I have the happiest time with you and am thankful to you for making me your friend. I have spent life in great isolation. As such I am additionally grateful to you and your family."

Dhanush and Savera were so lost in appreciating each other that they forgot that they were to leave for the party. But then the notes of music from a radio from the neighborhood shook them back to the world of reality.

"Where are you lost Dhanush? What are you thinking?" Savera asked him.

"I was thinking how lucky I am to have such a beautiful and lovely friend." He smiled at her.

"If you don't mind, can I hold you by the hand and take you to the car?" Savera asked politely.

"Sure, you can. It will be my privilege." They held each other's hands.

"And today, you will drive my new BMW." She pushed him to the driver's side.

"Oh, a new car? When did you buy it?"

"Only last evening. It was a good deal and I bought it," Savera told him cheerfully.

It was the first regular date of Savera and Dhanush. They had met each other so attractively dressed and made up. It was a pleasant breezy evening with light snow falling but with no likelihood of a snow storm. Washington D.C is one of the most beautiful historic cities in America. Its population is around ten million. The city hosts leaders of the world. There are famous buildings such as the Smithsonian, Lincoln Museum, DC Road, Creek Park and the U.S.A. Botanical Garden. Having seen them, Savera and Dhanush finally reached the beautiful Four Seasons hotel, situated near the Potomac River. The route to the hotel was the same they had traversed earlier and the togetherness on the occasion had made them friends.

The evening today was going to lead them to some new destination. Hope can take you to any limits. Savera was conscious of the fact that she was two years Dhanush's senior in age. Still, she was confident that she could have Dhanush as her life partner.

Dhanush parked the car in the hotel parking lot and quickly moved to Savera's side and opened the door of the car. He caught her hand and helped her out. He led her to the hall. Western music was playing. This Place was selected by the Event Management committee of The Company where Savera was working for.

"Savera, who is this dark handsome Indian Boy?" someone in the party asked her.

"Oh, Vicky, meet my friend Dhanush," she introduced Dhanush to Vicky.

"Hello Vicky, nice to meet you." Dhanush shook her hand.

"It won't do. You shall have to dance with Vicky," Savera prompted Dhanush.

"Oh no. I really don't know how to dance," Dhanush protested.

"Never mind. I will teach you." Vicky held his hand and led him onto the dancing floor.

Savera watched them dancing from a distance. Dhanush didn't do poorly for a beginner. After the dance was over, they came to the dining table. Dhanush was a vegetarian and teetotaler. Savera also abstained from eating meat. Dhanush noticed this. He was surprised and asked her, "Savera, today you haven't either eaten meat or taken a drink. Is everything ok?"

"Yes, Dhanush. There is a reason for my not drinking and eating meat today."

"What is the special reason?"

"Dhanush, there is a boy in my life and he is a vegetarian."

"Is he an Indian or American?" he asked calmly.

"He is both Indian and American. He can speak good Hindi."

"In that case, will you not introduce him to me?"

"Yes. Just wait a little. I hope to introduce him to you tonight," she said confidently.

"Is he not at the party here?" Dhanush was apparently a little sad.

Savera noticed his anxiety and sadness. She was pleased as her planning was bearing fruit. It was a confirmation that Dhanush too loved her as much as she loved him. At that moment there was an announcement that the couple that was the best dressed and excelled in dancing would be given a prize. Now Savera once again compelled Dhanush to dance with Vicky for more practice. Finally, Dhanush got ready to dance with Savera. He first took off his long coat and then removed Savera's coat too. As soon as he took her coat off and saw for the first time her half-unbuttoned blouse, her slim waist and soft arms sandwiching two full breasts, he could not move his eyes off her. His eyes moved to her white throat, a firm chin, thick lipped mouth, the eyes and the dark hair. Very slowly his gaze moved down to her lower part and imagined a lot of treasures there; he felt proud and lucky. Now he had no eyes for any other beauty in the crowd. Savera also noticed the male muscular body in white shirt and black trousers and lost her feminine reserve. Her heart missed a beat. Dhanush caught her by the hand and took her to the dance floor. Whitney Huston's song 'I will always love' was playing.

They started dancing. Savera was swinging in Dhanush's arms and simultaneously she was looking into his eyes. She found the smile on his lips and the dimples on his cheeks very attractive. Now and then she placed her palms on his lips and he kissed them. Savera whispered in Dhanush's ears, "I wonder how I have changed. I don't know when I started liking you.

In return, he also whispered in her ears, "I shall never forget your dazzling beauty and an equally dazzling night. Today is my night. You have come into my arms without any reservation. I am proud of you and very lucky. ``

"Dhanush, don't leave me in the arms of time. Please take me into your arms."

"Savera, never before have I had such a sweet experience. Anyone who looks into your eyes is sure to forget his identity. I am inclined to spend my life in your arms holding me tightly against your bosom." He pressed her tightly against his chest.

"Dhanush, I am madly in love with you. My whole being is for you."

"I, too, love you from the depth of my heart, Savera. Your name is imprinted on my heart," he confessed, looking at her beautiful face closely. They could feel each other's warm breath on their faces.

"Dhanush, you have a claim over every bit of my existence. I want to assure you that I shall always be with you through thick and thin."

The music stopped but Dhanush and Savera were still dancing. Then an announcement was heard, 'Today's winning couple is Dhanush and Savera.' But the winning couple had no ears for such announcements against the announcement of the hearts that were so loud and clear. It had suppressed the mundane announcement of their victory. They danced unmindful of the curious and amused onlookers. Dhanush's hand was round Savera's slender waist and her head leaning on his shoulder. Her nipples pierced his chest. Their lips touched each other's and they had no eyes for anything around. At last Vicky advanced and tapped on Dhanush's shoulder and when he looked up, Vicky gestured to them to stop as the dancing had been over for a considerable time. She said, "You are the winning couple, the best dancing partners and the best dressed."

It was a memorable night for Dhanush and Savera. With the fewest words they had written the history of love. They heard the beats of each other's heart beating in harmony. It was one of the best nights for both. It seemed the divine grace too was with them.

After the party this couple went to the Potomac River. They strolled on the road that was close to the Four Seasons hotel. Dhanush usually visited the river for fishing, boating and canoeing. He had seen blue fish in the river. He had many American friends with whom he used to come here. Now Savera suddenly insisted on going canoeing. She said, "Dhanush, you are fond of canoeing. Let us do it now."

"Savera, I suggest that we come canoeing during the daytime. Then we can see beautiful birds and ducks swimming in the water. We can also see George Town from a distance." At night the river presents a heavenly sight. The dancing waves create sweet music, and the twinkling lights of Washington impart a fairyland scene. Dhanush and Savera felt as if they were walking in heaven, not on the earth.

"Dhanush, I would like to watch you surfing in the river someday."

"Sure."

"By the way, aren't you afraid to surf in the river?" Savera asked him.

"What fear? Furthermore, from now on, there will never be any fear as far as I am concerned."

"Why no fear now? Were you never afraid before?" she said.

"No, I was never afraid. But not afraid now because I have a brave girl named Savera with me."

"Dhanush, I find it difficult to believe that we are so close to each other," she said, placing her palms on his chest. "When you raise your shy eyes and look at me, I feel as if you have brought along heaps of dreams in my house."

Snowflakes were descending like flower petals. The music of the waves wafted to them. The green and blue lights played with the waves. The other waves in two hearts were binding them together. Their bodies felt so light as if they were dancing on the playful waves of the river. They started dancing on the road. At that moment a couple in love happened to pass by. When they saw them dancing, they said, "Hey, both of you are made for each other and are so cute."

"Thank you," Savera and Dhanush said in one voice and waved to the couple. They had been together for quite a long time. Dhanush looked at his watch and said to Savera, "Let us go home, Savera. I am sure Satnam aunty will be worried."

They left in their car. Dhanush reached his apartment. Savera was to drop him there and drive home alone. Dhanush didn't want her to drive alone and wanted to propose that he could drive her home but felt that she might misunderstand him. As such he only said, "Savera it is late. Please drive carefully and don't forget to phone me so that you have reached home safely."

"Dhanush, I promise that lost in your thoughts I shall reach home safely but…"

"What is a Savera?" He moved forward and took her in his arms.

"Dhanush I am a bit off my hinges and also obstinate. Obviously, I am likely to make mistakes. Please keep forgiving my mistakes."

"If what you did today was a mistake, I would like you to keep repeating such mistakes." Dhanush kissed her passionately.

"Dhanush, your smile is so charming. Let there be perpetual spring in my life with your smile."

"And you know what? Tonight, when it is snowing, let there be light with your love."

"And your presence is like moonlight. Your touch sends a thrill through every pore of my body."

"Savera, I have nothing to offer to you except true love."

"I want nothing more. I just beg this love for you."

"In matters of love, one doesn't have to beg. My love is for you. Keep it with you away from the jealous eyes of the world."

"I promise, as the moon and its light are inseparable, I shall keep your love with me in my heart, body and soul."

They would not have separated from each other if the weather had been limited only to snow. But there was a gust of wind and it was a strong reminder that they would have to go to their nests. Savera left for her home and Dhanush moved towards his apartment.

CHAPTER 15

Dhanush carried the hangover after drinking the wine of youthful love. He returned to his apartment, mechanically opened the apartment door and entered. The world of romance in which Dhanush had spent the time did not represent the whole world. There was another world in which numerous other things were happening. As he entered the apartment door, he heard the phone bell ringing and lifted the receiver.

He said, "Hello."

"Dhanush, where have you been? I have been trying to contact you for such a long time but you didn't receive the calls."

"Bhanu didi, I have just returned to my apartment. Are you fine? Why are you so agitated?"

"Dhanush, do you know the stalker that had been writing me notes from Los Angeles to Greece, has come to Canada too?"

"Oh! How dare he harass my sister so much? You need not worry. I am coming to Canada tomorrow to set him right."

"But my dear cutie pie little brother Dhanush, there is no need to be so scared. He is not a stalker at all. In fact he is a doctor. But I have done what was necessary in the circumstances. I boldly told him that if he did not discontinue stalking me, I shall call the police."

"What was his reaction then?" Dhanush felt proud of his didi.

"He was scared and assured me that he would never chase me. But…"

"What do you mean by but?"

"The strange thing is that though he gave his name as Dmitri, he can speak Urdu, Hindi and Rajasthani."

"Didi, don't feel nervous. Maybe he is alone and may have been seeking company and maybe he likes you."

"You naughty young man! How dare you pull my leg? But where were you, Dhanush? Were you busy working in the hospital?"

"I don't know how to put it, Bhanu didi. I think I have fallen in love. Actually, I am in love."

"Bravo, my little dear brother, you have fallen in love. I shall just inform Mom that in Washington you not only study medicine but also have learnt how to fall in love."

"No didi, don't tell Mom yet. Savera will herself phone you and talk to you."

"Hurray! So Savera is the name of my to-be sister-in-law, the queen. Looks like you have had a hot date tonight."

"Bhanu didi, I am to go to hospital for work tomorrow. Please take care." He felt shy in confessing that he had.

Bhanu disconnected the phone and forgot the love story of Dhanush. She instantly started thinking of Dmitri. These days she rarely talks to Purnima and Amita. Bhanu was happy and soon fell asleep. She got up early in the morning and found Nadia ready to go to school. Nadia noticed that Bhanu was very happy that morning and was humming cheerfully. She asked, "Won't you share the good news that makes you hum so sweetly this morning?"

"Nadia, my brother Dhanush is in love. Can you believe it?"

"Oh, so I have lost the chance to have some romance with your brother," Nadia laughed good-humoredly.

"Nadia, he is younger than me in age. But he is soon to be a doctor and will bring me a sister-in-law too."

"He will certainly bring your sister-in-law but when will you think about yourself?"

"Nadia, what do you want to say?"

"I want to say what you don't want to hear. Dmitri is also a doctor and loves you. The minimum you can do at the moment is not to reject his friendship."

"Nadia, you also have a boyfriend. Why don't you marry him?"

"I have that boyfriend just to amuse myself. I am not serious about him."

Engaged in this chit chat they reached the car and were soon in school. Bhanu and Nadia had been living in the same room and working in the hospital. One good thing about Nadia was that she considered Bhanu to be a nice innocent girl. As such she never brought her boyfriend home. She also knew that Dmitri would come to teach human anatomy class in the current semester. The new semester had commenced that day. Dmitri was to take his first class. When he came to teach, Bhanu and Nadia were also in the class.

"Nadia, this stalker doctor has also become a teacher."

"Bhanu Devi ji, why do you think so negatively about Dmitri?"

"Nadia, I fail to understand how this man has come to Canada all the way from Greece and Los Angeles."

"Look here, today we shall go to bid him hello after the class."

"You can go to say hello to this stalker doctor and teacher. But I shall not go to him."

"All right Miss, don't say hello to him but you can at least accompany me."

"Nadia, but I must confess that he delivers a good lecture," Bhanu said in a low voice.

"Thank God that at least you like something by Dmitri."

"Nadia, why are you pushing me to Dmitri?"

"Why should I tell you that?" Nadia teased Bhanu.

As Dmitri was still taking the class, he was distracted by the whispers of the two girls. He said loudly, "Silence please."

After the class, Nadia went to Dmitri to apologize and Bhanu watched her talking to him.

"Sir, forgive us. Me and Bhanu were talking about you," Nadia said.

"I am very lucky that you were talking about me. But please, don't talk in the class. You can talk in the park."

"What a surprise that you are going to the park with us. But right now we are going to the cafeteria. We are very hungry."

"I am also very hungry. Ok, today let it be a treat for both of you from me."

She called aloud, "Bhanu, O' Bhanu, what a miracle that sir is taking us to lunch."

Bhanu felt angry and wanted to say that she would not go to the cafeteria. But she controlled her anger and followed them. Dmitri mostly talked to Nadia at the cafeteria. Nadia told him that when Bhanu hummed, it seemed she should have been a singer in Bollywood, not a nurse.

"Bhanu, do you know that I love singing too. My grandfather was a good poet. My mother also used to tell me that she sang and did modeling on the college stage."

"So that is it, Sir Dmitri. Bhanu also does modeling on the stage and sings," Nadia told Dmitri.

Nadia and Dmitri tried their best to have Bhanu open up but Bhanu responded only by nodding or shaking her head and kept looking at her toes. When they were leaving after lunch, Dmitri addressed Bhanu and said, "Occasionally, at least raise your head to look at the sunshine and the chirping birds if not at people. You won't lose anything."

"Great Sir Dmitri! We are sure to be enjoying this semester. What if we have a picnic?"

"Why not Nadia? Make a program and only the three of us will go."

"What do you think about Niagara Falls, Bhanu?" Nadia said.

Before Bhanu could answer, Dmitri said, "All right, I would like to leave now. But don't forget to do your homework."

Dmitri left but Nadia was in suspense expecting Bhanu to express her protest against the program. However, Bhanu neither protested nor said anything. On reaching her room, she started doing her homework. The old routine was on. Now and then, Nadia teased Bhanu about Dmitri. Now Nadia, Bhanu and Dmitri usually had lunch together.

Though Nadia had proposed going on a picnic, yet the anatomy class was tough, they didn't get time for it. Off and on Bhanu looked at Dmitri from the corners of her eyes and would make eye contact with Dmitri. She would at once lower her eyes out of bashfulness.

Time passed steadily and the semester had only two weeks more to go. The whole class made a program to visit Niagara Falls after the semester. Bhanu had seen every spot worth seeing in Canada except Niagara Falls, an important destination for every tourist. But it had evaded her for two reasons. One was her preoccupation with studies and the other with thoughts of Dmitri. Now, whenever Nadia teased her, she just smiled and kept quiet. One day Bhanu was studying in the library and was alone. Dmitri also happened to be sitting at the table opposite hers. Once he noticed Bhanu looking at him. He left his table and approached her. He sat down on the spare chair and said, "Bhanu, would you like to ask any question about human anatomy?"

"Yes sir, I would like to ask some questions but not about human anatomy. It is about you."

"Go ahead. My life is an open book."

"Why did you follow me and if you followed me, why didn't you speak to me? I am not a bad girl."

"Who says that you are a bad girl?" Dmitri said.

"I apologize for calling you a stalker." She kept quiet for a few moments and looked after him thoughtfully. Then she continued, "You are not a stalker and I am lucky to have you as a frie…n … d I mean a very good teacher in you."

"On the contrary, it is for me to apologize. I wrote you notes which I find offended you... I saw you first in Greece; then we came across each other in London. The moment I set my eyes on you, I was convinced that you are my destiny."

"Yes, sir. The meeting when we met in Canada was a surprise for me."

Dmitri looked at her and she noticed his face getting sad. Then he seemed to have made up his mind and said, "Bhanu, I have not seen my childhood and youth with my father. Only my maternal grandparents and my mother inculcated Indian samskaras (culture and tradition) in me. Naturally I believe in fate and karma and phal (actions and their fruit)." Dmitri's eyes became tearful.

"Oh please sir! Don't weep. I cannot see anybody weeping. My own life has been a long series of shocks, suffering, and pain from childhood to youth."

"Bhanu, just address me as Dmitri. Drop this 'sir'. Count me as a friend when not in the classroom."

"Sir, I mean Dmitri, I can become a good friend. In fact I already am one but I think I cannot become a life partner. I had another young man named Pankaj. He wanted to be my life partner but…he died. Fate snatched him away from not only his loving parents but from me forever as he was killed in a Car accident,

"Bhanu, if I have to give up my life for the sake of your love, I shall take that day to be auspicious."

"Oh Dmitri, please don't utter inauspicious words." She placed her hand on his mouth to close it and he took it. It was done only as an impulse but before she could remove her hand, Dmitri caught both of her hands and said, "My dear friend, let us go out of the library and talk outside, otherwise the librarian will throw us out."

They rose from their chairs and came out of the library.

"Dmitri, how did you learn to speak Hindi?" Bhanu asked.

"Bhanu, I liked your addressing me as 'you' minus sir. As for my learning Hindi, I have been educated in India."

"I, too, can speak Hindi but can't write it," Bhanu said with regret.

"As you are my friend now, I shall teach you how to write Hindi. Please confirm once again that you are my friend, aren't you?" he pressed the question.

"Yes, we are friends," Bhanu said shyly with lowered eyes.

Dmitri felt a strong urge to kiss Bhanu's shy eyes. But his intuition warned him that if he did this, he would lose not only Bhanu's friendship but also Bhanu. He controlled the urge. They sat outside the library on the lawn and talked about everything concerned with their respective lives. Finally it was time to leave and they went home.

Both had no sleep. Dmitri turned in his bed thinking of Bhanu and Bhanu too wondered about this new development in her life. She felt spontaneously attracted to Dmitri. She had noted that he was six feet tall. His eyes were big but he seldom opened them fully. He had neither very fair color nor very dark. Above his dark eyebrows his curly hair made him look very attractive. Whenever he looked at Bhanu, her heart beat accelerated. Dmitri too had the same experience when she looked at him. He would watch Bhanu's innocent beautiful eyes and her reticence with sadness on her face. Recalling her looks and her aloofness of demeanor attitude made him sleepless.

By and by the final test of human anatomy class was over. The following Sunday the whole class was to go to see Niagara Fall. That day Nadia too was to bring her new boyfriend.

"Nadia, how will your boyfriend reach the bus stand?" Bhanu asked.

"He will go by his own car, for I know if he were to share my car, you would refuse to come with me."

"No, I shall ask Dmitri to come to the bus stand where I shall wait for him," she said in a very low voice.

"It means that you will walk to the bus stand in this cold," Nadia jokes.

"Nadia, my best friend, I am proud to think how concerned you are about me."

"Bhanu you too are so nice and innocent and… pure," Nadia praised her.

"All right, now stop showering praises on me and let us move."

"Get ready quickly as Dmitri will be waiting," Bhanu said with some emphasis on Dmitri.

"Oh great, but let me see your blushing cheeks that have reddened and the lowered eyes at the mention of Dmitri," Nadia teased her.

"Nadia, I regard Dmitri as a good friend only. I don't intend to try to know him more than what we already know and am determined not to cross my limits," Bhanu said firmly.

"What limits are you talking about? Not an apsara (a female heavenly entity) can stand any comparison to you in beauty."

Tears appeared in Bhanu's eyes. She hugged Nadia like a sister and friend and said, "Today you have opened my eyes. I had never considered myself to be beautiful."

"How I have done that miracle can be told on the way. But let us first get moving right now. And yes, don't forget to take sandwiches with you," Nadia said, picking up her bag and car keys.

Both the friends reached the bus stand. Nadia's boyfriend had already arrived there. All the teachers and students got into their cars when they saw them coming. Nadia occupied a seat with her boyfriend.

Dmitri wanted to lift Bhanu physically and make her sit by his side in the bus but Bhanu preferred to sit alone on the last seat in the bus. She hadn't yet overcome her shyness. She closed her eyes and started thinking that she alone knew what. Dmitri sat on the front seat and the bus moved towards its destination.

A hundred million people of all faiths and cultures lived in that city. Canadians are very proud of CN Tower. It is a five hundred feet tall free-standing monument. The bus halted there for some time for them to see the tower. Then the driver took the party to see all the three universities of Toronto, namely Ryerson University, York University and University of Toronto. Bhanu was clicking her camera to take pictures of these universities alone. Nadia was fully preoccupied with her boyfriend. If there were any lone travelers, they were Bhanu and Dmitri. Occasionally Dmitri turned round in his seat and when their eyes met, they smiled at each other. Sparks of love had put the hearts of both on fire. But still they were not yet ready to open up in the company of other people.

The bus moved via Royal Ontario to Brampton. There a few Indians had their shops. Some of the picnickers ate a little randomly and made odd purchases. They again boarded the bus. Most of them were tired by now and began to doze off in the bus. Bhanu and Dmitri would close their eyes or when opened, look at each other and smile. But their heart beats never slowed down. The bus was running to cover the last lap of 56 kilometers to Niagara Falls.

Finally, following highway number 405 and 420, it reached Niagara Falls. At the sight of the Niagara Falls, its flying water sprays and its grandeur, the faces of all were shining with pleasure. Each made their own observation about Niagara Falls. But all the first-time visitors were wonder struck at this natural marvel. When the initial excitement had subsided, the party divided itself into two groups. One group wanted to have a Maid of the Mist boat tour. The other group that could not afford the sails chose to go through a cave to reach Niagara Falls. At that moment Dmitri came to Bhanu and asked her, "Bhanu can you swim?"

"Yes, I can swim but it is very cold and I haven't brought my swimming trunks."

"I didn't want you to swim. I just wanted to know whether you would like to go for the Maid of the Mist boat tour."

"No, I would like to enjoy the sight of Niagara Falls," she said.

"Look, everybody is going according to their choice. I would also like to enjoy the sight of Niagara Falls sitting by your side. But there is one more choice…," Dmitri said.

"What is that?" Bhanu asked innocently.

"It is a journey behind the falls. Let us have an elevator and we can reach the Horseshoe Falls."

"I think there is a fee of ten dollars too," Bhanu said, counting the money.

"Bhanu, I am afraid to ask something," he was a little hesitant.

"What are you afraid of? You are my friend. Besides Nadia and you, I have no one else in Canada as my own."

Dmitri thought that he should embrace Bhanu and say, "Bhanu I also have no one in Canada."

After his mother, Bhanu was the only love he had. But he said nothing. He watched his friends boarding the Maid of the Mist boat. This boat goes via American Falls to Horseshoe Falls and has a halt of ten minutes. The noise here surpasses the thunder of clouds. Dmitri and Bhanu took an elevator and put on plastic over coats and moved in the tunnel together. Along the way Dmitri told the entire history of Niagara and American Falls. "Bhanu, though there are many bigger falls in the world, yet Niagara Falls has a beauty of its own," Dmitri told her.

Both reached the platform where the water fell noisily with great force. It presents a very romantic scene. But the two had another romance to take care of. During their sightseeing both were weaving dreams not exactly known to each other but one could imagine they were on similar lines. They looked into each other's eyes, smiled but said nothing.

Nature itself was in collusion with the fate of the two lovers. A strong gust of wind sprinkled a large amount of cold water on Bhanu and Dmitri. Bhanu instinctively clung to Dmitri's chest. Totally drenched, she was shivering with cold. Water continued playing madly with her shivering body. But Dmitri had found the long-awaited opportunity in holding Bhanu to his heart. He relished every moment spent in Bhanu's company now. The feeling that could not be expressed in words was expressed by the two hungry bodies. Even the angels seemed to be rejoicing in this union. The water of the Niagara Falls was playing Cupid. Dmitri and Bhanu clung to each other as if in a trance.

Before Bhanu could detach herself from Dmitri, he lifted her up as if she were a child and kissed her eyes. The setting was perfect for romance. To one side there was Niagara Falls with a rainbow and on the other side was a full moon in the clear sky. Dmitri carried Bhanu in his arms and slowly came out of the tunnel.

Someone passing nearby observed, "What a lovely couple! Let me take a picture of the two lovers."

The noise of the waterfall was still very loud. Once out of the tunnel, Dmitri seated Bhanu against a wall and said, "Look over the flow of the water of Niagara Falls there is a rainbow. You may close your eyes and make a wish."

"I don't need to make a wish. I have already got today what I wanted."

"What have you got? Let me share this treasure."

"Dmitri, look, over there. To one side there is a full moon. Round it there is a circle of dark clouds and to the left there is gurgling water. I wish…"

"Yes Bhanu, today, in this hour of bliss, I take this rainbow in my heart and jump into the water of Niagara Falls."

"No, please don't say this." Bhanu trembled with unseen fear and placed her palm on his lips. Dmitri kissed her fingers one by one. He began to set her wet hair in order. Then he took her face in his hands and said, "Your inviting eyes are compelling me to kiss them again and again."

"Dmitri, am I dreaming or are you really demonstrating your love for me?"

"Come on. Place your hand on my heart. Do you feel its beats and hear its voice?"

Bhanu blushed. She could not bring herself to confess what she had in mind. She hid her face with her hands.

"Bhanu, don't be so cruel as to hide your beautiful face behind your hands. Let me feast my eyes on this angel's face. I have waited for this moment for ages."

"Dmitri, I am beside myself with joy and my feet won't touch the ground. The moon in the sky has brought down to me my own personal moon. The moon in heaven has lost its shine now."

"In a little time, my Bhanu has come so close to me that I will never let her go away from my life. I shall go to Greece next week and bring along my mother."

"But next week I am going to California on vacation."

"Then make a promise, Bhanu," he said, holding her hands.

"What promise, my love? I shall fulfill the promise about which the poets sing even at the cost of my life."

"My goddess Sparta, my queen of Sparta, has become so bold in love that she makes me feel as if I were not a doctor but a Spartan king." He laughed aloud.

"Dmitri, what are you saying about Sparta? I don't know a thing about it," the innocent girl said.

"Bhanu, Sparta is the name of a famous city in Greece."

"And...?" Bhanu asked.

"Greek history is full of legends and wars. According to Greek history, women are looked down upon as second-rate citizens," Dmitri said.

"I don't know why it is always women that are the victims of injustice and tyranny," Bhanu said gloomily.

"But it is also said that in the seventh century BC the status of women was raised," he added.

"Dmitri, did in Greece too people follow the system of marriage as in India where parents decide the matches?"

"Bhanu, though I am not a historian, I have heard that in Greece to the parents arranged marriages of their children and there was nothing wrong in it."

"I went to India when I was quite young. Now my brother Dhanush and I want to visit India and see the ancient temples there."

"Dhanush is a very sweet name. What is he studying, Bhanu?" Dmitri asked her with great interest.

"My brother is very intelligent and loving. He is going to be a good doctor."

"That's great. All of us will go to India and build a big hospital there. We shall serve the poor at their doorstep," Dmitri said happily.

"Dmitri, your dream is very lovely indeed. I too would love to serve the poor."

"How can the Spartan queen be behind?" Dmitri smiled broadly.

"But you have not told me who Spartans were."

"Bhanu, an elite section of Greece was known as Spartans. Their women folk were very brave. If there was a single daughter in a royal family, she would rule the community empire."

"Oh, my king of Sparta, I am not the only daughter of a royal family. But could you let me live in a corner of your heart as a slave?" Bhanu said pleadingly with her gaze lowered.

Dmitri's heart-beat accelerated. Greek, American, Canadian and Indian beautiful nurses, doctors and others would die to get his attention. But now the same Dmitri kneeled down on his knees and, holding Bhanu's hands, said, "Bhanu you are not a slave. You are the queen that would reign over my heart. My queen, I would like to serve you as a humble servant at your royal feet. Please don't reject this appeal, my sweetheart."

This confession of love was totally new to Bhanu. She could not believe her luck that she was destined to have such a handsome lover. The evening was gradually approaching and the picnickers were now eager to return home. Multicolored lights created kaleidoscopic patterns around Niagara Falls and gave it a heavenly sight. It was not mere imagination. It was a reality created by nature. All marveled at this divine creation and came closer to have a parting look at the beauty.

It Was time to return home and everyone started packing up their belongings. Nadia looked around for Bhanu and Dmitri and saw them approaching, holding each other's hands. She found it difficult to believe in this fast progress in the intimacy of the two lovers. Nadia had also had a good time with her beau. She was very cheerful. Nadia's boyfriend also came along. Nadia and he got onto the bus and sat together on a seat. Dmitri and Bhanu also sat very close to each other this time.

As all were tired, most of them went to sleep at once. The driver closed the windows and pulled down the shades. The bus moved and without much ado this time, Bhanu went to sleep in Dmitri's lap. Dmitri looked at Bhanu's face. Her closed eyes, full lips and long pointed nose made her look like a Greek beauty. He could not believe that luck had smiled on him so quickly. He had been looking for the beauty of his imagination in various corners of the world but she was lying innocently forgetful of the concerns of the world. It was his great luck. He was convinced that nature had connived to make the union of the two feasible. He pitied the people who had never found true love in life. The two young hearts had come together to exchange their romantic love and the miracle had happened.

In about four hours the bus dropped the passengers in front of the nursing college. Nadia also got down and waited for Bhanu near her car after her boyfriend had left in his car. But Bhanu was still asleep in Dmitri's lap. He gently shook her and whispered in her ears, "Bhanu my life, we shall have to part now. We are at the college." Bhanu opened her eyes and lingered a little longer in Dmitri's lap. She raised her hands and pressed Dmitri down to bring his ears close to her mouth and said, "Dmitri, what have you done to me? The darkness that had surrounded me from all directions in my short life has been cleared and a pleasant sunshine engulfs me."

"My love, conceal our love in your heart and don't let it be betrayed to the world around lest there should be prying eyes and ears to turn the sacred gift of heaven into a scandal."

"Dmitri, I could not even have a glimpse of you in Greece. You did your best to come to me but I feared you as a stranger and kept running away." She clung to his neck with her hands.

"Bhanu, you are my destiny, the queen of Greece, Rome and Cleopatra of Egypt. I want to make sure that you are in my arms." He embraced her with warmth. He hadn't bothered even to see whether they were alone in the bus or not. The driver waited a little away from the bus and blessed the two lovers in his heart. Then he coughed lightly to indicate that it was time for them to get down. Bhanu was startled and said, "Dmitri, I must leave now. I am sure Nadia will be waiting for me." She reluctantly eased herself free from his embrace and sat up. Dmitri also realized that the meeting was to end after all. He helped her down the bus and said, "Ok, but ring me up at once on reaching home."

"Yes, I promise, and what's more, I shall talk to you daily."

Dmitri took her aside out of people 's gaze and kissed her passionately. He said, "It should be a firm promise, not a formality."

"Yes, it is firm, firm, firm. Now please let me go," she said, looking into his eyes.

"Suppose I don't let you go?" He tried to detain her by blocking her path. But she dodged him and quickly reached where Nadia was waiting. Dmitri looked at her going away. Nadia was appreciating the diamond ring on her finger and sat lost in her own thoughts.

A child is born and grows up in the care of parents, passing through various ups and downs of life. It learns to walk, holding the parents' fingers, parents who hold him when he misses a step. By and by it learns to run. But youth replace childhood that surpasses childish joys in other mature attractions. Love steps in and every moment becomes lovely, adding luster to life. Dreams become rosy and one finds oneself very happy.

Rita was unaware that her children were now grown-ups and had been blessed by the god of love. Parents wish their children to have everything they want and that can make them happy. The two children of Satnam and Ravinder were passing through this phase of life. Both their children were successful in their career. Subodh had a girlfriend who was Bengali but Satnam wanted both her children to marry in Punjabi families. Savera was studying law and was very intelligent. Along with getting education, she was working as a junior clerk in a lawyer's office. As a part of her job, she had to interact with Hindi and Punjabi speaking clients. That's why her mother had taught her the languages. Off and on she made fun of the faulty accent of Dhanush in Hindi and Punjabi. He was madly in love with her. Savera's company had created interest for Hindi films. Whenever he saw the heroine in any film, he saw the picture of Savera in her.

For some time Savera and Dhanush had not seen each other as Savera was preoccupied with her court work. On the other hand, the final tests of Dhanush were approaching. Savera would satisfy her urge to see her lover by looking at his pictures with which she had adorned her room. One day, on an impulse she visited a jeweler and brought two diamond rings. She faxed a letter to Dhanush. It read:

> Friend and partner of my life, I know that both of us are busy in our career and can't see each other as frequently as we would like to. But in your absence, I feel very insignificant. I am conscious of the fact that I am senior in age to you by a few years. I am worried lest your sister and mother, who would soon be a mother-in-law herself, should disapprove of our marriage.
>
> I hope you know that I would find life impossible to carry on. You are synonymous with my existence. You are the embodiment of all my womanly desires and happiness. I dream of reclining my head on your chest and forgetting everything. I would wish not to see anything else when I raise my head and open my eyes.
>
> Will you not oblige me by coming to Potomac River this evening so that I may see your moonlike face to soothe my soul? I promise that I shall not detain you long. If you don't come, I shall be angry with you and you will not be able to make up with me even when you sing numerous film songs. I miss your captivating smile. Please come to the river bank as

Krishna used to come to see his Radha.

Your Radha in waiting,

Savera

In the morning when Dhanush came to his office, he was thrilled to find Savera's letter. He read and re-read it many times and kissed it. He held it to his heart as if it were a treasure that could be snatched away from him. Finally, he wrote a letter to Savera and faxed it to Savera at her office address. He wrote:

My dear Savera,

Hardships and misery seem to have turned away from me now. Your love has banished them and has filled the vacuum left by the age-old miseries. I have talked to my mother and my sister Bhanu. Both are happy. I have also sent my picture that you took with your cell phone and the one Vicky took to my mother and Bhanu. They have claimed that you have ushered in a new dawn in their life.

Your gestures and acts have a deep impact on my life. I have seen that lovers often make promises never to meet them but I am different. I will come to see you. Under the light of the stars in the silence of the night I shall confess my love to you and tell you that you are my life.

Your own,

Dhanush

Savera was beside herself with joy when she read Dhanush's letter. She wanted to make herself up in a manner that Dhanush would go mad after her and would never let her be away from his eyes and heart. With these things in mind, first of all she visited a beauty salon for facial make up. She had her hair colored a little brown with a tint of golden highlights. Then she decorated her hands, feet and nails. Then she bought a new light violet colored long skirt with a matching blouse. On return home she went to her room and switched on the tape recorder that played Indian music softly. Then she entered the bathroom.

Satnam called Savera a number of times but without any response. She wondered whether Savera was dancing to the tune of Hindi music. She went to check. She knocked at her door. But there was no response. Out of curiosity she opened the door and went in. She was surprised to see the walls of the room covered with pictures of Dhanush. Then she found Dhanush's letter on the bed. Satnam was an educated lady but she had never so far thought that her daughter was now grown up and needed privacy. She read the letter and tiptoed to her bedroom. She said, "Ravinder ji, do you know what our daughter is up to?"

"What is she doing? But I think that by making her up as her mother does, she is about to go out for a stroll."

"But I say you had better take Savera and Subodh to India and find suitable matches in order to have families for them, have them married without any delay."

"What's that? Do you take your children for dumb cattle? Anyway, what is the matter? Why are you so concerned for Savera and Subodh today?"

"Ravinder ji, Savera has fallen in love with Dhanush," Satnam told him.

"Dhanush is a nice boy. I have talked to him a couple of times. His father is an engineering degree holder from a good university."

"But Dhanush is from a broken family. His father used to beat his mother," Satnam said with emphasis on her words.

"But Satnam ji, how is Dhanush to blame for what his father does? Why do you want to punish Dhanush for his father's actions?" Ravinder said angrily.

"The son has seen his father beating his mother. The chances are that he too will follow his example. Have you forgotten the case of my younger sister?"

"Satnam, the husband of your younger sister, had not beaten her. It was she who had exploited the fights between her in-laws."

"Ravinder, you, being a man, naturally side with men. The father-in-law of my younger sister beat her mother-in-law." Satnam was flustered.

"Yes, it may have happened but your younger sister never missed a chance to remind her husband of this and when he protested loudly, she impressed on him that he had the habit of his father. It was not right on the part of your younger sister."

"I shall right away warn Savera that she should stop seeing Dhanush."

"Satnam, don't commit this mistake in your haste. I shall talk to Savera and Dhanush in this regard," Ravinder calmed her.

It was seven o'clock and stars twinkled in the sky. Multicolored lights falling in the water added to the beauty and romance of the scene. Dhanush dressed in a dark blue coat, matching jacket and light blue shirt and dark blue trousers looked dashing. He was moving to and from on the bank of the river waiting for Savera. Savera got out of the car. She herself looked like an angel from heaven. She saw Dhanush moving about impatiently waiting for her. But she wanted to test his eagerness to meet her and was deliberately a little late. Savera had involved her friend Vicky in the plan to test Dhanush's love for her. She was expected to reach with her camera to take pictures but hasn't come yet.

Exactly after half an hour she approached Savera. Now Savera quietly took out the diamond ring and tiptoed to where Dhanush was moving about. She sat down on the ground and said in a dramatic manner, "My Dhanush, I pray to you that taking the sky as a witness, accept this ring and marry me."

Dhanush was elated at this development. He removed the stray hair from the face of Savera and said, "My Urvashi (a celestial female figure in Indian mythology), you are my world; you bring spring in my life. I sincerely wish to be your life partner." He extended his hand to her.

Savera put the ring on his ring finger and added, "Dhanush, won't you ask me for it?"

"Savera, I don't have a diamond ring. But if you like, I can sever my heart out of the chest and present it to you. You will hear every heartbeat repeating your name," Dhanush said, kissing her hand.

"Here is your ring. When you become a doctor, you can pay the price of this ring," Savera said, smiling. Dhanush sat down on the ground facing her and taking the ring from her, he said, "The day dawns in Washington with my Savera (morning). Savera is the most beautiful flower of Washington. Today, on the land of Washington, on the bank of Potomac River, I asked Savera, will you marry me?"

Savera got up and frolicking round Dhanush she said, "Your Urvashi, coming down from the heaven, says, "Yes, yes, my Dhanush, I shall marry only you and from today I shall call you aap (formal word for you used for seniors or in a formal manner) I shall not call you 'tu' (informal mode of address for close acquaintances or younger ones). But right now, lift me in your arms and hold me against your heart."

It was the happiest moment for Dhanush. He had found a sweetheart that loved him dearly. Dhanush was ignorant that Vicky was taking their pictures from a hiding place. The dazzling lights around the Potomac River had hidden everything except the face of Savera to Dhanush. After both Savera and Dhanush had had the rings on and were appreciating them, Vicky shouted, "Surprise, surprise!"

"Where is Vicky shouting from, Savera?" Dhanush asked.

"My going to be hubby, I have invited Vicky to take our pictures," she laughed.

"Oh, I see. That means my Savera had come fully prepared to formalize the engagement with the ring and all. I am overwhelmed by your endearing gesture." Dhanush kissed Savera.

"Congratulations Savera and Dhanush on your engagement. Dr. Dhanush, look, there is an arrangement for your dinner in the boat anchored to your right. You two go there and enjoy the dinner. It is an engagement gift from me," Vicky said.

"Vicky, the first thing is that I am not a doctor yet but you have started calling me Dr. The second thing is I wonder from where you have leant to speak in Hindi."

"Ask your would-be wife. She has taught me all the dialogues I have just delivered. In addition, I could understand a little myself."

All of them laughed at this. Vicky took leave of Dhanush and Savera. Dhanush and Savera occupied their seats in the big grand boat. The boat was tastefully illuminated. Their seats were close to a window and the twinkling stars reflected in the river presented a beautiful scene to them. It appeared Cupid had done his duty very meticulously. Dhanush and Savera were unaware of the fact that near the dining table there was an arrangement for the lovers for a slow dance. At that moment someone shouted. "Congratulations to Savera and Dhanush." But the lovers heard nothing. Savera was saying, "Dhanush, one thing is bothering me at this hour of rejoicing. I wonder if my being a couple of years older than you and the love marriage will be acceptable to your mom and sister."

"Don't bother your beautiful head, my doll. From my mother and sister, you will get nothing but love and respect. They are very simple and sincere people. But I am afraid of your parents, Satnam aunty and Ravinder's uncle. They belong to the elite American society. They are likely to look down upon my broken family. I fear lest following their example you too should start behaving like them," Dhanush said.

"Banish such ideas from your mind, Dhanush. I have found in life a man who has trusted me and whom I can trust. I have had the opportunities to date about half a dozen young men but I found not a single one of them who was as honest and frank to talk about his family. I am really lucky to have you."

"I love you Savera and feel grateful to the Almighty that you too are so frank." He kissed her hand.

They were lost in each other when a beautiful American lady came to them and said, "Are you Dhanush and Savera?"

"Yes, Mam," both answered simultaneously.

"Some woman named Vicky has asked us to sing a special song for you. Will you please come to the dance floor so that I can sing as she has desired?"

Dhanush and Savera came onto the dance floor and began dancing and Celine Dion started singing - 'My heart will go on...'

Doubt sometimes shows its ugly face by creating situations never expected. Man is frightened out of his wits and forgets even his future happiness. People of this nature are themselves responsible for killing their happiness. While Savera and Dhanush were dreaming of a happy life together, Satnam found sleep eluding her. She was torn between two emotions. One was that in the core of her heart she liked Dhanush. She would go to the room of Savera again and again, look at the handsome and innocent face of Dhanush and a smile would spread over her face. Nevertheless, on the other hand she would be reminded of his broken family and feel sad. She would go to Ravinder and say, "Look here Ravinder ji, please make enquiry about Dhanush's father, his brothers and sisters. I shall also gather as much information about the family from Dhanush's mother as possible."

"Satnam, from where have you caught the fever of being a paper correspondent and a detective? You'd do well spread rumors among friends and families. Please go to sleep now. In the morning I shall find out where Sudhir is and have the father and son patch up their differences." He tried to calm Satnam down.

But Satnam could not be calmed. Then she recalled that her friend Geeta had a travel agency in Los Angeles. Satnam usually bought traveling tickets from her. Geeta had interaction with many people in California. Geeta was widely known in the Indian community. Satnam consulted her watch and guessed that it would be about 9 o'clock in the evening in California. She quietly went to Savera's room and using her phone, she called Geeta, "Hello Geeta, how are you? It is Satnam from Washington D.C."

"Satnam ji it must be about midnight in Washington. What is the matter that you have chosen to call me at this late hour?"

"Geeta, please arrange four tickets for us for India."

"Satnam ji, the moment you place an order for the tickets, rest assured that four first class tickets are ready. But you sound as if you were nervous. Is everything alright?"

"Geeta, I am concerned that my children should be married now. As such we shall go to India and find good matches in well to do families there and have the children married at once. Grown up children create problems, you know. The matches from India respect Hindu traditions at least," Satnam explained.

"But Satnam there is a lot of change in India too. The modern youth there too are highly westernized. They are no longer interested in their language and religion. Most of them want to marry our children to uplift their families or bring their lovers whom their family denied them to marry. But you have still not answered my question why you are disturbed."

"Geeta, please treat what I say to you as confidential. Do you know some Sudhir and Rita?"

"Satnam, I know them very well. Theirs is a very notorious family. Sudhir is a very short-tempered man. He regularly beat Rita. I have also heard that Rita has a doubtful character. She doesn't enjoy a good reputation. It is also heard that both their children were fed up with their mother's conduct and have run away to God knows where," Geeta said.

"Oh my God, Geeta! Rita's son has entrapped my innocent daughter Savera. Give me Rita's phone. I would talk to her. I would teach her a lesson once and for all," Satnam said to Geeta.

"Sure, I shall give her number in a minute. She is a prostitute, she is a whore, she used to allure her daughter to flirt with older men when she was barely fifteen, she even dated younger men who like to date her daughter at the same time Please keep your children away from her." She gave Rita's phone to her.

It's amazing that people from all over the world from different cultures, religions and races came far away to settle down in America. They love America for opportunities for a better life; yet one thing few of them have not learnt is not to speak ill about each other. One does not need to forget their culture when one is living in the west, but imposing their cultural beliefs, values on a democratic country like America is really disrupting the whole system of American political structure. Immigrants need to respect American diversity as one doesn't have in one's own motherland. Some Americans think Hinduism is a cult, but it's not a cult - it's a way of life. Immigrants from India also have freedom of religions in India as Hinduism respects all sects. Immigrants from other nations have to understand America is a Christian nation as they are tolerant to others' beliefs as well.

Satnam Kaur rendered a lot of social service among the Indian community. She sponsored fashion shows in clubs and through radio programs. She also donated generously to all Hindu and Sikhs temples, churches and to homeless people and organized langars (community feeding as a humanitarian service). She frequently organized big parties and had become very popular among the Indian community in Washington. But out of ego and a suspicious nature, she had not learnt how to understand the problems of helpless and suffering women. On hearing negative comments from Geeta, she was so furious that she at once rang Rita up. Rita took the call and said, "Hello, Rita speaking."

"Hello Rita, I am not your customer because I am a real noble woman from good Sikh families," she said, without introducing herself to Rita.

"What do you mean by customer and real noblewoman? Who are you anyway? This is not a shop. It is a house. No customer phones here. You must have got the wrong telephone number. Only cultured brothers, sisters and friends call here." Rita was about to hang up the phone on her.

"Look here, I am Satnam Kaur, Savera's mother. I find a mother like a son. Your son Dhanush, assuming an innocent face and postures and with his eye on our wealth, has befooled my innocent daughter Savera."

"Satnam Kaur ji, I think you have some misunderstanding about me in your mind. Please calm down. Your daughter Savera has talked to me and my daughter Bhanu many times. I am sure that everything is in order. Now as you have called, I would like to acknowledge my gratitude to you for treating my son as a member of your family," Rita said very politely.

Satnam had lost her composure and was saying very unsavory things to Rita without knowing that Savera had returned home. She also didn't bother that Ravinder and Subodh were awakened by her loud talking. As soon as she disconnected the phone, she was startled to see that the whole family was watching her contemptuously and Savera was shedding tears.

"I have not said anything wrong. Geeta has told me that Rita sells herself. There is not a single man in Los Angeles who has not slept with her at least for a night," Satnam went on.

"Satnam, you forgot that you had run away from home without informing your family to marry me. In India such a girl is always termed as characterless and notorious," Ravinder ji said.

"But Ravinder ji, both of us belong to respectable families. Our only problem was that we belonged to different castes and religions," Satnam countered Ravinder.

"Satnam, after listening to your diatribe against Rita, the three of us, Subodh, Savera and I have taken a unanimous decision."

"What decision? All of us will go to India next month."

"No, Satnam, you will go to India alone. We three will sleep in the other vacant house. In future too, you will live alone like the mother of Dhanush. Then people would talk about you too as they do about Rita. Then only you will realize what the meaning of bad days is. You will know how painful it is to cheat on marriage vows," Ravinder firmly told her.

"No, Ravinder ji, you can't do that to me. Whatever I have done is for the good of the family," Satnam said adamantly.

"You call it 'good' by adding salt to the injury of a suffering woman, Mom?" Savera said, weeping.

Ignoring Satnam's pleadings not to leave her alone, Ravinder ji, Subodh and Savera packed their belongings and left the house. Savera was in a bad shape from weeping inconsolably. She was so disturbed that she could not find time to talk to Dhanush, thinking that he might not marry her now as he loved his sister and mother very much and her mother Satnam had left hardly any choice for the family but to move back from the proposed marriage of Dhanush and Savera. Dhanush was preparing for his final exam. He had told

Savera a number of times that he expected his wife to give him regard and nothing else. Because of his final exam, he found no time to see Savera. He would write 'I love you' and fax it to Savera. Savera also reciprocated in a similar manner. Dhanush was extremely busy in preparation and didn't attend any phone calls. As a result neither Rita nor Bhanu could contact him.

Bhanu and Dmitri never had a single day when they did not see each other. Nadia had told Bhanu that her boyfriend had given her a promise ring and assured her that he would marry her. But Nadia didn't know that Bhanu's brother had also promised to marry a girl.

Dmitri was scheduled to go to Greece to see his mother. Bhanu was going to California to see her mother. Although Dmitri had talked to Rita, yet Rita phoned him, "Dmitri, don't tell Bhanu what Savera's mother had said to me, as otherwise Bhanu and Savera would quarrel. If Savera was to be the daughter-in-law, they were to take care that nothing was done to cause pain to Savera." Rita continued, "Dmitri your mummy Tripta is a very large-hearted lady. She has understood the situation of our family."

"Rita aunty, you are not only like my mother but in fact you are my mother too. In your family I shall not be a son-in-law but your son and a brother to Dhanush. I shall disclose the incident to Dhanush myself and persuade Savera's mother that she was not to go by what she had heard. Leave the matter to me," he asked Rita.

"Dmitri, you are not an ordinary human being. You are an angel. I have talked to your mother too. She is a very understanding, kind lady," Rita said.

"Aunty, please don't disclose my plan to Bhanu. She is under the impression that I am going to Greece. But I am coming to Los Angeles to see you. My mother will reach Los Angeles straight from Greece and I and Bhanu will land on the same day in Los Angeles." Dmitri shared his secret and the plan of giving a surprise for Bhanu with Rita.

Rita liked Dmitri's habits very much. Dmitri had had his mother speak to Rita over the phone. Although Tripta was from a rich royal family, ego and partiality had not touched her. Though she had been living in Greece for a long time, in her heart she had a dream of opening hospitals in India for the benefit of the poor. She also dreamt of someday helping in India's having broad clean roads and to awaken patriotism among Indian children to love their mother land India. Being from a royal family, she had heard stories of freedom from the members of her family. She had taken care that Dmitri too was not affected by the idea of discrimination between people on the basis of caste, creed, the rich and the poor and one's status in society. She had fed Dmitri with the idea that he should open a hospital in India for the poor where the poor, women and children could get treated at a very low cost. Rita had found a friend in her. Now whenever she was sad, she would talk to Tripta and find consolation. Satnam had used such abusive language that Rita would weep for a long time at night.

On such occasions she would remember Sudhir's injustice and cruelty and curse her fate. Then she would become calm on her own as there was none to soothe her.

Rita had never given up her relationship with her husband but destiny had behaved with her in inscrutable ways. Except for reading what love is in books or listening to love songs, she had never known love genuinely. She was happy that what she could not get herself was, at least, coming to her children.

She badly felt the absence of Sudhir. She felt that if her husband had been with her, Savera's mother wouldn't have dared to open her mouth against her and her character. She felt inclined to forgive him for all the wrong things he had said and done to her. She got up and fished out old pictures of their marriage. She looked at them and like an old film the times they had spent in love and in disputes came before the eyes of her imagination one by one. She also recalled how Dhanush and Bhanu would suffer and cry when their father beat their mother. She trembled and started thinking that it was she who was to blame for the situation she was in and not Sudhir. Whatever Satnam had said of her and Dhanush was only because her husband was not with her and she could not ensure a secure childhood for her children.

Rita was lost in these musings when the telephone rang. She picked the receiver. It was Satnam on the line.

"Hello, Rita speaking."

"Rita, my sister, please forgive me for hurting you and your innocent son with my abusive language. Please also forgive me for my false allegations." Satnam was weeping and asking for forgiveness.

"Satnam ji, when a person asks for forgiveness, nothing is left to be said." Rita was short of words on how to respond to Satnam.

"No Rita, my sister, I am your defaulter. I am a mother too. I am also a wife. Yet I regret that I failed to understand a woman's Pain My husband and my children have forgiven me," she told Rita

"Where is Savera?" Rita asked.

"Rita Bahen ji (dear sister), Savera, Dhanush and my husband are standing by my side at the moment. Talk to Savera and Dhanush yourself," Satnam said.

Rita wondered what Dhanush was doing there so late at night. She also did not know that it was Dmitri whose efforts had brought about this peaceful denouement of the whole problem. It was he who had advised the family not to drag the incident of the relationship of Dhanush and Savera unnecessarily. Dhanush, Savera, and her brother had reconciled the matter between Savera's parents. There are times when parents behave like children and children behave like parents. But Rita had suffered at the hands of the society very much. She had seen nothing but tears and suffering. The call of Satnam gave her consolation that Satnam would at least treat Dhanush with love and respect. Talking to Savera and Dhanush, Rita said, "Savera and Dhanush, my children, may you always be happy. I am trying to find out where Sudhir is and hope to reach him somehow."

"Yes, Mom. The presence of my father at my wedding will be a great thing," Dhanush opined.

"Savera, you may rest and Dhanush you had better go to your apartment now. But first let me speak to Satnam and Ravinder ji."

Satnam and Ravinder held parallel lines and said, "Rita Bahen, from now on, please don't take yourself as alone. You are a member of our family now. We would prefer to hold Subodh and Savera's marriages simultaneously."

"Satnam and Ravinder Kumar ji, I ask for the hand of your daughter for my son Dhanush. As soon as I find Sudhir, we shall come to you with mehndi (henna) and sindoor (vermillion) for dear Savera," Rita said.

Bhanu was getting ready to go to California. Dmitri told her that at the time she was to board the flight for California, he too was catching a flight for Greece. The two flights were scheduled at the same hour. As such they would leave home together. On the day they were to catch their flights the weather was not bad in spite of a light snow.

Bhanu was standing before a mirror with nothing on. She was observing her face and body for the first time so closely. A new desire, a sweet pain and eagerness invaded her. Then she noticed her thick lips and touching them she mumbled to herself, "Dmitri these thirsty lips want to say something to you. They are shielding a fire behind them. They don't know how to read the dictates of fate. I am waiting for you but I find it very hard to control myself. If you don't believe me, ask this breeze and the silver white snow, as they know what I have in my heart."

Then she noticed her pure innocent body from top to toe and felt shy. She at once covered herself. The drops of cold water fell from her wet hair and she felt that the drops were the cotton soft loving fingers of Dmitri that were massaging her gently. She went to her room and opened her cupboard and while putting on white and dark under garments, she thought how her body would look to Dmitri.

She tried to visualize in which under garments Dmitri would like to see her. In order to present a perfect figure before him, she changed into garments of various colors turn by turn and scrutinized herself in the big mirror. Her hands moved up and touched her young breasts which were so firm and silken smooth skin and made her proud. Then she spread her legs and looked at her treasure between them. She pressed her lips and felt her whole body squirm uncontrollably. A sigh escaped her wide open mouth. Then instantly she blushed when she realized what she was thinking about. Bhanu dried herself with a soft towel and put on a red blouse over a yellow cotton skirt. She wondered where Nadia was that day. She had bidden goodbye to her and left her with her boyfriend.

Bhanu packed her bag and took out her long gloves. Then she placed her long snow boots to one side. It was still three hours to leave for the airport. But suddenly someone rang the doorbell of her apartment. Bhanu would never open the door before first verifying who the visitor could be.

Today she also followed her routine. She looked out of the window and saw a big bouquet of yellow lilies and multicolored tulips. She at once opened the door and found a card in the bouquet. It was written on the card – 'My greatest love, my soul, my life, my breath, I love you. I am right next to you, the queen of my heart.'

Nobody had ever sent Bhanu flowers. She took up the bouquet, touched the flowers to her eyes and started running down the steps barefooted calling, "Dmitri, Dmitri." She didn't even notice that there was snow on the steps and she was about to fall down, when suddenly Dmitri caught hold of her in his arms and said, "Do you know that you would have slipped and fallen down the stairs? If you had hurt yourself, what would have been the consequence?"

"If you are around to hold me in your arms, I would prefer to slip down again and again. Please support me and hide me in your heart. Don't ever let me be away from your sight." Bhanu clung to his broad chest.

Dmitri carried her to her room, seated her in a chair and helped her in wearing her socks and shoes. Then he handed her the gloves and finally the full coat. He held the coat in a manner that she thrust her arms into the extended sleeves and wrapped the coat round her throbbing body. Without any warning he embraced her in a tight grip and put his lips on hers. The kiss lasted a long time. This over, when he was taking up her baggage, she said, "Dmitri, there is a lot of time yet. Why are you taking the baggage so early?"

"You are right. But I want to eat something before we board our flights to our separate destinations. I don't like the food on the plane, you know," he said.

"In that case we can eat something at the airport," she said innocently.

"Bhanu baby, my life, leave every decision of life to me now," Dmitri said, kissing her again.

As soon as Dmitri took her to the car, she was surprised to see his Lamborghini. She asked, "Dmitri, it is a Lamborghini. How did you come by it?"

"This car has been bought with my own earnings," he laughed.

Dmitri was very happy today. He was bent upon giving Bhanu surprise after surprise. The land of Canada is heaven on earth. When it snows here, the ground becomes snow-white and when it rains, the weather becomes very romantic. In spring, when there is sunshine, various colored flowers bloom on the margin of the lakes and birds of different hues and sizes make their advent. Ducks swim in the water and birds fly in the sky.

All these add to the natural beauty of Canada. Dmitri took Bhanu along the bank of river Humber and then going over the Dam Bridge, he stopped the car in front of the famous Palace Hotel. Two employees of the hotel came forward to open the door of the car to receive Bhanu and Dmitri. Bhanu had no idea what was to follow. Dmitri kneeled in the middle of the road and taking Bhanu's hands in his own, went ahead to put a ring on her finger and said, "My destiny, the embodiment of my dreams, the queen of all the Indians in America or in India, will you marry me?"

Bhanu found it difficult to swallow the flood of happiness. She just kept looking into his eyes with apparent bliss on her face. She could not utter a single word. But Dmitri didn't give up. He continued, "Bhanu, today you have to decide whether to make a mark on my life. If you are still reluctant to accept me, you can say this plainly."

Bhanu felt inclined to cling to Dmitri and shout to the world that she was blessed that day. She extended her hand and said, "You are the captain of the boat of my life. You steered it in the past life; will do so in this life and will do it in the lives to come. Here is my hand for you to put the ring on."

Dmitri lifted her up as if she were a kid and carried her into the hotel. He had reserved a corner table for both of them. The place offered a beautiful panoramic scene of the lake surrounded by flowers. Small duck swam in it and lights played with the rippling water. The sky had cleared in a short time. Bhanu was silent but the glow on her face betrayed her happiness. Dmitri knew that as soon as they reached California, he would ask for Bhanu's hand from Rita. Dhanush, Savera, her brother's Bengali girl friend and their parents were also to arrive there. All had decided to perform the marriage that very week. Dmitri was still keeping everything as a secret from Bhanu so that he could give her surprise after surprise to make her as happy as he could.

After dinner, Bhanu and Dmitri went for a stroll on the river-bank. Bhanu suddenly said, a bit worried, "Dmitri let us go to the airport. We are getting late. If I don't go today, my mother will be sad and I cannot bear this."

When they reached the airport, Bhanu questioned him, "Which airport is this? Are all private airplanes here?"

"Yes, but I have suddenly changed my program. I have decided to travel to California with you. Now as you are my fiancée, I cannot leave you to travel alone."

"But what do you say about your mother who is waiting for you in Greece? Will she not be sad when you don't go to Greece?"

"My mother is also reaching your mother's place to meet Rita today. Not only she, but Savera, your brother Dhanush along with your Bhabhi's parents are also reaching California today," Dmitri said, smiling.

"Oh, my master, my angel, my life, you have showered so much happiness on me that I am afraid lest someone's evil eye should harm it."

Rita was waiting for her children, her son-in-law, daughter-in-law and their parents and relatives. But she highly regretted the absence of Sudhir. She had checked with all agencies in Korea and made enquiries about him but to no avail. She recalled her past spent in penury, pain, the absence of love and security without Sudhir.

The past scenes made faces at her. The bitter memories were potent enough to deprive her of happiness. Rita had been trying to make a success of her life and the life of her children. But her cruel fate had always pushed her into vast desolation. It waited in hiding to pounce on her whenever she made her next move to set her life in order. It had always added to her difficulties and problems. One problem was hardly tackled when the next would come storming to her.

Rita again started thinking about Sudhir and took out the old pictures of her marriage. She remembered the routine when she would leave her home for college and return straight home. Her parents had never allowed her to visit a cinema hall to watch a picture. But Rita was thinking that the modern parents were very understanding and broad minded. Children found their own life partners and got engaged without even telling their parents about such important steps in life. Rita was no exception. Her children had found their life partners without her intervention or permission but still they wanted to solemnize the marriage vows in the presence of their parents. It was a great relief to her. She felt proud of her children.

When Rita found out about the choice of their life partners and their future, she was satisfied. The children wanted to get married according to Hindu rites. But their father was nowhere around. She again acutely felt the absence of Sudhir. She phoned Sudhir's friends and enquired about him but no one had any information about his whereabouts. On an impulse she phoned his elder sister-in-law. She took the call. Rita asked, "Bhabi, how are you? I need Sudhir's address and phone number. Please give this information to me."

"Rita, so you have remembered your husband now when he is in hospital close to the place where you live. He is suffering from cancer."

"No it can't be. You can't be serious. Nothing can happen to my Sudhir. My Sudhir can't cheat me on our marriage vows. Please give me his number." Rita started to weep.

But the sister-in-law abruptly dropped the receiver onto the cradle. Rita started looking for Sudhir in every hospital in her area where she lived. She was cursing herself. Her helplessness was so intense that forgetting all humiliation she had received at Sudhir's hands, for the last time she went to his elder brother to get Sudhir's phone number. But as soon as the door was opened, she found Sudhir standing there. She gave out a scream and like a mad woman rushed to him and put her arms around him. She said, "Sudhir, you can't leave me like this. May God take away my life as I don't deserve to live."

Sudhir noticed how agitated and miserable she was and said, "Rita calmed down. What has happened to you? Dhanush's future father-in-law had rung me up."

"What are you saying? Ravinder Kumar ji rang you up? How does he know you? But your eldest sister-in-law was saying…" She tightened her hold round his waist.

"I had visited the hospital just for a routine checkup. The sister-in-law must have played a trick on you, a crude one I admit. She should not have gone to that extreme. Anyway, Ravinder Kumar ji knew a close friend of mine. He got my contact number from him and told me everything about Dhanush," Sudhir said.

"Sudhir, I am glad that you are back. Kindly forgive me and overlook my shortcomings. See the sun is setting in the sky though the sun of my prime of youth is setting without your love." Rita started weeping chaotically.

"No, Rita, wipe your tears. I am your defaulter. I can't imagine how you have brought up the children. I also can't guess how you have faced the criticism and taunts of the people. I am proud of you that you have never deviated from the marriage vows. Our scriptures have always held the marriage vows as sacred and inviolable." Sudhir's eyes became tearful and he wiped them quietly a number of times.

"I had reconciled with the idea that defeat was my fate and my life was as fragile as glass that could be broken even with a gust of wind." Rita kept weeping.

"Rita, I have been cruel to you in life. I whipped you, tortured you and my children suffered as a consequence. I now realize how cowardly I am that I kept beating, accusing my innocent wife. My dear Rita, please forgive me." Sudhir kneeled down on his knees, humbling himself before Rita. This unprecedented gesture on the part of Sudhir was a great surprise to the other members of the family who had come out and were witnessing the drama. They could not believe their eyes.

Sudhir led her to a chair. They sat down. Pointing to Sudhir's hair she said, "Your hair has turned gray. Time has left its footprints on your face too. My face also bears witness of the ravages of time. The sun is setting," she said, pointing a finger at the sun.

But she meant to say how their youth had vanished and they have stepped into old age already. "Let us pay our respect to this life change in us. However, the cheating on marriage vows has not happened. Let us express our gratitude to the God Almighty."

"No, my dear wife, look there, the moon is rising, bringing along new hope. It will illuminate the sky in a little while." Sudhir's voice was hoarse. He took Rita into his arms.

After years of a family remaining broken, it was again uniting them, promising to fulfill the vows made in front of the sacred fire. The two hearts had united into one again. A wind of change promising happiness had started blowing again. They had realized that cheating on marriage vows is like cheating on one's very life. It was likely that even God was happy in this reunion of Rita and Sudhir. The whole of nature had risen to bless them. All the happiness was in their lap that the world had tried to deprive them of.

End

www.ingramcontent.com/pod-product-compliance
Lightning Source LLC
Chambersburg PA
CBHW032145050726
47591CB00001B/90